THE 5TH DEMON

Demoneyes

BRUCE HENNIGAN

The 5th Demon: The Elixir of Lies By Bruce Hennigan Published under imprint Area613

An imprint of 613media,LLC

Cover and layout design by ebooklaunch.com

Author's website www.brucehennigan.com

All scripture quotes are from the NIV version.

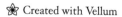 Created with Vellum

Hope Again: A Lifetime Plan for Conquering Depression (with Mark Sutton)
    The Homecoming Tree
    Our Darkness, His Light

Death by Darwin (Jonathan Steel Prequel)
    The 13th Demon: Altar of the Spiral Eye
    The 12th Demon: Mark of the Wolf Dragon
    The 11th Demon: The Ark of Chaos
    The 10th Demon: Children of the Bloodstone
    The 9th Demon: Time of the Cross
    The 8th Demon: A Wicked Numinosity
    The 7th Demon: The Pandora Stone

Ebook only:
    Praxis Makes Perfect

To son and daughter-in-law, Sean and Jennifer for their inspiring devotion to foster children. You bring love to the unloved in the name of Jesus! Love you guys!

*Then Joseph said to his brothers, "Please, come near me," and they came near. "I am Joseph, your brother," he said, "the one you sold into Egypt. And now don't be grieved or angry with yourselves for selling me here, **because God sent me ahead of you to preserve life**. For the famine has been in the land these two years, and there will be five more years without plowing or harvesting. God sent me ahead of you to establish you as a remnant within the land and to keep you alive by a great deliverance. **Therefore it was not you who sent me here, but God.** He has made me a father to Pharaoh, lord of his entire household, and ruler over all the land of Egypt.*

Genesis 45:4-8

FOREWORD

This is the final half of "The Unholy Triad" and picks up right after the events of "The 7th Demon: The Pandora Stone". You may note there is not a book entitled "The 6th Demon". These two books cover the 7th, 6th, and 5th demons. If you are interested in reading the books in order, pay attention to the top line on the cover: "The Chronicles of Jonathan Steel Book #".

PROLOGUE

For almost a century, the mansion had crouched at the foot of the mountain range, tucked up against the rocky slopes and scrub bushes of the hill country. Teenagers had a long tradition of approaching the evil mouth like entrance to the mansion and knocking on the door only to be greeted by the creepy old housekeeper. Some teenagers over the decades had dared to climb down the mountain side to the back of the mansion where its ancient brick façade met the broken stone of the mountain. There, rumor had it, one could find a cave that led into the depths of the mansion where once upon a time, an evil practitioner of the dark arts had overseen human sacrifices. This rumor was spurred on by the discovery of a skull in a small cave uphill from the mansion.

If one were to stand on the highest tower of the mansion and look down upon the valley surrounding the mansion grounds on one particular night, that person would have seen the wary approach of a taxi, it's wan, yellow light casting shadows on the roadside as it wound its way up the serpent shaped driveway. That same light would illuminate the ghastly "face" on the front of the mansion and the animals poised around the circular driveway representing creatures that had only existed in man's wicked imagination.

"You sure you want to go into the haunted mansion?" The cab driver asked through his open window.

Dr. Nigel Hampton paid the cab driver. "My dear boy, this is my other 'homeland'." Hampton waved the cab away and turned to regard his home away from home. He had financed the renovation of the old mansion many years before and had not been back in quite some time. In the absence of current occupants, he had retained the staff to keep the place livable. True, in the dusk, it conveyed a decrepit, mysterious quality. Of course, the man who had designed it had intended for the building to do just that.

A semicircle of steps led up to two double doors of wood. Carved into the doors' surface were leaves and vines that only Hampton would recognize as they were based on an unknown plant species yet to be discovered by modern science. Contrary to the rare plants carved on the door, the old red brick walls had been covered along the first floor by creeping vines of a well-known variety. Three stories towered above him with turrets and arched windows and lightning rods camouflaged as bronze spinnerets and copper flowing banners. Topiaries lined the driveway and the circular turnaround depicting animals from the world of imagination. Hampton paid a very special gardener monthly to maintain the topiaries.

The stairs were meant to resemble the plates in the lower lips of a remote South American indigenous population. The doors were framed in an oval entryway that resembled a mouth. Above the doors two large slits resembled a nose. And two of the largest windows on the second floor poured forth meager light and reminded one of eyes opened in surprise. The mansion had been copied from a similar mansion in Brazil and the very foundation of the home was built into the base of a small mountain. What lay beyond the rear of the house inside the mountain was of more interest to Hampton than almost anything else in the world. Once upon a time, he and his demonic companion had the power to teleport but Hampton had convinced his powerful ally the cost to his own person was too risky. He valued the time to slowly move from place to place as ordinary humans did. It gave him time to think. And, plan! One had to take in the simple niceties of life!

The doors opened and a gray face peeked out. "May I help you?" The elderly man's voice was barely audible. Wispy hair covered his aging scalp.

"Hobbs, my good man, it is Dr. Hampton. The owner."

The doors slowly crept open and the older man was silhouetted against the light from inside. His skeletal figure was clad in a house coat over pajamas. He straightened his house coat and tried to stand straighter. "Welcome Dr. Hampton. It has been a while."

Hampton hurried up the stairs and removed his bowler hat. His breath steamed in the cool air. "Thank you, Hobbs"

Hampton hurried past the harried man and walked into the spacious foyer. Two winding stairways surrounded the oval room, and their steps were starkly white like a plethora of teeth. The arched doorway leading from the foyer into the living room beyond even had a special light fixture dangling from its apex that for all the world reminded one of the uvula.

Hobbs closed the door behind him. "We had no idea you were coming, sir. I regret we have not prepared a meal. And I am not properly dressed."

Hampton shrugged out of his outer coat and handed it and his bowler to Hobbs. "Not to worry, my good man. I will only require a simple sandwich and coffee. Black."

Hampton walked across a spacious living room and paused in front of two double doors. The doors were of hardy wood and carved into their surface were mythological creatures: centaurs, unicorns, trolls, fairies, and elves. Along the bottom of the doors more arcane and macabre creatures seemed just out of sight, reaching up with talons and claws and tentacles toward the more

3

sedate fictional creatures. "Ah, the doors to the library are as enticing as I remember. The stuff of dreams."

"Or nightmares." Hobbs whispered.

Hampton glared at the old man. "Now, Hobbs, where would we be without our imagination, hmmm? Now, has anything been changed in the library since I left?"

Hobbs shook his head and his wispy gray hair floated in the breeze. "No sir. No one has entered the library since the former occupants left. As you requested, we have maintained the rest of the house. If you require a tour, I can arrange it."

"Not now." Hampton grasped the handles of the library and paused before pulling them open. He closed his eyes and tried to recall that fateful night when he had returned a certain item to the occupants of the house. Since that night, things had not gone as he had hoped. But now his plans were falling into place. He reached out with his tainted spirit. Ah! It was still there, hidden away among the books and art. He opened his eyes and nodded. "Perhaps later, Hobbs. Just get me something to eat. I'll take them in the library."

Hampton turned doorknobs shaped like eyes on stalks and opened the doors. The odor of old paper, leather book covers, and a hint of sulfur and brimstone wafted over Hampton, and he inhaled it with great relish. "My good friend, I am home."

❦ I ❦

Night had also embraced the North Dallas Tristate Clinic sitting unprotected in the midst of vast untouched acreage. Joshua Knight awoke from his dark, smothering nightmare and searched the room for Dr. Nigel Hampton. The man had called him a living "petri" dish and he desperately wanted to get out of his hospital bed and out of the clinic.

He tried his best to push upward in his bed concentrating on wiggling his toes, there was no movement beneath the covers. As always, the infusion had restored most of his upper body function, but his lower body might as well not exist! If the past few times were accurate, he had about an hour before the paralysis returned to his upper body, creeping up his chest and neck until once again he would fall into dark slumber. He moved his arms and hands and ran his fingers over his face. He could feel the touch of his fingers. He could feel the stubble of whiskers on his cheeks. He could feel his face for now!

The revelation from Hampton had been terrifying. Hampton had told him his mind was a laboratory experiment for creating a virus that would destroy the part of his brain hardwired to believe in God! And the presence of Pandora on top of that? She was to become the world's 'goddess'?

Josh reeled under the implications of all that was happening to him. He couldn't get up and walk out of the room. There was no escape! He needed someone to help him. But who? His nurse practitioner, Faye Morgan entered his room. She wore a white coat over a dark blue pair of scrubs. Her long, dark hair hung around her shoulders and her intense brown eyes were focused fully on Josh.

"So, you're awake."

"Faye, can I please get out of this bed for just a few minutes?" Josh said. He had to see just what he was capable of. Or more like it, what he was NOT capable of if he was going to escape this hospital. As long as he was a prisoner here, they would have control over Jonathan.

"Josh, your legs are too weak."

"Then take me for a ride. Just put me in a wheelchair and take me outside for just a few moments. Please."

"It's dark already."

"I don't care. I can see through the window the back area is lit up, right? Besides, I'd like to see the stars. The moon. Clouds. Anything!"

Faye frowned. "We have a courtyard for the patients that is open until eight."

"What time is it?"

Faye glanced at her watch. "7:30 P.M. right after shift change."

"Don't you rotate off at seven?" Josh asked.

Faye stifled a yawn. "I'm working a double shift."

"Then the cool, night air might revive you. Please, Faye?" Josh said.

She nodded. "It would do you a lot of good. I'd have to check with Dr. Shutendoji first."

"You know what she will say." Josh said. "Why can't I go

outside? For just five or ten minutes? Don't you think it would be good for me?"

Faye paused and studied him and then smiled. "I am a nurse practitioner which gives me more clinical discretion." She nodded and then smiled. "Okay. I'll just have to get Dudley to change your diaper." She said as she removed the I.V. line from his I.V. adapter.

Josh tensed. "My what?"

Faye tried to hide a smile. "How do you think you've been going to the bathroom?"

Josh looked down at his body beneath the covers. "I can't feel anything."

"Well, there shouldn't be anything wrong with your smell."

"I thought the whole freaking place smelled like that." Josh said. Was he the source of that horrific smell? "Oh, my Lord, is that me?"

"That would be you." Faye said. She pushed the alert button and talked to someone about coming to Josh's room and bringing a wheelchair. Josh studied her face. Could he trust her? Was she a part of the demon team? There was one way to find out.

"Faye, while we are waiting to, uh, change my diaper." Josh swallowed. "I never dreamed I would say that. Can I ask you a personal question?"

"Shoot."

"Are you a Christian?"

Faye blinked and crossed her arms. "Well, I was raised by two very loving, faithful parents who got into fostering because they thought God wanted them to."

"I don't mean your parents. I mean you. I need to know. It's very important."

"Well, I surrendered to Christ when I was twelve. Hung out with the youth group until college. To be honest, I haven't been that faithful since then. My Mom and Dad nag me about it. And my three brothers. My two sisters not so. Why is it so important to you?"

Josh glanced at the drawer in the bedside table. Earlier, Dr. Hampton had revealed the "Pandora Stone" he had hidden away in the drawer. The stone was the source of the spirit of Pandora invading his mind while he slept. "It's just something I need to know."

Dudley showed up wearing gloves and a mask and a wad of diapers under his arm. He was a short, slight man in green scrubs. Josh's eyes widened. "Dude?"

Dudley paused and winked at Josh. "You can call me, dude, my man. Or bro. Whatever floats your boat."

Josh's heart leaped and for the first time he felt an unmistakable tremor of hope. The man standing before was no mere mortal. Dude was his guardian angel! He had first met him during the encounter with the eleventh demon and then again on the airplane to London right before Numinocity.

"Dudley" frowned and held his nose. "Josh, you stink worse than the older adults. Ms. Faye, step out or prepare to gag."

Faye almost laughed and she patted Josh on the shoulder. "We'll get you cleaned up."

Dude pulled down the covers and Josh turned his head so as not so see what was going on *down there*. "Dude, where have you been?" He whispered.

"My man, I am right where I need to be."

"Oh yeah! Then why am I still here in this stink hole, Bro?" Josh's face warmed with anger, but he refused to look at Dude as the odors worsened. He could feel movement, but could feel no sensation from the waist down.

"Josh, this is all part of God's plan. Don't lose hope. Have faith. All things work together for good." Dude said quietly. "As long as I am standing beside you, they can't hear you. But you need to understand your room is under audio surveillance. They will hear anything you say above the level of a whisper." He finished and pulled the covers up over Josh's lower body. He suddenly appeared in Josh's field of view and Dude pulled his mask down. "Help is coming soon."

"And what about Pandora?"

Dude's forehead wrinkled. "Who?"

"The medieval chick in my head." Josh said his voice tight with anger. "Is she part of their plan? Hampton wants to rewire my brain, Dude! You gotta get me out of here."

Dude straightened and seemed deep in thought. "I will have to check on that. I wasn't aware something else was going on."

"Hurry up! Why aren't you helping me? Dude, I'm dying in here." Josh raised his voice. Was God going to let Dude just stand by while Pandora took over his mind?

Faye opened the door. "Is something wrong?"

Josh glared at Dude. "Just get him away from me! This is the most humiliating thing ever to happen to me. Wiping my butt! Changing my diaper!" He was all but in tears and he couldn't look at Faye when she returned to the room. Dude quietly left the room and Faye came to his bedside.

"I'm sorry about that, Josh. We usually change you when you're asleep. Dudley will help get you into the wheelchair."

"I don't want him around me! Just leave me alone." He whispered.

He felt Faye's hand on his shoulder. "Hey, it's okay. You're getting better. You're more alert between treatments now."

Yeah, and my brain is turning into the brain of a sorceress named Pandora who wants to rule the world, he thought. And even an angel of the Lord doesn't know what to do about her. Maybe he was losing his mind after all. Was the virus doing permanent damage despite the treatments? He managed to look back at her and his face burned with embarrassment. "I don't think I'll ever get better."

Dudley rolled a wheelchair into the room and before he could protest, picked him up and slid him into the chair. Josh's teeth rattled and his head lolled. He fought for strength and the muscles in his shoulders and neck responded. He straightened a little and even began to feel his arms and legs.

"Sorry about earlier, Josh. I'm on it." He said.

Faye put a blanket across his lap and legs. Josh glanced once at Dude and refused to answer.

Faye motioned to the door. "Thanks, Dudley, that will be all for now. Now, Josh, for a quick ride before you start to weaken again."

Josh drew a deep breath and fought back the despair. He had to overcome this. He had to find the strength and the will to get out of this place. His anger at Dude only motivated him more. He drew a deep breath and nodded. "Let's go."

Faye rolled him down the hallway and Josh tried his best to take in every detail. If he was ever to escape this place he had to know where the entrances and exits were. A tiny blinking red light came from a rotating camera in the ceiling. They passed a janitor closet and for a second, Josh sensed something, a wave of goodness and hope, for reasons he could not explain. They passed a double door with the sign, "Conference Room".

"That's where your doctors are right now. Some kind of conference. We have about thirty minutes. I'm hoping you'll last that long." Faye said. She turned down a side hallway and paused at the door at the end. She pulled her badge down on a retractable line from her jacket pocket and swiped a panel beside the door. Josh heard the door unlock and open automatically.

Faye rolled him out onto an covered porch lit by several hanging lights. The porch overlooked an enclosed courtyard illuminated by several lampposts. Only one other patient sat in a chair before an outdoor fireplace. Wood crackled with heat and smoke lifted into the evening air.

Josh looked out over an open lawn surrounded by short, stunted trees and only darkness lay beyond. "Where are we?"

"In the big middle of Texas nowhere. North of Dallas in the scrub land. Closest building is two miles away. The clinic owns over 1200 acres of land. Mostly undeveloped, of course. That's why you don't see any lights out there."

Josh pointed to a taller tree with bright red leaves in the

corner of the courtyard. "Take me to that Sweetgum tree. I like the red leaves."

Faye pushed him down a walkway and off onto the hard packed ground covered with Sweetgum balls. She paused beneath the tree and turned Josh to face the porch. "The residents don't like the spiky Sweetgum balls. It hurts to walk on them. But you are right. I love how the leaves turn from green to yellow to orange and then to red."

Josh tried to glance over his shoulder into the darkness. No doubt the land stretched open and undeveloped for miles around them. Even if he did escape, where would he go? How could he make it to the nearest help? He turned back to the clinic and realized this had all been carefully planned. What other people were being held hostage here in the guise of incurable illnesses?

Above the porch, the clinic towered four stories and spread out from the center porch. To his left, a harsh sodium lamp illuminated a loading ramp descending to the basement level. Could he get down to the basement? Maybe hide in a delivery truck? It all seemed so hopeless.

"Faye, can they hear us out here?" He looked up at Faye.

"What?"

"I need to know. I must tell you something and if they hear me, you would be in danger. You said you were a Christian. And I don't sense evil coming from you. You're not one of them."

"Them?"

Josh glanced back at the clinic. "Okay, look in the drawer with my clothes. There is a necklace with a red jewel." Why hadn't he asked Dude to get it? Because he had lost his temper! Way to go, Josh. "My real father had one just like it when he died. Jonathan saved part of the jewel and gave it to me for my birthday. It's special and I need the necklace around my neck."

"We don't allow jewelry on our patients. Especially around your neck. It might choke you in your sleep."

"No, this necklace will protect me because Dude won't."

Faye raised an eyebrow. "Dude?"

"Dudley? He's not human. He's my guardian angel. He calls himself Dude." Josh said.

Faye squatted in front of him. "Josh, you have to come to grips with the fact that many of the things you perceive are fictional. Your mind will reinterpret what you see and hear. You brain is sick, and it will lead you into delusion."

Josh's face burned. "I'm not delusional, Faye. Look in the top drawer of my bed side table. There is a shining stone in there that is messing with my mind."

Faye raised an eyebrow and stood up. "I think it's time for you to get back into your bed."

"Wait!" Josh said. "Faye, I'm caught in the middle of spiritual warfare. I don't know what is going on, but the reason Jonathan is not here is because they are making him do things he wouldn't ordinarily do, or they would let me suffer. They are using me as leverage."

"They?"

"The seventh, sixth, and fifth demons!"

Faye pushed his chair back onto the walkway. "Josh, you have to think clearly now. None of this nonsense."

Josh tried to look back at her over his shoulders. They were growing dangerously close to the back porch. Patients and their attendants would hear what he had to say. "Okay, listen. Why are the doctor's names Shutendoji, Gumijo, and Santelmo? Look up their names. I bet you'll find their names have something to do with the numbers seven, six, and five. It's because they are in league with the seventh, sixth, and fifth demons. There is a Dark Council. Google it. It's real and Jonathan is fighting them. But, right now, I think he's being forced to do what they say because of me. Don't you get it?"

They were back under the porch and Faye was silent as she pushed him through the door and down the dark hallway. As they neared the conference room, the doors opened and out stepped the three doctors.

Josh watched silently as they paused, turned their heads in unison and focused on him.

"What is the meaning of this?" Shutendoji said to Faye.

"I thought a little outside air might help Josh." Faye paused.

Shutendoji's face reddened and she glanced at her colleagues. "You are never to do anything with Mr. Knight without our express permission! He is not to leave his room. He is never to leave this building. Do you understand?"

Her face suddenly twisted and a bizarre, inhuman countenance with multiple eyes, red skin, and horns flashed and then disappeared. Shutendoji put a hand to her face and pointed to Josh's room. "Put him in his bed. Now!"

Faye pushed Josh past the three doctors and into his room. Faye helped him back into his bed. Her face was pale and sweaty, and she was uncharacteristically silent. Her gaze shifted toward the drawer and then back to Josh.

"You saw it, didn't you? For just a second, you saw who she really is." He whispered. His heart pounded. "Faye, whatever you do, don't let them know or you'll disappear."

Faye put her hand to her mouth and hurried from the room. Josh closed his eyes in despair. "I'm sorry, God. Please help us all."

❦ 2 ❦

Hampton's Museum of the Weird sat on a side street not far from the Tower Bridge on the side of the Thames opposite from the famous Tower of London. Steel and Cassie had walked across the street from the pizza parlor to his hotel and Steel had checked into his hotel and dropped off his luggage as his room was not yet ready. He and Cassie took a cab along the Thames and past the Tower Bridge before turning into the old city proper.

The museum sat tucked in between two three-story buildings older than the United States. The building housing the museum was four stories high with dark, soot-stained brickwork and arched windows. A double glass door bore the Museum name and that was it. Very plain and nondescript.

The cab dropped them off on the street and Steel followed Cassie inside. The foyer smelled of old paint and a bit of mildew. A simple desk had a sign advertising the upcoming shows. To the right, an arched open doorway led into a long hallway and the sign next to it said, "This Way to the Path of Evil!"

A woman sat behind the desk. She was short and her eyes were magnified behind large round glasses. Her hair was teased in an old-fashioned set of curls right out of the 1950's and she wore a severe gray dress with a single pink fabric rose on a lapel. She glanced up at them with owlish eyes and slowly stood up. At her full height she wasn't much taller than the desk.

"The Museum is not currently open for visitors." She said tersely.

"Margaret, it's me. Dr. Sebastian. I was just here this morning."

The woman lifted an eyebrow. "And the two of you left your breakfast dishes in the break room. I had to clean up the mess. Now, may I see some identification from you and your companion?"

Cassie mumbled something and took her ID out of her purse and handed it to Margaret. Steel slipped his out of his wallet. Margaret peered at both ID's for the longest time through her thick glasses. She glanced up at them and grunted. "Dr. Holmes is on the fourth floor in the apartment." She handed the IDs back to them. "I don't think you've been up there before. Or have you?" Margaret squinted in her direction.

"No. I've never been above this floor." Cassie glared at Margaret.

"You can take the elevator or climb the stairs." Margaret pointed to a nearby elevator door and then sat back down and crossed her arms.

"Thanks." Cassie said. A single button sat in an ancient bronze plate next to the elevator doors. She pressed it and a rumble shook the walls as the elevator arrived. The doors slid open with a screech. The inside of the elevator could barely hold three people. Steel followed Cassie inside and an old panel with large black push buttons had labels for each of the four floors. Cassie pressed the button for four and the doors screeched closed on Margaret's smile.

"She's enjoying this way too much, the old crone." Cassie said.

The elevator shook and trembled as it slowly ascended. Cassie reached out and grabbed Steel's arm as the elevator lurched once like a dinosaur's hiccup and then carried on. When they reached the fourth floor and the doors had finally opened, Cassie rushed off and Steel was right behind them.

"You should have taken the stairs." Dr. Montana Holmes waited for them outside the elevator. He had let his beard grow out in the week or so since Numinocity and his unruly long black hair kept falling into his face. He wore a simple black tee shirt and frayed blue jeans and sandals.

Cassie ran to him and embraced him. She kissed him on the cheek. She suddenly pulled back. "Hey, Monty. I've never been up here before."

Monty pointed to the elevator. "That's why. Jonathan!" Monty shook his hand.

"It's good to see you, Monty." And so is Cassie, he thought.

Monty motioned behind him and brushed the hair out of his face. "Let's sit in the conference room. If you want to call it that." He led them into a large room with a pocked, dark wooden table. The chairs were somewhat rickety when they sat.

"The whole building seems about to fall apart. I take it things went well in Switzerland? So, what's up, Jonathan?"

Steel glanced at Cassie. "I like that. Cut to the chase. I'm looking for four artifacts, Monty. They might be in Cephas' crates."

Monty nodded. He turned in his chair to a nearby table and picked up a small black notebook. "I have a copy of the manifest right here. I keep a copy up here and the crates and another copy down in the theater. That way I don't have to go back downstairs if I need anything. It's creepy down there."

"Oh, and it's not creepy up here?" Cassie said.

Monty frowned. "Down there is Margaret."

"Right." Cassie took the notebook and opened it. "Jonathan is looking for Moses' rod and the bronze serpent."

"Really?" Monty said. "Funny you should mention it. There are over one hundred items listed in the manifests for two of the crates. And if you look on the third page, I believe you will see a listing for a rod and a bronze serpent."

Steel actually smiled and drew a deep breath. "Thank God!"

Cassie turned to the page. She frowned. "But they are listed as missing!"

"What?" Steel said.

"No!" Steel pounded the table, and it shook. Dust drifted down from the ceiling.

"Jonathan! Calm down. It doesn't mean they are not here. There is a third crate for which I do not have a manifest. It is possible some of the missing items are in that crate." Monty said.

"What about the urinal and the thimble?" He turned to Cassie.

"Urim and Thummim." Cassie said. "Jonathan, no one has ever found them."

"That's the other two artifacts? You don't mess around. Like Cassie said, they've never been found." Monty said.

Steel tried to calm his racing heart. "I vaguely remember something about them in the Old Testament. Just what are we talking about?"

Cassie glanced at Monty. He nodded. "I'll get my laptop."

He disappeared into another room. "I'll let him tell you. He knows much more about this than I do." Cassie said.

Monty returned and opened his laptop and tapped on the keys. "We have to start with the priestly garments." He turned the laptop toward Steel and Cassie. The image of a priest from the Old Testament days filled the screen. He wore a long robe with a breastplate covered with colorful stones and a covering on his head.

"In the wilderness, God commanded Moses to set aside the Levites as the official priests for the new tabernacle. Moses' brother, Aaron was anointed the high priest by Moses and this garment, and its coverings were detailed by God to Moses. The details are in Exodus and Leviticus and are also mentioned in Numbers."

Monty pointed to the breastplate. "There is a covering over the white tunic called the ephod."

"Yeah, but we aren't sure of its exact dimensions." Cassie said. "All we know is it hangs from the shoulders over the chest and the back and is attached by gold threads at the shoulders."

Monty raised an eyebrow. "To be a little more specific, it was made of fine linen, and consisted of two pieces, which hung from the neck. It covered both the back and front and hung above the tunic and outer garment. It was embroidered with several different colors and the two pieces were joined together over the shoulders with clasps of gold, as Cassie said."

"Or precious stones." Cassie said. "We aren't completely sure."

Monty sat back. "I thought you wanted me to tell this story."

Cassie shrugged. "Sorry. Couldn't help myself."

"Anyway," Monty continued pointing to the image, "The ephod was fastened round the waist by a girdle of gold, blue, purple, and fine twined linen."

"Where do these stones come in?" Steel asked glancing at his watch. Time was precious to him.

Monty tapped on keys and changed the image to a close-up of the priest's breastplate. "Before we get to them, let's talk about the breastplate. The breastplate is made of a gold plate, doubled over, so that it forms a square of about nine inches on a side. And, on the breastplate are four rows with three precious stones in each row. Beginning with the top row there is a ruby, a topaz, a beryl, a turquoise, a sapphire, an unidentified stone."

"Probably an emerald." Cassie said energetically.

Monty paused. "Or maybe a diamond."

"Okay, yes, maybe a diamond." Cassie said.

"I don't need all the details." Steel said tersely.

Monty nodded. "Of course, but the remainder of the stones were jacinth, an agate, an amethyst, a chrysolite, an onyx, and a jasper. Each stone contains the name of one of the twelve tribes, and all are mounted with gold filigree."

"The Urim and Thummim?" Steel said.

"I'm getting there." Monty brought another image of two blue stones. "Now, the breastplate had a gold filigree border with gold rings at each of the two upper corners to attach the breast-piece to the shoulders of the ephod. The breastpiece of the priest then has the purpose of shielding the ephod and remains fastened tightly to it. And it also contains a pocket in order to hold the Urim and Thummim in a position near the heart of the priest."

Cassie pointed to the stones. "We don't know what they looked like. But there has been a lot of speculation of the nature of the Urim and Thummim. Some believe these were two special stones that were kept by the high priest within a fold of his ephod in his priestly garment for the purpose of cleromancy."

"Clero what?" Steel said.

"Jonathan, cleromancy is simply casting lots to determine the will of the gods. It is found in most ancient religions." Cassie said.

"Wait a minute." Steel said. "Are you telling me God plays dice?"

"Hang on." Cassie put a hand on his. "It's not that simple. So, let me give you an example from Chinese religions. In the case of 'poe' in Taoism, round stones have a flat side and a curved side. When they are cast before an idol with a question for the god to answer, they may land three different ways. If both land on the flat side, then the answer was 'yes'. If they both landed on the round sides, then the answer was 'no'. And if one landed on the round side and the other on the flat side, then then the answer was ambiguous."

"Or, the god laughing and mocking the priest." Monty said.

"So, the priests cast the Urim and Thummim on the ground to see what God's will would be?" Steel said.

"Well, no." Cassie said.

"A view has been presented that the two words are hendiadys of two supercharged words, 'lights' and 'purities'." Monty said.

Steel shook his head and abruptly sat back in his chair. "Hen what? What do chickens have to do with this?"

Cassie put a hand on Monty's hand. "Let me handle this one, Monty." She looked at Steel. "What Monty is talking about is the idea that the stones together would indicate a shimmering brilliance that would be a divine sign. So, when Moses went before Yahweh with a question, it is possible that he would speak to the high priest who would pray to Yahweh. Then, when the priest received a divine answer, he would turn to Moses with the stones of his ephod shining in dazzling light." Cassie said excitedly. "Jonathan, a pure and divine light was a signal from God that the response communicated by the priest was a divine response and not some random throw of the dice."

"Jonathan, the dazzling light from the stones on the ephod would validate the message from the priest. This dazzling light would be the visual sign of Yahweh's revelation." Monty added.

"So, what happened to these special stones?" Steel asked.

"The Urim and Thummim appear five times in the Bible and nowhere else in extrabiblical literature." Monty said. "In Deuteronomy, the care of the Urim and Thummim was given to the Levites. They are mentioned in passages from Ezra and Nehemiah."

Cassie nodded and looked into Jonathan's eyes. "Don't be concerned about the idea of casting lots. Focus on the fact the Urim and Thummim helped the priests know the answer and will of God. The ultimate decision always remained with God."

Steel sat forward and studied the images of the two stones on the laptop screen. "These stones are lost in history, then."

"Yes." Monty said.

"Why would a demon want these two stones? Why would they think these stones would somehow tell them God's will? This makes no sense."

Cassie shrugged. "I'm not sure, Jonathan. They would only be useful to a priest."

"And we are no longer under the covenant of the law instituted by Moses with the Ten Commandments. We are under a new covenant with Jesus Christ as our high priest. And with Jesus we need no casting of lots or a high priest to confirm God's will in our lives. The Holy Spirit serves that function now." Monty said.

Steel slid the notebook over and began to scan the list of items in Dr. Lawrence's crate. "I don't suppose there is a listing for the Urim and Thummim."

"I don't recall them being listed. And if they were, I would remember." Monty said.

Steel paused and pointed to a listing. "Collection of arcane stones. Description: One dozen varied stones of unusual nature of unknown origin." He looked up at Monty and Cassie. "Could the Urim and Thummim be one of these stones?"

Monty pulled the notebook over and nodded. "I guess it's possible. I haven't made it to this part of the list yet."

"Can we go look?" Steel asked.

"Absolutely." Monty said.

Steel touched the fountain pen from Max in his pocket. Should he activate the dampening field now? Max had loaned him the pen to shut out and of the unholy triad's demonic insect drones. But, no insects had appeared since he had arrived at the museum. He had demanded the unholy triad demons stop surveilling him. Perhaps they had. But he couldn't take a chance. "What are we waiting for?" Steel stood up.

Monty closed the notebook. "We're not waiting for the elevator, that's for sure."

❦ 3 ❦

J ason Birdsong's inner clock stirred his mind to wakefulness, and he glanced at his watch. Four A. M. He had hidden away in the janitor closet on the North Texas Tristate Clinic after sneaking into the clinic in the guise of a replacement nurse for the evening. He had managed to avoid being recognized by Faye Morgan from their earlier visit when he was pretending to be a police officer accompanying Dr. Jack Merchant.

By five A.M., the nurses and physician's assistants would be hurrying to finish up the night's work before the new shift arrived at seven. He stood up and stretched and then peeked out the door to the hallway. The rotating camera in the ceiling was just pointing away from this end of the hallway. He put his surgical cap and mask on and slowly walked to Josh's room.

Birdsong pushed the door open and stepped quietly into the room. He could hear Josh's ragged breathing. The room was dark except for red and green light from the intravenous line pump. He withdrew three twenty c.c. syringes from his scrub pocket and moved quietly over to the side of Josh's bed. He quickly inserted a needle and syringe into the port of the bag hanging from the pole and withdrew two syringes of fluid. That should be enough, he thought. Just to be thorough, he drew two more syringes of blood and placed the blood in vials. Dr. Merchant had seemed pretty rattled when he talked to him earlier. All of the original samples were missing from the laboratory where Dr. Merchant's colleague had apparently been murdered. Birdsong tried not to think about the growing complexity of this entire affair. He had seen worse in his life. But those heinous events had not involved the forces of darkness until after he met Jonathan Steel, his partner.

"Jason?"

Birdsong jerked and dropped an empty syringe on the floor. He glanced down at Josh's glittering eyes.

"Shh! Don't make any sound, Josh." Birdsong said.

"Where's Jonathan?"

Birdsong glanced around the room. Would there be surveillance? He didn't see a camera. He squatted down so his face was at Josh's level. "We need to be very quiet, Josh. Don't move and talk quietly. They can probably hear us."

"What is Jonathan doing to stop them?"

"He's cooperating."

"No!" Josh almost raised his voice. "Don't let him do it, Jason."

"They're going to let you die, Josh. He has no choice." Birdsong placed a hand on Josh's arm. It was hot to the touch with fever. "But you know Jonathan. He's going to turn everything around on them, right?"

"I hope so with your help."

The door creaked as someone stepped into the room. Birdsong dropped down out of sight and slid quietly behind the bedside table.

"Mr. Knight? It's Dr. Santelmo. Who are you talking to?" Dr. Santelmo stood just a couple of feet away from where Birdsong crouched out of sight. The diminutive doctor leaned over Josh and then looked up at the intravenous fluid bag. The woman looked exactly like the other doctor. Steel had said they were triplets. He had called them the unholy triad! Something tickled at the back of his neck and a cold chill ran over him. He was experiencing what Steel had described as a wave of evil. His spirit responded to the presence of this evil being!

"I was talking to Jonathan." Josh said hoarsely. "Now, he's gone. When will he be back?"

"Soon, Josh. You must concentrate on getting better."

A shadow appeared behind Dr. Santelmo and Faye Murphy stepped into the room. "Dr. Santelmo? I was just coming to check on Josh."

"It was Pandora's box, wasn't it?" Josh said a little more loudly. "Dr. Hampton made me get it out of the crate. Something was inside of it, and I stuck my finger. If you find that box, you'll know what is infecting me."

"We already know, Josh." Santelmo looked back at him. "And you're just hallucinating from the swelling of your brain tissue. We have everything under control."

Josh sat up weakly in the bed. "I'm ready to go home. I can't wait to tell Jonathan all about my dreams and the weird things I've been hearing and seeing, like Pandora taking over my mind. It's what Dr. Hampton wanted."

Santelmo froze and studied Josh's face. "Pandora?" For a moment fear etched her face and she licked her lips. "You are hallucinating, Mr. Knight." Santelmo turned to Faye.

"He is delusional. His mind is so muddled by the influence of this fantasy about Dr. Hampton, I am afraid he will have a psychotic break soon. And taking him outside earlier subjected his mind to unanticipated stimuli. I want to start sedation around the clock."

Faye shook her head. "Sedation? But isn't that a bit of an overreaction?"

"I fear that he is not resting in between treatments anymore. And this delusion about some mythical being taking over his mind is dangerous." Santelmo said.

"Wait! Don't put me to sleep yet. I need to talk to Jonathan about Dr. Wulf. His blood was so delicious. It made all the difference in the world." Josh said weirdly.

Santelmo raised an eyebrow. "Wulf? I'm afraid you're not making any sense, Josh." Santelmo glanced once more at Faye. "See what I mean. Start the sedation immediately."

"Sorry, my mind drifted off again back to the vampires and their tainted blood and Renee Miller and the prions. I really miss her. I want to tell Jonathan about her." He laid back down in the bed and pulled the covers up over his chest. Josh's eyes closed and he fell asleep.

Santelmo opened her hand for the tablet chart and Faye handed it to her. Birdsong watched Faye's finger trace along the doctor's hand, and she flinched. Dr. Santelmo took the tablet and glared at Faye.

"What was that?"

"Static electricity." Faye said quietly

Santelmo tapped on the tablet and put in her orders. She handed it back to Faye. "Get that sedation started now, nurse." Santelmo whirled and strode out of the room.

Faye Murphy glanced at the tablet and then paced across the room mumbling to herself. "I felt it. Something about her was off." She glanced at the tablet. "What was it? Not static electricity." She stopped and looked over at Josh. "And I did see something in Shutendoji's face earlier."

Faye slowly came to Josh's bedside and whispered to herself. "I'm not sick. I don't have fever. My head doesn't hurt. This virus you had is over so I couldn't have it. Why would I hallucinate?"

"She's a demon." Josh whispered as he opened his eyes. "I told you."

Faye leaned so close Birdsong was afraid she would see him. "Josh, what is going on with you?"

Jason put a finger to his lips. He mouthed, "They're listening." He pointed to the drawer on the bedside table.

Faye opened the drawer to the bedside table slowly and

looked in. Birdsong saw golden light play across her features. The woman gasped and put a hand to her mouth. She slowly closed the drawer and hurried across the room to the console on the wall. She pulled open the top drawer and rummaged around inside. She turned to Josh and held up her hands and mouthed.

"Your necklace is not here."

"No!" Josh whispered.

Birdsong had enough. He slowly stood up and Faye stiffened when she saw him. He put a hand up to stop her from reacting and pointed to Josh and mouthed. "I'm his uncle. I'm here to help." Technically, this was all true as Birdsong's grandmother or "hu'lu" had made Jonathan his brother.

Faye breathed deeply and suddenly the door to the room opened again. Santelmo stuck her head in, and Birdsong dropped quietly out of sight. "And hold off on his next infusion until an hour after the sedation." Santelmo glanced at the open drawer behind Faye. "What are you doing?"

"Looking for some diapers. He has soiled himself." She closed the drawer. "I can get Dudley to bring some."

"Dudley has been terminated. He was not an exemplary employee, nurse. Remember that! Now, I don't care if he has poop up to his ears, I want that sedation started now!"

"Yes ma'am." Faye said. The door closed.

Birdsong slowly stood up from behind the table. Faye made a motion with her hands. Birdsong smiled. She knew sign language!

He tapped his chest and she looked at him. He signed, "You know sign language?"

Faye smiled and answered back. "Yes. I am the interpreter for the deaf for the clinic. One of my sisters is deaf."

Birdsong frowned. "My auntie was deaf. I'm a bit rusty. It's been a long time since she passed away."

"Sorry. We don't have much time. Who are you?"

"I am Jonathan Steel's partner. He sent me to check on Josh.

I need to get these samples back to Dr. Merchant. He wants to analyze them." He held up the vials and syringes.

"What's your real name?"

"Jason Birdsong."

"I thought you said you were Josh's uncle."

"It's complicated. My grandmother made Jonathan my brother and that makes Josh my nephew. Oh, never mind. It's an O'Odham thing. Indigenous Americans from Arizona."

Faye raised her hands to stop him and moved to the bedside. "Things are confusing enough already."

Josh raised his hand to interrupt them. "What are you saying?" He whispered.

"No time." Birdsong whispered and looked up at Faye. "They are using Josh to make Steel do things. Bad things. Evil things. Josh is a hostage."

"That's what he was trying to tell me. He was looking for a necklace given to him by his father."

Jason glanced at the door. "Oh, no! If they found the bloodstone then we may be in even more trouble."

Faye shook her head. "Bloodstone? Glowing rocks? This can't be happening." She stopped and drew a deep breath. Her eyes filled with fear. "But I do know I saw something, and I felt something when she touched me that makes no rational sense."

"We're not dealing with rationality at all. These creatures can teleport through space."

"Jason, did you hear what the doctor said? They fired Dudley!" Josh whispered.

"Who is Dudley?"

"Josh said he was his guardian angel." Faye signed.

"Dude?" Birdsong signed rapidly. "He was here?"

"But it sounds like they fired him." Faye signed.

Josh closed his eyes. "Jason this is my fault. I got mad at Dude." He yawned. "No! I'm going back under, Birdsong. You have to stop them."

"They said you needed sedation." Birdsong glanced back at Faye. "If he is so sleepy then why the sedation?"

Faye had closed the bedside table drawer and reopened it. Golden light played over her features. "Josh said this stone was put here to manipulate his mind. He sounded like he was fighting something in his mind while he slept."

"Close that drawer before it affects us, too. Can you move it?"

"Later when they aren't watching me this closely. They suspect something and if they were listening before, they know about the stone in the drawer." Faye signed.

"Why the sedation?" Jason asked.

"If he sleeps and dreams, then this Pandora person can enter his dreams, maybe?" Faye shrugged.

"I know a lot about dream walking. An O'Odham tradition. With the sedation, he will not dream. This isn't making any sense." Birdsong said. "Look, do they know you know you're helping us?"

"If they did, I would have been let go. Jason, we have to get Josh out of this clinic." Faye said.

"No! What happens if he doesn't get his treatments?"

Faye looked down at Josh. He had closed his eyes and his chest rose and fell in a slow cadence. "He will die."

"Then he stays. Dr. Merchant will find out what is wrong with him so we can treat him once he gets out of here. Until then, he needs someone to look after him." Birdsong said.

Faye paused and bit her lip. She studied Josh's sleeping body and nodded. "It's my calling. I will watch over him."

"Here is my cell phone number. When you're away from here call me." Birdsong handed her a business card then paused and put out a hand and touched Josh's shoulder. "You stayed an extra shift to watch over him, didn't you?" He looked back at Faye.

She nodded. "I knew something wasn't quite right. I thought it was his delusions. Like I said, he talked about somebody being in his head. This Pandora."

"And now, he just mentioned Pandora's box." Birdsong stiffened. Josh had mentioned other people too. Wulf? Wasn't he the twelfth demon? And drinking blood? Prions? Was Josh trying to tell him something? He had to remember everything Josh had said.

Faye walked around the bed and turned Birdsong to face her. "What is this all about?"

"Josh mentioned several things they may have something to do with his illness." Birdsong looked at her and shook his head. "No! You are already way too involved. Your life is already in danger. The less you know the better. I have to get out of here without being seen. Earlier I was able to get in without anyone noticing. But if they are this suspicious, I can't just walk out. They'll spot me in an instant."

"You're right. The halls have cameras." She signed. She glanced at the only window, hurried over, and looked out. "Trash truck. Backing into the loading dock below the window." She motioned to the window. "You can jump from the window."

Birdsong joined her and glanced out the window. "Into the trash?"

"It's not medical waste. Just ordinary trash. It's your only way of getting out of here without being seen." She tried to open the window and it wouldn't budge. Birdsong put his hands beside hers. They were warm and moist. He glanced at her face once, the deep brown eyes, the black hair.

"Thank you." He whispered.

Faye smiled at him as together they pulled open the window. "Take care." She whispered.

A ledge outside the window gave Birdsong just enough room to stand. Below him was a sub-level for deliveries. A trash truck sat right beneath him filled with black bags of trash. Birdsong stepped out onto the ledge and Faye closed the window quietly behind him. He heard voices in Josh's room. Another nurse had arrived with the sedation.

Taking a deep breath, he stepped off the ledge and landed in the trash truck. The smell was atrocious, but he burrowed himself beneath the bags as he cast one last look at the window to Josh's room.

The trash truck started up and pulled out of the driveway and headed for the main entrance. When the truck was stopped to turn out of the clinic's driveway, he hopped out on the side away from the clinic and made his way down into a ditch along the highway. He was already covered in rotting food so what was mud, now? He lay down in the ditch until the trash truck pulled out onto the highway. He duck-walked along the ditch until he was clear of the sight of the clinic. He ran down the highway to the hidden truck. He would have to wash and fumigate Jonathan Steel's truck after this, but at least he had gotten away without being seen. He reached into the scrub pants pocket and pulled out the syringes. Along with this and the help of an unanticipated ally, Josh's chances for survival had just gone up.

$\approx$ 4 $\approx$

Margaret gave them a caustic look when they emerged from the stairwell. Monty led them silently past her and down another stairwell into a large, open room. Two rows of benches encircled the open circle of pale light that shown up from below. Steel walked down three steps to a railing and peered over. On the level below was an ancient surgical operating suite. A few rows of chairs circled the central floor.

"What is this place?"

"In the old days, medical students and doctors would come to watch famous surgeons perform their surgery." Monty said. "This building was once part of a medical school. Up here were the students. Down there closer to the surgical table were the surgery residents and esteemed surgeons of the day."

"Not very sterile." Cassie added. "Wouldn't happen today, of course. At least not under these conditions."

Steel pointed to three crates sitting around an old operating table. "And those are the crates?"

Monty nodded and led them down a spiral staircase to the back of the lower observer section. Steel followed him down to the main floor. A half a dozen objects sat on the operating table with labels attached. Two were statues of glaring demonic faces.

31

One was a platter with an obscene sensual scene carved into the face. The last item was a black, multifaceted stone.

"This black stone was one of the twelve in the manifest." Monty bent over an open crate and took out a metal box. "The rest are in here. I take one of them out at a time to try and determine as much about them as I can."

Monty placed the box on the table and pushed back the lid. He adjusted an old-fashioned surgical light above the table to point into the box. Bubble wrap protected each stone. Monty took them out one at a time and lined them up along the table-top. He paused and glanced back into the box and then hurried over to the crate.

"What is it?" Steel asked.

Monty rummaged around inside the crate. "There are only ten stones in the box. The manifest says there are twelve."

"Could they have fallen out?" Cassie joined Monty and glanced down into the box. She gasped. "Monty, what is this?"

She straightened and held a wooden box. She placed it on the table and tapped the top. "A woman sitting before an urn with demonic vapors coming out! Monty, this is Pandora's Box!"

Monty returned to the table. "I saw that earlier, but I hadn't got to it yet."

Steel reached over and quietly took her hand. "I think we've seen enough. I'm hungry. Let's do dinner."

Cassie glanced at him and before she could say anything Steel motioned to his lips and mouthed. "They are listening."

Monty froze and glanced around the room. Cassie stiffened and her face turned red. She paused and fought for control. "Good idea. Let's go eat."

Steel motioned to the spiral staircase, and they climbed to the upper observation level. He motioned for them to stop and took out his fountain pen. He clicked it and a tiny green light blinked from the shaft. He pointed to the pen.

"We can talk now." He hurried back down the staircase. "A

gift from Max. A dampening field for any type of electronic surveillance including demon spider drones."

Monty followed after Steel and Cassie. "Spider drones?"

Steel nodded. "Even if they were here the dampening field would stop them. I'm not certain if I am still under surveillance but we have to talk."

Steel motioned to the box. "Josh said he stuck his finger on Pandora's box from one of these crates and that is how he was infected."

Monty stepped back from the table. "What?"

Cassie, on the other hand, stepped toward the box and gingerly picked it up. Steel tried to stop her from handling the box. She shook her head and pushed his hand away.

"I've done this kind of thing many times, Jonathan. I know how to handle a dangerous artifact." She pulled back her blonde hair and secured it with a tie then lifted the box by the corners and slowly turned it over, studying every inch. She placed the box upside down and leaned over the underside. "Here. Look. Tape residue along the edge close to the corner."

Steel's face turned red, and he swore loudly. "He did it! Just like I thought."

"He?" Monty said.

Steel whirled and his anger surged. "Hampton! He's working with the unholy triad. That would be Seven, Six, and Five, Monty. He infected Josh as leverage over me!" He poked his chest. "I'm so sick and tired of these demons! This has to stop."

Monty put a hand on Steel's arm. "Hey, man, calm down. Dampening field or not, we don't want Margaret to show up."

Steel jerked away from Monty and fought for control. He looked up at Cassie. "They are making me do three tasks, Cassie."

"The four artifacts?" She said.

"Yes. Number Six's demands. I've already taken care of Seven's task."

"Which was?" Monty asked.

"Raven's dossier." Steel said.

"What are you talking about?" Monty said.

"Raven, the assassin you told me was dead?" Cassie said gently.

"Well, she's alive." Steel said. "And no longer dangerous. Monty, Dr. Monarch tried to reset her mind and erased it."

Monty blinked. "What? And this dossier?"

"A record of every assassination and its details. Blackmail material for sure. The Council of Darkness wants a member on the Penticle." Steel said.

Cassie laughed. "The Penticle? That's just a myth."

Steel glared at her and then sighed. "Sorry, but it's not. It's real and the unholy triad, as I call them, want the dossier to blackmail one of the five members so they can put a demon controlled person on the Penticle."

Monty shook his head. "Conspiracy theories, Jonathan. I've fought them my whole career. The Penticle can't possibly exist."

"Then why am I helping a demon controlled operative get information to blackmail Dr. Faust?"

"Faust?" Monty stiffened. "Did you say Dr. Jorgen Faust?"

"He's the member of the Penticle FBI Special Agent Ross is investigating." Steel said.

Monty ran his hand through his dark hair. "If that is true, then I'm in big trouble."

"Why?" Cassie said.

"Not now! No time for that. Long story." Monty turned back around to the crate. "We have to find those stones for Josh's sake."

They worked in silence for almost an hour looking through everything in Lawrence's crate. No other stone surfaced. Steel wiped sweat from his forehead and looked at the closed crate. "Could they be in that crate?"

Monty leaned against the operating table. "Not likely. The two stones would have been with the other twelve. No other stones are listed."

Steel walked over to the third crate that resembled a metal coffin. On the surface a glass plate gleamed in the light. "Is this how you open it?"

Monty joined him and Cassie stood at his other side. "The crate will not open unless the appropriate person puts their palm print on the surface."

Steel nodded and placed his right hand on the glass. A pale light sprang from the faceplate and the shadow of Steel's hand played across his face as a red line moved from top to bottom, scanning his palm print.

"State name for voice recognition." A robotic voice said.

"Jonathan Steel."

The entire window pulsed a bright green and then went dark. Steel stepped back and with a thudding click, the top of the crate opened an inch on their side. Cold vapor seeped from inside.

"What?" Steel stepped back from the vapor.

"Just liquid nitrogen for preservation." Monty stepped forward and pushed the lid back and up. He fanned the vapor away. "Cassie, pull that surgical light over here, please."

Cassie grabbed the light on a levered arm over to the third crate. She pointed the light into the vapor filled interior. They all leaned over in expectation.

"It's empty!" Steel said.

Monty leaned deeper into the crate. "What? It can't be empty."

Cassie laughed. "Dr. Lawrence has the last laugh after all."

Steel drew a deep breath and pounded the lid closed on the crate and screamed until he was hoarse. Monty and Cassie stepped away from him. Steel's heart felt like it would explode. He leaned forward onto the cold metal lid and fought to control his anger and his ragged breath. What was he going to do now? "No serpent! No rod! No stones!"

"I'm sorry." Cassie said.

Monty put a hand on Steel's shoulder and Steel resisted the

urge to rip it away. He slowly stood up and slowed his breathing. "Jonathan, I'm so sorry they aren't here."

Steel turned around and slowed his breathing. "I'm sorry. You didn't deserve that. You are my friends, not my enemies."

His friends! There was a time he could never say that. These two friends were here for him. He put a hand on both of their shoulders. "Thank you for trying. Those artifacts must exist if the triad wants them so bad. I don't think they would send me for them unless they were certain they existed. If they are not here in Cephas' crates, they must be somewhere else."

"Like?" Monty said.

"Dr. Gomijo mentioned the Ark of the covenant. And the Ark of Chaos."

"You mean the Ark of the Demon Rose." Cassie said.

"I know about the demon rose, but not the change in name." Steel said.

Cassie looked at Monty. "Jonathan, they are two different things."

"What?" Steel clasped his fists. "That's not what Vivian said. She was the last one to have it. Minus the metal compass rose from the lid. She called the thing both names."

Monty snapped his fingers. "You're right, Cassie. Who was it that wrote about it? Mustaffo? Syed?" He tapped his forehead. "Think, Montana."

"I'm not sure where the definitive information is, Monty." Cassie said. "I only remember reading about the two arks in a blog post. I thought it was spurious at best. They were on my list to look for. Before. You know, when I didn't care how I spent my time. I hadn't thought about it since."

"Okay." Steel took Monty by the shoulders and looked into his eyes. "Think, Monty. If there are two different arks, then we need to know where I can find the Ark of the Demon Rose. We know the Ark of Chaos was taken by Vivian. Just don't know where. And Vivian is missing. She might even be dead."

"I know, I know." Monty gently pulled away from Steel. He

went to another worktable at the edge of the amphitheater and picked up a tablet. He brought it to life. "I know it's here somewhere. I found a photograph of scrolls from a 1700 Bible. Where did I put it?" He swiped the screen of the tablet and sweat beaded on his forehead. He stopped and smiled.

"Here it is. It's in Latin so I'll translate."

"You read Latin?" Steel said.

"So do I." Cassie joined Monty. The light from the tablet lit up their faces. Monty began to read slowly and erratically.

"Be it know in regard to the two Arks of evil intent that each has found its way into our hands. The priests have tried to approach the arks several times and the evil within withers their minds and blinds their eyes. They have sent for me knowing that my own soul was once tempered by the evil of Satan. For a fortnight as a teenager, I was under the extreme influence of the Second Demon. The reason for his name he chose not to reveal to me but my familiarity with evil even though my soul now belongs to the Savior, gives me the strength and stamina to approach the Arks."

Monty paused and swallowed. "He goes on to describe the two wooden boxes' appearance." He continued to read. "Both boxes are identical in appearance save for the lids which bear a bronze circular compass rose."

Cassie looked at Monty. "They both have compass roses?"

"That's what it says." Monty read out loud again.

"The Inscription on one compass rose is composed of evil and arcane symbols of all twelve demons on the Dark Council. The other compass rose contains the numbers one through twelve along with symbols I would associate with the twelve apostles. Truly these two arks are at the center of a war between good and evil."

"If one of the arks contained a compass rose of the apostles." Cassie said.

Monty smiled. "Then it would contain artifacts that are not evil."

"Like the Urim and Thummim." Cassie nodded.

"Wait, we don't know that, do we?" Steel said.

"No." Monty said.

"Finish reading." Steel said. Monty nodded and continued.

"Upon touching the compass rose of the Ark of evil intent which I will call the Ark of the Demon Rose Compass, my hands instantly blistered under the onslaught of brimstone and sulfur! It took hours of cold water and compresses to relieve my pain so that I could once again approach the arks. This time I used a metal utensil to pry open the lids. This was without success. Both arks are sealed beyond any human capacity to open. After consultation with the committee, it was decided that there was truth to the legend the Ark of the Demon Rose contained talismans of each demon. Destroying the arks was out of the consideration in view of their obvious indestructability. It was after reaching this impasse that the Spirit relayed to me a solution.

I left the committee chambers and hurried to the examination room. The priests hurried after me shouting many questions and objections. I arrived at the arks and ignoring the pain and suffering to my bandaged hands, I removed the compass rose from the Ark of the Demon Rose with a sharp twisting motion. The pain was exquisite and can only be compared to the most minimal of pain suffered by my Lord. When I touched the compass rose of the apostles, my hands cooled instantly. The pain subsided. I removed the compass rose from the lid. The priests behind me were trying their best to talk me out of my plan. But their fear of the arks prevented them from approaching. I placed the compass rose of the apostles onto the Ark of the Demon Rose and seated it into place. I covered my ears as such screeching and screaming as no human has ever heard issued forth from within the box. My soul writhed in agony at the screams of Satan's handmen. The screams eventually died, and all grew silent. I picked up the Demon Rose. It burned my already blistered hands but not as severely. I placed the compass on the lid of the Ark of the apostles and snapped it into place. The compass glowed a sickly red for only a few minutes and then all was silent. I felt a hand on my shoulder and turned to find the priests had approached the arks.

I had neutralized the evil for now! Two members of each committee decided to take each of the arks and separate them and hide them from the world. We spread the rumor that both arks were still evil even though both arks had been neutralized. To prevent the uninformed from trying to open either ark we allowed them both to have ominous names, the Ark of the Demon Rose and the Ark of Chaos for truly chaos now rules supreme in the Enemy's world once the Ark of the Demon Rose had been contained and hidden."

Monty looked up at Steel. "I don't know how this helps us."

"The Ark of Chaos in our possession contained the Compass of the Demon Rose." Steel said. "It must have been the original apostles' ark." He whirled and faced them both. "Which means that Vivian had the ark that means the most to us! It is the one I need."

"Then where is the other ark?" Cassie asked.

"I don't know. Cephas probably knew. He also played his cards close to the vest when we talked about the ark. He even has the original compass of the Demon Rose in his basement."

Steel froze and pointed excitedly at Monty. "In his basement! If two stones are missing, could they have been in the ark? If so, then why did Cephas list twelve stones? Somewhere between the basement and now, someone took the stones from the crate. I have to find those two stones and since they were listed in the manifest, they are NOT in the arks." He spun and grabbed Cassie by the shoulders. "But they were in the crate when it was back in the basement. You said you had found Dr. Maize?"

"Maize? The mad scientist who sent us back in time?" Monty stepped up beside them. "Cassie, you never mentioned that."

"I found out he was here, near London." Cassie gently pulled away from Steel and backed up.

Monty closed his eyes and shook his head. "And I thought you were here for me."

Cassie hurried to him and hugged him. It looked like she was hugging a tree. "I'm sorry, Monty. That was the old me. I thought if Maize was still around, he might have the prototype machine and that maybe, just maybe." She pushed herself back from him and her face was streaked with tears. "I could save Renee and the Children of the Bloodstone."

Monty melted and pulled her into his grasp. Steel walked over to him, once again uncomfortable with unfamiliar emotions. Cassie pulled from Monty and turned her tear-filled eyes on him. "Oh, Jonathan. I miss her so much."

She fell against him, and he put her arms around her trembling shoulders. He hugged her tightly wishing away the fear and pain and loss they both felt. He held her until she stopped crying. Showing his concern for someone was becoming increasingly easier. She pulled away and leaned against Monty. He looked up at Steel and the connection between Monty and Cassie couldn't have been more obvious. But for Steel there was no time for sentiment or grief.

"I hate to break this up, but I have an idea." Steel said. "Monty, remember right before we opened one of these crates in Cephas' basement after we returned from Jerusalem?"

Monty nodded. "Yes. You said something about Josh seeing you in the basement while you were in the past."

"Yes." The memory returned.

Steel opened his eyes. He was standing in a bedroom. The morning sun peeked through the slats of a window. As his eyes adjusted to the darkness, he made out a sleeping figure in the bed. Joshua Knight rolled over under the sheets and mumbled something in his sleep. What was happening? And then, to his shock, another figure moved out of the shadows in the corner of the bedroom. It was a man with his back to Steel. Something about his stance, the way he held his fists, the tilt of his head filled Steel with dread. Steel tried to move but couldn't.

"My dear boy." The man said quietly, and the tone of his voice was

far too familiar. "I am sorry you have gotten mixed up in all of this." He reached forward with his right hand and Steel tried to move. The air of menace and danger drove his heart rate up, dried the spit in his mouth. But the man did not harm Josh. He merely pulled up the sheet and covered the boy's bare shoulder.

The man turned, and Steel gasped. It was himself! He was looking at himself as the man walked right toward him and passed through him as if he were a ghost. Steel felt the control return to his body, and he spun to follow the man out of the room and down the stairs into the kitchen of the lake house. The man looked around the kitchen and made his way toward the double doors leading into the basement where Cephas kept his treasures.

What was happening? Steel had experienced flashbacks to his past. But this was different. It had a different feel to it. Could this be a flash forward? Was the trip through the Portal somehow showing him the future? He hurried down the steps behind himself into the basement.

The other Steel figure flipped on the overhead lights. The confusion and disarray that had been left behind shortly before Cephas' death were gone. Liz Washington must have been busy straightening the room and putting back the contents of the crates.

The other Steel walked from crate to crate. He squatted down to glance at the labels on the crates. He would shake his head and move on to another crate. What was he looking for? Finally, the other Steel paused before a crate and smiled.

"Gotcha!" He said out loud.

"Got what?"

Steel whirled. Josh stood at the bottom of the stairs. "Jonathan? When did you get back?"

The other Steel froze and reached into the pocket of his jeans. He took something out of his pocket and pointed it at Josh. Steel's heart froze. It was a small pistol.

"I'm sorry, Josh." The other Steel said. "I have to do this." He pulled the trigger even as Steel tried to throw himself between Josh and the other Steel. A tiny flash of silver passed through him as if he were a cloud. He whirled. A small dart protruded from Josh's bare chest, and

the boy slumped forward onto the floor. The other Steel ran over and retrieved the dart.

"You'll wake up with a headache and wonder how you got down here." The other Steel said. "But you won't remember the last few minutes."

As the other Steel stood up, he heard movement at the top of the stairs. "Josh! Are you down in the basement?" Liz Washington's voice echoed down the stairs.

The other Steel swore loudly and glanced around the basement. He hurried through the crates to one of the small windows at the top of the basement walls. He climbed onto a crate, popped open the window and wiggled through just as Liz Washington came down the stairs.

"Josh?" He heard her shout and then the light began to grow around him, filling the room with white noise. He tried to scream for Liz but he had no voice, no air and he tumbled back into darkness.

STEEL LOOKED AT MONTY. "WHEN YOU WERE AT THE LAKE house we went into the basement and found the coins."

"Yes."

"Do you remember. Josh said something about seeing me." Steel said.

They walked down the stairs into the basement of the lake house. Steel paused at the bottom of the stairs and surveyed the room filled with partially opened crates and stacked books. The hair on his neck stood on end. The dream or flashback or flash forward resurfaced in his memory.

Josh stopped beside him holding a partially eaten pork rib. "Hey, Jonathan, I had this really weird dream while you were gone and I woke up right here in the middle of the basement with Mama Liz beside me."

"What?"

"Yeah, I was in bed, and I thought I heard your voice. I got up and

came down to the basement, and you were standing by one of Uncle Cephas' crates. You took out this gun and shot me with a dart, I think, and I passed out."

"You weren't supposed to remember it." Steel said automatically.

"What?"

"I had the same dream, Josh only I was watching it all take place like I was an observer."

"Dude, let me get this straight. You dreamed the same thing, and you saw yourself shoot me with a dart?"

"Yeah, right after I passed through the Portal into the past."

Josh looked around the basement. "You know what this means, don't you?"

"No."

"Dude, you were coming from the future! That's the only thing that makes sense. You said the scientist who made the machine went into the future. Maybe one day, he'll send you back in time to that moment to get something from the crate."

"Speaking of crates." Holmes wandered over. He was gasping and sweating. "Do you realize what a mess this is? There are books over five hundred years old just lying about sucking up moisture!"

"Calm down, Dr. Holmes." Dr. Liz Washington patted him on the shoulder. "I'm working with my university to catalog and store everything appropriately. There's just so much, and Cephas had his own bizarre catalog system."

Steel pushed past Holmes and walked over to a partially opened crate. "This is the crate I saw myself trying to open. It's been partially pried open. Liz," He looked back at her. "Was this crate opened when you started cataloging?"

Liz joined him. "Well, I'm not sure. It might have been."

"That's the one you were opening when I had my dream," Josh said.

"YES, I REMEMBER." MONTY SAID. "WHAT IS YOUR POINT?"

Steel hurried over to the open crate. "This is the same crate.

Those stones were there within this crate, Monty. I know they were."

"How do we find them?" Cassie asked.

Steel froze and turned to Cassie. "By going back to that moment in time."

Cassie stiffened and backed away. "No way!"

"*You* were going to do it." Steel said.

"Do what?" Monty looked at them both and then ran his hands through his hair. "Go back in time? You're both crazy!"

"Can you get me there?" Steel asked.

For a fleeting second, a hungry, ambitious look filled her eyes. "Yes. I have it all mapped out. But I don't have a vehicle. We can't very well take a cab to a time machine."

"Jonathan, you can't do this." Monty said.

Steel whirled and glared at him. "Josh is dying. I have to get these artifacts, or he never gets well. What would you do?" Steel advanced on him and Monty backed against the metal crate. "What would you do to save your only son, Monty?"

Monty looked away. "We all know the answer to that. All three of us were in Jerusalem."

Steel felt Cassie's hand on his arm. "God gave his only Son. Yes, we know, Jonathan."

Steel turned and looked deeply into her eyes. "God put himself into a human body and turned himself over to us! Horrible, sinful, murderous humans! Josh is in that same situation right now. Surrounded by three demonic beings who are slowly killing him. I can't let that happen. God may have turned his back when his Son died on the cross, but I will not!"

"That was different." Monty said.

"How?"

"He had to turn his back on his only Son when he took on all the wrongdoings of the entire human race for all time." Monty said. "God cannot look upon imperfection. In that moment Jesus was totally alone and abandoned by everyone. Josh is not, Jonathan. We are all here to help you."

"And if they find out you know what is going on, then Josh is in more danger." Steel said. "That dampener is protecting us from surveillance right now. I demanded they stop watching and listening to me. But if there is one thing I know about Satan and his demons it is this: they are liars."

Monty paused and seemed deep in thought. "So, you are assuming you were there in the past which means you're going back in time in the present. Here. Now. I can't argue with that no matter how fantastical it sounds. So, if you are determined to go through with this, Hampton has a delivery truck out back. If I can get the keys from Margaret, we can take it."

"Not we." Cassie put a hand on Monty. She looked at him and ran a hand through his hair. "I know where to go. Jonathan is right about one thing. If they are watching, the fewer of us involved the better."

"She's right." Steel said. "I hate to admit it, but I need Cassie to take me there. I have no idea how to drive around in this country and I'm so exhausted I would probably have a wreck and injure someone in the meantime. It's bad enough I am putting her in the line of danger."

Monty took Cassie's hand and leaned into her. He put his forehead against hers. "Okay. I don't like it. You will take care of her, won't you, Jonathan." He looked up at Steel.

Steel's heart pounded with fear and anger against the circumstances. It was so obvious now that Monty and Cassie had a deep, abiding love for each other. And he was pulling one of them into the pits of hell with his actions. He reached out and took them both in his arms and held them tight as tears filled his eyes. This emotional outpouring was getting exhausting. But it was so natural now.

"Why, why, why?" He moaned. "I'm so sorry to have involved the two of you. Can you ever forgive me?"

They pulled away from him and Cassie held Monty close. "Jonathan, if not for you I would still be dying a horrible, lingering death." Cassie said.

"And I would have never had the opportunity to see my fragile faith so strengthened by an encounter with my Savior. This is the least we can do." Monty said.

Steel nodded. "Then I will take care of Cassie. I promise. And I always keep my promises."

5

Faye Morgan pulled out her laptop and placed it on the table in the break room. Her hands still shook after what she had seen. And Jason Birdsong had shaken her world to the core. Demons? Really? Was all of this really happening to Joshua Knight?

She glanced at the break room door as Travion stepped in. "What you doing, girlfriend? Looking for love on the Internet?" He laughed.

"Just browsing for gifts for my sisters. Christmas will be here before you know it." Faye lied with surprising ease.

Travion opened the refrigerator and took out a one-liter bottle of soda. "I would join you, but I need to keep an eye on the monitors. The three sisters were in a tiz last night!" He left the room and Faye released the breath she did not know she was holding. She glanced at the clock. Almost six A.M. The next shift would be arriving soon, and she had to get this done before leaving the clinic. If what Josh said was true, she had to consider whether leaving him alone was the best option even if she had not slept in over 24 hours.

Okay, first, Dr. Hampton. Her search yielded a website for Dr. Hampton's "Museum of the Weird". She read about his unusual collection of "ancient arcane objects". But what did this museum have to do with the clinic? She clicked on a tab and images filled the screen from some of the museum's displays. She scrolled down the page and froze. She gasped and put a hand to her mouth.

One of the exhibits was for "Pandora's Box" and showed a woman with red hair and a flowing white gown hovering over an elderly lady in a poofy robe and old-fashioned night cap. Both figures were mannequin type reproductions. But what took her breath away was the object the elderly woman held in her hand. It was a blood red stone etched with veins of gold and the caption read:

> "The spirit of Pandora hovers over Mary, the Jewess, the first alchemists who holds the Philosopher's Stone in her hand, the source of the Elixir of Life."

Faye sat back as a cold shiver ran down her spine. The stone looked exactly like the stone she had seen in Josh's bedside table drawer! She went to the contact tab and scrolled through Hampton's contact information. At the very bottom of the page was a notation that read,

> "If you have a serious illness, Dr. Hampton is the co-founder of one of the premier specialty medical clinics in the world. For more information go to this website."

She clicked on the link and the website for the North Dallas Tristate Clinic filled the screen. Josh was right! Hampton was a founding member of the clinic!

Faye sat back in her chair. Her heart was racing, and she glanced around the break room. It was ordinary. It was normal. And yet, behind the façade there was a man named Hampton who owned a Museum with Pandora's Box in a display and was a founding member of a clinic in Texas! Josh was not delusional. He had suggested she look into the names of the three doctors.

Faye then searched for the name, Shutendoji along with the word "demon". The image that popped up filled her heart with dread. An ancient etching showed a huge, red skinned demon with multiple eyes and horns hovering over an unsuspecting man. She read the description.

> *"Shutendoji was a Japanese demonic being standing 50 feet tall with a red body, five horns and fifteen eyes."*

Faye's hands trembled as she put in Dr. Shutendoji's first name. "Schichi is the Japanese word for the numeral seven." She stood up and backed against the wall. What had Jason said? There were three demons from some kind of council; seven, six, and five?

She sat back down and did a search on Gomijo. The seductive image of a young girl appeared and from behind her one could see nine fox tails.

> *"Gumijo is a fox tailed demon from Korea. According to the oral legends of Korea, if a fox lived a thousand years it would turn into a gumijo, and this means a nine-tailed fox. Gumijos transform themselves into beautiful women who seduce boys and then eats their hearts or livers."*

Faye swallowed again and searched for Gomijo's first name. "Yeosut" was the numeral six!

The next search revealed Santelmo was a creature that seemed to be covered in flames. And, of course, the first name Lima meant the numeral five.

Faye closed her laptop with trembling hands. She had seen something in the face of Shutendoji that had shaken her world and that image corresponded to everything Josh and Jason had claimed. Were the three doctors truly demons? Were they in some kind of evil plan with Dr. Hampton? It all sounded like a bad supernatural thriller novel. The problem was, she was in the middle of it, and it was all true! She glanced at her cell phone. She had to call Jason Birdsong but she didn't dare do so from the clinic. She had the next thirty-six hours off and in spite of not wanting to leave Josh in the hands of these creatures, she had to get some sleep. IF she could sleep!

Faye hurried from the break room and down the hall to Josh's room. She paused outside the door and drew a deep breath. "Dear God, I've been complacent for too long. Protect me now. And watch over Joshua Knight."

Faye moved into the room and the sight before her drove her heart into her throat. All three doctors were positioned around Josh's bed: one to the right, one to the left, and one at the foot of the bed. All three doctors turned in unison to look at her.

"Is there a problem?" Shutendoji said.

Faye swallowed hard. "Uh, no. I was checking on Josh one last time before I left for the day." She moved over to the counter. "Should I change his diaper?" She pulled open the top drawer. Before, when she looked through the drawer, she had been unconvinced about the presence of the 'bloodstone'. But now, she saw a faint reddish glow from beneath a folded tee shirt. She brushed the tee shirt aside and the red jewel sparkled with some kind of inner power. Just as Josh had said, the sliver of a red jewel hung from a silver necklace. She closed her hand around the jewel just as she felt the presence of someone behind her. She turned slowly, holding her closed fist behind her back. All three doctors stood before her.

"What are you doing?" Gomijo said.

"Looking for a diaper." Faye said hoarsely.

Santelmo glanced at her watch. "Your shift is at an end. The next shift will take care of Mr. Knight."

Gomijo pointed to the window. "Did you open that window earlier?"

Faye nodded nervously. "Since you don't want me taking Josh

outside, I thought some fresh air might help. But the window is almost frozen shut. It hasn't been open in years."

Shutendoji looked at her sisters. She tilted her head as she looked back at Faye. "Nurse practitioner Morgan, although your clinical privileges exceed those of most nursing staff, we are still Mr. Knight's attending physicians. You will not make such drastic changes in his environment without our consent."

"Or you may join Dudley in his unemployed state." Santelmo said.

Faye nodded. "Of course. By the way, Dudley had formed a rapport with Josh. May I ask why you fired him?"

Gomijo raised an eyebrow. "You may ask. But we do not have to answer."

"Is there any chance he may return?" Faye said.

Santelmo looked like she was chewing on glass. "According to his contract, he will have a few more days in the next week of employment and we cannot forbid him from showing up for work. But I do not want him anywhere near Mr. Knight. Understand?"

Faye nodded and felt heat grow in her closed fist. Was the jewel heating up? "Of course. I'm off for the next thirty-six hours and I hope that Mr. Knight will do well."

"As long as he is sedated, he will be fine." Gomijo's lips lifted in a false smile. "You may go."

Faye cast one look at Josh and breathed another silent prayer as she left the room. Like hungry predators, the three sisters of the unholy triad returned to their vigil over the sleeping boy.

$\mathcal{H}$ 6 $\mathcal{H}$

Warehouse on the Thames

DR. MONARCH SAT IN NEAR TOTAL DARKNESS. OLIVIA AND Steven had gone upstairs, and she was alone in her lab with all the lights off. The only illumination came from the computer monitor. Steel had mentioned a word that nibbled at the corner of her memories. Penticle. Where had she run across that word before?

Monarch signed into a highly secure cloud service and accessed her saved folders. She studied the folder names. The information in these folders had been saved from her various experiments. Somewhere in these notes there was a reference to the Penticle, she was convinced. She did a search and came up empty.

She sighed and leaned back wearily in her chair. The memory card entrusted to her by Jonathan Steel sat on the desk before her. It contained the names of every person who had hired Raven to perform an assassination, including the time Raven had attempted to kill Monarch only to take out her husband. Steel had begged her not to tamper with it. But the temptation was growing by the moment. There had to be a way to safely access the data.

She stared back at the monitor deep in thought and noticed one of the file folders near the bottom of the list contained a strange name she did not recognize.

"ProtoOne? This isn't one of my folders."

Monarch double clicked on the folder and a video window opened. Her husband stared back at her. Monarch gasped and put a hand to her mouth. Her eyes watered. He had left her a message? He had hidden this video in her experiment folder which she had not opened in a long time! Her hand drifted toward the mouse, and she hovered the cursor over the play button. Her heart thundered in her chest. She closed her eyes and clicked the mouse button.

"My dearest, I have left a message for you in the event I do not make it back from my latest conference. I hid this video in one of your, uh, experiment folders. You know, the ones about your brain research. Anyway, one day you will search for one of about a dozen words that should trigger this video. Of course, if you are seeing this folder then I must be, well, indisposed. I placed it here purely out of a need for redundancy in the event I am in some way, uh, detained."

He paused and Monarch fought back a sob. "You meant dead." She whispered.

"Open the folder and its contents and all will be self-explanatory. Keep it safe. Keep it secret. I love you. And the kiddos." His image froze and Monarch sat back as tears poured down her cheeks. She closed the window and it blinked out of existence. She gasped again. No matter how many times she searched for the name "ProtoOne" the search came up empty. Her husband had made sure the video would disappear after she listened to it. She had lost the last message from her husband!

Monarch stood up and paced around the lab until she could

contain her sobbing. She washed her face in the lab sink and dried it with a towel. Why would the name "Penticle" matter to her husband? He was a marine biologist and a virologist by training. Somewhere, somehow, sometime in the past her husband must have searched for the Penticle! Time to see what was so important!

She sat before her computer again and double clicked on the folder again. The video was no longer in existence as she had discovered. She searched the trash again, and it was not there. She ran a recovery program again. No video. It was gone. Forever. What did the video have to do with her search for the word, "Penticle"? She went back to the folder labeled "Proto-One" and examined the dozen or so documents and graphic files. There were too many to just start opening files randomly. She would be at all night.

"Ah!" She smiled. When she had run her search for the word "Penticle", she had not included *this* folder. It had remained hidden. She ran the search for "Penticle" on the folder contents and got a hit.

Monarch looked at the document name. "Snoball? Sno, not snow." The name seemed very familiar and it was tied to the memory of her first encounter with Jonathan Steel.

※

DR. MONARCH LOOKED AROUND THE SURGICAL SUITE IN DISGUST. *Who would put such a room in a prison in Africa? The conditions were less than sterile. And yet, she had agreed to do the surgery. She had to know if her methods were successful for the sake of her daughter. The things a parent would do for their children!*

The tall, dark man carried a baseball bat and shoved her patient into the room. The man was of medium height with reddish blonde hair and a tightly coiled muscled body. His tee shirt was stained with sweat and blood and he reeked to high heaven of the latrine. Monarch pulled her surgical mask up to cover her nose. She pushed her dark hair up into a surgical hair cover and glared at the man standing beside her as he pulled a pipe out of his pocket.

"No smoking, Captain." She barked at him. "We have pure oxygen in this room."

The Captain turned his bright, turquoise eyes on her. He was dressed in a khaki shirt and pants, and he put a meerschaum pipe into his mouth. The Captain raised an eyebrow and glared at her. "Dr. Monarch, I am not a fool. I will not light the pipe."

The tall African pushed his prisoner down into a chair. The prisoner's eyes were filled with a murderous lust, and she caught her breath at their intense turquoise color. This was indeed the Captain's son! What kind of man would subject his son to this kind of surgery? She couldn't afford to asks such questions. She couldn't afford a conscience right now. She closed her eyes and recalled the image of her daughter as the bullet entered her daughter's skull. This was for her! She would do anything to help her daughter, including working for the Captain.

"I knew you were here!" the man growled.

"I told you not to try and find me." The Captain motioned to the table. "Maxi, if you would escort my son to the table."

Mazi, the tall African, shoved Steel toward the table, and the Captain pointed to Steel's hands. "Remove the bindings."

"He will try to escape."

The Captain shook his head. "Why should he try to escape? He has found what he has been looking for. Right, son?"

The man continued to glare at his father while Mazi removed the cord from his wrists. Mazi pointed the bat at the man. "Just in case," he muttered.

"Kito!" The Captain spoke. "Dr. Sno."

Another shorter man in blue scrubs came through the door. His intense black eyes were filled with fire. "Yes."

"Keep Mazi under control. I don't want that bat to ruin my son's brain." The Captain said.

Mazi glared at Kito and took his bat. "If he tries to escape, it's on you." Mazi growled. Sweat rolled from his forehead.

Kito took the bat and tucked it under his arm. "Shut up and listen."

The Captain took the pipe from his mouth and paced back and forth in front of his son. "I told you to stop looking for me, or you would have to pay the price. Do you know where you are?"

"Somewhere in North Africa," The man whispered. "Some kind of biological weapons facility."

The Captain stopped pacing and pointed the pipe at his son. "No, son, this is a prison camp. You're lucky the militia didn't cut your head off. It cost me a lot to get them to spare your life."

The man looked around at the surgical suite. "This looks like a hospital. More of your experiments?"

The Captain smiled. "Oh, no. Not my experiments. Dr. Monarch has made some impressive advances. A marvelous technological advancement. Dr. Monarch is going to let you be one of the first patients to experience it."

The man tried to push up from his seat and Mazi jerked the bat from Kito's grasp and caught the man across his back with the bat. The man gasped for breath and thudded onto the floor. Mazi turned him over onto his back and picked him up like he was a rag doll. He placed him on the surgical bed.

"Kito, please take Mazi out of here before he kills my son." The Captain said.

Kito motioned to the hallway. "Let's go, Mazi. Or, I trigger your implant."

Mazi growled at the man on the ground and reluctantly followed Kito from the room..

The Captain leaned over his son. "Let me tell you what your future holds. You will undergo this surgery. And then, one day, you will escape from this prison camp and come after me again. On that day I will whisper something in your ear, and your life will end. Everything you hold dear will disappear in a puff of smoke. Think about that. Your devotion to your precious God will vanish. Your 'transformation,' as you call it, to your new life will be forgotten. You will have nothing left but an empty page. Do you want that? Do you want to forget your God? That is what will happen if you come after me again. Do you understand?"

The man gasped for breath and whispered. "Nothing can separate me from the love of God."

Monarch blinked away tears. How could this man still cling to his belief in God when that very God had allowed him to fall prey to his father's experiments? How could God have let her daughter suffer? Because there is no God, she thought. There was only what she could make of it at the moment and right now, the Captain was god. Monarch picked up the anesthesia mask as she had to do both the job of the anesthetist and the surgeon. She put the mask over the man's eyes and his intense eyes focused on her.

"Why are you doing this?" He said hoarsely.

She pushed the mask over his nose and mouth. "Don't fight it, and it will all be over in no time."

Monarch wasn't the only doctor at the clinic. But she was the only one performing neurosurgical procedures. However, there had been one other doctor present who had shown an interest in her procedure. The oaf named Mazi had called the other man Kito. Kito was a small, diminutive man probably from India or Pakistan. He had been in the room when she started Steel's surgery and had watched attentively.

When the inmate breakout occurred later, she remembered running for her life and she had seen Kito free Steel from his cell and then take the life of Mazi. What she had not noted at the time but now came crashing back to her was seeing the man in the hall right after.

"Run, Dr. Monarch. I will protect your retreat." Kito said *hefting his gun.*

Monarch had her messenger bag slung over her shoulder with her laptop and all her research. "I couldn't get the implants or the electrodes, Kito. I can't let anyone have them."

His back was to her and he faced the empty hallway from which the escaped inmates were coming. "I'll destroy them." He turned and nodded at her. She remembered gasping at the sight of his totally white eyes. She barely thought about it as she ran out of the prison and into the brush to a waiting ATV she had hidden just for such an emergency.

MONARCH SAT FORWARD AND PUT HER HEAD IN HER HANDS. The man had white eyes? Kito, Kito what? What had been his name? She gasped and sat back. The Captain had once called the man Dr. Sno. And in London they had learned that the Captain was working with a female Dr. Sno with white eyes. What had Steel called them? Vitreomancers! A Council of Darkness and its opposition the Vitreomancers. What had she stumbled into? It sounded like a worldwide conspiracy. Just like the Penticle!

She opened the document labeled "Snoball" and began to read. The document spoke of a cartel of five individuals who comprised the Penticle and controlled various aspects of govern-ment and commerce. If she had not heard the word from Steel, she would have passed it off as a fictional conspiracy. But now a chill ran down her spine when she read off the five names listed in the document. One of them was Dr. Sno and the image in the document was that of a woman, not the man. And she recalled Steel mentioning his father, the Captain was working with a Dr. Sno. Dr. Sno was one of the members of the Penticle!

What if her husband's inquiries into this Penticle had trig-gered the assassination and the target had been her husband after all? Or maybe both of them? Could it be *she* was targeted because of her husband? Was it possible they were both targets of assassination? Now that Raven's mind had been wiped, the only answer lay in the dossier on Raven's memory card.

Monarch picked up the memory card and held it up before her. "All my answers are in the palm of my hand."

"And so is Josh's life." The lights came on overhead.

Monarch whirled in her chair and Olivia stood in the doorway to the stairs leading up to their living area. She wore a pair of Star Wars themed pajamas and held a cup in her hands. "I decided to get some chamomile tea to help me relax and was coming down here to offer you some. I'm glad I did. Mom, you can't do this."

Monarch placed the card back on the console before her and minimized the windows on the monitor before her daughter could see them. "I know. It's just so many answers are right here in that dossier. I could find out who wanted me killed. I could find out if it's true I was the target and not your father."

Olivia came to the console and leaned against the edge. "Mom, Mr. Steel gave you that memory chip to keep it away from someone. If you access it, who's to say it won't alert someone?"

"It might alert Max. But whoever is making these demands on Jonathan is a separate threat."

"The next demon?"

Monarch glanced at her. "You don't believe in demons, remember?"

Olivia massaged the tea cup in her hand. She shivered and sipped some tea. The fragrance wafted over Monarch and for a moment, seemed so normal. But their lives had not been normal since the assassination of her husband. Olivia ran a hand through her short hair.

"I'm not so sure about these demons anymore. You weren't there inside Numnocity. You weren't on that slab in Thakkar's warehouse." Olivia sipped some tea. Her eyes glittered with emotion. "Mom, I saw things in this world that cannot be explained."

"Honey, you know how your seizures affect you sometime. You have auras. You see things. You hear things." Monarch said.

Olivia sipped more tea and sighed. "I know, Mom. But there was something about all this that was different. I knew something was wrong. I felt evil. It was different from anything I've ever experienced with my seizures. It was as if I sensed the wrongness of it in my soul, my heart."

"Soul? You know how I feel about that word." Monarch said.

Olivia rolled her eyes. "I know. We are our brains. There is no soul." Olivia bit her lip and looked into her teacup. "I think you're wrong, Mom. I've been reading about consciousness and the soul and the mind. There are plenty of scholarly articles that make a convincing case we are far more than just biochemistry."

Monarch sighed and rubbed her eyes. "I don't want to argue, honey. I'm too tired."

"No matter what, I want to go home. I want to check on Josh." Olivia said firmly.

Monarch looked up at her daughter. Her short hair had grown back after the fire had singed some of it. The minor burns on her face were clearing. Her heart ached with love for this child. Was that feeling of love nothing more than just biochemistry? For a moment, she hoped not. She put a hand on Olivia's arm. "Olivia, if we go back to the states, whoever is after Jonathan may be waiting for us."

"Jonathan gave you that memory card because he knew they had no idea we were involved. I think we will be safe." Olivia said.

"You can't know that."

"I can go back by myself. I can get Jonathan's partner, Mr. Birdsong, to watch over me." Olivia said. Olivia pulled her cell phone from her pocket. "He's staying in Shreveport for a while. Wouldn't tell me why. I can ask him if he could meet me at the airport and watch over me so I could check on Josh."

Monarch stood up and tightened her lips. She shook his head. "You're not going anywhere without me, young woman!"

Olivia sighed and slid the phone back into her pocket. "It was worth a try. I'm heading to bed. Mom, don't do anything you will regret later."

7

Jason Birdsong was back in Shreveport and paced up and down the hallway of Merchant's hospital. Inside a nearby office, Dr. Jack Merchant was busy at work doing his job as a radiologist and he had assured Jason he would be finished soon, and they could go to lunch.

"Can I help you, sir?"

Birdsong paused and looked down at the woman in green scrubs. She had bronze colored skin and short, brown hair highlighted with maroon streaks.

"I'm a friend of Dr. Merchant. He's taking me to lunch."

She smiled. "Well, it might be a few. He's not in the office. He's down the hall performing a CT guided lung biopsy." She paused and shook her head. "Sorry, I'm Pam, one of the radiology nurses. Want me to give him a message?"

"Sure. Just tell him I'll wait for him in the main waiting room by the cafeteria."

Pam laughed. "He won't eat there. He'll eat in the doctor's cafeteria on the third floor."

"You've eaten there?"

"Oh, no. I've just had to chase him down on occasion. And don't plan on any better food up there. The only difference between their cafeteria and ours is they get real silverware instead of plasticware." She turned and headed back down the hallway. She paused and turned back to him. "Sorry. Didn't get your name."

"Jason Birdsong."

Pam's eyes widened and she hurried back to him. "Birdsong? Indigenous American?"

"Yes. O'Odham. I'm from Arizona."

Pam smiled. "I'm close to full blood Caddo Indian." She then said something in a foreign language and laughed.

"Sorry, didn't get that."

"I said you are a pleasantly big man. Technically, strong man." She blushed and turned away and disappeared around the corner.

"Jason?"

Birdsong looked to his right down an intersecting hallway. Dr. Jack Merchant walked toward him stripping off a face mask and a surgeon's cap. "Sorry I'm running late. Let's get out of here."

"To the doctor's cafeteria?"

Merchant wore black scrubs and a white coat. "Still hospital food but it's quiet. How did you know?"

"I met Pam."

Merchant raised an eyebrow and smiled. "Ah, Pam." He motioned to a nearby bank of elevators and Birdsong followed him. "She's single. Sweet girl. Goes to church. Loves softball." Merchant punched a button for the elevator. "Softball church teams are the rage in Louisiana. More intense than the majors."

Birdsong followed Merchant into the open elevator. "Are you trying to fix me up?"

"No. She's my fiancée. Although I'm not so sure anyone is safe around me." Merchant punched the button labeled three. Birdsong noticed the tremor in his hand.

"Doc, you okay?"

Merchant shook his head and remained silent. He led them through the open elevator doors and down a hallway to the

"Doctor's Cafeteria", a small room with large windows overlooking the air conditioning units on the roof of the second floor of the emergency room. The food was served cafeteria style and Merchant nodded to the server behind the counter.

"He's with me. Charge his meal to my account."

Birdsong loaded up on black eyed peas, corn on the cob and fried chicken. He seldom got that in Arizona. Merchant had chosen a salad and a bowl of tomato basil soup. The sat at a table in the farthest corner. Merchant flexed his hand.

"Look, Jason, you might be used to these supernatural things but I'm not. Right now, I'm pretty shaken up. I think about someone like Pam. She's living out her ordinary life with friends and family and church totally oblivious to these creatures among us. I want to go back to that. I want to be oblivious."

"I'm sorry, Jack. Once you're let the demon out of the bottle you can't put it back." Birdsong chewed some cornbread. "I met someone at the clinic. Nice girl named Faye. A nurse practitioner. I think she will help protect Josh. I saw her reaction to things she has seen. I'm sure she's trembling right now, too."

"Pam and I are engaged. I was nervous after my first wife passed away." Merchant drank his water and swallowed hard. "Now, I'm beginning to think marrying me is a mistake. How do you go on with normal things when you realize there are these monsters who can animate dead flesh and possess innocent people?"

"What do you mean animate dead people?" Birdsong paused.

"At the morgue. I went to get my tablet." Monty looked over his shoulder like he was expecting a ghost. "One of the bodies tried to take the tablet from me. A dead body, Jason! It walked and talked and moved! I hate zombie movies. The human body isn't supposed to move like that." His hands shook again, and he placed both in his lap. "I don't know if I can do this."

Birdsong placed his fork on the table. "Okay, Doc, I used to teach senior high school boys in church. I've learned a thing or two about spiritual warfare. First off, Doc, there are no innocent people. We are all broken. And broken vessels leak. We also let other disturbing stuff seep in. Second, we live in a technologically advanced world where the supernatural seems to be just another CGI special effect. Cling to the normal things." He picked up his fork and ate some more peas. "Normal is the only way to keep from losing your mind. That, and staying spiritually strong. Put on the whole armor of God. We literally did that in Numinocity."

"When I died, I had a near death experience. I went through the tunnel of light. I saw Jesus. I saw my dead wife. And I saw a red shoe." Merchant said.

Birdsong paused. "Red shoe?"

"Yep, on a window ledge of the hospital where it was impossible for anyone to see it from the ground or from any angle other than hovering out over the street!" He paused and drank some of his water. "I found the shoe. Just where I had seen it. No way I could have known about the shoe. And, yet I had seen it while having an out of body experience, Jason."

"Then, you shouldn't have any problem with the supernatural. I mean, you believe in God, right?"

"Yeah, I do. Once, I told God I would find time for him when I felt like it. The last three years have changed all that. I go to church." Jack looked down at the table. "But I guess I didn't really believe in all that weird stuff in the Bible."

"Until now." Birdsong said. "I was in the same boat, Jack. I've seen things in the past and things in virtual reality that make me question my grasp of reality. But there is one thing I know. What you read in the Gospels really happened. It happened just as it was written."

Merchant looked up. "I still can't believe you went back in time. Did you really see Jesus?"

Birdsong smiled. "Looks like we both did. And if we saw Jesus, then why should it surprise you that you met a demon possessed corpse? Jack, I've met angels and demons. I've traveled through time because of the permission and work of God. I faced a demon who created a quasi-spiritual virtual reality that threatened to take the minds and souls of millions. It's all real. Way too real, dude." Birdsong sat back. "Like the song says, you gotta serve somebody. I've seen both sides and I know which side I want to serve on. And it is the side of the angels."

Merchant nodded and began to eat his soup. "I just needed to know I wasn't losing my mind. I've been close to that before."

"Jack." Birdsong said.

Merchant looked up from his soup. "Yes."

"Serving God will cost you something. There'll be more than the shakes ahead. You gotta be prayed up, confessed up, and read up on the Bible. Because these demons have always been here and you just didn't believe it. I need to know you are willing to go the distance. I would march into hell for Jonathan Steel and Josh Knight. Will you be by my side?"

Merchant nodded. "Even with the shakes."

Birdsong's phone rang and the name 'Faye Morgan' appeared. "It's about Josh!" He said and put the phone on speaker. "Faye, is something wrong with Josh?"

Faye's face appeared in a Facetime chat. Her hair was in disarray and her eyes were puffy. "Other than being in the hands of, and I hate to say this, demon doctors, no." She put a hand to her mouth and stifled a sob. "Mr. Birdsong, I looked up the names of the doctors. They all refer to demons with the same names. And their first names are seven, six, and five." She drew a shuddering breath. "I only slept a few hours! I'm exhausted and confused and scared. I have to get back to the clinic!"

"Faye, take a deep breath." Birdsong said calmly.

"Take a breath? Are you kidding me? If what you guys say is happening, this changes everything in my world!" Faye struggled to breathe. "Okay, I'm hyperventilating."

Merchant took the phone from Birdsong. "Ms. Morgan, this is Dr. Merchant. I had no idea these things were happening either until a couple of days ago. I have had to rethink my world-view. Are you a religious person?"

Faye fought for breath. "Yes. Sort of." She paused and slowed her breathing and her eyes opened wide. "One thing is for sure. I will be more dedicated from now on. I haven't been to church in a while. My parents are Godly people who adopted foster kids because they saw it as their mission. We were raised in the church, but I've never wanted to be that committed. Until now!"

"I'm in the same boat. Although it sounds like I made a deeper commitment before you did after things happened after my wife's death. I've seen some things, Ms. Morgan."

"Faye. Call me Faye, Dr. Merchant." Her breathing was regular now.

"Call me Jack." Merchant continued. "Like I said, I've seen some things just in the past day that will haunt me for the rest of my life. If there are demons, as Jason just told me, there must be angels on the side of God and of good."

Faye's eyes widened. "Dude! Josh said one of our orderlies was really his guardian angel named Dude."

Birdsong slid over so the phone would pick up his face. "I've met the guy."

"What?" Faye said.

"He rescued Josh and me in London. He can help you. If he's there, he'll watch over Josh."

"No!" Faye put a hand to her mouth. "No, they fired him! They must have known he was an angel!"

Birdsong took the phone from Merchant. "May I? Faye, you have to get some sleep and then go back to work. Nothing bad will happen to Josh as long as they have Jonathan Steel under their control. They will make sure he is alive and well. But we don't know where this thing is headed. Jack is working on the fluid and the blood. If he can find a way for Josh to survive without this infusion, we can get him out of there and free up Mr. Steel to do what he does best."

"Which is what?" Faye asked.

"Kick demon butt!" Birdsong said.

❧ 8 ❧

"Cutting off the top of a man's head is not what we had in mind! We told you to keep a low profile!" Shutendoji shouted at the image on her tablet.

"I was hungry."

"Oh, spare me the melodramatics!" Santelmo walked behind Shutendoji, glared at the tablet and then sat at the conference room table next to Gomijo. "This isn't fiction! You're not that character in a muzzle, whatever his name was."

"We all have our role models." The man said.

Hampton had returned from his mansion after hearing about the murder in Shreveport. Now, he paced around the conference room until he paused just out of the man's visual range. "I can take care of this." He said softly. "Let me talk to him."

Gomijo glared at him and turned the tablet to face Hampton. Reginald Drake's face filled the tablet screen. As always, his eyes shocked Hampton. His right eye was a pale, icy blue and his left eye a deep chocolate brown. His handsome face was framed by silver hair making him look much older than his young age. He wore a shiny, silver Armani suit with a burgundy tie held back by a tie tack shaped like a scorpion.

"How?" Gomijo said.

"Simply teleport him out of the country." Hampton said.

"Ah, that may be a problem." Drake said lazily. "My current, uh, associates are quite ineffective in that respect. My previous associate moved on."

"I don't blame it." Santelmo said.

Drake laughed. "Problem is, we were too much alike!"

Hampton cleared his throat and the three women glared at him. "I know a certain host with extraordinary abilities. She can transport herself around the world. It takes the human part a while to recover, but she is extraordinarily powerful. I think we can whisk Mr. Drake out of the country. He will be indisposed for a while but that may be a most agreeable situation."

"He is wearing a tracer anklet. They will know where he is. I say we kill him out right." Shutendoji hissed. Her normally sedate features twisted once again into the multi-eyed, multi-horned creature.

"Well, I wouldn't exactly consider that a viable option, dearest." Drake said from the tablet. "I record all of my video transactions and I can assure you if anything happens to me, they will be made public."

"And we would all be heroes!" Gumijo said tersely.

Santelmo put up a slim hand to calm them all down. "Then we go with Hamptons' option."

"I like the idea of leaving the country." Drake said. "I would love to visit that furnace. How many bodies were burned there over decades?"

Hampton paused. "Hundreds. Cadavers from the medical school. I will have my assistant take you out of the country within the hour. I will need your location and you can text it to this number." Hampton relayed his number and then smiled at the triplets. "I will take care of this."

Santelmo glanced at her sisters. "Before we go on, we have a question. Who is Pandora?"

Hampton froze. "Pandora? A mythical being."

"Josh said he pricked his finger on Pandora's box. We understand that is how you inoculated the boy. But he is claiming Pandora invades his mind when he dreams."

Hampton laughed. "What an absurd accusation. How would such a thing happen? I think this development is due to the brain swelling."

Santelmo moved slowly over to him as she spoke. "Dr. Hampton, do you have our best interests at heart? Or yours?"

Hampton frowned. "Yours, of course. We have an agreement. Doctors, I submit that since Josh pricked his finger on Pandora's box, he naturally would hallucinate about Pandora."

Santelmo nodded. "Then you will not object to keeping Josh sedated while he sleeps to prevent him from dreaming? That would prevent this Pandora from manifesting."

Hampton hid his shock. He looked away. "Of course I don't mind."

The three triplets glanced at each other and Santelmo nodded. "Very well. Proceed with your plan with Drake."

Hampton left the conference room and walked out into the chill air of the courtyard. A couple of patients sat under the covered porch smoking. Hampton hurried to the shade of the tree with the red leaves. His phone beeped with the arrival of Drake's location. He dialed a number.

"I need you to take care of someone for me, Margaret." He said as a blood red leaf settled on the back of his hand. Now he would have to decide how to remove Josh's ongoing sedation or his plan would fail!

9

Faye Morgan stared at herself in her bathroom mirror. Her eyes were surrounded by deep circles of black, but she had taken some acetaminophen with Benadryl after her conversation with Birdsong and had gotten deep, but restless sleep. Her hair hung wet and listless around her face after a steaming shower that had done nothing to change the reality that she was about to go to work to protect a young man not from disease, but from demons.

She went through her morning routine of makeup and drying her hair, but her heart was not in it. What did it matter how she looked to a demon? What she had to do was find Dude and make sure he came back to work as they said he would. But how? And how was she to face the three doctors knowing they were in league with extra dimensional spiritual beings? She needed something to bolster her confidence.

Faye dressed in her scrubs and pulled her still moist hair back into a ponytail. She sat on her bed in her small apartment and opened the drawer of her bedside table. She half expected to see a glowing red rock with gold veins but instead saw her brand new Bible her brother had gotten for her last Christmas. She had put it away in the drawer and forgot it ever existed.

Faye picked up the Bible and felt a tear in her eye as the look and feel of this new Bible reminded her of an older Bible. When she had finally met her biological mother, she had wanted to hate her; to blame her for all that was wrong with her mind and spirit. After all, her mother had allowed Faye to be abused by her father while she was zoned out on meth.

Much to her surprise, her biological mother had cleaned up her act and had been sober for ten years. Her biological father was still in prison for killing a fellow drug dealer and good riddance to the beast! Her mother had asked for forgiveness and Faye had been rather cool about it. How could she forgive this woman who had allowed her to suffer such trauma?

Her mother had said very little. She recalled the conversation.

৩৯৩

"You don't have to call me mother." The woman said as she sipped at her coffee. "Call me Rachel."

Faye fidgeted with her own coffee cup and glanced around at the bustling crowd in the coffee shop. How many of these people around her had suffered a childhood like Faye? More than she could imagine? Or not at all?

"I was strung out on meth." Rachel said. Her face was thin but healthy. Her teeth had been replaced with implants and her black hair was shot through with strands of gray. But she was clean and sober, and her eyes were surprisingly sharp. "Monica, I don't expect you to forgive me."

"It's Faye." Faye said tersely. "I changed my name. All three of them. I had to erase that garbage from my memories, Rachel!"

Rachel flinched. "Faye? That's a nice name. Keep it. You deserve a new start."

"Why are you here?"

Rachel sipped more coffee and put her purse on the table beside her. "I'm not asking for forgiveness because I don't deserve it. But you deserve a new life and peace." She dug in her purse and pulled out a small wooden box and put it on the table. Faye gasped and put her hands on her face.

"Grandmother's jewelry box?"

"I want you to have it. Mother kept it hidden or I would have hocked all her jewelry. She's dead now." Rachel's voice broke and she put a fist to her mouth. "I don't even remember the funeral. I was in rehab." She drew a deep, shuddering breath and pushed the small box toward Faye. "I want you to have it. She loved you so much and she tried to warn me many times about what was happening to you. And I know if mother and father had been healthy enough, she would have taken you instead of letting child protection put you with a strange family."

"They are not strange." Faye said with less venom than she wanted to. "They loved me and cared for me and helped me heal." Faye opened the box and a tiny ballerina popped up. The melody of Cinderella's waltz filled the air between them. Faye's eyes watered and she slowly closed the lid. "Thank you." She whispered.

Rachel stood up and reached into her purse for one more item. She took out a brown leather book. "Your grandfather's Bible. I wish I had paid more attention to the truth he shared with me from the Bible. It would have spared so many from so much pain." Rachel placed the Bible on the table by the jewelry box and a lone tear splashed on the cover.

Rachel turned and rushed out the door into the cold winter air. Faye sat still and silent as she stared at the Bible. Her mouth twisted into a frown. "And where were you, God, while I was in hell?"

❁

FAYE WENT TO HER CLOSET AND TOOK DOWN A STORAGE BOX. She carried it to her kitchen and placed it on the table. Inside the box she found her grandfather's Bible. Since she had received the Bible from 'Rachel', she had found a way to work through the pain of her mistreatment. She had made a tentative peace with God. But it had been a while since she had read the Bible. In fact, she had never opened this Bible putting it and the jewelry box away with her haunting memories.

Faye opened the cover of the Bible and found a folded piece of paper. Monica was written on the outside. She touched the paper and breathed in the faint fragrance of Old Spice and old leather. A note left for her? She picked it up and slowly unfolded it.

"Dear Monica. Your grandmother and I want only the best for you. One day, this Bible will make its way back to you. We regret that out health prevents us from taking care of you and we are very sorry for the evil done to you by your mother and father. If we had known, we would have acted sooner. But such things were not in our world when we grew up. We were naïve to think your troubles were because of you learning disabilities. Now we know the truth and we have decided it is best we sever all contact with you. Putting this horrible past behind you is necessary for you to heal. Your new mother and father are Godly people and are called to the ministry of helping those who could not help themselves. We hope that one day you will also choose such a path. Until then, know that we love you and pray for you and only want the best for you. We want to share our favorite verse with you, Isaiah 40:29-31.

'Do you not know? Have you not heard? The Lord is the everlasting God, the Creator of the ends of the earth. He will not grow tired or weary, and his understanding no one can fathom. He gives strength to the weary and increases the power of the weak. Even youths grow tired and weary, and young men stumble and fall; but those who hope in the Lord will renew their strength. They will soar on wings like eagles; they will run and not grow weary, they will walk and not be faint.'

Soar, Monica. Soar!"

FAYE SLUMPED INTO A KITCHEN CHAIR AND LET THE TEARS pour. She hugged the letter to her chest and sobbed, gasping for breath.

"Are you everlasting, God?" She said. "Do young men stumble and fall?" She held the letter before her and wiped at her tears with a free hand. "I will not stumble! I will not fall! I will soar!" She folded the note and placed it back in the Bible. Closing the Bible she slid it into her work backpack.

Faye opened the jewelry box and the ballerina popped up and spun lazily as the final halting notes of the waltz filled the silent room. Tangled in old earrings and bracelets she found her grandmother's necklace. It was golden and from it hung a cross formed from four nails. She had made the cross for her in Vacation Bible School one year when she was seven. That was the year she almost died and help finally came. That was the year she left her hell and found a taste of heaven. She undid the clasp and put the necklace around her neck and felt the cold cross touch her chest. She held the nails in her palm and felt one nail pierce her skin. She winced and glanced at her palm. No blood! Then she thought of the necklace Josh had mentioned. He said Jonathan had given it to him and it was all Josh had left of his biological father. The two of them were in similar situations. Lost from their biological parents and under the care of new loving, caring parents. Adopted. Taken in. Family. From the depths of her memory a verse came to mind. Leaving her grandfather's Bible in her backpack, she went back to her bed and found the Bible given to her by her brother. She looked up the verse Ephesians 1:4-6.

"For he chose us in him, before the foundation of the world, to be holy and blameless in love before him. He predestined us to be adopted as sons through Jesus Christ for himself, according to the good pleasure of his will, to the praise of his glorious grace that he lavished on us in the Beloved One."

She gasped as she saw a handwritten note in the column of the Bible next to that verse. "Sis, I know I drive you crazy, but I love you cause we are family!" It was a note from her brother!

God had chosen her before the word began! Oh, how she had doubted God and blamed God and tired her best to keep Him at arm's length. All the while, God only wanted to love her, and hold her to himself! She closed her eyes and smiled. She would take care of Josh as if he were her adopted brother! And she would find the power and resolve to do that because she herself was a part of the family of God! Between the cross necklace and the Bible, she hoped that she had some meager protection from the unholy triad as Birdsong had called them. It was time to go to work and save Joshua Knight!

⚜

FAYE STOPPED OUTSIDE JOSH'S ROOM AND GLANCED AT THE BAG of fluid. It was time to start his next infusion. In her other hand was the syringe with the sedation. The back of her neck crawled and she whirled.

"Ms. Morgan?" Gomijo appeared beside her. "What are you doing?"

Faye felt something strange. The cross beneath her scrubs almost tingled! Was she sensing the presence of evil? She tried to smile. "Dr. Gomijo? I was double checking the medication to make sure it was correct."

"You seem hesitant. Are you questioning my medical judgment?" Gomijo glared at her. "Perhaps this case is getting too personal for you. I can reassign a new nurse practitioner."

"No! Please. I have built a rapport with Mr. Knight."

"Rapport means nothing when he is constantly sedated, Ms. Morgan." Gomijo said.

"I understand that. But I know his case very well. I would prefer to stay involved. Now if you'll excuse me, it is time for his infusion." Faye turned quickly and went into Josh's room. Gomijo stayed outside.

Faye hung the infusion bag by Josh's bed and examined the boy's sleeping figure. He was pale and sweaty. His eyes were motionless beneath his closed eyelids, so he was not dreaming. Heavily sedated. His breathing was slow and his heart rate only forty beats a minute. When she had signed in at the nursing station, she had checked the surveillance desk. Josh's room was not on video surveillance, only audio. Faye glanced over her shoulder. Gomijo had remained outside.

Faye changed out the fluid bag and began the infusion drip. She put a blunt tip needle on the syringe and pushed the needle into the injection port of the I.V. line. She stood between the line and the door just in case. She loosened the needle hub from the syringe and injected the sedation. It spilled around the base of the needle and dripped harmlessly onto the floor. She took the needle out of the injection port and turned.

Gomijo stood right behind her. Faye gasped and dropped the syringe. She stooped quickly to retrieve it and put a shoe over the spilled sedation medication. When she stood up, Gomijo had her hand out.

"May I see the syringe?"

Faye handed the capped syringe to Gomijo. Gomijo held the syringe up to the light and it was empty. She dropped into the nearby red disposal box. "Ms. Morgan, you are not performing this procedure correctly."

Faye tensed. "Pardon me?"

"You should never recap a needle, even a blunt tip. Dispose of both immediately in the red container." Gomijo turned abruptly and started toward the door and left the room.

Faye blew out her breath and she felt Josh's hand on hers. She bent over Josh and whispered in his ear. "They are listening, remember. You are supposed to be sedated but I will not be giving you any more sedation. You will be awake, but you must not let them see or hear you are awake."

Josh squeezed her hand. He licked his lips. "The sedation keeps Pandora away. But I know how to handle her now."

❧ 1 0 ❧

Eాast of London, Cassie drove into the evening until arriving at a small village surrounded by rolling hills. They passed through the quaint village until Cassie directed the truck north along a narrow, winding lane. The lane ended at an iron gate in a long, dilapidated stone wall that undulated out of sight in the growing darkness.

"Where are we?" Steel asked.

"One of Boone's properties here in the U.K. I doubt there is any surveillance. Why would anyone come here? I checked the legal status, and it is still a frozen asset pending the outcome of multiple lawsuits." Cassie turned off the engine and got out of the truck. Her hair was pulled back into a ponytail and she wore a one piece gray jumpsuit and boots.

"And Maize is here?"

Cassie undid the simple chain on the fence and pulled it open toward her. "I've been monitoring electricity usage at all of Boone's properties in the U.K. Why would an abandoned old manor have ten times the usage of the entire nearby village? He's here, Jonathan."

"So, what's the plan? We walk up to the front door of this manor and knock?"

"Why not? Where is he going to go? We're in the middle of nowhere." She headed through the gates and down a winding driveway lined with tall, leafless trees. Steel followed and after a short hike, the manor came into view. In the waning sunlight, the ancient stonework was dark and mottled with mold and dirt. The two-story manor had typical parapets and arched windows. The driveway was riddled with weeds. But, as they neared the building, Cassie pointed out a lone light gleaming from a first-floor window.

"See, someone is at home." She trudged up the sloping driveway to an ancient wooden door covered with peeling paint. Without hesitation, she tugged on the handle and the door creaked open.

The foyer smelled of mildew and rotten vegetation. Dirt and scattered papers covered the marble floor. Cassie pointed to the large living area beyond the foyer. The light came from an open door. Stairs led down into a basement.

"The mad scientist is in his basement?" Steel said.

Cassie nodded and led the way down a winding set of slippery stone stairs illuminated by two bare bulbs along the walls. At the bottom of the stairs, they paused at the sight of the machinery filling the basement.

Steel recognized the framed portal Maize had constructed on Boone's island. But the computer monitors and consoles were less numerous and older than the ones from Boone's machine. In contrast to Boone's aseptic and well-constructed machine, Maize's machine was wieldy and lopsided.

The slumped figure of a man sat at the main console with his head resting on his arms. He did not move as Cassie approached.

"Dr. Maize?" She said.

Maize's head stirred and he lifted it shakily. He turned slowly. "Who's there?"

"Dr. Sebastian." Cassie said. She gasped at the sight of Dr. Maize as his face came into view. Dark circles surrounded his eyes. His hair had come out in tufts exposing pink, shiny scalp.

Crusted blood leaked from his nostrils. "Dr. Maize, what is wrong with you?"

"Sebastian? Who's with you? I can't see too well."

"Jonathan Steel." Steel said.

"Steel?" Maize coughed wetly and blood trickled through his fingers as he covered his mouth. "I should have listened to you. Look what has happened to me."

"What has happened?" Cassie said. "You need a doctor."

"It's too late." Maize turned back to his console and tried to type on a keyboard. "The machine is almost charged and when it is, I'll head far into the future where they will have a cure."

"Cure for what?" Steel asked.

Maize pointed a shaky finger at a dull, black metal trunk in the corner. "Bradwell Nuclear Power Plant" was stenciled on its sides. Cassie gasped.

"We have to get out of here, Jonathan! Now!"

"You're perfectly safe." Maize wheezed and coughed again. "In 1966, twenty natural uranium fuel rods were stolen from Bradwell. Harold Sneath, the idiot that stole them was going to sell them for scrap. But his vehicle had defective steering and he was caught."

He coughed wetly and continued. "What they did not know was there were two more rods stolen that actually fell out of the van. They were brought here and hidden in the manor inside that container by the real thief who put Sneath up to it. That thief was never discovered and two of those rods lay here for decades safely sealed inside that box. When Boone bought this manor, he found the rods in the basement and was going to have them removed but he got sidetracked."

Maize coughed some more. "This is where I came so I could perfect my first version of the time travel machine. But we moved all the new equipment to the island. Only the prototype remained here. When it all fell apart, I tried to send myself farther into the future to land here hoping that this area of the United Kingdom would not have changed much."

"You didn't come too far into the future." Steel said.

"I know. I brought with me a hand full of Sunstones and I had to adapt my original machine to use their power. I found the trunk not long after that. Someone had come in and opened the lid. By the time I found it, I had been exposed to lethal levels of radiation. I moved them shortly after that back to the Bradwell Nuclear Power Plant which has been decommissioned. I was afraid they might mess with my Sunstones. As for me, the damage was done."

He tried to stand up and wobbled then collapsed back into his chair. "There is no hope for me in today's medical environment. I will go far forward in time."

Cassie looked around and found a Geiger counter sitting on a nearby counter. She picked it up and turned it on and warily leaned over the open lid of the coffin shaped trunk. It was empty. Only a few ticks sounded from the instrument. "We're safe, Jonathan."

Steel walked over to Maize and studied his pale, sweaty face. "Dr. Maize, I need to use your machine."

Maize glared at him and shook his head. "Oh, no you can't! Not this time. This machine is my only hope, Steel."

"You're out of hope, Maize. The only reason the machine worked in the first place is through supernatural intervention."

"Yes, the Sunstones." Maize pointed to a nearby gray metal container. "There are six of them left. Six, Steel. If my calculations are correct, they will be enough to catapult me at least a century into the future."

"How do you plan on getting out of the middle of nowhere in the future?" Cassie said.

"My machine can also translate one through time and space."

Steel reached for a nearby clipboard and picked up a pen. He scribbled onto the pad and showed it to Maize. "This is where I need to go, and this is the time and the day. How many Sunstones will it take?"

Maize tried to focus on the clipboard. "Maybe one. But why don't you appeal to your precious angel, what was his name?"

Alar San Angelo had appeared to be a pilot but was revealed to be an angel sent to watch over Steel. Steel glanced at Cassie and then around the room. They were truly alone. No eaves-droppers from Dr. Gumijo.

"I'm afraid I am on a mission that any one of my guardian angels would not approve. I can't count on an angel for help. Maize, if you don't let me go back in time, there may not be a future for you to go to."

Maize blinked and then laughed. "That is so cliché, Steel."

"It's true." Steel said.

"Okay, for argument's sake, let's look up your little location." He tapped at his keyboard and brought up a map program on the computer monitor. He zoomed in several times until the lake house appeared from a satellite image. Steel pointed to the boat house just yards from his own back porch.

"Put me there on this date and at this time." He tapped the clipboard.

Maize made entries on his keyboard and studied the readout on another monitor. "Well, I was right. One sunstone should to it." He pointed to the entry key on the keyboard. "All I have to do is touch this key and the portal will open." He motioned to a pile of equipment nearby on the console. "Put on one of those bracelets and you'll return in thirty minutes."

Maize leaned back in his chair. "But I need all six of the remaining sunstones for my trip to the future. And the keyboard is biometrically attuned to me. Only I can start the sequence, Steel. Anyone else touches the keyboard and the machine self-destructs. You see, I can't take a chance on someone else discov-ering my secrets once I go into the future. My trip will be one way and then this machine and this manor will burn to the ground."

Maize coughed again and this time, blood splattered across the computer monitors. More coughing racked his body and he gasped for breath. His eyes widened and he grabbed Steel's arm. He tried to stand and stumbled backward falling over his own chair. More blood poured from his mouth and nose. Cassie tried to help him up and Maize shoved her away, lurching to his feet and clawing at the console. He missed the keyboard with his hands and then fell backward onto the floor. With one last gasp, he stopped breathing.

Cassie knelt beside him. "Jonathan, he's dead."

Steel looked at the computer monitor and the keyboard. "I can't say I'm sorry. But the machine is ready for me to go back in time." He snared a bracelet from the console table and slapped it onto this right wrist.

Cassie stood up. "You can't be serious!"

"Cassie, look at this man. Look closely. He has no one to blame for his death but himself. If I don't do this, Josh's fate will be the same. Help me put him in the chair."

"What?" Cassie said.

Steel lifted the man's astonishingly light, wasted body and sat him in the chair. "Never mind. All I have to do is press the return key with his finger and the machine will be activated."

Cassie shook her head. "I didn't sign up for using a dead man."

Steel glared at her, his heart racing. "I know. But if you would, at least make this place safe by removing the sunstones from the machine in case I'm mistaken."

Cassie glanced at the metal container containing the sunstones. Steel opened the lid and bright, yellow light filled the room. He grabbed a coat tossed on the console, no doubt once belonging to Maize. He gingerly picked up one of the glowing orbs with the cloth, reluctant to touch the thing. As he had seen Maize do in the caverns of Boone's island, he located a tube shaped structure with an opening on the end and placed the sunstone in the opening. It rolled out of sight and came to rest at the bottom of the left-hand side of the portal frame. The frame came to life with glowing lights and flashing diodes. Steel shut the lid to the container.

"Can I count on you to keep these away?" Steel said.

Cassie gasped and tears ran down her cheeks. "Jonathan, don't do this."

Steel tossed the coat aside and rummaged through another pile of stuff until he found a backpack. "Cassie, I have no choice. I must take a chance. I must do this to save Josh. If I die in the process, then it is God's will. Now, hurry before Maize's body gets too cool to activate the biometric reader."

Cassie wiped tears from her eyes and picked up the metal case of sunstones. It was surprisingly light. "Fine. But I may not be here when you get back. I can't do this, Jonathan."

"I never asked for a partner." Steel took Maize's right hand, extended the index finger and poised with it above the return key. "Now, go. Hurry."

Cassie ran from the lab up the stairs. Steel drew a deep breath and looked around him. "God, I need a little help even though you know I shouldn't be helping the enemy. But this is for Josh." He pressed Maize's finger onto the return key.

❧ 11 ❧

Steel stepped through the familiar mirrored interface of the portal and was glad the machine had not exploded. The tingling effect of the mirrored surface played over his skin and then he was through into a dark, humid night. The sound of water lapping against the ski boat and the distant croak of frogs told him he was in the right place, the boat dock behind the lake house. The glimmering light of the portal vanished as it closed behind him.

He glanced up at the dark, cloudy sky. No moon. No stars. The dock creaked behind him, and the darkness seemed to move toward him, swallowing up what little light reflected from the water. Like a cold wave of death, the black cloud of memory engulfed him.

HE WOKE UP IN TOTAL DARKNESS. CONFUSION FILLED HIS MIND. *He tried his best to blink away the cobwebs. Where was he? He had just finished lunch in the school cafeteria and had gone outside for some air with his best friend, Clay. He vaguely remembered sitting on a bench in the quadrangle courtyard. Now, he was in total darkness and his head*

pounded. The air reeked of disinfectant and detergent. He fumbled around him and felt the wet end of a mop. Through a metal grate in front of him, he heard his name being called. He was in a closet.

He pulled himself up and fumbled for the door handle. He pushed the door open with an ever-growing sensation of nausea. He stumbled into the school hallway just outside the gym. Coach Beason heard the door open and whirled. Clay was with the coach.

"There you are? JJ, where have you been? We've been looking for you for two hours." Coach Beason hurried toward him, and he felt the nausea build. Just as the Coach grabbed him by the arm, he vomited all over the man.

THEY MET IN THE EMPTY GYM. *JJ* SAT FORLORNLY ON A BLEACHER *while Coach Beason stood by. JJ looked up at the reddened face of Assistant Principal Moore. The woman was short and wide with the face of a frog. Clay was standing next to her.*

"I tell you Ms. Moore, he was with me the last two hours." Clay said. His sandy blonde hair was long and fell constantly into his face. Moore glared at him.

"I suppose you were hiding in the closet with him? Your English teacher said you were in class and your friend was not! Now, you can leave this room." She pointed to the door out of the gym. Clay cast one forlorn look at JJ and shrugged. He hurried from the gym.

"You stink!" Moore wheezed. "Where have you been?"

JJ looked over at Coach Beason, his white tee shirt and running pants stained smelled to high heaven.

"I ate lunch and then, I don't know what happened." He stammered.

"You don't remember? You're one of our brightest freshmen and you can't remember?" Moore's eyes bulged with anger. "Let me refresh your memory." She handed him three Polaroid snapshots. He tried to focus but the headache was growing worse. The snapshots showed Stimpy Malone in a pose reminiscent of a mug shot. His left cheek was bruised and his left eye swollen shut.

"What happened to Stimpy?" He looked up at Moore.

"*You happened. You beat him up.*" *Moore planted her short arms on her hips. "I've suspended him because the witnesses said he started it. They claim you were only defending yourself. But you know what the rules are for fighting on school grounds."*

JJ studied the pictures and tried to wrap his aching brain around what she was saying. "But I don't remember hitting Stimpy. I woke up in the closet."

"We have witnesses." Coach Beason interrupted. "I always knew you were a troublemaker!"

Moore put out a restraining hand and hesitated before touching the coach's wet shirt. "JJ will be suspended three days for fighting."

"But I didn't hit anyone!" JJ shouted. His head throbbed with pain, and he felt another wave of nausea. Moore opened her mouth to speak and the door to the gym screeched open. His mother entered.

She was tall and thin with reddish blonde hair. Her milky white skin was reddened with anger. "That is enough, Lydia."

Moore's face whitened. "Christine, I am in charge of discipline in the school, and you will not interrupt me."

Christine rushed across the gym and bent over him. "You were a bully when we were in school and you're still a bully. Honey, are you all right?"

JJ looked up into his mother's jade green eyes. "I don't feel good. I threw up. My head is killing me."

Christine stood up. "I'll take my son home, now."

"Don't bring him back until next week. He is on suspension." Moore crossed her short arms across her chest.

STEEL SAT UP GROGGILY ON THE DOCK. HIS HEAD POUNDED and nausea gripped him. He leaned over the edge of the dock and retched. What happened? A flashback? To high school? Tears filled his eyes. He had remembered his mother! More than just a passing moment.

In Numinocity, his "other" self claimed Steel had killed his own mother. That was impossible! Then there was the memory of her consoling him in the library. And here she was freshly returned to his memories. He sat up and clung to the image of her face, her hair, her eyes filled with concern. Why had the flashback come back now? Was it the portal? Had he been exposed to radiation despite what Maize had said?

Steel looked up at the back of his lake house and saw a figure moving along the perimeter of the basement windows. For a second, the figure was silhouetted against the light coming from the basement window and then his bracelet began to blink.

"What?" He looked down at the bracelet. The blinking meant he only had a minute until the portal returned. Had he been out the entire time? When he looked back at the lake house, there was no one to be seen. Probably just a bunch of shadows?

Light gushed from behind him, and the portal reopened. He swore and climbed shakily to his feet. Could he use another Sunstone to return? Josh's life depended on it. He stepped through the mirrored surface of the portal.

Steel's feet echoed on the wooden dock. He looked around. He was back on the lake dock! How? He glanced behind him at the portal surface, and it shimmered and died. He was in the past. Again. He glanced at his bracelet and a tiny green light gleamed. Somehow, he had gone back in time again?

Steel glanced up at the sky. A full moon painted the lake in silver light. Stars gleamed in a cloudless sky.

"What? There were clouds." He shook his head. Maybe it had all been a dream, a hallucination caused by going through the portal? He was here at the lake house in the past and he had only a few minutes. Maybe less than the thirty minutes he had started with.

Steel hurried across the back yard to the back sliding doors and peered into the darkened den beyond. It should be the middle of the night according to what Josh had recalled. Liz and Josh should be upstairs in their bedrooms. Steel glanced inside the door and noticed the security system had not been armed. He would have to talk to Josh about that. If they both survived.

He slid the door open as soundlessly as possible and made his way across the darkened den and into the kitchen. The clock on the microwave gave meager light to the kitchen and in retrospect, he should have made note of the time.

A set of double doors at the rear of the kitchen opened onto a wide staircase that led into the basement containing Cephas' crates. He padded down the stairs into complete darkness and felt his way over to Cephas' desk. A small desk lamp sat there, and he turned on the light. But, when the small light clicked on, the overhead lights also came to life.

"Jonathan?"

He whirled. Cephas stood at the top of the stairs. His bushy, white hair was as wild as ever and he wore a tee shirt and his favorite robot covered pajama bottoms. "I thought you went to bed."

Steel froze. This was wrong! He was supposed to have come back when Cephas had already perished in Cobalt's space station! He almost swore out loud. According to Josh, he had come through one of the small windows at the ceiling level of the basement.

"Cephas." He said hoarsely. Cephas made his way down the stairs.

"I woke up and needed a midnight snack and heard someone in the basement. I thought it might be Theo or Josh."

Cephas made his way slowly across the room toward his 3-D printer. "My back is killing me tonight for some reason. Must be a storm coming. Or it might be because of what I went through at the farmhouse this afternoon."

Steel opened his mouth to speak but couldn't. Cephas was talking about the encounter with the eleventh demon. He wanted to run across the basement and embrace the man but knew that would be very out of character for where he had been emotionally at that point in time. He acted as nonchalant as he could. "What are you doing?" He managed.

"Ah, my replica of the Demon Rose is finished." He removed a pale, plastic disc from the printer. "I wanted to make sure we had a three-dimensional image of the demon rose in case some frisky demon showed up to take the original."

Steel nodded and glanced at his watch. He had only fifteen minutes before the bracelet activated and opened the portal again. "I was just doing a recon of the house to make sure we will be safe tonight." Steel said.

Cephas opened a cabinet above his desk and placed the disc inside. "Until the tenth demon shows up, we should be safe, Jonathan." He turned to Steel and put a hand on Steel's arm. Steel almost flinched. "Once I decipher the images on the demon rose, I will have a better idea of this Council of Darkness and its members." As he was closing the cabinet, Steel caught a glimpse of the original demon rose compass Vivian had given to them from the Ark of Chaos. "I'll put the real demon rose in the safe in the morning."

Steel recalled the last time he had seen the Ark of the Demon Rose in Ketrick's old office. He recalled the memory.

۞

BILE PLACED THE WOODEN CHEST ON THE DESK BEFORE VIVIAN. IT was beautiful. The ancient wood had been worn down to a dull shine, and the bronze cornice pieces were intricately carved. A circle of shiny bronze sat on the top. It was the Demon Rose, in all of its glory.

"You had the Ark? All this time, you had the Ark?" Vivian flew out of the chair and around the desk.

"It's for you, Miss Vivian." Bile smiled. She glared at him and slapped him hard across the face. Bile's eyes widened in shock.

"You're a stupid, helpless shell of a man, Bile." Vivian shoved him

and he stumbled and fell. He reached for her feet. She placed her foot on his forehead and pushed him away. "Get away from me!"

Bile glanced at me, his face smeared with tears. I almost felt sorry for him. Almost. He crawled away into a corner and continued to sob. Vivian turned her back on the poor man and leaned over the Ark of the Demon Rose. Her eyes widened as she examined it.

"Innocent people have died for this, Vivian," I said. "Destillo, Zoe Reynolds, and Lynn Alba."

"I would hardly call Lynn innocent!" She glanced once at me and then at Cephas. "I don't know where your little document is, old man. But it would seem that we both want to stop these Vitreomancers and the Council. So I'm going to give you a little help."

Vivian placed her hands on the Demon Rose and twisted. With a click, it released from the lid of the Ark. She held it up and it gleamed in the light of the office. It looked almost three-dimensional, deeper than a simple flat circle. She handed it to Cephas.

"We're even, Steel. What is inside is more important than the Demon Rose." She slid the Ark back into the canvas bag. "Now, it's just the Ark of Chaos. Let's go, Bile. I have a plane to catch." Vivian stormed out of the room dragging the Ark of Chaos behind her. Bile picked himself up from the corner and followed her out, sniffing and panting.

❦

STEEL GLANCED ONCE MORE AT THE REAL COMPASS OF THE Demon Rose inside Cephas' cabinet and a plan was forming. But first, he had to find the two stones. "Cephas, I was down here because I was reading my Bible." Steel started haltingly.

"Good for you! The Word of God is our best protection right now." Cephas patted Steel's arm.

"Yeah, it was about the Urim and the Thummim. You know, right after Moses' serpent and rod. What do you know about that?"

Cephas raised an eyebrow and rubbed his huge mustache. "Well, I have a box with twelve stones in that crate over there.

I'm packing them up to loan them to an old nemesis who lives in London. There are twelve stones, Jonathan and there is a remote possibility two of them are these Urim and Thummim. I can't be sure, and I am hoping that Dr. Hampton may be able to sort it out for me. But the discussion of their significance would take an hour or so and I'm very tired." He started up the stairs. "Right now, I'm going to grab a warm glass of milk and head to bed. You coming?"

Steel swallowed and fought moisture in his eyes. "As soon as I make one more sweep of the perimeter." Steel pointed to the crates before him. "Cephas, are these the crates you're packing up to send to Hampton?"

Cephas nodded. "Two of them are ready. The third will have something very special once I put my hands on it. Why do you ask?"

"Just want to make sure the windows are secure, and no one will try and get in here. The security system has not been armed."

Cephas waved a hand at him. "I know. I forgot. Josh and Theo were out by the pool when I went to bed, so I didn't turn it on. Talk to Theo. He's supposed to be looking after Josh. Good night, Jonathan."

Steel started to say more and glanced at his watch. Five minutes! Cephas disappeared up the stairs pausing once to say, "Turn out the lights, will you?" He paused at the top of the stairs. "Oh, and by the way, the serpent and its rod are in the crates, too. Again, I have no idea if they are genuine."

Steel hurried over to the wooden crates. He peered inside. He dug through packing peanuts and found several items sealed in plastic. One was a wooden box. Could it be Pandora's box? If he took it now, would it not be there when Hampton asked Josh to remove it? But Cassie seemed to think Hampton had put something else on the box. It was not the box itself that had stuck Josh's finger.

Steel's hand strayed across a rough burlap bag, and something hard made of metal inside. He pulled the bag from peanuts and peered in the top. A bronze serpent! He took out the serpent gleaming and shiny, coiled upon itself over a length of two feet. The serpent was segmented and separated into two pieces. Attached to the bag was a leather strap and at the end of that strap was a heavy brown pole. Could this be Moses's rod?

Steel tucked the serpent into his backpack and threaded the rod through the backstrap to hang behind him. He shoved the empty burlap sack back beneath the packing. He bent over the crate again and found the metal box they had found in Hampton's theater. He took out the box and opened the lid. The stones were indeed wrapped in bubble wrap. But unlike in the future, two stones were enclosed in one wrap. Their dumbbell shape stood out from the other stones. They had to be the ones! He placed the wrapped stones in his backpack and closed the box and placed it back in the crate.

His hand brushed against Pandora's box and for a moment, he felt a jolt of electricity. He glanced at his hand to make sure he hadn't stuck himself. Strangely, the surface of the box glowed. The figure of a woman sitting before an urn from which vapors issued glowed with golden light. Around the edges of the lid, a tiny golden circle glowed for a second and he blinked as an after-image burned into his eyes. He saw the Compass of the Demon Rose!

He stood up and gasped and then his bracelet started to beep, and a yellow light flashed. He had one minute. Could Pandora's Box be one of the arks? Before he ran up the stairs he stopped before the cabinet and pulled open the doors. He grabbed the metallic disk that was the real demon rose compass and started up the stairs. Behind him, something crashed to the floor. He turned and saw a broken vase from the shelf. For a second, he was certain a shadowy figure moved out of view.

"Cephas?" He asked. Of course, Cephas wasn't here. But who was? His bracelet beeped faster. He ran up the stairs and across the living room and hurtled through the sliding doors and saw the shimmering mirror of the portal form on the boat dock. The bracelet was flashing red now and picking up speed. The portal would soon close, and he would be stranded in his own past. Would that be so bad? He could hide from himself and prevent so many deaths! He slid to a halt and almost stayed but then at the last second threw himself through the portal.

12

Josh sat in a chair in Pandora's laboratory. He blinked his eyes. He was supposed to be sedated. If he had been sedated, then his mind would not be active. As Faye had mentioned, she had fooled the doctors and withheld his sedation. Which raised a good question. Hampton wanted him dreaming and the demons wanted him sedated. That meant their goals were opposed to each other. Hampton's agenda was not the same as the demons. What did that mean?

More importantly, what day was it? What time was it? Had Jason made any progress with the nature of his disease? And where was Jonathan? He had played possum for hours and his sensation of time was blurred. He had told Faye he knew how to handle Pandora and he had a good idea. He just hoped it worked!

The door to the laboratory opened and Pandora walked into the room with a dramatic flourish. She wore a long, billowy evening gown. Her fiery red hair fell around her bare shoulders. She whirled and stopped in front of Josh.

"How do I look?"

Josh ignored her. Pandora sighed and snapped her fingers. A sharp pain lanced through Josh's abdomen, and he bent over. He gasped for breath.

"If you vomit while you are asleep you could die, Josh. Do not ignore me." Pandora said.

Josh blinked away the pain. Maybe dying in his sleep wasn't such a bad idea. It would certainly stop Pandora. He sat back in the chair and looked at her. Play along.

"Yes, play along, Josh. I can hear your thoughts, remember?" Pandora said.

Jesus, I need help, he thought. Pandora froze and glanced at him. "What was that? I didn't catch it."

"I said you need my help, it seems." Josh tried not to think about what he had just tried.

"I do need your help."

"Then don't hurt me. I've been through a lot and there is no need to do that again. I'll cooperate." Josh said. "But I want to ask you a question.

Pandora swirled in front of him. "Fine. But first, how do I look?"

"Ravishing." Josh said.

"I chose this outfit because of a memory you had. It was your mother? At a military ball type thing?"

Josh stiffened. Photos of his mother and his father surfaced in his mind. He recalled his mother in the same dress asking a young Josh how she looked. He thought she was the most beautiful woman in the world at that time. He felt the sorrow take him, the overwhelming sense of loss and despair. The room grew dark and shadowy. Pandora froze and glanced around.

"What are you doing? Stop it right now or I will hurt you."

Josh stood up from his chair, his legs suddenly strong and he strode across the room to Pandora. "That memory is of my mother, and you will not taint her memory with your evil presence, do you understand? I'll just say one thing. Jesus Christ is my Lord and Savior!"

Pandora flickered and suddenly disappeared from sight. Josh nodded. "Thank you, Jesus." He had just learned how to fight back!

❧ 13 ❧

"Well, well, what do you have?"

Steel picked himself up from the floor of Maize's laboratory and glared at the woman standing in the middle of the room. Her red hair was pulled back into a bun on the back of her head. She wore a tight, black jumpsuit and her bionic arm gleamed in the meager light of the machinery.

"Snake?"

"You're a hard man to follow, Steel. Fortunately, I put a tracker on your little girlfriend thinking you might seek her out."

Steel glanced around the interior. "Where is she? What have you done to her?"

Snake rolled her eyes. "Please. I don't kill everybody, Steel. She's outside in your truck with a stash of glowing tennis balls. Tied up, not harmed, don't worry. Now, that notebook was not what I risked life and, ahem, limb for in Zurich. And, you didn't have it on you on the flight back to the states. So, here's the deal. I will let you pass, and you and your girlfriend can tootle on out of here if you give me what I want."

Steel's grip on the rod attached to his backpack tightened

and the demon rose cut into his side from gripping it so tightly. "I don't have it with me even if I decided to give it to you. Why do you want it?"

"Not your concern." She sauntered toward him. "You know this bionic arm has over twelve different settings finely tuned for torture?"

Steel backed up until he hit Maize's console. Maize's dead body slumped in the chair beside him. What to do? He glanced down at Maize.

"Did you kill him?" Steel said.

Snake laughed. "He was dead when I got here, and you knew that. Don't play games with me. What is this machine, anyway?"

"A time machine." He stepped aside to reveal the monitor. "I just went back in time to retrieve an item from my past." Steel motioned to the keyboard with his chin. "Just think, Snake. You can go back in time and stop whatever it was that cost you an arm. You can be whole again."

Snake froze and confusion clouded her features. "I heard about this through some back channel chatter. Is this Dr. Maize?"

"Yes. He worked with Boone."

"The mysterious exploding island?"

"Yes. This machine is the original prototype. The final version was destroyed by Vivian Darbonne."

Something clouded her features and she looked away. "Vivian? Well, I don't believe you."

Steel slid aside some more to reveal more of the keyboard and monitor. "Just put in a date and the coordinates for a location and hit the return key."

Snake moved closer and shoved Maize's chair aside. It rolled across the room and dumped the man's body onto the floor. She examined the keyboard. "There's blood on the return key."

"His last act was to send me back in time." Steel said. "He died from radiation poison. See that open lead box over there? It contained uranium from a decommissioned nuclear power plant. It's empty now and totally safe. There's a Geiger counter over there if you want to check. So, you see, I wasn't the one who killed him. He did himself in."

Snake examined the open trunk. "You could put his body in it. Not much smaller than a coffin." She came back to the console. "Okay, let's see if you're telling the truth." She tapped on the keys and filled in a date and time. She pulled up images on the map and Steel had a hard time following the exact location. She paused. "Why are you telling me this?"

"I can't give you the dossier, Snake. I don't have it anymore. My job was to obtain it. If I hadn't, my son would suffer. Do you think I would put his life in jeopardy for a dossier? Why do you think I risked going back in time? These items are my second task and if I don't leave here soon, Josh will suffer."

Snake regarded him coolly. "You wouldn't try to stop me?"

"I don't care what happens to you at this moment in time. This isn't our fight, Snake. Let our bosses fight this out. I have to go. Take a little trip down memory lane and you can always find me through Cassie's tracker. But, let me go. Now. Please."

Snake looked at him, deep in thought. She tilted her head toward the stairway. "Go."

Steel ran across the room; the demon rose cutting into the skin of his hand. He hurried up the stairs and heard a distinctive click as Snake pressed the return key. He rushed through the living room, through the foyer, and out the front door and had just cleared the stairs when the ground convulsed beneath him. He tumbled across the dead grass toward the driveway and the explosion shook the earth behind him.

Steel struggled to his feet as the manor began to crumble and flames shot up through the roof. Bricks and broken stones began to fall all around him, and he ran for his life down the winding lane toward the distant truck hoping against hope that Snake had not lied to him about Cassie.

Steel gasped for breath as he ran down the rough terrain of

the driveway away from the flames and falling debris. He topped a little rise in the driveway and saw Cassie standing before him. Her face was illuminated by the flames of the burning house. She ran to him and tried to hug him, but his hands were not free.

"Jonathan! Thank God! What happened?"

"Snake." He gasped for breath.

"She tied me up in the cabin of the truck, but I got free." Cassie said. "What happened to Maize's machine?"

"Snake pushed the button." Steel straightened. "Set off the self-destruct."

Cassie pulled away from him. "Then, she is dead? Good riddance! We have to get out of here, Jonathan. That fire will alert the nearest village and a fireman crew will be here soon."

Steel nodded toward the truck. "Let's go. I have the artifacts."

Cassie led him to the truck, and he climbed in the front seat. He placed the backpack between them along with the compass of the Demon Rose and the rod. Cassie looked at the objects with a shimmering glint in her eye as she sat in the driver's seat.

"Is that?" She started.

"The rod, yes. The serpent is in the backpack along with the two stones."

Cassie reached for the rod. Steel stopped her. "Not now. Drive."

Cassie started the truck and pulled out onto the road. They rode in silence for a few minutes until a firetruck appeared over the hill. Cassie pulled over to let it pass. Once it was gone and they were down the road she drew a deep breath. "Is that the compass of the demon rose?"

"Yes." Steel said.

"I'm sorry I doubted you. That must have been painful seeing your past again."

"I saw Cephas, Cassie." Steel felt the shaking take him and the trembling.

"Do we need to stop?" Cassie slowed and he shook his head.

"No, keep going. Get us to the museum, Cassie."

She drove on in silence as Steel felt his body shake and tremble. He closed his eyes and felt into a deep, dark well of silence and stillness.

🦋 14 🦋

"Jonathan?"

Steel opened his eyes. He sat up and the bed in which he lay shook. He looked around. Monty stood up from a chair and came to the bed. "You're okay. You passed out and Cassie brought you back. We put you in my bed."

Cassie stood up from her chair on the opposite side of Steel. "I was so worried I almost took you to the hospital. But there would be so many questions. Like, why you were covered in dirt and soot for one."

Steel slowly sat up in the rickety bed. "Water?"

Monty left the room and returned with a bottled water. "Take is easy. There is no telling what going through that machine did to your body."

Steel sipped the water. His mouth tasted like rotten eggs. "What time is it?"

"Noon." Cassie said. "We took turns watching you."

"Where are the artifacts?" He drank some more water.

"In the conference room." Monty said. "Let me get you some breakfast."

"No time." Steel stood up and wobbled toward the door. Monty followed behind.

"Steel, you've got to rest. You can't go on like this." Cassie said.

Steel finished the water as he made his way down the hall to the conference room. "I can." Was all he could manage.

The backpack lay on the table unopened. The rod sat next to it. The compass of the demon rose lay next to the rod. At the end of the table stood the tall, black rectangular box holding the Sunstones. "You brought the Sunstones?" He said to Cassie.

"What else was I to do with them?"

Steel nodded and sat weakly in a chair. "Okay, let's think." He squinted his eyes and pinched his nose. "On second thought, Monty, I will take something to eat." Steel glanced over at Cassie. "And some tea with caffeine. Then let's get all of this down to the theater. I have a plan."

"We'll have to check with Margaret first." Monty said. "I think we know who the real boss is around this place!"

৩৯৩

AFTER EATING SOME SCONES AND SOME STRONG TEA, STEEL felt better, and they took the objects down the scary elevator to the lower level. After the exploding house, the elevator seemed absolutely tame as did the glare from Margaret.

"Don't go beyond the room with the crates." She glared at them. "We had a fumigation last night. The workmen used some chemicals that might burn out your retinas." She went back to writing something in a registry book. For a moment, Steel felt his palm grow warm. He glanced down at the slight glow from his palm as he followed Monty and Cassie down the hall. Why had his palm glowed? He was still a bit groggy from all the flying and fleeing from an exploding house. The glow faded as they entered the amphitheater.

In the theater, Steel placed the rod and the backpack on the operating table after Monty moved the artifacts back into the open crate. Steel removed the bronze serpent from the backpack.

"Oh my!" Cassie said. Monty put a hand on her arm.

"Could it be?" Monty said.

"I don't know, Monty, but it is exquisite." Cassie's eyes lit up.

The bronze serpent was in two segments each a foot long. Monty put on white gloves and placed the ends of each piece against one another. They snapped into place. The bronze serpent was hollow, and the tail was shaped into a spiral. The head looked out over the spiral tail with two red jewels as eyes. The mouth was closed. Cassie donned gloves and picked up the rod.

"This rod is amazing. It is heavy and almost has the consistency of petrified wood. Do you think it will fit inside the serpent?"

"Let's find out." Monty placed the assembled bronze serpent on the table and Cassie inserted the rod. It fit perfectly through the spiral of the tail and the end slid into a hollow at the base of the head. She smiled and grabbed Monty in a hug.

"It fits!"

Monty patted her hand. "Of course, there is no way to know where or when this originated. Cephas does not give any details in the manifest." He looked at Steel. "Remember we told you that many ancient societies had serpent imagery after the days of Moses in the wilderness."

Steel reached for the serpent and Monty put a gloved hand in his way. "Jonathan, don't touch this thing."

"I already have, Monty. I carried it from the crate." He ran his hand along the highly polished wood of the rod and his fingers strayed along the coils of the serpent. Nothing. He felt nothing. No presence of good. No presence of evil. He turned his left palm toward him. No light. No sensation. He was hoping the special light, whatever it was, would signal the rod was the real thing. He sighed. "I don't guess this thing can heal Josh after all. It's just a thing."

"That's what I told you." Cassie said. "I'm sorry."

"I don't care. They wanted a serpent and a rod, and they'll get just that." He turned to the metal crate and pressed his right hand on the glass plate and opened the crate. He picked up the rod and serpent and placed them in the bottom of the empty crate.

"What are you doing?" Monty asked.

"Carrying out MY plan." Steel turned back to the backpack and removed the bubble wrapped stones. He placed them on the table and motioned to Cassie.

"Have at it."

Cassie removed the bubble wrapping. Two bright blue stones emerged from the wrinkly wrap, and she placed them on the table. Both were about the size of a walnut. "Look, Monty. Flat on one side and convex on the other."

"True cleromancy stones." Monty said. "But just like the rod and serpent, there is no way to know if these are the original Urim and Thummim."

"There is one way." Steel said. He picked up a stone with his left hand. The dark, blue rounded surface suddenly burst forth with pale light. His palm lit up the stone. Cassie and Monty stepped back.

"What is happening?"

"I wish I knew." Steel said as blue light played across their faces. "Something is happening with the palm of my left hand. It helped me defeat Major in Jerusalem and push Thakkar away in Numinocity." He stopped short of telling them about the Grimvox.

"Then these are the real thing?" Cassie said in wonder as the blue light flickered in her eyes. She reached for the stone and suddenly winced. "Ouch!"

She pulled the glove from her hand and looked at the tips of her fingers. "That burned."

"I wouldn't touch these if I were either of you." Steel said. He placed the stone in the crate and picked up the other stone.

It let forth a blinding, white light and they each had to close their eyes against the intensity. Steel placed the second stone next to the first in the empty crate and the light died out.

"I don't guess they have any special healing properties." Steel turned to Cassie and Monty.

"They were only manifestations of communication with God." Monty said. "And it would seem God is speaking to you."

Steel frowned. He really had nothing to say to God right now until Josh was better. If God wanted to reveal something to him, why not show him how to heal Josh? He glanced at the other crates. "I have another idea. There are times when this strange light in my palm reveals something from the past. Perhaps Pandora's Box holds secrets that might help Josh." He crossed to the second crate and put his hands on Pandora's Box and suddenly, he was somewhere else.

JJ SLUMPED IN THE PASSENGER SEAT AS THEY PULLED INTO THE long, winding driveway that led up to the manor. What had just happened? He remembered eating lunch and talking to Clay. Stimpy had been there at the table and had made some offhand comment about his mother. He had gotten angry, but he had walked away. He refused to let someone like Stimpy take up any of his time. He was a low life and a worthless bully. But now there was a two hour hole in his memory. And the headache and nausea had come out of nowhere.

"Are you feeling better?" His mother asked.

"My head is hurting less. The nausea is going away." He sat up straighter in the seat. "What are you going to tell dad?"

His mother shook her head as she pulled into the garage. "He won't be back from Bolivia until next week. He doesn't have to know you were suspended."

"Mother, I didn't beat up Stimpy. Look," JJ held up his right hand, "no bruises or cuts."

She examined his hand and sighed. "I know. I believe you."

"But why can't I remember?"

His mother's eyes held something haunted and distant. She blinked. "I don't know, son."

A shiver ran over him and he looked out the car window at the huge garage. "Am I going insane like grandfather?"

"No!" Christine shouted. "No, you are not going insane, do you hear me?"

JJ glanced back at his mother and there were tears in her eyes. "Then why are you crying?"

ॐ

"So, HOW MANY OF THESE 'ABSENCE' SPELLS HAVE YOU HAD IN THE last three months?" Dr. Noah Franks looked up from his notebook. He had a huge combover that draped across his ample forehead like a cape.

"Four or five." JJ said and shrugged. "I don't know. Maybe ten?"

Franks nodded and scribbled on his pad. He wore thick glasses that made his eyes look like raw oysters swimming in brine. "And when was the last one?"

"Two days ago."

His mother put a hand on JJ's leg and patted it. "He has been accused of doing some terrible things and I know he is innocent."

Franks looked at his mother. "Your son's record is growing. Petty theft, assault, pranks, vandalism, just to name a few. Fortunately, no one has pressed charges."

"He just turned sixteen. He is a minor." Christine patted his leg again.

JJ felt terrible. In the past three months, the headaches had come and gone. The nausea had disappeared. But he had still awakened several times after a two hour lapse in memory. In each case, witnesses said he had done something terrible. "My grandfather was crazy." He blurted.

"Honey, don't say that!" Christine gripped his leg.

"It's true! He went mad and killed people. My father still keeps the rooms locked where it all took place." JJ leaned forward, desperation in his voice. "I need to know if I am following in my grandfather's footsteps!"

JJ heard his mother sobbing beside him, and he ignored her. As much as he loved her, he had to know the truth before he hurt someone he truly cared about. So far, the incidents had been petty. Those who had been affected deserved it. But something had to be done to stop these spells.

Franks leaned back in his desk chair and gazed at him through his thick glasses. "I am aware of your heritage, my son. I researched the medical records of your family. Your grandfather was accused of using mind altering drugs for some kind of experiment. I doubt his 'insanity' is hereditary."

JJ sighed. He had heard those theories before. It didn't change anything. The door was still locked and sealed off in his father's library. The events of the night of his grandfather's death were still a closely guarded secret. His father had never told him what really happened. "Then what is happening?"

"You may be suffering from seizures. Absence seizures or what we call petit mal can give you moments of 'blackout'. Characteristically, these type of seizures only last for a few moments. But your prolonged loss of consciousness is somewhat unusual. You may be suffering a long 'post-ictal' state. That means the confusion and sleepiness after a seizure. The other possibility is a physical one. We need to do some tests on you. I recommend an MRI of the brain and an EEG to trace your brain waves."

"An MRI?" His heart started to race, and he glanced at his mother's reddened eyes. "Do I have a brain tumor?"

Franks blinked behind his glasses. "I cannot rule it out. There is also a very remote possibility you may be dealing with a multiple personality disorder. Have you been hearing voices?"

JJ swallowed and looked away. "No!" He lied.

"Jonathan!"

Steel stood up and looked down at the box in his hands. He had another flashback! He looked into Cassie's concerned eyes. "Sorry, I just had another flashback. It had nothing to do with Pandora's Box."

Cassie glanced at Monty and then back at Steel. "Are you okay?"

"I'll be fine." Did he have multiple personality disorder? Would that explain the man he had met in Numinocity? Was there a violent, and yes, he would say it, evil version of himself lurking just behind the curtain of his broken memories? Steel took out 'Pandora's Box' and placed it on the table.

"What are you doing?" Monty asked.

"If I am correct, the compass of the demon rose should fit perfectly on this lid." He took the golden compass engraved with arcane symbols representing each of the twelve demons and placed it on the lid. He twisted the compass slightly and there was a firm click. The symbols began to glow, letting forth a red light. Steel stepped back as a wave of evil cascaded over them. Cassie grabbed Monty and they stepped away.

"It's the Ark of the Demon Rose." Cassie whispered.

"And now you've reconnected it with the proper compass, Jonathan. What have you done?"

Steel ignored the glowing symbols and picked up the box. The light in his palm flickered and matched the ruddy light coming from the compass. Pain shot up his left arm and he ignored it as he lowered the Ark of the Demon Rose into the third crate. He stumbled back and gasped for breath while his heart raced. He looked down at the light from his left palm. It was not the normal pale blue. It was red and pulsating and fading fast.

"I don't know what to say." Monty reached out and held Cassie's hand. "I've never seen anything like it."

"Me, either." Cassie said. "But after being healed, I don't question God's mysterious ways."

Steel nodded and slowed his breathing as the pain lessened down his left arm. "I still question enough for all of us."

Monty took Steel by the shoulder and led him away from the crate. "Jonathan, I know it's no consolation but remember, God's ways are not our ways. The worst evil that could ever happen in the history of humanity brought about the best good that we can never imagine. We killed God, nailed him to a cross and in that profane action God assured our salvation."

Cassie took Steel's left hand and examined it. The light had faded. "I don't know what is happening to you, Jonathan. But remember that Satan thought in crucifying Jesus of Nazareth he was winning the war. He may have won what he thought was a battle, but in Jesus' death on the cross he was totally and forever defeated. You may not understand why Josh is being put in this situation. But Monty and I have to believe it is for a greater good. And so should you."

Steel nodded and closed his palm. "Yes, I know this in my head. Just not in my heart. Now I need both of you to disappear."

"Why?" Monty said.

"I'm about to call the Sixth demon and tell her I've performed her task."

"No! You can't give her these artifacts!" Cassie said.

Steel stepped away from them. "You must trust me, Cassie. Now both of you go upstairs and wait for me. Whatever you hear down here don't come down. Promise me."

Monty reached over and took Cassie's hand. They looked at each other for a moment and she nodded. Monty looked back at Steel. "We will be praying for you."

💥 15 💥

Steel texted Dr. Gumijo on his phone and he was notified of an incoming video chat. He answered it and the face of Dr. Gumijo appeared.

"Success, Mr. Steel?"

"Are you alone?" Steel asked.

Gumijo's features were emotionless. "Yes."

Steel walked over to the crate and pointed the phone toward the rod, serpent and the two stones being careful to keep the Ark of the Demon Rose out of the field of view. "I found these in Cephas Lawrence's crate. I believe they are what you seek."

"How can I be sure?" Gumijo said.

"Well, if it isn't, I have something else that may be of more value." He turned the phone back on his face. "You mentioned a certain ark earlier during our initial conversation."

Gumijo gasped, her normally impassive features betraying her excitement. "You found it?"

"Yes, the Ark of the Demon Rose complete with the demon rose compass."

The air sizzled behind him and Gumijo appeared from thin air. She stumbled for a second and caught herself against the table. She gasped for air and blood trickled from a nostril. She wiped away the blood, looked at it and then licked the blood from the back of her hand.

"Ah, this human host is too weak to teleport this far. She will suffer but it is worth it." Gumijo straightened and caught her breath. Her face was pale and sweat trickled from her forehead. She blinked several times and fox tails appeared behind her. Her features transformed into a seductive face. She shook her head and the very human face reappeared. "Now I have reasserted control. Show me."

Steel motioned to the crate and Gomijo stumbled across the floor and caught herself on the edge of the crate. She leaned forward and her eyes widened. "Yes! The Ark of the Demon Rose!"

"I understand there are talismans for each demon left on the Council of Darkness." Steel said.

She turned deadly dark eyes on him. "Yes."

"And with the Ark you alone would have considerable influence over the Council, wouldn't you?" Steel said quietly. He saw the hunger fill her eyes, saw her hands flex in eager anticipation.

"With the Ark, I will have absolute power over the remaining Council members. I can become head of the council." Gumijo said.

Steel reached over her and slammed the lid shut on the crate. It hissed and locked into place. Gumijo stumbled back and her human countenance broke. The fox tailed vixen appeared only her face was no longer young and beautiful. A horrid hag hissed at him.

"What game are you playing, Steel?" She growled.

"No game. I found the artifacts for you. They are sealed in the crate only I can open, and I can easily have them transported to the other two of your unholy triad." He stepped toward Gomijo and fear filled the ancient eyes. She stepped back as Steel raised his glowing left hand. "You don't like this, do you?"

"Mr. Steel, do not forget I have control over Josh."

"No, *three* of you have control over Josh. And all I have to do is tell your two sisters you now possess the Ark of the Demon Rose, and you weren't going to tell them. What would they do?"

Gomijo's face twisted in anger, and she hissed and spit venom. The drops of venom sizzled on the floor. Steel held his glowing palm closer. "The decision is yours, Gomijo. I got you what you wanted, the rod, the serpent and the stones. If you want the Ark, only I can open the crate. Try to open it without me and the contents will be incinerated."

Gumijo shook her head in a rapid blur and the hag disappeared. The tails faded from view behind her, and she was once again the calm human. She drew a deep breath and crossed her arms. "You have me at a disadvantage. I told the others it was not wise to try and bargain with you."

"I want Josh healed. I want the cure to be completed so he can go home and be away from your influence."

Gumijo shook her head. "That is not possible. The other two would know. The best you can hope for is to continue the treatments'."

Steel swore and looked away. "Fine! Then the contents of this crate will have to be our secret. So, you will tell them I have completed the second task and the objects are safely hidden away until I complete the third task."

Before Gomijo could say anything, Steel pressed the call button on the very first number for the unholy triad and put the phone on speaker. "Mr. Steel?" The voice was identical to Dr. Gumijo's voice.

"Who is this?" He asked.

"Dr. Shutendoji. Where is Dr. Gomijo?"

Steel glanced up at Gomijo. "She is here with me in Dr. Hampton's Museum of the Weird. She has just inspected the items I was to obtain, and we have safely sealed them in the crate to keep them away from your, uh, competition."

A hiss came over the speaker. "That was not our deal!"

"Neither was having a Vitreomancer stalk me. I did what I

was asked. Dr. Gomijo is satisfied with the results. Aren't you?" Steel pointed the phone at Gomijo.

Gomijo pursed her lips and glared at him. She started speaking in a guttural language and Steel pushed the mute button. "Nope! English!" He unmuted the phone.

"The rod and serpent are here along with the two stones. I am satisfied Mr. Steel has completed the second task." Gomijo growled.

"You sound angry." Shutendoji said. "Are things truly satisfactory."

Gomijo drew a deep breath and Steel held up the glowing palm. She blinked. "It is this human host. She is weak after so far of a teleportation."

"Then return at once and I will let Santelmo inform Mr. Steel of his third task."

Gomijo popped out of existence leaving behind the fragrance of brimstone and sulfur. A drop of blood hovered in the air and then splashed on the surface of the third crate. Steel's phone warbled and the phone call ended replaced by a Facetime request. One of the three appeared in the screen. She wore scrubs and a white coat.

"Dr. Santelmo here, Mr. Steel. I am giving you the third task."

"Not until I see Josh." Steel said.

"I thought as much." Dr. Santelmo turned and handed her phone to someone. Josh's face appeared. Steel touched the record button on his phone. He wanted to record this conversation.

"Jonathan, where are you?"

Steel gasped at the sight of Josh's dark rimmed eyes and his gaunt face. "I'm at Nigel Hampton's museum in London. Are you okay?"

"Weak but awake for now. When will you be back?"

"Soon. Hang in there."

"Hurry. I'm beginning to hear the bird's song." Josh closed his eyes and slumped back in the bed. Someone snared the phone before it could hit the floor.

"Wait! What happened?" Steel said.

"He is very weak, Mr. Steel." Santelmo returned to the screen. "He will receive his next dose in two hours. That is assuming you agree to continue to fulfill these tasks."

"Yes." Steel gritted his teeth. "What is it I must do?"

"Vivian Darbonne, Mr. Steel. She is a thorn in my side. I want her neutralized. She has been seen since the disappearance of number eight. We believe she is planning something heinous to take apart the Council. You will find her, and you will take her out of the equation. Do you understand?"

Steel tensed. "You mean, eliminate her? I am not an assassin."

Santelmo raised a small eyebrow. "I wouldn't be so sure of that, Mr. Steel. We do not want Vivian to return to the Council, Mr. Steel. She has special status with our master so only you can deal with her. It must seem as if you are the avenging angel, if you will. And, hurry, Mr. Steel. Josh is growing weaker by the hour."

The screen went blank, and Steel slumped against the table. He ended the recording and saved it. Find Vivian? And kill her? He had no idea where she was or even if she were alive! But there was one thing that did give him hope. Josh had sent him a message. Jason Birdsong was watching over Josh, and it should be the demons that were concerned about the future, not Steel.

❧ 16 ❧

Josh had to be still. He was supposed to be sedated. The infusions still took him under and now he had to contend with Pandora. But he had a plan and without the sedation, he was able to think in a conscious state. It was just humiliating to pretend to be sedated. His feelings of paralysis and numbness came and went with the infusions.

He felt Faye beside him as she hung another bag of infusion. "Josh, I know you can't hear me but it's time for your next infusion. Good news. Dude is back and will clean you up. Have a nice rest."

⋇

Josh waited patiently for Pandora to appear and when she did, her reaction was priceless. She looked around at the interior of the truck. Josh sat behind her in the back seat and Pandora sat beside the woman driving the truck. Outside, the rolling hills of northeast Texas passed by. Josh looked at the back of her head and Pandora twisted her head completely around in a gut wrenching manner.

Josh raised an eyebrow. "Uh, that's gross!"

Pandora turned her body sideways and assumed a more normal position. "Sorry. But where are we?"

"Is this your friend?" The woman in the driver's seat turned said.

"We are in my mother's truck on our way to Lakeside." Josh felt the power of his mind grow slightly with her confusion. His skin crawled for a second and he felt the piercings again in his face as the memory fully gelled. He smelled the odor of his unwashed body. For a moment, he felt guilty. He had put off showering on purpose to tick off his mother. Now, she was gone, and he would never have a chance to tell her how sorry he was. He pushed that sorrow away before Pandora could sense it. He had to keep focused on this one moment in time.

"Yes, mother. This is Pandora. She wants to learn about quantum physics." Josh said.

Claire Knight glanced at him in the rearview window, her eyes hidden behind sunglasses. She smiled. "Well, it is refreshing for a change to see you actually curious about my field of study." In reality, Josh had tried his best to ignore his mother on that ride. She, on the other hand, had been so excited that her Uncle Cephas had called about a mysterious supernatural phenomenon the old man had described as "extra-dimensional". He had tried to shut out her lecture on quantum mechanics. Now, he tried his best to recall every word.

Pandora nodded and smiled. "I see you've decided not to fight me anymore."

"Doesn't look like I can hold out forever. You wanted to learn about how consciousness changes reality? Well, my mother and I had this very conversation on the day she took us to Lakeside to meet Jonathan Steel. Go ahead and ask her anything."

Pandora crossed her arms and leaned back against the side door. "I need to know how to transform thoughts into action. How can I make the things Josh thinks become real."

Claire pointed to the car moving in front of her along the interstate. "Okay, if you were to ask that car what state it was in, it would say, 'Ahead of Claire'." Claire accelerated and passed the car and pulled in front of it. "Now, if you ask it about its current state, it would say it was behind Claire. In the macroworld, each of those statements are mutually exclusive. But in the quantum realm, that is, the ultra-microscopic world of particles, we have learned that particles can be both a particle and a wave at the same time. Two things at once."

Pandora's forehead wrinkled. "I don't understand."

Josh leaned forward. "It's like us. I'm Josh. But according to you I am also Pandora. When my mother asks you a question you answer as Pandora. When she asks me a question I answer as Josh."

Pandora looked between Josh and Claire. "What does this have to do with my mind having the power to control reality?"

"Well, that is a misperception." Claire said. "You see what happens is when we interrogate a particle it forces the particle to assume one state or the other. Our process of observing the particle must utilize some kind of interactive medium, say an electron microscope or a particle accelerator. And the very process of interrogating it, forces it into one state or the other. In that way, one can think they have affected reality."

Pandora glanced at Josh. "This is making no sense."

"Welcome to quantum mechanics." Claire smiled. "It seems to defy the laws of logic. According to the law of noncontradiction, A thing, A, cannot at once *be* and *not be*. A dog cannot be a dog and be a non-dog. Light is both a particle and a wave. Think of a grain of sand and a wave passing through the ocean. Light can be either or both or one. Confused?"

"Yes." Josh said at the same time as Pandora. Good! Her mind was in sync with his. He had to keep it that way.

Claire laughed and Josh's heart skipped a beat at the memory of the sound of her laughter. How he missed it. How he had taken it for granted. "Josh, quantum mechanics is the branch of physics relating to the tiny, the very small. And because of that there appears to be some very strange conclusions about the world. You see, at the scale of atoms and electrons, many of the equations of classical mechanics, which describe how things move at everyday sizes and speeds like the cars on this highway, cease to be relevant. In our larger world classical mechanics apply and objects exist in a specific place at a specific time." Claire glanced back at Josh and smiled again. "How am I doing?"

"Great, Mom." Josh managed to say.

"The problem arises because, in quantum mechanics, objects don't exist in constant defined states. Instead, they exist in a haze of probability. The car we passed is behind us thirty percent of the time and ahead of us seventy percent all at the same time. So, on the quantum level it would seem that logic would not apply because A can be both A and non-A seemingly at the same time."

Pandora's looked down at her arms and shook her head. "I'm trying to understand." She glanced at Josh. "Do you understand?"

Josh shrugged. "Sort of. At least, there is a strong probability I understand."

"Josh, if I were to try and simplify it, I would say that quantum mechanics is counterintuitive to our notion of how larger objects behave. But it is not a violation of the laws of logic. You see, the laws of logic are necessary and unavoidable because all thought, correspondence and actions have to presuppose truth and its application, or we would not be able to function in our reality."

Claire looked over her shoulder at Josh and took off her sunglasses. For a moment, he saw the freckles on her cheeks, saw the warm color of her eyes and also, the pale skin that hid the disease killing her. Like the quantum mechanics that were not visible to the naked eye, her hidden illness could have been readily apparent to him if he had only looked beneath the surface; past his arrogance and self-centered nature.

"That's why we can't change reality by thinking. Our thoughts are playing out in the real world, not at the level of quantum mechanics. Sorry, Pandora, you can't change reality merely by willing it be."

Before Pandora could respond, Josh said. "Please Mom, don't!"

In the past, he knew what was coming and had heard it so many times. He had begged his mother not to say it again! Now, he couldn't wait to hear her say it again.

"Josh, the creed." She looked at him in the rearview mirror.

"What is she talking about?" Pandora glared at Josh.

"You wanted this memory. You have to take it all. This is her favorite part of this 'lecture'. Don't you want to hear it? Or, are you afraid? Did she shoot down your theory of changing all of reality with a mere thought?"

Pandora shook her red hair and sneered at him. "I can take anything you can bring up."

"Mom, please not the creed. Not again." He said and he was back in the truck seat with the air conditioning on high and the green hills passing by and Ida's presence dwindling in the journey to another of his mother's obsessions. How he wished he could really relive this moment. How he wished he could tell his mother how much he had grown; how much he had learned about love and sacrifice. How much he longed to tell her what a wonderful mother she had been.

"You have to say it with me. After all, if a particle can exist in two states at once why can't God exist as three in one?" Claire said.

Pandora put up her hands and panic filled her face. "No! You will not do this, Josh. I will hurt you!"

Josh felt the pain build in his abdomen. "Too late. You wanted it all. You can't stop this. You can't pick and choose what you want me to remember." He grimaced and bit his lip to keep from screaming as the pain took him. He had to say the words; he had to bring to life the creed that solidified it all. God in three persons. It all made sense even with the merest understanding of quantum mechanics.

"I believe in God, the Father almighty, creator of heaven and earth. I believe in Jesus Christ, his only Son, our Lord. He was conceived by the power of the Holy Spirit and born of the virgin Mary. He suffered under Pontius Pilate, was crucified, died, and was buried."

The pain intensified and all he could see was red. Pandora's hair seemed like fire blossoming around her twisted features. He focused through the red haze on the face of his mother reflected in the rearview mirror and the sound of her soothing voice as they spoke together.

"He descended to the dead. On the third day he rose again. He ascended into heaven, and is seated at the right hand of the Father. He will come again to judge the living and the dead."

Pandora was fading into translucency and the pain was beginning to abate. Josh spoke the words with his mother, their voices joining as one.

"I believe in the Holy Spirit, the holy Church, the communion of the saints, the forgiveness of sins, the resurrection of the body, and the life everlasting. Amen."

Pandora was gone and he now sat in the front seat of the truck where he belonged. His pain was gone, and he looked over at his mother. Tears were trickling down her cheeks. He had made fun of those tears. He had said so many harsh words.

"Mom, can you ever forgive me?" He whispered.

His mother turned her face toward him, and she smiled. "Of course I can, Josh. I love you."

❧ 17 ❧

Vivian Darbonne Ketrick Wulf fell and fell, gyrating and tumbling through cold air and never slowing. Around her, walls of psychedelic color swirled, and the air was filled with the fragrance of lilacs and roses. She screamed and nothing came out of her mouth. She thrashed at the air, and it became hot. Blisters formed on her skin. The blisters ruptured and blood burst forth dotting her body with beads of crimson.

"Stop!!!" She tried to scream, and the heat filled her mouth and her lungs, and the walls became flames that licked at her clothing until all was burned away exposing her blistering skin.

A man appeared in the air floating effortlessly. He wore a white tuxedo and when the blood burst from her blisters, it rolled off him as if his suit were made of Teflon. He had no hair, and his eyes were an intense blue. He steepled his hands.

"So, you called out to God, my sweet?" He said quietly.

She tried to answer, and only hot breath exploded from her mouth. She nodded her head as she continued to fall and fall, and the man hovered along with her.

"Yesssss!" She finally managed to say. "Why am I burning?"

"One must consider your original destination. Has it changed?" The floating man said. He man waved a hand and she found herself sitting on a folding chair. She wore a one-piece bathing suit and the chair creaked beneath her. Waves pounded just meters away on a pearly white sand beach. The water was turquoise. Palm trees swayed above her, and the man sat in a similar chair beside her.

"Is this better?"

Vivian gasped for air and ran her hands over her arms. The blisters were gone. No blood. "What?"

"Not every near-death experience is a pleasant one." The man said. "I'm Traveel. I was sent here to rescue you from certain death." He motioned to the sand around him and the blue water. "It's not exactly a tunnel to the Master but I think it is pleasant enough. We don't have much to work with right now since your brain is damaged from tearing the goggles off. You were warned."

Vivian swallowed. "Where am I?"

"Somewhere between heaven and hell. You called out to God. You asked for forgiveness. It must have been genuine, or I would not have stopped your fall."

"My fall. You mean into hell?"

"Well, there are many ways to experience separation from God. Imagine falling into flames for an eternity."

Vivian felt her heart race and she sat forward. "I did ask for forgiveness. Jonathan took the stinger meant for me. He suffered for me. " She blinked and realized that for the first time in her life she felt a glimmer of peace. "Like Jesus did. I saw him from a distance in Jerusalem."

"You were offered forgiveness then and you rejected it." Traveel said.

"Yet, it was offered again?"

"Again and again and again." Traveel said.

Vivian held up her hand. The tiny shards of the Grimvox were no longer imbedded in her palm. "This time it was for real. I was so tired of fighting it. So tired of bowing down to Satan. He's not going to be happy with me."

"Well, that is true. Once your mind heals and you wake up from this in between state, you will face a great ordeal." Traveel said.

"Deservedly so." Vivian couldn't believe she was saying it. But she realized it now with all her heart. The regret, the guilt, the shame washed over her like the waves at her feet. "I have much to answer for, honey child."

"Let's be clear. This is not some kind of Purgatory. If you were really dying, there would be no in-between. It is appointed man once to die and then the judgment. You are not quite dead and if you had not ripped those goggles away, your mind would be sound, and you would not be teetering on the brink of death." He smiled. "The Savior has decided your job is not yet done. In going back to reality, yes, you will face adversity, but it will be to help those you have wronged. Your story is not yet at an end."

"I made the right choice just in time?" Vivian said.

"In God's time, yes. You are one of the fortunate to have seen beyond the veil of reality to what is waiting."

Vivian leaned back in her chair. "What now?"

"We wait. But, be warned. As your mind awakens, you will experience things that no person should. It will be painful. It will be upsetting. You will beg to go mad. You will wish it had all ended. You might even wish you had continued to fall." Traveel looked out over the water. "His eyes are the same color as the sea."

"Jonathan?"

Traveel laughed. "No, Jesus."

"Jonathan is no Jesus." Vivian smiled and laughed. "Honey child, he is one messed up dude."

"God uses those, too."

Clouds rolled in with a sudden burst of cool air. The waves thrashed and the water turned a dark bluish gray. Traveel nodded. "And now it begins." He faded from view.

Vivian stood up as the wind picked up threatening to blow her over. "Traveel? What is happening?"

A wave in the distance heaped upward out of the dark sea and fingers of water appeared. It hurtled toward her, and she tried to run but the sand sucked at her feet, and she stumbled and fell. The hand of water paused over her and slowly lowered to touch her face.

"My dear Vivian, what am I to do with you?" A voice echoed in the distance. The hand touched her cheek and she tried to pull away, but the sand had piled up and over her body, holding her to the ground. For a brief second she saw snow white eyes gleam above her. The hand and the eyes disappeared. Water trickled over her cheek, and it was no longer cold. Tears. She was crying even though she could not move.

The sand receded like water and the sky grew black. She felt cold, hard metal beneath her. She was no longer on the beach. She was in a room with black walls and a black ceiling above her. The only light came from beneath the slab on which she lay. She tried to move but her muscles refused to respond.

Her tormentor appeared beside her slab, a cadaverous, sore pocked woman with long, greasy gray hair and totally black eyes. The woman leaned over Vivian and her breath reeked of death and decay.

"Hello, sweetie. Finally getting what you deserve?"

"Mother?" Vivian tried to say but her lips would not move. No, this wasn't right! Her mother was dead. Vivian had seen visions of her mother while in Numinocity but this creature was far too real, too tangible.

Her mother's hand appeared arthritic and missing half the flesh. White bone and pink muscles moved as she stroked Vivian's cheek. "Now, I can have my revenge. I always told you what a worthless sack of meat you were. But your father and I fought over you for years. He was too soft on you. That's why Sudie gored him. He deserved it!"

The touch of her fingers felt like cold electric shocks to her skin. Each stroke sent painful waves across her face. Tears collected in her eyes and ran down the side of her head.

"I am suffering for my sins, daughter. It is time for you to suffer too. Time for you to feel the pain and the loneliness and the unending tedium." She cackled and her nose fell off and landed on Vivian's chin.

Vivian tried to close her eyes against this nightmare, and nothing happened. She had been forgiven! So, why did she have to endure this torture? Was this the price to pay for following the Son of God? The smell of decaying flesh and the stench of death wafted over her. She drifted back in her memories to ancient Jerusalem. That day of death smelled like this, brought back memories of flayed flesh and tortured minds.

She saw him walking and stumbling under the cross, his back muscles torn open by the flogging. She saw him fall again and again. She stood on the hill of Golgotha as they lifted his naked body up onto the cross and it thudded into the ground. She saw his eyes again looking at her down the long alley and they did not condemn her as her mother's eyes did. They were filled with love and compassion, something she had never received from this specter that hovered over her. And yet, in spite of all Vivian had done, he still suffered for her. He still had died for her. He still forgave her.

Tears spilled out of her eyes and her vision cleared. She looked again at her mother's decaying face and black eyes. She wanted to hate her. She wanted to kill her, but she was already dead and suffering something far worse than Vivian could ever devise. Could her mother have asked for forgiveness from the Savior? And, if she had, would he have forgiven her?

Vivian replayed so many of the decisions she had made that hurt others. There were too many to keep count. And, yet with one request, she had been forgiven for all of them. What kind of love was that? Not human, she realized. Holy. Divine. God.

She was forgiven! It was still hard for her to believe it was so, but her heart felt different. Her mind felt different as if she no longer had allegiance to the evil one, Satan himself.

And she no longer cared what happened to her. Every pain

she would suffer from this moment on was nothing compared to the pain she had inflicted on her victims. And, with startling clarity, she realized that every pain she had ever experienced and every pain she had ever caused was nothing compared to the death of the Son of God on the cross. And, it had not ended there. She was sure of it. If Jesus had stayed in his tomb, there would be no need for a Council of Darkness. If Jesus had stayed in his tomb, there would be no sending demons to Tartarus. He was real. His death was real. His resurrection was real. And so was his love and forgiveness.

Vivian realized what she had to do, and it would be the hardest thing she had ever attempted. If she could just open her mouth and speak. She concentrated on her mother's nose less face and the beetle black eyes. This was the woman who had given birth to her. This was the woman who had nurtured her and loved her until her mother's love of alcohol and drugs became the dominant love in her life. She felt movement returning to her lips and she drew in a breath.

"I forgive you." She whispered.

Her mother's eyes widened, and she stiffened and drew back. "No! I won't accept it. You're lying."

Vivian managed to swallow and cleared the dryness from her throat. "I forgive you!" She said loudly. And, with that proclamation, her body began to feel again, and her heart swelled with something so different, love. She did not like her mother, but she did love her, the essential her, the her before she self-destructed.

Her mother raised her bony hands to her face and screeched out loud. "No! No! I cannot be forgiven. I am damned and cursed." And she faded from view.

Feeling returned to Vivian's arms and legs and she carefully sat up on the slab. Her head swam and dizziness threatened to tumble her from the slab. She sat on the side of the slab with her legs dangling down. The dizziness grew and grew, and her head pounded with pain. Lights flashed in the darkness of the walls.

She felt her mind melting away and she tumbled back onto the slab in a faint.

Where was she? When was she? Who was she? She was certain that just moments before, clarity had wrapped its arms around her. But now, she was losing her mind. Again. What had the nice man said? Something about wishing it had all ended? Wishing what had ended?

The room grew brighter with suffused light. Vivian sat up on the couch and rubbed her head. She straightened the skirt.

"I really need to iron this." She mumbled.

A pair of high heel shoes sat by her feet. "No wonder my feet are killing me!" She said quietly. "I need to get a new pair of heels." Yes, that is what she would do. That would make all things better. Shopping.

A shadow eclipsed the bright light and she looked up into the face of the other woman. Her red hair hung down around her face in disarray. She wore a dark one-piece jumpsuit. Maybe she worked at the drive in. Yes, a hot fudge sundae would do the trick!

"Vivian, my dear, it is time to get you out of here. I have a trip to make east of here, but you have an appointment with the Overlord."

Vivian smiled and wished she had a compact to check her lipstick. "I can't wait to meet him."

❦ 18 ❦

Steel had returned to his hotel room after the encounter with Dr. Gumijo. Monty and Cassie had tried to talk to him, but he ignored them. "I need to rest, Cassie. I'm taking a cab to the hotel room."

Monty glanced at the closed crate. "What now?"

"You keep it safe, Monty. Only I can open it and all the artifacts are sealed inside." He said.

"You made a deal with the Sixth demon, didn't you?" Cassie said.

Yes, Steel thought, he had made a deal with the devil. Back in his hotel room, he stood at the doors to the balcony and stared at the cloud filled afternoon sky. A misting rain had turned to snow, and the air was filled with swirling white flakes.

How was he to find Vivian? She had disappeared after taking off her goggles while in Numinocity. When he had awoken in Monarch's lab, Vivian was gone.

"God, I know I'm working with the other side now, but I have to trust that you've got this. I need to find Vivian."

His cell phone rang, and he studied the caller ID and smiled. Dr. Cephas Lawrence, his mentor, often said there was no such thing as a coincidence.

"Hello?" He said.

"Mr. Steel? You may not remember me. I'm Reginald, one of Ms. Vivian Darbonne's assistants. Well, more than just one of her assistants now that Jerome is missing. I'm her personal assistant."

Reggie had been a tightly buttoned up assistant in Vivian's office and had sparred with the late Bile, once Vivian's closest assistant who had perished in the island debacle and relinquished the thirteenth demon to Vivian. "I remember you, Reggie."

"Reginald." He said crisply. "I'm calling out of sheer desperation. I got your cell phone number from Ms. Darbonne's contacts. We have weeks' worth of business to take care of and week after next is Thanksgiving and there are deadlines. And do you know where she is?"

"Why would I know?"

"Well, the two of you have a love hate relationship." Reggie said. "Mostly hate."

"Actually, I'm looking for her myself." Steel said. To kill her, he thought. He tried to banish the thought from his mind. "I last saw her less than a week ago when we were involved in one of Dr. Sultana Thakkar's projects."

"Ah, yes, the implosion of Thakkar's Third Eye Interface! I wondered if Vivian had anything to do with that." Reggie said. "So, you have no idea where she is?"

"When was the last time you heard from her?" Steel asked.

He told Steel a date and time. It was the morning before they had ventured into Numinocity. "Sorry, Reggie. I haven't seen her since that morning, either."

"I've tried to track her phone. I've checked on her credit cards. Nothing, Mr. Steel. It's as if she dropped off the face of the earth."

Yeah, in Numinocity, Steel thought. "Does she go somewhere to get away from you?"

"Away from me?" Reggie said testily.

"Go somewhere alone. Me time." Steel said.

"There is a private island in the Maldives. I checked. She's not there." He was silent for a moment. "Maybe I should file a missing person report. But, if she is merely being, well, uh, Vivian, then her anger is something I would not like to face."

"Reggie, if you hear from her, please let me know immediately." Steel said.

"Ah, so there is more love than hate? I figured as much." Reggie ended the call.

Steel looked at the empty screen of his cell phone. What now? At least he knew Vivian had not surfaced. How could he find her? Reggie had tried electronically, and no tech had found her. That meant she was either dead or off the grid. He looked down at his left palm and it glowed faintly. There was something different about Vivian than any other human being. She had fragments of the Grimvox imbedded in her hand. Could he use that to find her? The demon network?

The memory of an encounter with a man and his demon surfaced and for the first time in months, Steel swore. The man was a monster! But the man and his demon were ambitious. They wanted to be on the Council. Steel could use that to his advantage. With the man's connections, he might know how to find Vivian. Or maybe he had an angle on the Grimvox fragments imbedded in Vivian's hand. It was a testimony to his absolute desperation he would even consider contacting him! How far down the rabbit hole was he willing to go? Problem was, it wasn't a rabbit hole, it was a hell hole! He checked his watch to see what time it was in Dallas, Texas.

❧

"JONATHAN?" THE WOMAN'S SMILING FACE BROUGHT TEARS TO Steel's eyes. It has been so long since they had talked.

"Ruth, how are you?"

On the laptop screen Ruth Martinez brushed back the dark hair from her face. "Just getting back from my morning workout.

Why are you calling me at 5:30 in the morning when I haven't heard from you in months?"

"Sorry, I'm in London, England. I thought I remembered you loved your early morning workouts. Running?"

"Biking." Ruth drank from a water bottle. "But back to you. London? I guess that is why you haven't you called? I've reached out to you multiple times. Globe hopping, I guess? Grace was worried about you."

Grace Pennington was the head of the law firm where Ruth Martinez was a full partner. Grace had retained Steel to help investigate a murderer defended by Ruth Martinez. Her success had landed her the position of full partner. "I'm sorry, Ruth. I've been very busy."

"And you managed to adopt Joshua Knight, I see." Ruth smiled.

"How did you know?"

"I keep my eyes on you, Jonathan." She glanced away and almost blushed. "Truth is, I miss you. You were a tornado in my life that turned destruction into something good. I never really got the chance to fully thank you. The last time we talked, you and Dr. Lawrence were going to examine the mask lent to you by Grace. The thirteenth demon, right? Did you find him?"

Steel sat back and sighed. "Yes. I did."

"You seem different, Jonathan. Settled a bit, but still tightly wound. What's going on?"

Steel took the fountain pen from his pocket and clicked it and placed it beside the laptop. Just in case. "I have made peace with a lot of things, Ruth. I loved and lost. Cephas passed away. And Josh is my son, now." He fought the wave of sorrow and swallowed. "I need your help."

"What kind of help? Legal?"

"No." Steel sat forward and he was dreading what he was about to say. "I need to find Drake." The memory returned and he drew a deep breath.

৩৯৯

Roy Festivan's office address led me to a run-down strip
mall in Mesquite, Texas. It sat just a block or two away from a huge
shopping mall and housed a pawn shop, a sandwich shop and two
deserted stores separating the small office of "Roy Festivan, P.I.". The
snow had let up some as my car slushed through the empty parking lot. I
parked in front of the office where the glass windows were covered with
posters for local elections. Only the door was transparent with a "Closed
for Business" sign dangling from a rusty chain.

I peered inside the office and made out an old wooden desk with a
landline and a doorway leading to the rear of the office. I nudged the
door with my foot and it swung inward, unlocked. The odor hit me full
force and I choked. I used the flashlight setting on my phone and followed
the foul odor down the hallway to the rear office.

The room was shrouded in shadows and I heard the buzz of flies. Not
good. A large glass and chrome desk sat beneath a rear window. Pale light
cast shadows across the figure slumped over the desk.

"He just couldn't take it another moment." Someone said behind me.

I whirled and the man stepped out of the shadows. There are times in
my life when I have felt the unmistakable brush of evil. It is like a
powerful force that emanates from the darkest side of our human existence. But the wave of pure evil that washed over me made me step back
and reach for a gun I never had.

"What?"

The man stepped into the wan light from the window. "Sorry. Didn't
mean to startle you. Reginald Drake." He held up his hands and I saw
they were encased in blue latex gloves. His eyes were of different colors. So
much for my eyes making people feel weird. His were downright creepy.
"I'd shake your hand, but we don't want to leave any evidence that we
were here. I'm afraid Mr. Festivan ended his life a day or so ago." He
pointed over my shoulder. "There's a note. He was in great despair after
being fired by someone at the Institute."

"You are evil." I whispered hoarsely.

"Of course I am." Drake chuckled and his two disparate eyes glittered with malice. "I did not kill Mr. Festivan. But we did harvest his soul."

"Who are you in league with?"

"Oh, just a minor bottom dweller demon. Something that can give me access to past memories and limited powers. It doesn't realize I'm using it, not the other way around. Now," He reached into his blazer pocket and retrieved a small object. "This is the flash drive Festivan tried to give to Dr. Morrant just moments before she fired him. Seems she was displeased with his progress and never looked at the images on here. I think Ruth will find them very helpful."

He held out the flash drive and I let him drop it in my hand. It was hot. "Why are you doing this?"

Drake shrugged. "Ruth was able to obtain my acquittal. I'm still facing minor charges, but I've got a connection I think that can get them dropped." He stepped toward me. "You see, I owe her. But I don't own her. Yet." He smiled and his perfect white teeth shone in the weak light.

"I should call the police and report you."

"Oh, but you won't. You don't have time to go down to the department and fill out paperwork and make a statement, do you? Ruth needs that flash drive now. So, run along and don't touch anything."

He stepped to the side and gestured toward the hallway. What to do? I glanced once again at Festivan. The man was dead. His fate had been sealed when he made a pact with the devil. I turned back and Drake was mere inches away. He was studying my face, tilting his head side to side like some reptile.

"You really do have the most striking turquoise eyes. Rocky Braxton was right."

I flinched and stepped away. My hips banged against the edge of the desk and stirred up a cloud of flies. Drake gestured to the flies, and they spun and danced in a sphere above his head until the sphere formed into a perfect spiral.

"Braxton is dead." I hissed. "But the thirteenth demon is out there somewhere."

"I know." Drake swiped his hand through the air and the files fell to

*the floor, dead. "You won't stop pursuing him, I know. But far be it from
me to give you any hints as to his whereabouts." He stepped around me
and pressed the speakerphone button on the landline. He dialed 911.*

*"911, state the nature of your emergency." A man's voice echoed from
the speaker.*

*"It stinks really, really bad!" Drake grinned. His voice sounded like
that of a teenage girl. "Like, I think something is dead in that office.
Maybe a possum or a raccoon." Before the voice could answer, he killed
the call.*

*"They'll be here in about five minutes, so you best be hurrying on.
Give my best to Ruth." He saluted and disappeared from sight; just disappeared, leaving behind empty air and a snap that made my ears pop. I
glanced around the office. Drake was gone. Like that. I had forgotten
about my phone light, and I played it over the desk. Festivan's head was a
sea of gore, and blood and brain splattered a handwritten note on the
desk. In the far distance I heard a siren. Without touching anything I
hurried out and drove off from the office of death.*

◈

DRAKE HAD BEEN ARRESTED FOR MURDER AND THROUGH A
clever series of events, had managed to get his defense lawyer,
that had occurred long before Steel had been hired to help Ruth
with her defense of Dr. Frank Miller accused of killing his boss.
Ruth froze and her face paled. "So, you're not just checking up
on me. Or Grace."

"Ruth, the truth is, Josh is in trouble."

"And how can a serial killer who escaped justice thanks to
me, possibly help Josh?"

Steel looked away. "I can't explain it. I just need to know how
to get a hold of him. I assumed that with your, well, obsession
with him you might have kept track of him."

Ruth's features stiffened and her voice tightened. "Fine. He's
wearing a tracker. The district attorney tried to put him away,
but the man had some kind of connections and got away with an

ankle tracker." She looked away and mouthed an obscenity. She looked back at the tablet and focused on Steel. "Sorry for being so abrupt. I'm not happy about Drake. Look, I can have the police tell me his exact whereabouts. I'll be in touch." Her finger stabbed at the image and the window went blank.

❧ 19 ❧

The underground was more crowded than usual. Olivia hugged her backpack to her chest and glanced at her watch. She had less than two hours to make it to the airport and catch her flight back to America. Her mother had not touched the memory card for the entire day and had, instead, been occupied with research on the Penticle. Her mother had no idea Olivia knew this. Olivia had hacked into her mother's computer to keep an eye on the memory card and everything her mother was looking at had mirrored to her iPad. She could care less about a conspiracy theory. She only wanted to see Josh.

All three of them had spent a leisurely afternoon at the museum at her mother's insistence and she knew it was to look for more clues about the Penticle. Olivia never let on. Afterwards, Steven had gone to play soccer with some of his local friends excited about his "new" hands. Olivia, couldn't feel the same way about her "old" broken brain! Now, afternoon was turning into evening and Olivia had volunteered to go get pizza. Her mother seemed very preoccupied and merely waved her on her way without any hesitation. Her mother would regret that later.

Now, if she could just make it onto the airplane and it took off before her mother found out, there would be nothing to keep her from making it back to check on Josh. She knew something was wrong. Josh was in trouble, and she had to help him after all he had done to help her find her brother.

The backpack had two changes of clothing, her laptop, and a month's worth of medicine. Once she got back to Atlanta, she could go to her mother's safe house and get the self driving car hidden there. It would be a long drive back to Louisiana, but it was a safe bet her mother would keep her from flying to Shreveport. She was still a minor.

Olivia had learned how to be fiercely independent in the years since the head injury that had given her epilepsy. Her mother had taken her and Steven around the world, including three months on North Africa, in search of their father's assassin and all three had learned how to exist off the grid. Now, according to her mother, the assassination attempt had actually been against her mother, not her father. She touched the necklace around her neck and her fingers played over the whale's tail her father had given her from his many journeys. She closed her eyes and tried to remember his face, the sound of his voice, the smell of his aftershave as his beard tickled her.

Someone jostled her in the seat next to her as more people crammed onto the crowded train car. She glanced up at an Asian girl gripping the metal pole beside her as the train moved on down the underground tunnels. The Asian girl was probably in her early twenties with a pink sweater and black jeans. The girl glanced at her angrily and quickly looked away.

"She's mental, that one." A raspy voice said. Something dark and leathery appeared slowly from behind the girl's head. At first, Olivia couldn't understand what she was seeing or hearing. Then, red eyes in narrow slits gleamed through the girl's hair as a head raised itself above the girl's pink headband. The thing had a shortened snout like a pug dog and pointed, serrated ears. Its mouth stretched from one ear to the other and opened to reveal rotten teeth. The smell of the thing's breath played over Olivia, and she gagged at the odor of decay and death.

The thing made eye contact with Olivia and tilted its head like a curious dog. Olivia stood up abruptly and shoved her way through the standing crowd. The girl glanced at her once and with a triumphant grin, plopped into the empty seat. The thing behind her head became more visible now with a short, cockroach like body and multiple stick like legs imbedded in the girl's very flesh. It grinned and winked at her.

"You have demon eyes, eh? Good luck with your sanity." It rasped.

Olivia shook her head in confusion and stumbled over someone's feet and fell up against the door. Patrons around her cursed her and roughly shoved her back into a standing position. Olivia glanced back at the Asian girl. The thing was gone. Was she going crazy? Was she back in Numinocity? Maybe she had never left!

No, the past few days had been normal and painful as she had healed from the burns she suffered in the warehouse fire. She looked away from the girl and rubbed her eyes. Maybe her implants were malfunctioning, and she was having some kind of strange aura. Auras preceding seizures could involve odors and sometimes, sounds. But hallucinations? She had never seen things that didn't exist.

The train lurched to a halt and the door behind her opened. She grabbed a pole and held on like a drowning rat as people moved off and onto the train around her. She was swept away from the door as her hands slid from the pole and she fell into another seat. She glanced up at the electronic sign. She had a few more stops before she arrived at the airport.

An elderly man sat in an empty seat beside her. His white hair was wispy and filled with static electricity. He wore a leather jacket and khaki pants and leaned on a metal cane.

"People!" He growled at her. "Problem with this world is too many people."

Olivia tried to ignore his foul breath at least grateful it wasn't as bad as the creature on the girl's head. The man wiped at his face with his other hand and Olivia gasped as blood trailed across his skin. The man's hand was purple and knotty with six fingers; no not fingers, but more like talons? Yellow nails raked through the man's skin and blood poured down his face and dripped onto his lap. He glanced at the palm of his hand oblivious to the trickling blood. From the center of his palm, the flesh parted, and a bright green eye appeared. It swiveled as it studied the man's face.

Olivia closed her eyes and leaned away from the man. She was losing her mind! She had to get out of here. The train lurched to a halt, and she bolted out of the seat and shoved people aside as the door opened. She knocked people aside and she ran through the jostling crowd away from the horror in the train.

Olivia tried to make her way up the crowded stairs and a wave of conjoined grating voices swept over her. She glanced up the stairs at the crowd coming toward her. More of the things appeared crouched and attached to people's chests and backs. They were of all types of nightmarish creatures with wings and bony arms and tentacles and bulging eyes and long forked tongues. And, floating in the air above the surging crowd were spherical things with open maws that pulsated and gyrated. One came close to her, and she lashed out and her hand passed through the thing. A searing fiery pain lanced down her arm and the thing turned toward her.

"No! Go away!" She screamed. Olivia shoved her way roughly up the stairs and out into the snow filled evening air. She ran down the crowded streets with no regard to her location, her eyes averted to the ground to avoid more demonic visions. And, then it hit her, a powerful aura of flashing lights and she was gone.

"Hello, poppet."

Olivia opened her eyes and gagged at the smell that engulfed her. The man was short and round with matted hair and brown teeth. His right eye was clouded, and she felt his rough hands on her arm. She jerked out of his grasp and looked around. She had suffered an absent seizure.

"Where am I? Who are you?"

The man stood up and motioned to his left. "She's awake, love."

A woman stepped into Olivia's field of vision. Her hair was maroon and teased out like Medusa. Her bright, green eyes glittered with malice. "Good, she'll bring a nice price, what?"

Olivia tried to stand up and found she was tied to a chair. She looked around at the dark, grimy room. Windows had been blacked out. Furniture was old and broken and the air was filled with the odor of mildew and the nasty man. "You will regret this, whoever you are."

"Oh, I don't think so." The woman said. "I'm Mallificent, like the movie. Loved the name. Took it for meself. Only I added an extra 'l' because I'm loving it!"

"And I'm Prince Charming." The man laughed out loud. "And this is our castle."

Olivia's heart raced. "I had a seizure. Where's my medicine?"

Mallificent looked at Prince Charming. "Well, that explains how easy it was to bring you here. We just thought we'd gotten lucky, eh, love?" She nudged the man.

"Low hanging fruit. Theys always not thinking about wheres they are. Thinks they are immortal." He laughed again. "Well, our client will change all that. The Overlord is always looking for young ones."

Prince Charming walked over and ran a rough hand across Olivia's short hair. "Likes your hair, I do."

Olivia waited until his rotten breath bathed over her and his face was inches from hers and then she slammed his nose with a head butt. Prince Charming shrieked and backed away as blood spurted down his ratty clothes. "Oi! That's it! I say we finishes her right now, love."

"Oh, shut it, PC. Go wash your face and straighten out that nose. She's worth more than you ever had. Now, git." Mallificent shoved PC toward a door and he swore and swore as he disappeared down a hallway.

"Got lots of spirit, don't you?" Mallificent planted a hand on her hip. "You'll need it where you're going. The Overlord don't like slackers." She picked up a cell phone from a nearby table and dialed a number. She adjusted her hair and licked her lips.

"What?" A woman's voice came over the phone.

"I gots you a fresh one, love." Mallificent said.

"Don't call me love. Show me."

Mallificent pointed the phone camera at Olivia and took a snapshot. She typed on the phone screen.

"She's a pretty one. Probably sixteen. The Overlord will be very happy. Our usual price, what?" Mallificent said.

"I'm coming." The woman said and the call ended.

PC appeared from the hallway with a dirty, blood-stained rag pressed to his face. "She's coming?" He squeaked. "What did you do?"

Mallificent was frozen staring at her cell phone like it was a spider. "Don't know. Her coming is good, right?"

"No, it ain't good, love. It's bad." PC said. "She usually sends one of those white robed goonies."

"Just calm down." A raspy voice came from behind PC. Olivia groaned.

"No, not again."

Mallificent looked at her. "What? You having another go at a seizure?" Something bulbous and vile green bubbled up through Mallificent's maroon hair. It was like her brain had turned to green slime and the slime was forcing its way through her scalp. The green slime coalesced into a grotesque head with an open mouth and a single eye. The eye swiveled and focused on Olivia.

"Demon eyes." A high-pitched voice said.

"What you looking at, love?" Mallificent said. "Look like you've seen a ghost." She laughed out loud. "If you knews who's coming to get you, you'd be filling your diapers, love."

PC chuckled and nodded and spindly, jointed legs appeared over his shoulders. A spider like head slid over the top of his scalp. Bright red, multifaceted eyes glittered.

"She's fertile ground." The thing rasped.

Olivia closed her eyes and moaned in fear. What were these things? Why was she seeing them now? In Thakkar's warehouse, the nanobites had somehow interfaced with her implant and allowed her to enter Numinocity. But the nanobites only lasted six hours. They should be gone by now. Something in the process of infestation with the nanobites had healed Steven's scarred hands. But she still had seizures. No luck with any kind of healing. But, had the nanobites somehow altered her brain? Was she actually seeing demons?

"No!" Her eye flew open. "You're not real."

Mallificent glanced at PC. "She's mental, love."

"Oh, we are very real." The slime demon burbled. "You have the curse. The demon eyes. What a treasure you are."

"Yes, when we take you, the Master will be very pleased with us." The spider demon said. "Remove us from the Dregs, he will."

Olivia looked away. This could not be happening. She did not want to believe in demons. She did not want to believe in the supernatural in spite of all that had happened in the past weeks. Because if these things were real, it meant there was a spiritual realm in which these things dwelled. It also meant there was a God. She did NOT want to believe in God. And that was something she had worked very hard to achieve.

The door to the room opened with a bang and a figure moved through the shadows toward her. Mallificent and PC fell back away, their faces etched in obvious fear. The figure paused in the shadows and picked up Olivia's backpack.

"There's drugs in there." PC said.

"My epilepsy medicine." Olivia said. "And it's time for my next dose."

"Get some bottled water." The figure said.

Mallificent placed a hand on her hip. "Do I look like the maid?"

An arm shot out of the shadows and gleamed with a coppery metallic finish. The metallic hand grabbed Mallificent's throat and the Crimson Snake stepped into the light.

"You look like someone about to die. Get water now!"

"Snake?" Olivia said. She had only thought things couldn't get any worse!

The Crimson Snake released Mallificent and the woman disappeared down the hallway, swearing and grousing the whole way. PC just slinked away to a corner. Snake paused before Olivia. Her unruly red hair was braided into two long ropes of hair that hugged her back. Black wisps of burned hair showed at the ends of the braid. Her face bore at least four small cuts covered with strips. Her good arm hung in a sling, and she had limped as she walked across the room.

"What happened to you?" Olivia said. "Looks like you didn't make it out of the warehouse fire after all."

Snake glared at her. "Let's just say I barely escaped an explosion at the hands of Jonathan Steel by throwing myself into a lead lined coffin. I woke up a hundred meters from the explosion trapped in the box. Good thing I had this." She raised her bionic arm and snapped her metal fingers. "When I get a hold of Steel, he'll see just how strong this hand is. Now, how did you happen to fall into the clutches of these two?"

Olivia tugged against her restraints. "I had a seizure and woke up here."

"Girlfriend, you were in the wrong place at the wrong time." Snake pulled a clear bag of medicine bottles from Olivia's backpack.

"Which one?"

"Red top."

Snake handed the red top medicine container to Mallificent who had returned with a bottled water. Snake motioned to Olivia. "Give her the meds and a swallow of water."

Mallificent popped the pill in Olivia's open mouth and tilted the bottle. Olivia swallowed the pill and took more water into her mouth. When Mallificent pulled away the bottle, she spewed the water into Mallificent's face. The slime demon recoiled and Mallificent raised her arm to strike Olivia.

"Stop. You needed a bath anyway." Snake grabbed the arm with her metal hand.

"You can let me go, Snake." Olivia said. "You rescued me from the fire at the warehouse. I know there's some good in you."

Snake glared at her. "Hey, I'm not Darth Snake, okay. You have your own self to blame. Lucky for you your seizures will keep you from being put in the Harem. The Overlord will let me put you where you're most needed. We lost the Keeper yesterday. Tear in her glove and she was exposed to too much fentanyl. It's the best I can do, Olivia. At least no one will touch you."

Before Olivia could react, PC grabbed her roughly by the neck and shoved a gauze pad over her mouth and nose. The chemical smell made her gag and, as she gasped for breath, darkness took her.

✿ 20 ✿

Monarch had put it off for too long. After spending the day wandering around a museum in search of more information on the Penticle, she had to admit the journey had not been to find information. It had been to put off the inevitable. And to try and talk herself out of accessing the memory card. Her mind kept going back to the folder on her desktop.

She had been acutely aware her daughter had hacked into her computer so she had hidden the folder but had not hidden the fact she was researching the Penticle. The cat was out of the bag by the time she realized Olivia had infiltrated her computer. A chip off the old block!

Another reason to wander around London for most of the day. She had made up her mind! Sending Olivia out for pizza would buy her some uninterrupted time while Steven played his video games with his newly healed hands. She hunched over her computer console and stared at the card. Its contents were so enticing. It was time to find who had ordered Raven to attempt to assassinate her.

Monarch had promised Steel she wouldn't try and open the card. But, she reasoned, there had to be some kind of security software that controlled the contents of the card. Steel said if she tried to access the information, the contents would erase. Which meant there had to be a security process. Such processes had never stopped her before! One side of the memory card contained a metal disc. Fingerprint analysis, perhaps?

Monarch bit her lip and took the chip and carefully placed it into a card reader. She studied the icon that appeared on her computer monitor. She brought up a terminal and began typing. It took a minute or two, but she finally was able to read the card's file format. She had not opened the icon on the desktop, but she had found a readme file. She used a terminal program to access the readme without actually opening the icon that represented it. The read me file outlined the caution that anyone accessing the card without the proper biometric information would trigger erasing the contents.

She smiled. "Biometric, huh? Well, that's a little more complicated than a fingerprint." She continued to probe the contents of the readme file and found a menu list of options.

"Fingerprint plus something else." She muttered. As she studied the list three letters appeared. "EEG? Really? This thing reads the person's EEG?" How could this small card possibly read a person's EEG? She knew that it was possible to pick up some remote neuronal activity in the finger. Was that enough of a signature to satisfy this small thing's security requirements?

Monarch sat back. "Where am I going to get Steel's EEG? Or his fingerprint?"

Monarch got up and paced, thinking furiously. EEG was a brain wave tracing. Very complex and difficult to find.

"Wait a minute!" She turned back to another of her computers and opened the brain mapping program she had used for creating a link to Numinocity. Each person who had worn a pair of the goggles had also had their brain mapped in preparation for entering her program. She had used the brain map from Raven to attempt to bring back her memories.

Monarch paused and closed her eyes. Instead of bringing

back Raven's lost memories, she had inadvertently erased all her memories effectively rebooting Raven's mind. Raven was now in the hands of Max who was reeducating her. And Max would not be amenable to helping Monarch.

Monarch pulled up the raw data from Steel's goggles and ran it through her proprietary software. Ironically, it was the same software she had used to detail the placement of Steel's brain implant at the direction of Steel's father, the Captain, years before. For a second the guilt took her and she sat back away from the computer and ran her hands through her hair. How many times had she agonized over that decision? In taking the Captain's ill gotten money she had hoped to find technology to help her daughter. Instead, the many brain surgeries she had performed had taught her nothing! Other than to never agree to work for the Captain!

Monarch pushed away the memories and the guilt and focused on the task at hand. She generated a tracing of Steel's readings in the form of a standard EEG read out. Great! Now, she needed a fingerprint. Where could she find Steel's fingerprint? He had touched the memory card but so had she. Wait a minute! Steel's goggles!

Monarch retrieved the goggles from a storage cabinet and found the one assigned to Steel. Using techniques she had learned in her years on the run, she found a fingerprint and copied it using adhesive tape and then made a reverse mold to fit her own finger. Now, she had Steel's fingerprint on her finger and the EEG tracing. But, how to make the reader sample Steel's EEG instead of her own?

The answer, unfortunately, was the goggles. If she could tie the goggles to Steel's brain mapping software and put them on herself while touching the reader on the memory chip, hopefully the software would detect the goggle generated EEG and Steel's fingerprint. If it didn't work, she would lose everything. And Josh would lose his life.

Monarch placed the goggles next to the computer keyboard

and paced. What to do? If this worked, she would have a copy of the files and have unlimited access. She could make a backup copy of the dossier for her own use. If it didn't work, then all the information would be lost. But how was Steel to know it was really there to begin with? She could always tell him the card must have been erased in the process of passing it on to her. She could lie to him. Easily. In the past few years, lying had become a necessary tool to ensure the safety of her children. She froze. Was Steel any different from her? Working with demonic beings to save his son? She couldn't think about Steel right now.

Monarch climbed the stairs from her basement laboratory to the street level of her building. She paused to look out the grimy windows at the Thames River illuminated by scattered lights from the buildings along its stretch. Clouds had moved across the setting sun and already, snow flakes were drifting down onto the river's moving surface. Always moving. Never stopping. Unsettled. Ever changing. Like her life with her children. The information on the memory card could change that.

Monarch made up her mind and hurried back down the stairs. She attached the goggles to her computer and made the necessary modifications to the goggle input sensors. Instead of sensing her EEG, the leads imbedded in the goggles would pass through Steel's EEG tracing. She put the goggles on her head and activated them. Only in wearing the goggles could she make this work. For a moment, she was totally blind and then the goggles kicked in featuring HER software modifications and not the interface with Thakkar's now defunct Numinocity.

Monarch could see clearly through the goggle visual interface, and she double clicked on the file icon from the memory card. The read me file appeared, instructing her to place her finger on the exposed metal contact of the memory card. When Steel had rescued her from the plane crash she had used a very special bracelet to activate his brain implants and erasing his short term memory. She had modified the bracelet to sense Steel's EEG readings from the goggles.

Monarch pulled on the bracelet and the half fingered gloves. A tiny electrode stayed attached to her index finger. With one touch, she had erased Steel's memory. After he had saved her! She closed her eyes and resisted the urge to stop. She had to do this! She had to find out who was pursuing them for the sake of Olivia and Steven. She had just gotten Steven back and she was not going to lose him again!

Using the bracelet, she placed the fingerprint copy on the tip of the electrode at the end of her index finger. The electrode was now connected to the goggle output. The software was counting down from twenty to give her enough time to place her finger on the card. She knew she only had one chance before the data was erased.

Monarch placed her finger on the card reader and held her breath. A schematic of Steel's fingerprint appeared on the computer monitor and red lines traced the whorls of the image. When the image read 100%, the fingerprint turned green. The fingerprint had passed.

Now, a window showed the EEG tracing. As the wiggly lines played across the screen, Monarch hoped they were Steel's and not hers. The wiggly red lines finally filled the window and turned green. A voice said, "Welcome, Jonathan Steel. You have full access."

Monarch released her breath in an explosive "Yes!" She watched as the folder opened up listing one single file, the dossier. She double clicked on the dossier icon and a document appeared. As she paged through the document, she discovered it was incredibly dense and packed with enormous amounts of information. Raven had recorded a total of 43 kills! And they had been collated by the name of each victim. She spent over two hours sifting through about one fifth of the dossier and had yet to locate either her name or her husband's.

"Mom! Mom!" Steven burst through the stairway doors.

Monarch turned from her computer. Steven held out his phone. "You need to see this."

Monarch blinked and tried to clear her mind of the task in which she had been so engrossed. "What is it?"

Steven grimaced and drew a deep breath. "Before you get mad, it was Olivia's idea and she insisted. I had no idea she would go off task."

Monarch took the phone. It showed a red tracing overlying a map of London. "What is this?"

"Olivia booked a flight back to America." Steven said, his face filled with anguish. "She was supposed to be boarding her flight right now! I waited to hear from her and never did. So, I pinged her phone to see is she arrived at the airport and on the airplane."

"What? The airport?" Monarch lurched up from the chair. "Why did you let her do this?"

"She is determined, Mom. You know that." Steven ran an his hand through his unruly hair. "I tried to talk her out of it."

Monarch glanced at the map on the phone. "This isn't anywhere near the airport."

"I know." Steven said hoarsely, tears in his eyes. "Look at the part of town. She got off the underground and went into a very shady part of London and then, her phone shut down. Mom, I'm afraid she may be in trouble."

Monarch's heart sank. She slumped back into her chair. "No! Not now!"

Steven took his phone back. "What do we do?"

Monarch whirled to her computer and closed the dossier document and brought up her proprietary security programs. It took only five minutes to hack into the CCTVs in the region where Olivia had disappeared. No need to go to the police yet until she knew what had happened. They would only delay her. This wasn't her first rodeo, and she would avail herself of the power of the authorities once she had more facts.

"I can't believe you didn't stop her." Monarch said.

Steven paced. "Mom, I'm sorry. You know how persistent she -

can be. I didn't believe she would go through with it." He paused. "I'm going to see if I can find her."

Monarch grabbed his arm. "I can't afford to lose both of you. I just got you back."

"Mom, I'll be fine. I'll hire a cab and just cruise the area. I won't even get out of the car. I promise. Let me help. Please. This is all my fault."

Monarch studied his anguished features. Steven had been so much worse than a trip to that section of London. She sighed. "Okay. Go. But call me every fifteen minutes."

Steven ran out of the room and Monarch began sifting through the video footage. She glanced at the image she had captured from Steven's phone. She went to that time stamp and found at least twelve cameras in the area. The fourth one brought up an image of a woman running out of the entrance to the Tube. It was Olivia!

Olivia raced down the snow-covered sidewalk, shoving through people until she stopped abruptly. The crowd thinned around her, and Monarch drew a deep breath. Olivia was having an absent seizure! Olivia stood still for a moment and then slumped to the side, slowly crumpling like a balloon losing its air until she lay on the ground, her shoulders and head leaning against the wall of a building. Falling snow gathered on her inert figure.

People stepped around her as if she didn't exist until a couple walked into the image. A scraggly man and a woman with poofy hair. They bent over and examined Olivia and spoke to each other briefly. Then, the man picked up Olivia and tossed her over his shoulder and walked away. Olivia had been abducted!

❦ 21 ❦

Steel's phone warbled with an incoming video chat request. He opened the chat and Ruth's face appeared. She had done her hair and put on some makeup. Framed diplomas covered the wall behind her. She was in her office. Steel expected a verbal lashing but instead, Ruth wore a dismayed look.

"Uh, Jonathan, I don't understand you and your business. What was it Dr. Cephas told me? Something about coincidences?"

"There is no such thing as a coincidence." Steel said. "Ruth, you look like you saw a ghost."

Ruth looked down at something on her desk. "It's just that Drake has on a tracking anklet. He can go anywhere. But not out of the country. I don't know how he did it. He's not in the United States."

She tapped on a keyboard out of sight and light from a computer monitor painted her face in rainbow hues. "I checked it and double checked it."

"What is it, Ruth?"

Ruth looked back at him. "He's in London. England. Where you are."

Steel gasped and sat back roughly on his bed. "What? That can't be. I mean why is he here?"

"No coincidence? What exactly does that mean, Jonathan."

Steel looked away in thought. What had Monty and Cassie said about the Urim and Thummim? Did priests cast lots to determine God's will? Did God play dice? If so, the game was fixed, and the roll of chance had been neutralized.

"Cephas always felt like there was some structure, some plan, some story behind everything. He always told me that God planned everything; every encounter; every disaster; every joyful moment to fit his plan. Like pieces of a jigsaw puzzle that can only fit a certain way. And the pieces make up a huge picture that only the person manipulating the pieces can see. If Drake is here, there is a reason."

"I don't like this, Jonathan. I was angry earlier but now I'm worried. The man is more than dangerous. I need to alert the local authorities."

"No!" Steel blurted out.

Ruth paused her typing. "What?"

"I need to talk to him. Just give me a couple of hours before you notify the authorities."

Ruth tightened her lips and sat back. "You want to talk to him? Jonathan, this man is a psychopath! He's a serial killer. And I let him go!"

"If I don't talk to him, it might cost Josh his life." Steel glanced at the fountain pen. The dampening field was still working. "I can't lose Josh, Ruth."

Ruth shook her head. "No! I can't let you do that! Don't you get it? With this infraction I can throw him *under* the jail. He got away with murder by bribing a judge. He got away with a tracing anklet, Jonathan! And he was not supposed to leave the country! I've got him dead to rights! And he's in a country from which I can have him extradited."

Steel put up a hand to stop her. "Please, Ruth. Give me a couple of hours. Please. I promise I will not let the man get away. There is something only Drake can do that will help me save Josh. If for no other reason, do this for Josh. I'll take whatever consequences I have to face."

"Like aiding and abetting?" Ruth said.

"Ruth, please."

"I don't know."

Steel hated what he said next. "I did save your life, Ruth. You owe me."

Ruth looked back at him, and her face turned red. She opened her mouth to say something and then closed it. She turned back to her computer. She studied the screen. "Fine. So that's the game we're playing." She tapped at keys and her silence was deafening. Steel felt his heart sink. What was he doing to one of the few friends he still had in this world? Ruth's voice was neutral. "I'm tracking him down in London now." She studied the screen. "Looks like he's in a building. Name of the building is Hampton's Museum of the Weird? That certainly fits."

Steel dropped the phone and slid off the bed. He fumbled for the phone. "Jonathan? Jonathan? Are you okay?" He heard Ruth's voice.

Steel fought for breath and his heart raced. He snared his phone and climbed back onto the bed. "Ruth, I was just there a couple of hours ago. That can't be!"

"Who is Hampton?"

"The man who infected Josh with a deadly virus and is holding him hostage to control me. And Drake is somehow involved?" Steel wiped his face and his palm glowed brightly.

"So you're not globe hopping! I don't like this at all, Jonathan. You met him while you were helping me with the Darwyn murder trial." Ruth said. "I'm alerting the authorities. I don't care what you say. If he is where you were today that means you may be his next target. Why didn't I see this? Everyone I care about becomes a target of that monster!"

Jonathan leaned into his phone. "Give me an hour, Ruth. Just an hour. If I find him, I will text you and you can send in the troops. There is some information I can get only from him. And you know if he is about to be arrested, he'll clam up and then try to bargain his way out of being arrested and Josh doesn't have that kind of time. Please, Ruth. Do this for Josh. Please."

Ruth drew a deep breath and nodded. "I'll wait two hours, Jonathan. You watch your back."

"And my front and my sides. Yes, I'll be careful. Thank you, Ruth."

He ended the call and hopped off the bed. If Drake was at the museum, then Cassie and Monty were in danger. He dialed Cassie's number and she answered.

"Jonathan, what's up? Are you okay?"

"Where are you?"

"At dinner with Monty. Look, Monty is in the restroom, okay. I was going to invite you, but I needed some time with Monty. We have a lot to process." Cassie said.

"Great! Take your time. I was just checking on you."

"We need to talk some more, Jonathan. We want to help you with the next task."

Jonathan shook his head. "I'm afraid this task will have to be mine alone." He ended the call before she could say more.

❧ 22 ☙

Monty had given Steel the access code to the electronic lock at the front door. The sky was growing dark as the sun set and the earlier snow had stopped falling leaving behind a slushy mix on the sidewalk. The air was bitter cold, and Steel shivered inside his light jacket. Steel studied his reflection in the glass doors. His hair was in disarray and he needed a haircut as if that mattered. His face was gaunt and tense and his turquoise eyes almost glowed in unison with the pulsing light in his palm. He tore his gaze away from his reflection and he keyed in the lock sequence and opened the door to an empty foyer. Where to start? He had no idea what lay beyond the door to the exhibits. And he had four floors to investigate. Ruth had texted him a phone app for tracking the anklet and had given him the code to the anklet. He opened the app and typed in the access code.

The GPS signal was strong but not very precise. The map he brought up on the screen showed the layout of the base of the museum but gave no indication on the height above ground. A tiny blinking blip was somewhere in the southeast section of the building. He looked in that direction and the door to the exhibit opened into darkness. Of course! Drake would be hiding somewhere in the midst of Hampton's latest exhibit on evil, pain and suffering. More of God's plans? Or more of God's sense of humor?

Steel glanced once at the sign to the entrance to the "Museum of the Weird". Below the title was a hovering hand holding a glowing rock from which multiple arcane images seemed to spring: a floating severed head, a stereotypical horned devil with a pitchfork, a headless horseman carrying a flaming pumpkin aloft, and a hooked nose crone carrying a basket of moldy fruit. Steel looked away. He didn't have time to examine all the images. He walked down the hallway toward the exhibit "hall". The narrow hallway was a testimony to the age of this ancient building. The rooms off the hallway had been converted into dioramas. Steel jerked in surprise as the light came on in each diorama as he arrived. Sensors may have been installed to save electricity but more than likely were there for the effect of startling the viewer. Cheap tricks!

The first few dioramas were far from frightening. One carried a floating severed head dripping blood and muscles from a face filled with horror and pain. Behind the severed head sat a fat robed king and beside him stood a seductive young woman in a skimpy robe with a golden headdress. The caption read, "John the Baptist Lost His Head."

The next diorama showed three crones with hooked noses standing over a glowing cauldron from which hands and arms protruded. The caption read "Which witch is Which?"

The figures were poorly painted and dressed as if a toddler had been hired to complete the artwork. Frankly, the entire exhibit was hopelessly amateurish. After ignoring a dozen such dioramas, Steel reached the end of the first hall and turned to his right. He chose to ignore the displays and focus on finding the source of the signal. It was growing stronger as he neared what would have been the back corner of the building.

The lights went out in the display cases behind him, and Steel was plunged into darkness. The only light came from his phone. He froze and listened. Somewhere far away he heard laughter. Maniacal laughter! Another one of Hampton's tricks of the trade? Using the flashlight on his phone, he continued down the hallway and the distant laughter grew louder. He reached an open room at the end of the hallway. The laughter stopped. Silence. Darkness. Nothing moved as he stood in the center of the room. His light did not reach the walls.

Suddenly, the lights came back on, and he gasped at the sight around him. Six large dioramas surrounded a hexagonal room. A doorway near the back of the room held an unlit exit sign. As he made his way toward the door, he stopped at the sight of one of the dioramas.

He walked over to the glass window behind which stood a dowdy woman in a white robe with an old-fashioned bonnet on her head. Behind her was an ancient laboratory counter with a steaming set of metal containers. The woman held a red stone with glowing golden veins. The look on her face was of astonishment and the artwork and design was light years ahead of the dioramas in the other hallway.

Something glowed and glittered to the right of the woman and a huge stone jar began to shake. The lid shot off into the air on a hidden wire and a green glowing light burst forth from the jar. From within a figure began to emerge. She was hauntingly beautiful with long, cascading red hair and bright teal-colored eyes. She wore a silver robe and hovered up into the air above the jar. Her eyes turned in his direction and a voice came from within.

"Have you seen my box? Have you seen Pandora's Box?"

The figure of the woman now came to life, turning slowly to face the other woman. "I hold the Philosopher's Stone. The box is no more. You have come from the Elixir of Life!"

Steel slowly backed away. The placard at the base of the exhibit read, "Mary, the Jewess, the first Alchemist and the Philosopher's Stone."

The figures stopped moving and Steel continued to back

away until he thudded into the glass of the exhibit across the room. The Pandora exhibit went dark, and the entire room fell into shadows. He heard the figures resetting into their original beginning positions. Just a mechanical device!

The light in the display case behind him came on and he whirled. The setting was a jungle with huge trees and ferns. In the background a river was painted on the wall and in the corner a rock wall stretched to the ceiling with an open mouth to a cave about three feet across. Something glittered in the depths of the cave. The man standing in the center of the display was six feet tall and wore a pair of pants and a gauzy shirt. In his hand he held a pith helmet and standing beside him was a short, dark skinned man with long hair. He wore only a loin cloth. At the shorter man's side was a roughhewn stone jar as tall as his waist similar to the stone container in the other diorama. The indigenous man held a flask of some type in his hand. Steel tried to focus on the object, but it was obscured by shadow.

The taller man's expression was hard and ruthless, and his eyes gleamed a bright turquoise. Steel stepped back from the display and stumbled in confusion. At the bottom of the window a sign had these words: "Professor Stone locates the source of the Elixir of Life on May 5, 1832."

How could it be? The scene was almost identical to the photo from the album in his flashback! But his grandfather wasn't even alive in 1832. Could this be his great great grandfather? The eyes were unmistakable, and the figure was so lifelike Steel expected the man to turn his head and look right at him. It was at that moment the laughter came again. The lights in the display went out and Steel stood in total darkness. He illuminated his phone as the maniacal laughter echoed around him. It came from the exit door.

23

Steel hurried through the exit door glad to leave the disturbing displays behind. On the other side of the door a stairway led up and down. The laughter came from below and died out to an uneasy silence. Steel drew a deep breath as he started down the stairs. On his phone, the blinking light brightened. He opened the stairwell door and found himself in a smaller version of the operating theater. A table sat in the center of the room and the lower level was surrounded by a rail to separate standing observers. He used the flashlight on his phone and made his way back through an open door into the theater with the crates. He was back in the operating theater. The blinking light dimmed. Where could Drake be? Back in the smaller theater? The one Margaret had said NOT to enter? Surely whatever chemicals had been used for whatever reason had dispersed by now.

Steel paused and felt his heart race. He glanced at his watch. His time was running out. And Drake was a dangerous man! Steel had never carried a weapon with him. From one of his flashbacks, he knew he was an excellent marksman and the memory of holding the pistol on Max drove shame into his heart. He could have killed Max! Could he kill Drake if it came to it? Was he capable of cold-blooded murder? The flashback of the way he had treated his girlfriend cast doubt on his true nature. He feared when pushed to the extreme he would have no problem killing someone!

Several items were spread out on a smaller table next to one of the crates. The light from his phone reflected off something and he spied a golden knife. He gasped as the memories returned! He was back in the lake house confronting Robert Ketrick.

🍂

STEEL STUMBLED BACKWARD THROUGH THE FRENCH DOORS AND left blood on the handle. He glanced down, and only then did he notice the blood running down his fingers from the cut in his palm. Ketrick stopped at the open door and noticed the blood. He reached down with a long, bony finger and dabbed at a spot of blood on the door handle. He raised his finger delicately to his flaring nostrils and sniffed the spot of blood. Smiling, he placed his finger in his mouth and savored the moment as his eyes closed in concentration. He opened his dangerous eyes. "You have good blood, Mr. Steel. Very good blood. Take care of it. It tastes almost as good as the blood that was left on the knife Rocky used."

Steel blanched, and he squeezed his hand in a fist. His heart pounded with horror. When he had seen the picture of the knife on the desk in Ketrick's downtown office, he had thought it looked familiar. Now it all came back to him. The gold, curved blade covered with her blood. The mosaic tile of the handle shaped like the backswept wings of a hummingbird. He glared at Ketrick as his mind reeled. He was unable to find words.

Ketrick grinned, and the red blood outlined his chiseled white teeth. Ketrick pursed his lips and steepled his bony hands together. "The police returned the knife to me once the inquiry into poor Rocky's death was over with. But don't worry. I cleaned all of her blood off the knife before I displayed it. I wouldn't want to dishonor the dead. See you later, alligator."

Ketrick quietly closed the door, and Steel lost control, running dizzily across the yard to fall in the bayou. He swam away from the castle and away from the hideous beast who lived there, toward the brush, toward the less frightening prospect of hungry alligators, rushing onto the shore, tearing through the bushes and shrubs, briars and vines ripping at his flesh until lungs almost bursting, he collapsed against his car, fumbled in his pockets, and in a blind panic drove away from this most private hell.

☙❧

HIS HAND HOVERED OVER THE GOLDEN KNIFE. HE RECALLED the police had found it in the ashes after the church had burned to the ground. Cephas must have kept it.

He took the knife in his left hand and for a second his palm glowed a dull crimson then faded. The golden blade felt warm against his flesh and he heard the dying screams of hundreds! A label tied to the knife had writing on it.

"Recovered from the church basement of the church in Lakeside, Louisiana and curated by Dr. Elizabeth Washington. This knife is believed to be the implement of human sacrifices in the ancient Mayan culture."

The screams faded into silence giving way to a new sound from the smaller theater and it chilled Steel to the bone. It was the laughter!

He transferred the knife to his right and pocketed his phone. Darkness filled the larger theater. A small lamp in the corner of the theater gave him meager light to find the door leading into the smaller room. He moved slowly into the smaller room and his shadow preceded him, falling across the old dissection table. On the far side of the smaller theater opposite the door from the stairs was another smaller door barely visible in the grime covered wall. He had not noticed it earlier.

He made his way quietly toward the door and his shadow grew smaller as he approached. The door screeched as he pulled it open, and darkness lay beyond. He turned sideways to allow the faint light to enter the room. He could make out a hulking, black shape in the center of the room and for a moment he was back in the basement of the church in Lakeside standing before the huge furnace. Before him was a much smaller furnace.

Steel longed to illuminate the light from his phone but feared it would only make him an easy target. He quickly stepped through the door and to the side and pressed his back against the stone wall. The furnace sat in the center of the room with an old rusted iron door. A window in the center had been broken out. Was Drake here? Holding the knife before him, Steel approached the furnace. The air was cold, and his breath steamed before him. He stopped just a foot from the door.

"Boo!" A face appeared in the window and Steel stumbled back, dropping the golden knife. Two eyes stared back at him one blue and the other brown. Steel fought his racing heart.

"Drake!"

"Hello, my man of steel. It took you long enough to find me." Drake smiled at him. His normally perfect hair was greasy with sweat and the odor that came from the furnace was nauseating. "Forgive my appearance. It would seem that Margaret is immune to my manly wiles."

Steel removed his phone and checked the time. Twenty minutes until Ruth notified the authorities. He glanced back at Drake. "It can't be a coincidence you are here."

Drake frowned and put a hand on the bottom of the window. "I will tell you everything, Jonathan, if you will allow me out of this wretched prison."

"I don't think so." Steel said.

Drake tilted his head. "Then why are YOU here?"

Steel looked away. He was making another deal with evil! "I need your help."

"Well, isn't that convenient for me. I would be very glad to help a fellow deviant." Drake smiled.

"I'm not a deviant." Steel's face warmed with anger, and he

shook his head. "Never mind. I need to find someone, and I think only a powerful demon can help me."

The laughter was low at first and then built into an insane cackling and Drake fell back into the furnace. He laughed for minutes, it seemed, until his laughter fell into a chorus of coughing. When his face appeared again, tears streamed down his cheek. "You have no idea how happy this makes me! You want to talk to *my* demons. My demons want to talk to you. I want to talk to you. We have so much in common, Jonathan."

"We do not!" Steel growled. "I am not a serial killer."

"Well let's not quibble on that word 'serial' shall way? A killer is a killer! Right? Had any flashbacks lately? I understand you have amnesia so how would you possibly know if you were a serial killer or not? I'll tell you." Drake pushed his head through the broken window and his two glowing eyes focused on Steel. "Do you feel your pulse quicken at the anticipation? Do you linger at the fragrance of your victim? Does your palm itch to hold that blade?" A dirty hand appeared through the window and a finger points at the knife at Steel's feet. Drake smiled and tilted his head. "Do you have dreams of violence so satisfying, so fulfilling your heart could burst?"

Steel stepped closer to Drake. "No, I do not."

Drake rolled his eyes. "Well, it was worth the try. What can we do for you?"

"I need to find Vivian Darbonne."

Drake froze and his eyes shifted back and forth as he studied Steel. He closed his eyes and smiled. "Oh, I see. *They* are pulling your strings. What is it like to be a meat puppet, huh Jonathan? To dance and gyrate to their beck and call? At first it can be disturbing. You wonder why you let them in. You fight to escape back into a world of reality but then you begin to taste it, don't you? You begin to give in to the desire for chaos and destruction and decay. It grows on your soul like a gruesome fungus infiltrating every fiber of your being with its mycelia. I can see it on you. I can feel it on you." Drake paused as if listening to a nearby voice. "You had such influence in your past, didn't you? Your soul is tainted by the intimacy of the demons."

"My soul belongs to Jesus Christ." Steel said firmly.

Drake recoiled at the name and disappeared from view. "If you want my help, you will never mention that name again!" His voice came from deep within the furnace. His face appeared and he smiled.

"Sorry. My buddies don't like that name. Doesn't bother me personally. Good curse word!" He nodded as if making a great decision. "Now, here is what you are going to do. You are going to open this door and free me. Now!" He shouted.

Steel flinched. His heart raced. "Why didn't you just teleport?"

Drake's face twisted in anger, and he nodded back over his shoulder. "Weak demons. Poor choices." He put both hands before him and lifted a finger. "One, there wasn't much time after the murder. Two, a very powerful demon brought me here. Three, I was told everything not organic would be left behind, like my clothes. Four, they lied. I still have my anklet!"

"Step back!" Drake nodded and disappeared back into the darkness of the furnace. Steel drew a deep breath and put his hands on the rusty wheel set in the door. He turned the wheel and the metal braces retracted. He stepped back and Drake pushed open the furnace door. He stepped out and the odor of human waste and urine washed over Steel. Drake was completely naked, and his body was covered in black soot. He looked down at himself.

"Pardon my clothing. As I said, I lost them in the teleportation and ended up in there. I'm wearing old dead people. Ashes to ashes. How many cadavers did they roast in that furnace in the name of science? Can you imagine dissecting a dead body to learn the mysteries of the human anatomy so that one day you could be a surgeon?" He smiled and his eyes gleamed with an evil fire. "Or dissecting a live one!"

Drake giggled and pointed to his anklet. "Now I know that

Ruth, my sweet darling, gave you the access code so you could track me. You are going to remove the anklet and then I will give you the exact location of Vivian Darbonne."

Steel blinked and backed away. How could he do this? He promised Ruth he wouldn't let the man go. He gritted his teeth and pulled the phone from his pocket. He opened the app again and stared at the access code. He had to do this! "How do I know I can trust you?"

Drake rolled his eyes. "Really, Jonathan. We are brothers! I would never betray you."

Steel held up the phone. "I can give you the code now, but I have to know you are telling the truth."

Drake crossed his arms and his lips moved without sound as he looked to his left. Then he looked to his right and spoke silently some more. He nodded. "Phleabite and Toepain are not the sharpest knives in the kitchen, but they are all I have to work with right now."

"Oh. You lost your main puppet master?" Steel said.

Drake froze and his face twisted in anger, and spit shot from his mouth as he spoke. "I am the one pulling the strings, Steel!" He poked his chest with a grimy finger. "Me! I bow down to no one! I was the one who took care of Moshander. Phleabite and Toepain ran away while I opened the top of his head and scooped out his brains. Want to know why they ran? They're cowards! I frightened them, Steel. Me! A mere human can make a demon scurry away in fear. What does that tell you about me?"

Steel drew a calming breath and chose his next words carefully. "A man with determination and purpose." He hated what he had just said. But he had to get Drake's cooperation even if it meant soothing the man's insane ego. But he wondered who Moshander was. "I'm sorry I doubted you. Do we have a deal?" Steel said quietly while his insides writhed in disgust.

Drake's heaving chest began to slow with his breathing. He swallowed and turned around three times. He stopped and pointed a finger at Steel. He opened his mouth to speak and shook his head as if battling for control. "Okay, okay! Deal. I've sent them away for information. Checking the worldwide demonic web, so to speak."

Drake seemed to deflate, to slump as if the energy had left him. He looked at Steel with a strange expression on his face. "When they're gone, I have to deal with the guilt. I don't like it. I don't want it. They keep it suppressed, hidden, tucked away in their nasty little minds."

"Guilt? Drake, no one deserves to die. Not even you. Of course, you should feel guilt."

Drake blinked his two-toned eyes and shook his head. "No. I can't. I won't." Suddenly he stiffened and then grinned. "They're back!" He laughed. "Really? That's where she is? Oh, to be a fly on the wall." Drake flinched and wore a wounded look. "Oh, I'm sorry about that Mr. Steel. I know you have a thing about flies and spiders, don't you?" He looked around as if someone might be listening and he walked closer to Steel, putting a hand next to his mouth. "Here's a freebie. They're not watching you anymore!" He giggled. "Got bigger fish to fry! Oh, those three are way in over their heads, they are." He clapped his hands and danced around. "They have no idea what is really going on. How sweet! How precious!" He said this last word like the famous creature hidden away beneath the misty mountains. He froze and turned around, his face now serious as he pursed his lips.

"Now, as to our deal. I'm going to give you one number of geographical coordinates. You can put it into your GPS app and see the location is not far from the city of London." He recited a set of numbers. Steel memorized the access code for the anklet, closed the app and opened a global positioning app. He typed in the first set of coordinates and a line appeared across the map of Great Britain. Not very specific but the line ran north and south and was definitely to the east of London. He drew a deep breath and swallowed.

"The access code is 3366785."

Drake pointed to his ankle and slid his foot toward Steel. "If you would, please."

Steel shook his head. "I'm not coming near you."

"Yes, you are." Drake said quietly, his voice filled with malice. "I can't see the tiny keypad on my ankle unless you give me the phone light. I don't think you are going to do that, so we compromise." He wiggled his foot in the air. "I wear size 10, sir. Make sure the shoes are not too tight across the arch. I have delicate feet." Drake giggled again.

Steel slowly approached Drake and squatted down in front of him. Drake lifted his foot and smiled. "No, my good sir. I do not think the crystal slipper will fit." He giggled again.

"Hold still!" Steel hissed.

"You'll have to take my foot."

Steel recoiled from the man's odor, and he took the dirty, grimy foot in his right hand. He anticipated the left palm glowing, but nothing happened. Why? Because he was cooperating with this evil being! His soul felt cold and distant as if God had turned his back on him.

He put the phone in his mouth and put its light on the keypad and typed in the access code. A tiny green light blinked once and then went dark.

"If you would be so good as to remove the anklet?" Drake held his foot in Steel's hand. Steel glared up at the man and Drake only smiled. "It's the least you can do."

Steel took the anklet off and tossed it away. Drake jerked his foot out of Steel's hand and laughed as he danced away. "What do you think? River dance? Do I have a future?"

Steel stood up and wiped his hand on his pants. He was growing tired of this creature. "Now, the other number?"

Drake stopped dancing and walked slowly across the room to Steel. Waves of evil poured from the man. Drake paused inches from Steel and his two-toned eyes focused on him. "You could join us, you know. You're good material."

"I belong to someone else. Remember." Steel hissed and his cold breath steamed over Drake.

"Yeah, so how was it you could touch me without my skin burning. I'm told you have that effect on people of my kind? Huh?"

Steel breathed harder. "The number!"

"Want to know why? Because you're fallen. You've walked away from the empty cross, Steel. You have more in common with my kind than with them. A reprobate. An outcast. A traitor!"

Steel reached out and shoved Drake back toward the furnace. Drake stumbled and Steel shoved him again and again until drake fell across the threshold into the darkness. Steel's chest heaved with the effort and his heart raced. He glanced at his left palm. No light. Nothing.

Drake's giggling came from within and he slowly reappeared, his eyes shining with malice and evil. "Oh, I have what I want now, man of steel. I have you!" He stepped out of the furnace and brushed soot from his hands. "Now, the number. Yes."

Drake recited the second number and Steel keyed it in. The global positioning app zoomed in on a location to the east of London. Drake leaned forward over the phone and Steel jerked it away from him.

Drake pulled back from the phone. He bent over and picked up the golden knife by the tip and held it up into the dim light from Steel's phone. "I'll be going now. Tata!"

He stepped around Steel and ran out of the furnace room. Steel seethed and gasped for breath. He studied the map on the phone. "What have I done?" He whispered.

STEEL MADE HIS WAY THROUGH THE FRIGID NIGHT AIR AS HE walked away from the museum. His phone rang and he glanced at the screen. Ruth Martinez. He answered the call.

"Steel! What happened? Drake's anklet went silent. I lost the position."

"He escaped." Was all Steel could manage.

"How did he get the anklet off?" Ruth said.

"Demonic influence?" Steel said.

"Steel, what are you not telling me? Where was he last seen? I'm on the phone with your buddy Special Agent Ross right now who is coordinating with London police. Jonathan, we think he murdered a doctor in Shreveport, by the name of Gupta Moshander."

Steel paused and swallowed hard. Was the man an associate of Jack? Again, too much of a coincidence and the thread that tied Drake with the murder led back to the unholy triad. And Hampton!

He calmed his thoughts. What should he do? If he told Ruth where Drake had been the local police would arrive at Hampton's Museum of the Weird. If they did that, they would find the crates. They would confiscate everything as part of the crime scene. He couldn't afford that. He looked around at the dark, shadowy neighborhood in which he stood. Figures moved through the shadows. Criminals just like him. He had to lie to Ruth. Satan was the father of lies! He closed his eyes.

"I tracked him to an old abandoned building on the waterfront near Shakespeare's theater. The anklet app stopped blinking before I could find him, Ruth. He could be anywhere." At least that last statement was true.

He heard Ruth sigh. "At least that gives us a rough area to start with. I'll tell Ross. And Steel, be careful." The call ended and Steel closed his eyes in shame. He swore and almost threw the phone into the street.

"Mr. Steel?"

Steel froze at the sight of the young man walking up to him. He had last seen him in Numinocity and then afterwards in the hospital. Steven Monarch pushed his blonde hair away from his face and pulled a long wool coat tightly about him.

"Steven?" Steel said. "What are you doing here?"

"I'm looking for somebody. I thought you went home with Josh."

Steel sighed. "It's a long story. How are you?"

"I can't believe I just tumbled upon you." Steven looked away and stiffened. "Look, we need your help. Can you talk to my Mom?"

24

Detective Chief Inspector Malcolm Dewinter was a middle-aged man with dark skin and salt and pepper hair cut short to his scalp. He was tall and bony with dark, intense eyes. He fidgeted with his tie as he leaned over his desk and studied the video footage on his computer monitor.

"Looks like you're spot on, Dr. Monarch. If that's your daughter, then we have a kidnapping incident. I'll pull out all stops to find your daughter but as you know, the longer it takes." He stopped and glanced at Monarch seated in the hard plastic chair by the man's desk.

"Don't say it." Monarch whispered. "Just find my daughter."

D.C.I. Dewinter nodded and motioned to someone across the room of the police station. A uniformed woman stepped up to the desk and they began carrying on in police jargon. Monarch didn't hear a word. All she could think of was Olivia at the hands of possible human traffickers. All these years they had been so careful. What had made Olivia leave the tube in the middle of one of the most dangerous areas in London? She knew better!

Monarch's phone warbled and she answered it, putting a

finger in her other ear to blot out Dewinter's conversation. "Hello?"

"Mom, it's me, Steven."

"I'm at the local police station, Steven. I, uh, we found CCTV footage. Olivia has been abducted." Monarch's voice broke. "Where are you?"

"Well, that's just it. I met up with someone. He might be able to help."

"Who?" Monarch sat forward.

"I can't really say. Not on the phone, you know. He's a bit paranoid with an iron will."

Steel! Monarch's heart raced. Could he help find Olivia? "Well, where is he?"

"I'll text you a note from him, Mom."

"Good, get back to the, uh, house. I'll need you there in case we hear anything." Monarch said.

"I could keep looking for the kidnappers." Steven said. "I'm not helpless, you know."

"I can't lose both of you, son. Please. Just go home and lock the doors." Monarch ended the call and checked her messages. A link to an address showed up with the cryptic message beneath it: "PR4."

"Dr. Monarch." D.C.I. Dewinter was speaking to her. She looked up from the phone.

"Yes."

"I've put out alerts and we are canvassing that neighborhood. We're pulling out all stops to find your daughter. Why don't you go home and wait to see if she might possibly show up. Or call."

"I don't have a land line." Monarch lifted her phone. "But I will go and wait. You have my number?"

"I'll call you if anything comes up. Promise."

It was close to ten o'clock by the time Monarch walked from the tube station to the address on her phone. An ancient church corresponded to the address. The stained-glass windows were only dimly lit, and the doors securely locked. Steel wanted her to come here?

"It's in the back, love."

Monarch whirled. A gray-haired man with a walking cane gestured to the right side of the church. "The side entrance. Always open, it is." His breath steamed in the frigid air. "I hope you get your prayers answered." He turned and shuffled away with his walking cane crunching in the snow.

Monarch found the side entrance and it was well lit. A sign on the door said simply, "Prayer room." She opened the door and stepped into a hallway. The air was warm, and the fragrance of vanilla and spice filled the air from candles on a nearby table. A young woman in jeans and tee shirt was walking down the hall with a Bible in her hand, mumbling to herself. A desk sat to her right and a man in a security uniform looked up at her.

"Come for one of the prayer rooms?" He said.

Monarch looked around at six doors leading off the hallway. "What is this place?"

The security guard raised an eyebrow. "Well, you did read the sign outside, didn't you? It's a twenty-four hour prayer room. If a room is empty, you can have it for up to an hour to pray. I'm a church member and I volunteer my time to keep everyone safe."

"And the young woman?" She pointed to the woman who had turned around at one end of the distant hallway and was coming back her way.

"She's prayer walking. Binding up Satan and chasing away demons. Keeping the place spiritually clean. Someone volunteers to prayer walk around the clock."

Monarch showed the security guard her phone. "My friend wanted me to meet him here."

"PR4? Prayer room 4. He told me to be on the lookout for you." The security guard stood up and pointed to one of the doors and Monarch then saw the numeral 4. "Go right on in. You've still got thirty minutes."

Monarch nodded and stepped around the occupied prayer walker and knocked gently on the door. It opened and Jonathan Steel stood before her.

"Come in." He said, looking over her shoulder warily.

"Jonathan." Monarch's voice caught in her throat. Her relationship with Steel was not ideal. They had last seen each other on the day Monarch had inadvertently erased Raven's mind. She put a hand to her chest and fought back a sob.

"What's wrong?" Steel asked.

"Steven didn't tell you?"

"No."

"It's Olivia. She's been kidnapped! Maybe by human traffickers." She gasped for breath. Steel helped her into a seat. He sat beside her.

"Steven said something was wrong but didn't give me the details."

Monarch reached for tissues from a nearby box and her hand brushed the open Bible on the table beside them. "She didn't tell me what she was up to. She bought a ticket back to the states. She wanted to check on Josh. But something happened to her on the underground and she got off in a bad neighborhood. There's CCTV footage showing her after a seizure. Two people took her, Jonathan. I've called her phone and it goes to voice mail."

"The police?"

"They are looking but we both know if human traffickers are involved, I may never see her again." Monarch held the tissues to her nose.

Steel was silent for a moment. "I don't know what to say. I don't know what to do." He said.

"I need your help, Jonathan." Monarch said. She drew a deep breath. "Wait a minute. You didn't ask me here to help me?"

His turquoise eyes glittered with emotion. "I asked you to

come to this church where there is a continual wall of prayer to protect me from prying ears and eyes."

Monarch wiped her eyes. "What are you talking about?"

"They have Josh. Three demons have Josh. They've infected him with some kind of brain virus and if he doesn't receive regular doses, he'll die. So, they coerced me into working for them or Josh dies."

Monarch sat upright. "The memory card?"

"Number seven wants it to give them leverage over a member of the Penticle."

Monarch blinked. "That's just a conspiracy theory. I mean, a five-member cabal that controls world governments and major corporations?" She did her best to hide the fact she already knew this. If Steel found out she had accessed the card, he would be furious, and he wouldn't help her.

"It's true." Steel said. "And these demons want one of their kind to become a member. The dossier on the card contains information about one of the members hiring Raven to assassinate several people. With that kind of information, they can force that individual to leave the Pentacle and then they can replace them with a demon controlled operative."

Monarch looked over at the Bible. "All this talk of demons and angels and God. You know I don't believe that stuff, Jonathan."

"I don't care if you do or not." Steel said. "I care only about Josh. I sent the card to you for safekeeping. I turned the tables on them."

"Do they know about me?"

"No. I mean, at least not from me." Steel sat back and looked away. "I just happened to meet Steven on the street. He said you needed my help. Frankly, I don't know if I can help you. But I thought it was a good idea to make sure whatever was going on wasn't connected to the card. See I'm holding *them* hostage for the memory card. It was the only way I could see Josh and know he was still alive."

"So, this isn't about Olivia's disappearance?" Monarch said tersely.

"I didn't know about it until just now." Steel said. "I've got to find Vivian Darbonne."

Monarch stiffened and shook her head. "Jonathan, I have to find Olivia. I can't waste time looking for Vivian."

"I already know where Vivian is. At least a general idea of the area."

Monarch lurched to her feet. "So, that's what this is all about? You don't care about Olivia, just that your precious card is safe?"

"No, I care about Olivia. But these demons are ruthless and cunning. If they found out you have the card, you or your family could be a target. And I would lose what little leverage I have to protect Josh."

"I don't care about Josh right now. I need to find my daughter." Monarch almost shouted.

Steel's face reddened. "Time is not on my side, Dr. Monarch. Every wasted moment brings Josh closer to death."

"And my daughter, too." Monarch ran a hand through her hair and collapsed into her chair. "I don't know what Olivia's disappearance is about. Unless they know I have the card, her abduction seems totally random."

"So have a lot of events that have happened in the last few days." Steel said hoarsely.

Monarch fought back her anger. Josh was just as important to Jonathan Steel as Olivia was to her. "Look, Jonathan there has been no contact from anyone about Olivia. If these demons took her as leverage, I would have already heard." She swallowed hard to hide her next lie. "The card is untouched and totally safe. I promised I would safeguard it and I will."

"If they contact you, will you let me know?" Steel said.

Monarch nodded. "If they contact me, then we are both joined in the same purpose, saving our children from these demonic forces." She blinked. "I can't believe I just said that.

You know I have a hard time believing all of this superstitious nonsense."

"As I said, I don't care what you think. I only need you to help Josh." Steel paused and drew a deep breath. His turquoise eyes bored into hers. "Now I understand."

"Understand what?"

"Why you did it." He pointed to his head. "You operated on me because you were trying to help Olivia. You would have done anything to help her. I get it now."

Monarch drew a deep breath as she studied the man's moist eyes. Was this forgiveness? Was this clarity? She had long left the guilt behind for doing whatever it would take to help her children. Even if it meant working for the Captain. She sat forward and pointed to the Bible. "Do you really believe this book?"

"I haven't read the entire Bible, but I have come to believe it contains truth. Ultimate truth, Dr. Monarch." Steel said.

"Then perhaps it is time for you to use this room for what it was intended. Pray that you will find Vivian. Pray that I will find Olivia. And, while you are on your knees praying, I will be looking for my daughter just in case there is no God to hear you." She stood up from the chair and slowly closed the Bible. "I can't rely on how many angels can dance on the head of a pin. I have more reliable ways." She turned and walked out of the room.

Ishido watched Jonathan Steel leave the church and head back to his hotel. Since dropping off the drive with Monarch, Ishido had hidden from certain criminals for which he once worked. After the past couple of days, he couldn't stand hiding. Using Max's secure phone, he had tracked Steel to this church. He had no idea what was transpiring between Steel and Monarch.

His phone had been turned off until just an hour before and

now it warbled with Max's secure line showed up. He had avoided Max as long as was humanly possible. Now that the phone was back on, avoiding her was impossible. Walking slowly through the snow-covered streets he followed Steel toward his hotel and answered the call by touching his earpiece.

"Sorry, Max. I've been busy." He whispered.

"I know exactly what you're doing, Ishido." Max's tense voice came over the earpiece. "You could have at least told me after Jonathan revealed his plans. I need to know the memory card is safe." Max's voice came through the earpiece.

"It is safe. It is not with Steel and is in a location unknown to Steel's demonic bosses." Ishido said and his breath streamed in the cold night air.

"If there is one thing we both know, Steel has no boss. Not even God, I fear." Max said. "My informer from the church tells me both Vivian and Olivia are missing."

Ishido frozen not with the revelation Max had an operative at the church but with the mention of Olivia's name. "Olivia is missing? I was unaware of this. That explains why Steel met with Monarch just now."

"And the meeting did not go well. I have concluded that Olivia's abduction had nothing to do with Dr. Monarch having the card. While this is good news, Olivia's abduction is not."

Ishido gasped. "How did you know?"

"Really, Ishido? How long have we known each other? If I do not know now, I will know very soon. You know that. Anyway, I have been sifting through chatter and I understand both Vivian and Olivia may be at the same location. I'm not sure where that would be. If my suspicions are correct, they are now in the hands of human traffickers, and it will not be long before both of them are out of the country." Max said.

"What should we do?"

"You have an old contact with formidable warriors who could storm the citadel of the Overlord and rescue both Vivian and Olivia." Max said.

Ishido had lost sight of Steel and his heart froze in his chest at the mention of that name and the realization of what Max was asking of him. "No! I cannot go back to them!"

"I have asked a lot of you Ishido. I have given you a new life. I would understand if you don't want to get involved with the very people who killed your family. But time is of the essence. They may know of Vivian and Olivia's location and with enough money, you could hire them to invade the Overlord's operation."

"She would be worse than the Overlord." Ishido ran a hand across his suddenly sweaty brow. "*She* will want the spoils." And, he thought, my soul!

"That cannot be helped. We do what we can with what we have. I am sending you information on an anonymous bank account from which to draw funds." Max said.

"Max, they will not respect me."

"Assuming they even remember you, Ishido."

Ishida's mind whirled with plans and possibilities. "This source of money, would they be able to trace it back to you?"

"No! I have some anonymous sources who owe me a favor. All I have to do is access one of those accounts." Max said.

"Anonymous sources? As in illegal sources?"

"Highly. I would never think of doing such a thing but time is of the essence and these are truly disparate conditions. There is one source I can access who will not know the request is coming from me. Or Jonathan Steel." She said a name and Ishido blanched.

"Max, don't!"

"I have no choice, Ishido. And, you must see that the person who offers to pay for the invasion is Jonathan Steel. Only then will it be believable." Max said.

Ishido looked around at the passing crowds of people enjoying a night on the town. How he longed for such normalcy. He should have known he would never leave the other life behind. It would always come back to haunt him. But there was no other choice. "I will see to it, Max."

❧ 25 ❧

"**W**hy are we here? And no more reciting religious creeds or I will rupture your spleen!" Pandora squinted into the bright sunlight. The waves broke on the white sands beneath the deck on which they stood. Josh drew in a deep breath of the humid air. How he wished he were here instead of in a hospital bed.

"Let me show you a memory and you will understand." He said confidently.

⚜

"AND, THEN THE SPEAR PIERCED MY SKIN, JUST BELOW MY PECS." Josh Knight tried his best to contract the muscles underneath the two crimson scars on his chest.

"I am sure there is a logical reason why you are talking to your chest." Cephas Lawrence said.

Josh spun away from the beach and his face warmed with embarrassment. "I was just, uh, practicing."

Cephas looked down at the sand stretching away from the deck of Jonathan Steel's beach house. It amazed him how quickly people returned to the beach after a hurricane. Near the water's edge, two teenage girls threw a flying disc. "Ah, you were practicing recounting your near death at the hands of Rudolph Wulf, the twelfth demon so as to impress those two young women."

Josh massaged his scars. "Yeah, that's about right, Uncle Cephas."

Cephas held up two plastic zip bags filled with ice. He pressed them against Josh's bare chest. Josh winced and lurched away.

"Dude! What's up with the ice?"

"Originally, they were for your hands." Cephas wiped the condensation from his hands on his tee shirt. He wore baggy shorts below a shirt bearing the huge smiling face of Albert Einstein sticking out his tongue.

Josh held the dripping bags away from him. "There's nothing wrong with my hands. And, what's with the tee shirt. He looks like your twin. And, that pink sunscreen on you nose? Dude, really?"

Cephas massaged his bushy moustache and shrugged. "I deduced you must have had something wrong with your hands since you can't seem to tear yourself away from watching those two young girls frolic on the beach and help me finish packing. Perhaps the ice will bring down the swelling."

Josh frowned and cast one last look at the two girls. "Uncle Cephas, I just needed a short break. I mean, we're here on the Gulf Coast in August and the babes are really hot and you have me inside packing up dusty books and stuff."

"Jonathan said we needed to have all the boxes in the den packed by the time he got back." Cephas said. "And, you've been out here for over an hour. In fact, you might want to put your shirt back on. Not only do you lack the pectorals that would attract those girls' attentions, but you are quite sunburned."

Josh glanced down at his chest. "Ouch." He pressed the ice packs against his skin and sighed. "Ah, that's better."

"Indeed. Now, if you will come inside you can help me finish the packing." Cephas pointed over his shoulder toward the huge beach house. He glanced up at the sun. "It's a scorcher out here and if you don't help me, it will be a tad bit hotter inside when Jonathan returns and the boxes are not packed. You know how angry he can get."

PANDORA WATCHED AS THE SCENE PLAYED OUT BEFORE HER. Josh pointed to the chairs on the deck. "It's what happened just prior to this I want you to see. I was sitting on the deck admiring the girls on the beach and Cephas came out to join me. Let's have a seat, shall we?" Josh pointed to the two chairs before him. A third chair appeared beside them. "You can have the third chair. And you might want to put on something more comfortable than that hot white robe."

Pandora smiled. "Now this is more like it, Josh. You are coop- erating." She pulled her long, red hair up into a bun and the robe disappeared replaced with a one-piece black swimsuit and a lacy red swimsuit cover. "How's this?"

Josh glanced at her and shrugged. "Nice. Did you wear that around Mary?"

Pandora settled into the third chair and sunglasses appeared on her face. "No. I learned this from you. Modern times beat ancient times hands down. I would have been burned at the stake if I had appeared in this, as you would say, skimpy swim- suit. Now, continue."

Josh settled into his second seat and tried to remember what it was like on that day. He had survived the thirteenth, twelfth, and eleventh demon and all he cared about was being a normal teenager. How much had changed since then! He closed his eyes and brought back the memory.

The sun beat down on Josh's bare chest. In less than hour, he would be sunburned, and his Uncle Cephas would be complaining about it. But right now, his Uncle Cephas had joined him on the beach house deck with a glass of iced tea and his pipe. Josh opened his eyes and smiled as he studied the old, strange man who was his great uncle. How many times had he laughed at the pipe; coughed dramatically at the smell of the pipe smoke? Weird Uncle Cephas had been an enigma to him then. Now, he missed the old man with a fierceness that brought tears to his eyes.

Uncle Cephas lit his pipe and the smoke drifted up into the hot, humid air. No breeze! He glanced over at Pandora. "Who is this, Josh? A cougar, eh? She is a bit too old for you."

Pandora frowned at Cephas and took her sunglasses away from her fiery, teal colored eyes. "Now let's remember the rules, Josh." Pain blossomed in his chest, and he winced, his face twisting in agony. "Where is this going, Josh? I don't like being insulted. As nice as this setting is, I want to remind you who is in control."

Josh sat forward and gasped for breath. "You asked me about consciousness and reality. This is a good memory with Uncle Cephas. If you can't take the memory, then leave. Go somewhere else and hijacked somebody else's mind." Josh sat forward and groaned as the pain grew. "Or are you too weak to deal with the truth? You spent centuries stuck in an urn and then in a box and you can't handle a few offensive memories? Really, Pandora, if you are going to succeed at this, you've got to show a little backbone."

Josh sat back and felt nausea grip him. If he vomited in his sleep, he knew what the risks were. "So go ahead and kill me and see if you can be a parasite on somebody else. The way I see, I'm your best shot. So shut up and listen or go away!"

The pain slowly abated. Pandora sat back and slid the sunglasses over her eyes. "This had better be worth it." She said but her voice lacked its usual confidence. "Who is this insulting man?"

"My Uncle Cephas. He is a collector of artifacts and has a great deal of knowledge. On this day he was in a lecture mode about the mind. I thought you might be interested in it." Josh sat back as the pain went away and let the sun soak into him. Of course, he recalled how inattentive he had been to Uncle Cephas' rambling. But Josh had started off the conversation and then his attention had drifted back to the girls. If what Pandora claimed was true, his memory of this discussion would return in its entirety.

"Josh, my boy, I cannot deny that being young has its advantages. But your surging hormones have hijacked your inquiring brain. You are so smart and bordering on genius and yet you ignore the importance of exploring what you have learned in these recent encounters with extra-dimensional beings. You must think and pray about what you have been through so that you will be prepared for the next encounter. You must transform your mind." He held up a book and tapped the cover. "An excellent book by Dr. Sharon Dirckx entitled 'Am I Just my Brain?'. Aren't you the least bit interested in your own mind and the fate it will suffer the next time you meet up with a demon?"

Josh remembered glancing at his uncle on that day and shrugging it off. But now, he wanted to initiate the conversation, no, the lecture that was to come by taking control of those memories. He sat forward and faced his uncle. "Uncle Cephas, when I was in the basement and that demon had control of me, what would have happened to my soul if I had died? I mean, dude, what is my soul? What is my brain? What is my mind?" Josh asked.

Uncle Cephas puffed on his pipe. "Josh, my son, that is a very deep question for someone whose immediate focus is on the young women frolicking on the beach."

"Dude, I can't believe you said frolicking." Josh laughed. Oh, how he remembered that moment making fun of the old man. Now he would welcome another sit down on a beach house deck.

"What you are feeling when you look at these girls, yes, frolicking on the beach. Is it just a bunch of neurons firing in response to your hormonal state? Are you not in control of your own feelings and thoughts when confronted with these girls? Or is there some deeper desire for connection and community and friendship?"

Josh squinted at Uncle Cephas. "What are you talking about?"

"Physicalism. It is the idea that we are nothing but our brains. The affection I feel for you as my great nephew is nothing more than biochemistry. Physicalism states that consciousness is an illusion. Our consciousness exists but is a product of the brain and emerged naturally as humans evolved to become highly complex organisms." Uncle Cephas put up a finger and tapped the book. "But no one has ever been able determine the mechanism of how consciousness could have emerged! After all, how can mere matter originate consciousness? How does the material create the immaterial? Hmmm?"

It was at this point, Josh remembered glancing back at the beach and trying to focus on the girls. Fortunately for him, his 'unconsciousness' had continued to listen to his uncle. He remembered grunting every now and then and glancing at Uncle Cephas to pacify his need to lecture.

"There is an idea. Dualism. This idea is that humans are composed of a physical body and an immaterial mind. You might also say the mind is the soul. In fact, science has shown that the idea of what is called the 'Soul Hypothesis' is extremely natural and inevitable to the human mind and experience. You see, children express this type of thinking without any prior instruction on the issue. In fact, young man, the existence of a human soul is presumed throughout ancient history including in the Bible."

Josh glanced at Pandora. "So, what are you, Pandora? Are you a soul? Are you an immaterial 'mind'?"

Pandora shrugged. "Of course, I am. Unless you think I'm just a figment of your neurochemistry." She smiled and pain lanced through Josh's chest again then subsided. "Did you just make yourself hurt? I don't think so. No more questions of my existence. Get on with this memory and make your points."

Cephas tapped the book again. "The author of this book became convinced that a person could not be a scientist and also believe in God. The two were incompatible. But as we have discussed many times, the smartest people I know believe in the God of the Bible because they have ample evidence and she came to that conclusion. But that is not the discussion I want to have with you."

Josh nodded and said, "Okay." He glanced at Pandora. She was silent at the mention of God.

"Scientists can measure the activity of the brain and see the neural networks at work. But those activities merely correlate with thought. We have been unable to access a person's actual inner thoughts. In this book, the word used is 'qualia'. It means the quality or property that someone experiences or perceives."

Pandora sat forward. "Stop. Where is this going?"

Josh smiled. "Can you describe for me the taste of a strawberry?"

Pandora took off her glasses. "You know what strawberries taste like."

"Have you ever actually tasted a strawberry? I mean when you were physically alive, did you taste a strawberry?"

"As a matter of fact, I have."

"Then tell me what a strawberry tastes like." Josh looked at her.

A strawberry appeared out of nowhere and she plucked it out of the air. She held it out to him. "Like this."

"Exactly!" Josh said. "What Uncle Cephas is talking about is you can't *describe* it. But you can experience it. If our thoughts are just our brain, we could come up with the chemical composition of the strawberry. We could examine its structure and its physical makeup. But how do you describe the taste? You can't. You have to experience it." Josh sat forward. "That is why you have hijacked my mind. Not my brain. You want my experiences. The experiences that you can no longer have because you don't have a physical body."

"And, in time, our minds will merge." Pandora said with a vicious smile.

"Wait. There's more." Josh sat back and let the memory continue.

Cephas puffed on his pipe and sipped at his tea. "You know an article from Science journal talked about the fact that 15 to 20% of people in a vegetative state who are presumed brain dead are, in fact, fully conscious. This is even with the presence of external stimulation and the lack of physical response. This means we human beings are more than our physical brains. And that, my boy, is the danger of demonic possession. The demons can take possession of the physical brain, but they cannot possess your *mind*. They can push it into a state of control, of course. I presume that is because most demonic possessions are from a person willing to allow that possession to occur. It is only after they realize what they have done and find themselves in a state of imprisonment, that they wish they had not made that choice."

Uncle Cephas tapped the ashes from his pipe. "Josh, if you hear one thing I say remember this." He looked at Josh, his ancient eyes squinted against the son, his bushy white mustache stained from pipe smoke. For all the world he looked like a wise sage come down from the lofty towers of knowledge. "If God exists, then he is a conscious mind of unlimited power and intellect. The notion that such a mind would create other conscious minds like his that can look at reality from a first person perspective and can think about reality should not be a surprise. Unlike the naturalistic paradigm of Darwinism, only theism can conceive of and anticipate such self-awareness as we mortal beings possess."

Pandora glared at Josh. "I thought I told you no more talk about a creator."

Uncle Cephas froze with his pipe halfway back to his mouth. Josh stood up slowly as the pain built within and he turned haltingly to Pandora. He gasped as the pain grew and grew.

"You claim you are a mind. You claim you want to push my mind out of my brain and take over. And yet you maintain you are not a person; a reality; a physical being. The truth is, Pandora, you are just slime and goo from an ancient cesspool of mixed DNA and the only reason you can animate that and penetrate my mind is you have a mind of your own. Not a physical mind in the past tense of you being a human." He gasped again as a new pain lanced through his chest and Pandora's face twisted in fury.

"You are a spirit. And if you are a spirit and you are no longer human then there is only one thing left you could be. You are a demonic spirit, a fallen angel and nothing so special as Pandora! Get out of my head! Now! In the name of Jesus get out!" Josh shouted.

Pandora screeched at the name of Jesus and faded away. Josh gasped as the pain left him and he sat up in bed, his eyes wide open. He looked around his hospital room. Faye Morgan sat by his bed, her eyes also wide open. She put a hand over his mouth and bending over the bed pressed her lips to his ears. "Don't make a sound. You are supposed to be sedated. Lay back down slowly. I'll take you for a walk and we can talk. But you have to act like you're completely sedated."

Josh's heart rate slowed, and he lay back slowly in the bed. He closed his eyes but refused to allow his "mind" to drift back into sleep. He wasn't sure, but he was hoping Pandora was gone for good!

❧ 26 ❧

Big band music. The raucous brass tune pounded against Olivia's head. She moaned and tried to put her hands over her ears. She fought back nausea and dizziness as she gingerly opened her eyes. She lay on a couch whose leather surface was cracked and had allowed stuffing to extrude. She sat up slowly and blinked in confusion. A large wooden desk sat before the couch with an American flag in a flagpole behind the desk. Another pole bore a blue flag. The backdrop to the desk were windows in an oval configuration. A man sat in a chair behind the desk and his glasses reflected the meager light back at her.

"Sir, where am I?"

"He won't answer you." Snake appeared beside the couch. "He's just a mannequin. Supposed to be President Roosevelt."

Olivia glared at Snake. "Where am I? The oval office?"

"Well, it was supposed to be a reproduction of the oval office during World War II." Snake had taken her good arm out of the sling and was moving it through various motions.

Olivia smelled the man known as Prince Charming when he came into the room. He leaned over the back of the couch. The spider head appeared above the crown of his head. This time,

Olivia didn't flinch. After all, she had "demon eyes". And, if she was seeing real demons, she had a lot to rethink about the spiritual realm she had spent years persuading herself did not exist. Funny how survival can drive home the truth.

"Who is your friend?" She pointed to his head.

"What friend?" PC looked up at the ceiling.

"The spider demon on your head. Your partner in crime."

PC glared back at her. "I know what you're at. Playing games with me mind."

Olivia shrugged. "Suit yourself. Not much to play with. We know who is really in charge, don't we Spidey?" She winked at the spider demon head and it receded back behind PC's enormous skull. She looked at Snake and tried to put on her best cavalier attitude. If there was one thing she had learned in the past few years on the run it was how to survive. Do the unexpected. "What's for breakfast?"

PC blinked in confusion. "What makes you think you're getting breakfast, love?"

"I'm still alive, aren't I? You need me for something and I think the Crimson Snake, here, will be unhappy if you don't treat me with proper respect." She slid off the couch. "First, I need my medicine. Where's my backpack?"

PC laughed and the spider demon peeked over his head. A few oblong, ameboid demons came through the walls and pulsated around his head. "You ain't making any demands, love."

Snake finished her limb rotations and planted her good arm on her hip. "Get your stinky self out of here!" She glared at PC. He bowed in fear toward her and hurried out the door. The pulsating demons floated out after him. Olivia crossed her arms.

"You don't have a demon."

Snake raised an eyebrow. "Don't need one. You're coming with me."

"First, my meds. Then, food. Unless you want to carry me after I have a seizure." Olivia said.

"You are just as feisty as I recalled. You'll find there is no breakfast in the White House. It's all fake. You'll see." She stepped outside the room and came back carrying her backpack. A bottled water was tucked in a side pocket. "There's granola bars in your backpack. Have a couple and take your meds. It's time for you to find out how to conduct your new job."

Olivia took the backpack and looked inside. In the inner hidden compartment, she felt the goggles were still there. They were the goggles Josh had activated that started the whole affair with the eighth demon. If she could activate them again, they would find any wi-fi or cellular signal and try to connect. Problem was that the goggles were designed to seek out Thakkar's Numinocity network. Her hand also caressed the small pouch with the altered nannobites she had used to bring wasps to Josh's rescue. There had to be at least five more groupings left she could use. If she could find out just where she was.

Olivia retrieved her medication. She swallowed two pills and chased them with water. She tore open a granola bar. "Where are we?"

"The American Experiment. It was a theme park from the 1980's celebrating all things American. Back when Reagan and Margaret Thatcher were popular. Didn't last long. Went up for sale. Now the Overlord owns it."

Snake motioned to the door leading out of the Oval Office. "That's all you need to know. Lucky for you I stumbled upon those two idiots, or you would be working in the labs or locked up in one of the harem rooms waiting for your next romantic encounter."

Olivia started in on her second granola bar. "Lucky? What is this place? Human trafficking? Who do you work for?"

"My boss has a vested interested in this place. But the Overlord is someone else. You'll meet him in a little bit after you learn about your job."

"What is my job?"

"You're the new Keeper." Snake said.

"Keeper? What's that?"

Snake nodded toward the door. "Come on and I'll show you. And realize there's no place to run so don't even try to escape."

Olivia shouldered her backpack. "I wouldn't dream of it."

Outside the Oval Office, they entered a corridor and Olivia paused before a grimy glass wall separating her from a huge diorama. The back wall of the diorama had a large image of Winston Churchill next to FDR. The diorama was of a beach with ships in the water offshore and soldiers storming the beach on D-Day. Unfortunately, the ceiling tiles had collapsed, and the battlefield was littered with trash and broken tiles.

"The Overlord has a favorite toy. She's not quite right in the head." Snake said as she led them down the long, dark corridor. "So, she needs help in taking care of herself, dressing herself, feeding herself. You will be her Keeper and get her ready for an audience with the Overlord." Snake paused in front of an elevator door, and it creaked open. She motioned inside. "After you. We're going to the penthouse level where the investors and VIPs stayed during their visits."

The elevator shuttered and groaned as they ascended, and the doors opened on an atrium with dingy windows. Outside, churning, gray clouds filled the sky and snow cascaded against the windows. "Not exactly the tropics?" Olivia said.

Snake pointed to a corridor. "This way." Faded, torn posters along the way advertised "Frontier World" with images of stage-coaches and cowboys and "Space City" with images of a space shuttle docking with a wheel shaped space station. Another poster promised fun and frivolity from the "Roaring Twenties" complete with Great Gatsby inspired "flappers" and young men dancing in a club. Snake paused before a poster showing two teenagers in a 1950's car shaking in terror at a huge hulking giant Elvis Presley towering over the landscape.

Snake put a real, metal key into the lock of the adjacent door and opened it. The main room was huge with two sofas and several wing back chairs. Sliding doors let the grim, gray light from outside fill the room with a little bit of depressing light. Snake pointed to double doors.

"This way to the next room." Snake opened the doors and they stepped into another world. The adjacent room had been renovated and was divided into two sections, a kitchen/dining room and a small living room. The décor was right from the 1950's with orange and chartreuse furnishings. Linoleum covered the kitchen floor. In the living room, an old black and white television flickered as it showed an early 1950's family sitcom.

A woman stood with her back to them at the kitchen sink. She wore a flowery cotton dress that reached to her knees. She wore stockings with seams and high heel shoes. She was humming "Blue Suede Shoes" as she washed dishes.

"Honey, you have a visitor." Snake said.

The woman turned and Olivia gasped. She wore a light blue apron with a big embroidered daisy. Her hair was short and curled and teased into a tight face hugging style right out of a rock and roll movie of the fifties. She smiled at Olivia as she held up a sponge in one hand and a sudsy pot in the other. "I don't have the roast ready yet. But you're welcome to stay for dinner."

Olivia blinked. "Vivian?"

❧ 27 ❧

"This was a bad decision." Steven said as he shivered in the cold, morning air.

"I am desperate, Steven." Monarch said. "I wish you had stayed at home."

"You're not getting out of my sight, now." Steven said. "I'll fade into the woodwork, so HE doesn't see me." He walked away through the open door into the depths of Westminster Abbey. Westminster Abbey was supposed to be a church filled with the warm inviting presence of the Holy Spirit. Whatever that was! Monarch followed him and, as always, found the interior cold and sterile.

Somewhere in the distance she heard organ music somewhat muted and inscrutable. The only people present were tourists, not worshippers. She knew that Olivia had claimed to have experienced something of the divine. And Monarch had to admit Steven's hands being healed were a true, well, uh, miracle? But this atmosphere was more attuned to her own attitude toward the divine. If God did exist, he was a cold and distant as the farthest dead star.

Monarch paused in the main chapel area of Westminster Abbey. No news had come during the night and Monarch had slept a couple of hours. A tour group moved around them as a tour guide discussed the life and death of one of its famous interred kings. Or was it a queen? Monarch didn't care. She just wanted to be in a very public place with lots of people around when she met her contact.

She glanced down at the name on the floor beneath her. Charles Darwin was interred right beneath her. Odd that the man who brought down God would find his resting place not just in a graveyard but in a church. Life was full of little ironies.

The Captain walked out of a group of tourists toward her. He was shorter than she was and wore a full-length black wool coat. His every present Panama Hat had been replaced with a warmer fedora. His turquoise eyes flashed with anger as he joined her on Darwin's grave.

"I told you to never contact me again." He growled. His ever-present pipe was clenched in his teeth but issued no smoke. On one side of the Meerschaum pipe bowl was carved an angel and on the other side a demon.

"I'm desperate." Monarch hissed. "You left me an emergency email contact. I did your bidding with your son, and you owe me."

"I paid you in full." The Captain said. "Our business was concluded."

"Then why are you here?" Monarch asked.

"You mentioned something I might be interested in? Something to do with a person named Raven?" The Captain took the pipe out of his mouth and slid it into a coat pocket.

"Don't play games with me, old man." Monarch said. "I know you hired Raven for some very special tasks." She opened the messenger bag hanging from her shoulder and pulled out a single piece of paper and handed it to the Captain.

"What is this?" He studied the sheet of paper.

"One page printed out from a very complete dossier compiled by an assassin named Raven. Every kill she performed is listed in the dossier with damaging evidence against those who hired her. This dossier could bring some of the most powerful individuals on this planet down to earth. And bury them. Or?"

The Captain's face grew paler and he licked his lips. "Or what?"

"Or it could give someone great power." Monarch said. "Have you ever heard of the Penticle?"

The Captain tilted his head. "Legend."

"Fact. I've done my research and, of course, most of the information I found is highly suspect. But, when you combine what I learned about certain powerful and wealthy individuals with the names in the dossier, one comes to mind that sparks a very interesting conclusion." She reached out and tapped the paper with a finger. "The name on that piece of paper is a member of the Penticle, right?"

The Captain remained aloof. "And so, what if it is?"

"Oh, come on! You crave power. You want control. I'm handing it to you in the form of this dossier. With it, you can have this person removed from the Penticle and put your own person in their place. I don't care. I just need your help."

The Captain handed the paper back to Monarch. "Assuming I agree to your suggestion, what's in it for you?"

"My daughter has been kidnapped. Probably by human traffickers. You have your finger in all kinds of nefarious affairs. Find her for me and everything in the dossier about this member of the Penticle is yours." Monarch tucked the piece of paper into her pocket.

"What makes you think I can find your daughter?" The Captain crossed his arms.

"You have resources."

The Captain massaged his chin deep in thought and then stepped closer to her. "I want to know where Raven is. Find her for me and, along with the dossier, I will find your daughter."

"Fine. I know exactly where Raven is. I'm surprised you don't know. I tried to restore her memory and wiped her entire brain! Now, there's something you would find useful, eh? The Raven you worked with is gone. A child has taken her place. A blank slate!" Monarch looked away. "Now, I need you need to move quickly. Find Olivia and the dossier contents are yours."

The Captain did not move, his eyes roving over the contents of the church. "Death and rebirth. These are the themes of all religions. I will miss Raven if she is, indeed, gone. However, I would need to determine that for myself." He nodded and held out his hand. "I want the entire dossier, Dr. Monarch. Not just the member of the Penticle."

"Fine. I'll put the contents on a flash drive and the minute you find Olivia, we'll arrange a drop."

The Captain nodded. "Pleasure doing business with you again, Dr. Monarch. If you're interested, I have some new surgical candidates who would benefit from your expertise."

Monarch shook her head. "I already sold my soul to the devil when I met you the first time. We're done." She turned and walked away into the cold, marble tombs of Westminster Abbey.

❧ 28 ❧

"I dressed her earlier this morning. Almost impossible with only one good arm." Snake said. "That will be your job from now on."

"What is wrong with her?" Olivia said as Vivian turned back to the sink and continued to wash the dishes.

"She pulled off her goggles while in Numinocity." Snake said. "That is what I understand happened. If it doesn't kill you, it makes a mess of your mind. She's not quite the same woman you remember."

"That would be an improvement." Olivia said. Although she recalled Vivian calling out to God before she vanished. And her "conversion" had led to her banishing the thirteenth demon from Numinocity. "So, she's like a big doll. I get to wash and dress and feed her?"

"She'll follow your commands. She's pretty docile. It's what the Overlord wants her to wear that is important. Today, she's a 1950's housewife and it's time to take her to the throne room."

Olivia placed her backpack on the kitchen table. "Throne room?"

"The Overlord is a bit dramatic."

"But you work for someone else? So, why are you here?"

"At the request of the Overlord. The previous Keeper ended up on the drug lines and she had a small tear in a glove. The fentanyl killed her instantly. My boss told me to come and find a new Keeper. He and the Overlord are very close."

Snake went to a nearby closet and took out a bright green dressy jacket. "Viv, darling, it's time to pay a visit to the Overlord."

Vivian turned and smiled. She placed her sponge and pot carefully on a drainage board and took off her apron. "Well, we wouldn't want to keep him waiting. That would be so rude." She smiled again and her facial muscles were far too tight. It was a forced smile, a false smile and a muscle twitched in her right cheek. Snake handed the jacket to Olivia.

"Livvy is your niece who has come to visit. She'll be helping you out from now on."

"Livvy?" Olivia took the jacket and Viv crossed the room quickly in robotic steps and pushed her arms into the sleeves. "Oh, yes, I remember Livvy." She adjusted the jacket until it fit snugly. "Shall we go?"

Snake led them out into the corridor, and they took the elevator down to a lower level. Olivia followed Snake and Viv around the corner from the elevator. The walkway had rooms to the right and was open into a huge atrium on the left. Glass windows looked out over an exhibition area meant to depict a Civil War battlefield complete with cannons and warring mannequins. The cannons and mannequins had been pushed aside to make room for the long line of tables that ran the length of the huge chamber.

Hooded, gowned figures worked tirelessly over boxes of small bags and beakers of white powder. Standing away from the tables and watching over the process were a dozen or so men and women dressed in white, flowing gowns.

"Who are the guards?" Olivia asked.

Snake glanced over her shoulder. "Enochians, the Overlord

calls them. They once belonged to a UFO church and now they swear allegiance to the Overlord."

Vivian paused and leaned against the railing. Her gaze was directed toward one of the gowned guards. "Enochians?" She mumbled. A confused look came over her face. "Where are the Sunstones? There are Sunstones here, right?"

Snake nodded at Olivia. "Your job?"

Olivia swallowed nervously. She put a hand on Viv's arm. "No, you had a sunflower on your apron, remember? Viv, honey, we don't want to disappoint the Overlord. Come along."

Vivian tore her gaze away from the guards and began to wring her hands. "But, if we don't take care of the Sunstones, well, something bad will happen. And I rescued the Enochians already. They were going to die, weren't they?" She looked at Olivia and her eyes focused on her for the first time. "I know you."

"Yes," Olivia glanced over her shoulder at Snake. "I'm your niece, Livvy. Remember? Now, don't you worry about those Enochians. They're doing exactly what the Overlord wants them to do. I'm sure they have the, uh, Sunstones in safe keeping. Now, let's go."

Vivian allowed Olivia to lead her away from the railing and one hand trailed behind. Vivian nodded and smiled weakly. "Yes, all is under control. All is well. The Overlord sees that all is well."

Snake led them to the far end of the elevated walkway. They were outside now and followed a winding ramp down to ground level. The snow had lessened and thankfully the ramp was covered by a dilapidated covering. Snow had blown onto the ramp and Olivia had to slow Vivian down so her heels wouldn't slide in the slush.

A "Main Street" stretched away from the base of the ramp with two story store fronts right from the beginning of the twentieth century. Snake led them along a covered sidewalk. Olivia tried to look through grimy, dirt crusted windows at the merchandise and theme park clothing now faded. At the end of Main Street, a stature of a man on a rearing horse filled a weed choked square and a church with a towering steeple sat on the other side. Olivia had been to Jackson Square in New Orleans, and this was a dilapidated copy. Snake led them across the open square through and up the steps to the front doors of the church. They stopped before a huge set of gold gilded double doors.

"What's this?" Olivia asked rubbing her hands to chase away the cold.

"Once a reproduction of a church. Now, it's a throne room." Two of the robed Enochians appeared from a hidden alcove and nodded to Snake as they opened the doors. Cold, incense laden air wafted over Olivia and Snake led them into the darkness.

Dimly lit stained glass windows glowed from the walls of the church sanctuary. Wooden pews filled both sides of the sanctuary. The sound of moans and whispers filled the air with an almost reverent chanting sound. White gowned Enochians were scattered about the interior. Some were kneeling in the aisle and bowing toward the stage. Some sat in their pews with heads bowed and resting on the pews in front of them.

The pulpit had been cleared and an open, empty stage housed a huge throne. The back of the throne stretched upward into the figure of an angelic being with huge wings swept out to the side. The angel's arms were pointed down toward the seat of the throne. The angel's face was twisted in pain or anger. Olivia couldn't be certain which. Behind the throne, the gleaming pipes of an organ dimly reflected the meager light. Candles on stands surrounding the throne illuminated the person seated on purple cushions. He was the most bizarre creature Olivia had ever seen.

The man stood up and he wore a long, flowing white overcoat with silver buttons down the front. The coat had no sleeves and where his shockingly white arms hung by his side, blood and pus dripped down the sides of the coat. His head was hairless and his features as white as snow. Small wounds trickled blood from his cheeks and his neck. His eyes were blood red. He snapped his fingers and a child in a white robe emerged from an alcove and ran forward with a towel. The man took the towel and wiped the blood and pus from his arms and hands and tossed the soiled towel over the child's head.

"Viv, so good of you to come visit me this afternoon." He hissed as they arrived at the level of the raised stage area. The man motioned to a sofa to the left of the stage. Next to the sofa was an old fashion "fainting" couch where someone could recline.

"My dear Snake, you and the Keeper may take the sofa. Viv you may recline on the couch." He motioned to the sofas with a white hand that already dripped blood and pus again.

Olivia fought back nausea. "Who are you?"

The man froze and glared at her. "My dear, as Keeper you do not speak. You only follow commands. But I can see you are new. Let us hope you last longer than the last. I am Overlord Lucas Malson, head of the Enochian church." He bowed. "Now, if you speak to me again in the future, I will have your liver for dinner."

Olivia swallowed and tried to quash the fear. Suddenly, her vision clouded, and the room filled with demons. Hovering, pulsating demons surrounded Lucas' head. She looked out over the auditorium. Every Enochian had a hideous creature attached to their heads or necks. Some had two or three. When she glanced back at Vivian whose blank expression showed she was totally oblivious to the demons around her, she noticed that most of the hovering demons avoided her as she moved to the couch. In fact, there was a faint bluish glow about her like an aura. She swept her dress from underneath her and sat gingerly on the couch.

"Keeper, remove her jacket." Lucas said.

Snake had to nudge her and when Olivia glanced at Snake, she noticed that even she had fear in her eyes. Olivia hurried over to Viv and tried to smile at her. "Aunt Viv, let me take your coat."

Viv smiled emptily and slipped out of her coat. Olivia folded it over her arm and backed away from the pulsating demonic spheres around Lucas' head. Lucas walked calmly over to the fainting couch. He bent over and reached a hand toward Vivian. He paused before touching her skin and frowned. "Alas, I can no longer touch you, Viv. Too bad, because your skirt is wrinkled." Lucas stood up and snapped his fingers. Another child in a white robe appeared and pushed a rolling table laden with instruments. The child trembled as Lucas nodded at her and she ran back into the shadows.

Lucas pointed to something on the table. "Viv, I think we need to iron your skirt. Keeper."

Olivia stiffened. "Yes."

"Come and get this iron and plug it into that extension cord." Lucas pointed to a cord next to the fainting couch.

Olivia placed Vivian's jacket on the couch and moved over to the table. It was covered with ordinary kitchen items: butcher knives, potato peeler, handheld mixer, and an electric iron. She picked up the iron and plugged the cord into the power strip.

Lucas stood close to the fainting couch, his bloody hands clasped behind his back. "Now, if you would, Keeper, please place the iron on a lower setting. We don't want to burn Viv's skin."

Olivia's eyes widened. "You want me to –"

"Silence!" Lucas shouted. "I will not give you another warning. You do not speak unless I allow it. Now turn on the iron and stand next to the couch."

Olivia put the iron on a low setting and with shaking legs managed to stand next to Vivian. Vivian just smiled at her and straightened her skirt across her legs. "He's right. My skirt is much too wrinkled." Her vacuous smile was chilling.

Lucas pointed to her legs. "Now, iron the skirt, Keeper."

Olivia began to tremble. She couldn't do this! Even to someone like Vivian! A host of amoeba like demons floated closer to the couch. Three demonic heads popped out of the amoebas and mouths formed. Vile tongues licked purple lips.

"Can she see us?" One head said.

"Who cares!" Said another.

"Keeper! Iron Viv's skirt." Lucas commanded

"Yes, dear." Vivian said quietly. Tears were running down her cheeks. "Please get rid of the wrinkles."

Snake appeared at her side and took the iron from Olivia's hand with her mechanical one. "Perhaps this is too much on the first day, sir. I will take care of the ironing."

Lucas' red eyes widened and for a second, he glared at Snake and then at Olivia. "Just get on with it. If she refuses again, I'll put her on the fentanyl line."

Snake pressed Olivia back from the couch with her good hand. With her mechanical hand, she placed the iron on Vivian's leg and began to move it back and forth across the material.

Vivian's mouth opened and she tried to scream but nothing came out. Her face reddened and Lucas bent closer, his eager eyes taking in every tear, every silent scream, every grimace.

"There, there, Viv. It is the price we pay for perfection." Lucas sneered.

A wave of weakness passed over Olivia and she felt a seizure grip her pulling down into welcome oblivion.

❧ 29 ❧

Monarch walked slowly through the line for the London Eye. She glanced around her in search of the Captain. She glanced at her watch. It had been six hours since her meeting with the Captain and he had wasted no time requesting she meet him on the London Eye at precisely 6 P.M.

She arrived at the top of the ramp and the operator motioned her forward. "Your ticket is taken care of, milady." He smiled and motioned to an open door into one of the pods. A man sat inside on the bench. Monarch stepped onto the pod and the door closed behind her.

"Isn't this a bit dramatic?" She asked.

The Captain stood up and walked over to the railing on the outside of the pod. "You can see so much from up high. Parliament, Big Ben, Westminster Abbey, not to mention the Shard."

Monarch joined him as the pod moved up along the giant wheel. "Your point?"

"We scurry about like ants. Building, spending, planning only to die in bitter despair." He turned his turquoise eyes on her.

"I don't plan on dying in despair." She said.

The Captain shrugged. "No one ever plans such a thing. But

no one escapes this life unscathed. You asked me for a favor, and I will deliver. But I need something else in return other than the name from the dossier."

"That wasn't our deal." Monarch stiffened.

The Captain frowned. "It is now. When this pod returns to the station below, you can get off with the information of where your daughter, and incidentally Vivian, are located or you can go away empty handed. I can find out my own information since you have now revealed that one of the people listed in the dossier is a member of the Penticle. That was your mistake letting me know that tidbit of information. However, I am not a fan of patience. I would rather have the information now than wait. But I can wait, my dear."

"What do you want?"

"When this is all over, I want the method you used to erase Raven's mind. I will find that most useful." He turned his gaze out over the Thames. "Ah, what a lovely sight from the very top. I'm afraid it is all downhill from here, Dr. Monarch. You have a choice to make."

She took the notebook out of her purse. It contained the printed dossier. She had been unable to duplicate the memory card. She held it out for the Captain. "I could not duplicate the memory card. This is all you get."

The Captain studied the notebook in her hand. "We are both negotiating on this deal, are we not?"

"I need to know something that is not mentioned in the dossier. Who hired Raven to kill my husband?"

The Captain froze and his turquoise eyes widened. "You haven't found that information in the dossier, have you." He took the notebook and opened it. "If was an off the books job. Raven had only a few of those." He scanned the pages. "Ah, as I suspected. This will be very useful." He glanced back up at her. "Your daughter and Vivian are both prisoners of the Overlord. His exact location is highly guarded. But I have discovered that a certain criminal mastermind has been offered payment to raid that location and rescue them both. In return, the Geisha, as she is known, will take over the Overlord's business."

"The Geisha?"

The pod was nearing the base of the wheel and the Captain tucked the printouts into his jacket. "My son is on his way to meet with her now and will succeed in hiring her and her warriors to raid the operations."

"Jonathan?"

"Yes, it seems he can play the criminal when it is necessary."

"Something he learned from you?" Monarch said.

The Captain shrugged. "I did my best. I trust you will send me the other information? If not, I will tell the Geisha to pass on the deal with my son."

The door to the pod opened and the Captain stepped off onto the platform. He glanced once back over his shoulder. "By the way, I'm the one who hired Raven to kill you AND your husband."

Before Monarch could react, the Captain disappeared through the line of patrons for the London Eye and into the gathering dusk. At least now she knew Steel was about to rescue Olivia. And that brought some comfort.

30

Birdsong studied the strange objects scattered about the basement of the lake house. Only one lamp was illuminated, and he had covered the three small windows at the top of the wall along the lake side of the house with foil to eliminate any light. A flashlight beam danced down the stairs ahead of Dr. Jack Merchant.

"Did you close the door?"

"Yes." Merchant said as he arrived at the foot of the stairs. "And I didn't turn the flashlight on until after the door was closed."

Birdsong nodded. "Hopefully we weren't followed."

"You drove all over Shreveport and half of Bossier City." Merchant collapsed into a desk chair and turned off the flashlight and placed his backpack on the table.

"I know how to shake any pursuit."

"And just how do you avoid invisible, inter-dimensional demons?" Merchant glanced around the basement. "How do we know they are not here?"

"I prayed over the truck before we left the hospital. And while you were in the bathroom upstairs, I prayed a perimeter of protection around the house." Birdsong sat on the desk. "It's the best I can do."

Merchant rubbed his face. "Pam wanted to know why we weren't going to dinner tonight. What if they find out about her?"

"Hey, man, we can't cover every eventuality. But I prayer for her safety."

Merchant leaned his head down on the desk. "Someone cut the top of Moshander's head off. Sam did the post and said they had taken part of the man's brain! What kind of people do this thing?"

"You said you had seen a lot as a deputy medical examiner."

Merchant looked up. "There hasn't been a murder like this in northern Louisiana since a serial killer murdered three people back in 1989. Things like this just don't happen around here. What if whoever did this finds out about Pam?"

Birdsong slid off the desk and pulled a chair up beside Merchant. "Can she leave town? Go see somebody? More importantly, since we've been back from Dallas have the two of you been seen together?"

Merchant shook his head. "No. She's been working twelve hour shifts and, of course, I've been occupied. We have a date this weekend. She can't just up and leave town. What do I tell her? A demon possessed murderer is stalking you?"

Birdsong sighed. "Jonathan warned us about getting involved. Why don't you let me handle it from here? Call Pam and the two of you disappear for a few days. Go someplace very public where he won't do anything in plain sight."

"No. As long as Pam is working she'll be okay. She lives with two other women right now. She sold her house and once we get married, she's moving in with me." Merchant plopped back. "Of course, now her roommates are in danger!"

"Jack!" Birdsong put a hand on the man's shoulder. "Stop! We have to focus on a plan to save Josh. We get Josh out of there and they lose all leverage on Jonathan and this thing ends."

Merchant nodded and he rubbed tired eyes. "I did warn Pam I was working on a case with the coroner's office and to be extra vigilant. I hope and pray she will be fine."

Birdsong sat in the other chair. "Moshander's death was meant to be a warning. As long as we keep a low profile, they won't make any other moves. After all, Moshander's death has alerted the local police that something bad is up."

"I am duly warned!" Merchant sighed.

"Tell you what. I can call Franklin Ross with the FBI. Get him to post someone outside their house. I'll tell him I've heard some chatter about Mosander's killer targeting women working at your hospital. I'll keep your name out of it."

"He'll know it has something to do with Jonathan." Merchant said.

"Of course he will. And as much as he acts like he despises Jonathan, he will help us out without question."

"Thanks, Jason. Now I might be able to concentrate." He unzipped his backpack and pulled out his tablet and pushed his gold rimmed glasses up on his nose. He tapped on the screen and slid the tablet over to Birdsong. "I had one of Sam's techs take a look at the fluid and blood your brought back from the clinic. We have access to laboratory tests most hospitals do not. I should have used them in the first place. After the 'zombie' sighting, the office is on lock down with extra security."

Birdsong studied the tablet screen. "What am I looking at?"

"First, Josh's blood is clean. No viral particles. A slightly elevated white cell count but not enough to raise a red flag." Merchant sat forward and tapped the screen. "The type of white cells is consistent with an ordinary mild viral infection. If he was still suffering from the autoimmune process, the white cell mix would be different."

"Meaning?"

"He is over that episode."

"So why is he still paralyzed?"

Merchant took the tablet and tapped the screen again.

"Because of this." He showed the tablet to Birdsong. "These are the ingredients in his infusion. Vitamins. Amino acids. And that strange combination of neuropeptides."

"I got the neuro part." Birdsong said.

"A protein associated with the brain. Why is it in the infusion?"

Birdsong sat back. "Josh tried to tell me something. He mentioned Pandora's box and something stuck his finger in Hampton's museum."

Merchant nodded. "Yes, he would have had to been exposed to some kind of viral agent at the beginning to induce his comatose state and then create the illusion of paralysis. But what kind of virus? We never detected the usual viral immune response. We tested his blood for every known viral agent that could have developed into the autoimmune state. Jason, as I said before, this viral agent is unknown to us. It could be very dangerous."

"And in the possession of Hampton and his mysterious box in London." Birdsong crossed his arms deep in thought. "Josh also mentioned the twelfth demon."

Merchant shrugged. "I couldn't keep them straight. Which one was he?"

"Rudolph Wulf of Wulf Pharmaceuticals. He bioengineered a type of agent in the blood of his victims that rendered them temporarily very suggestive. He surrounded the whole endeavor with the story of vampires." Birdsong sat forward and pointed a finger at Merchant. "Prions. Josh mentioned prions."

Merchant froze. "Prions? Prions are related to these neuropeptides."

"Just what are prions?"

Merchant tapped on the tablet. "Ever heard of mad cow's disease?"

"Years ago. I was scared for a time because I love my beef." Birdsong said.

Merchant turned the tablet screen to Birdsong. "Prions are

abnormally folded proteins. They have this weird ability to transmit their bizarre shape onto normal variants of the same protein. We don't know what causes the normal protein to mis-fold. But the structure confers infectious properties and collapses nearby proteins into the same shape. These abnormal proteins then aggregate into what we call amyloids which accu-mulate in normal tissue, particularly the brain and cause tissue damage and cell death. Mad Cow's disease comes from ingesting prions from infected tissue of the cow's brain. There are many other such neurodegenerative diseases caused by prions."

Merchant pointed to the strange fold shape of a protein on the screen. "And the problem, Jason, is there is no treatment and there is no way to kill the prion. They can't be destroyed by ordi-nary disinfection or cooking." Merchant took back the tablet and did some more tapping on the screen. He studied the results. "Okay, so Wulf's prions have been investigated! The CDC identified a prion that had a very brief effect on the brain and was quickly broken down by the body's immune system. Very unusual that the body could recognize the prion and elimi-nate it rather than it building up in the body to cause permanent damage." Merchant glanced up at Birdsong. "A bioengineered prion indeed, Jason. This is not a typical prion. It was something else."

Merchant reached into his backpack and pulled out a laptop. "Go make coffee. I need to do some research before we take Steel's truck and try to break Josh out of his prison."

Birdsong stood up. "I'll take black coffee. Without the prions!"

🐾 31 🐾

"Jason!"

Birdsong jerked awake in Cephas Lawrences's desk chair. He hurtled to his feet, his body and mind suddenly awake. He reached for his pistol and blinked in confusion. He was at the lake house.

"Jason, I found out what is happening!" Merchant pointed to his laptop held precariously in his hand. Birdsong glanced at the clock on the desk. It was three o'clock in the morning.

"Doc, don't ever wake me up like that! If I had my pistol, I would have shot you!" Birdsong rubbed the sleep from his eyes and pulled his hair out of his face.

Merchant hurried across the room and sat in one of the other desk chairs. "Sorry. Look, the neuropeptide in the infusion has characteristics like a prion. But, like Wulf's prion, it quickly breaks down. Whoever made this infusion had access to Wulf's prion and modified it." Merchant turned the laptop toward Birdsong. He tried to focus on the numbers and graphs on the screen.

"English?" Birdsong settled back into his chair.

"The infusion is making Josh paralyzed! It's not the cure. It's the disease!" Merchant said. "All we have to do is get him out of that clinic and away from the infusion and he'll recover completely."

"Okay, then I can handle it from here. We have an ally in the clinic, Faye Morgan. Once she finds out about the infusion, we can take him out of there."

"And once he is out of their clutches." Merchant said.

"Did you just say clutches?"

Merchant paused. "Okay, a little dramatic. Once he is out of the clinic, these demons have no further influence on Jonathan."

Birdsong nodded, his mind already whirling. "Okay, let me think on this. Come up with an approach to that clinic. We'll have to be subtle. Can't afford a full frontal assault. No telling what the unholy triad would do to stop us. Maybe even kill Josh."

Merchant nodded. "They took out my colleague! So, I agree. They are ruthless. And the question is why are they doing this?"

Birdsong rubbed his eyes in thought. "Simple. They wanted to control Jonathan Steel. Give Josh the initial virus to make him deathly ill and once he was in the hospital, fool Jonathan into thinking that only Hampton's clinic could cure him. Then keep Josh sick with the infusion until Jonathan completes their tasks."

Merchant nodded. "I had concluded as much. But this neuropeptide in the infusion is overkill. They could have used a dozen different pharmaceutical agents to create the same condition. Why this prion like particle?"

Birdsong stood up and paced. "Josh also mentioned Pandora's box."

Merchant was tapping again on the laptop screen. "I should have done this long ago." He studied the screen of his laptop, the light reflecting in his glasses. "Nigel Hampton's Museum of the Weird in London. Let's see. Yes, there is a display of Pandora." Merchant's forehead wrinkled in puzzlement. "But it isn't about Pandora's Box. It's about alchemy and the Philosopher's Stone." Merchant squinted as the read the screen. "The Elixir of Life. The display is all about one of the earliest alchemists who supposedly created the Philosopher's Stone and used it to create the Elixir of Life."

Birdsong glanced again at the clock. They would need rest before saving Josh. "Sounds like a bad wizard movie."

Merchant was silent as he typed on his laptop keyboard and shuffled through screens. He stood up and paced. "According to my search, the elixir of life was also known as the elixir of immortality." He paused and turned his chair toward Birdsong. "It was always associated with the philosopher's stone in ancient mythology. The elixir supposedly granted anyone who drank it eternal life. Or eternal youth depending on the legend."

Birdsong moved back to his chair. "I need that coffee to stay awake. Did Hampton create this Elixir of Life?"

"Pandora's box was in reality a large, stone urn filled with all the afflictions of life, so goes the legend." Merchant continued. "It is also associated with the same pseudoscience as the elixir, alchemy. Is there a connection?" Merchant hurried to his laptop and swiped through screens. "Aha! Josh's hemoglobin is low."

"What does that mean?"

Merchant glanced up at Birdsong. "He's not bleeding anywhere. And there is no evidence of hemolysis. Uh, that means his body breaking down red blood cells. Jason, they are taking his blood! They are removing his blood for some reason."

"Are you telling me that Josh is a test tube?"

"Exactly!" Merchant said. "This protein in the infusion is causing Josh to make something specific to his blood. Josh has been through a number of physical challenges, right?"

Birdsong stood up and paced again. "Well, he was possessed by the thirteenth demon for a short period of time. No telling what that does to a human. Jonathan said demons have limited ability to teleport. That has to be rough on the body. And then there was the tainted blood from Wulf."

"Cobalt!" Merchant stood up. "I read about him after you told me. He dabbled in genetic manipulation to create his 'children of the bloodstone', right? I doubted your story. Children who at the age of ten are already as large as grown humans? But with the proper genetic manipulation it is possible to achieve rapid growth."

"Jonathan said the fathers of these children were demon possessed when the children were conceived. Could demon possession also change a person's genetic makeup?"

"If so, then something could have happened to Josh's genome." Merchant paced with Birdsong. "And Josh was in Numinocity with you."

"Thakkar used some kind of nanotechnology as part of her deception. But Josh was not exposed to that." Birdsong paused. "None of us were."

Merchant paused. "Neuroplasticity! We know that changes in the body can elicit changes in the brain. Jason, there is no telling what changes occurred in your brain just be being exposed to the virtual reality of this Numinocity. And Josh was the youngest."

"Olivia and Steven are teenagers. They were exposed also."

"Did they experience any changes?"

Birdsong smiled and nodded. "Steven's hands were injured in the assassination of his father. When he woke up from Numinocity, his hands were back to normal. But Jonathan said it was a spiritual healing, not due to this neuroplastic stuff."

"His hands were healed?" Merchant froze. "That is not possible in current medical environment."

"Olivia has epilepsy. She was unchanged. No change in her brain."

"That we know of! Who knows what changes may occur in the coming months?"

"Does that mean Josh's brain will change also?" Birdsong said.

Merchant nodded. "And maybe this prion like particle is meant to induce more rapid changes in Josh's brain. If so, then harvesting the metabolites might, in some way they suspect, help create this elixir of life."

"Can it?"

"I doubt it, Jason. This is all pseudoscience to the nth degree. Nonsense."

"You thought demons were nonsense just a month ago." Birdsong said.

"Granted." Merchant was silent as he thought. "But why would the three demons do this to Josh instead of just keep him sedated in a state that resembled his disease? Are they trying to do two things at once?"

Birdsong froze. "Wait! It was Hampton that authorized the transfer of Josh to the clinic. It was Hampton who claimed to have the cure. That means there are two things going on here. The unholy triad has one agenda."

"And Hampton has another. This just got more dangerous, Jason. Josh is basically a lab experiment and the longer he is exposed to this infusion the more likely he is to have alteration of his brain! We have to get him out of there as soon as possible." Merchant pointed to the laptop screen. "Hampton is using Josh to produce his 'elixir of life' and he may bleed him dry before Jonathan completes his tasks."

Birdsong looked down at his cell phone. "I need to get a hold of Faye Morgan. She's got to stop his infusions!"

32

A cool, wet rag soothed Olivia's face and her eyes flickered open. She looked up into the empty gaze of Vivian.

"Livvy, are you okay?" Vivian said. "I've made some warm milk for you."

Olivia sat up weakly and looked around Vivian's "apartment". Snake was nowhere to be found. "I'm fine, Aunt Viv." She whispered. She spied her backpack in the corner and pointed to it. "I need my medication, Aunt Viv."

Vivian stood up stiffly and tilted her head as she studied Olivia. "You have epilepsy."

"That's right. I need my medication, or I'll have another seizure."

Vivian retrieved the backpack and handed it to Olivia. "That warm milk?"

Vivian smiled vacuously and brought a mug from the kitchen cabinet. She offered it to Olivia.

Olivia took her medicine from a pouch in her backpack and swallowed her pills with the warm "milk". She almost spewed it across the room but had to swallow the vile concoction to get down her pills. It was warm, soapy water!

"Vivian, that's not milk! This is dish water." She thrust the mug back into Vivian's hands. Vivian stared down at the mug.

"You have epilepsy." She said again. "Seizures."

Olivia wiped the water from her face and tried her best to keep it down. "That's right, Vivian." She looked around the room and spied the surveillance camera in the corner. "How did you know that?"

Vivian placed the mug on the counter and pulled up the hem of her skirt. Her legs were red where the iron had touched them through the fabric of her dress. The skin was not blistered. Lucas had been careful not to cause permanent damage, only pain. "When Missy ironed my skirt, you passed out. But it was not like a normal faint. It was something else." Vivian dropped the skirt and for a second, the empty look faded from her eyes. She blinked and Olivia's eyes widened. Was she coming back to herself?

Olivia stood up as quickly as her dizziness allowed her and grabbed Vivian in a hug. She pressed her lips right next to Vivian's ear. "You're remembering who you are. They are watching and listening."

Vivian stiffened for a second in Olivia's grasp and then relaxed as Olivia backed away. "Thank you for my milk, Aunt Viv."

Vivian blinked furiously and nodded. Olivia directed her eyes over Vivian's shoulder at the camera and nodded slightly. "It was good. I think I might try and get some sleep. Why don't I help you get ready for bed?"

Vivian licked her lips and nodded. "Of course, dear. I'm tired and my legs are sore from all the work of cleaning the floor. It is shiny, isn't it?" She gestured to the kitchen floor with a sweep of her arm as if she were a model in a television commercial.

"Spotless." Olivia held out her hand and Vivian took it. She led Vivian across the kitchen to an open doorway through which she had seen a bed. They entered Vivian's bedroom and Olivia sat her on the bed. A nearby closet held several shiny nightgowns. Olivia fought the urge to vomit in disgust all the while imagining Lucas watching them. She helped Vivian into the nightgown and Vivian laid back on her bed. Olivia pulled the covers up around her shoulder and bent over to give her a good night hug.

"I'm remembering." Vivian whispered in her ear. "It was your seizure. I remember Numinocity."

Olivia felt a thrill and stood up. Vivian smiled and closed her eyes. "Good night, Livvy. Don't forget to say your prayers."

The demons appeared suddenly in Olivia's vision hovering around the periphery of the room. The mention of prayer seemed to have triggered her ability to see them. She glanced around the room.

"I'll pray for us both." She said. "That will keep the boogie man away." And his demons she hoped.

Vivian blinked and a tear ran from one eye. "That would be nice. Do you want me to pray for us?"

Olivia knelt by her bed and felt the brush of otherworldliness as one of the demons moved close to her. It was time for her to abandon her hatred for God. It was time for her to realize that there was something beyond this reality from which these evil beings originated. And, with startling clarity she remembered something Josh and she had discussed.

"HOW DO YOU KNOW SOMETHING IS EVIL?" JOSH HAD SAID. "C. S. Lewis said the only way he knew a line was crooked was because there was a standard, a straight line. We can't know there is evil in this world unless we have an appreciation of good. And that means good comes from a transcendent source, God."

She felt Vivian's hand close on hers. "God, I don't know what to say or how to say it but protect this little girl from harm and give us a good night's sleep. Amen." Vivian's voice was quiet and filled with emotion, far different from the robot she had been just hours before.

The air around Olivia grew warm and a bluish aura emanated from Vivian and for a moment moved up her arm. She felt the warmth, the comfort, the unrelenting love in that light. This was a touch from God. And, as she slowly disentangled her hand from Vivian, she realized she wanted more. She wanted it all!

۞

Olivia slept in a small bed next to Vivian's. She was so exhausted; she fell into a deep sleep immediately. She awoke to the fragrance of bacon and toast. She sat up slowly. Vivian's bed was empty.

Vivian had set the table with two plates and bacon and scrambled eggs were piled in each plate. Vivian turned away from a toaster with a plate covered with the fragrant warm bread. She placed it on the table.

"Breakfast, Livvy?" She pointed to a mug. "Warm milk for real, this morning."

Olivia sat in her chair and glanced into the mug. Milk! She sipped it gingerly, and it was warm and slightly sweetened. Her medicine pouch lay on the table by her plate, and she took her pills.

"Aunt Viv, you must be feeling a lot better to have cooked all of this for us." Olivia said.

Vivian sat down and began eating her eggs. "I think it is having you back at home again, Livvy. I missed my niece so much. You have inspired me to do my best." Vivian smiled.

Olivia ate her eggs and bacon and glanced around the kitchen. No demons. Not yet, anyway. Vivian's prayer still echoed in her mind. She cleaned her plate and motioned to

Vivian's bedroom. "Do you want to get cleaned up and I'll help you get dressed?"

Vivian nodded. "You can help me with my shower, dear."

Vivian cleared the table and Olivia took her by the arm and led her to a bathroom off the bedroom. Vivian stepped into an old fashion tub with a white shower curtain. Olivia pulled the curtain around the tub.

"Just hand me your nightgown and undies, Aunt Viv and I'll have a towel ready for you."

Vivian started up the shower and Olivia dumped the nightgown into a clothes hamper. She went back to the closet. More dresses! She chose a bright, red dress and brought it into the bathroom. Vivian leaned her head out of the shower curtain.

"Livvy, darling, can you hand me the soap? I left it by the sink."

Olivia picked up a bar of soap and was handing it to Vivian. Vivian leaned close to her. "Fake a seizure. Now." She whispered.

Olivia was so shocked, her eyes flew open, and she leaned forward allowing her body to relax. Vivian took her by the arm and tugged her toward the shower curtain. She fell over the edge of the tub into the shower and the curtain collapsed on top of her and Vivian.

Olivia spewed water out of her mouth and Vivian's face was right next to hers. "I had to create a diversion. When we get to the throne room, stay back from Lucas. I'm ending this." She said in what Olivia realized was Vivian's real voice. The woman was back!

Vivian picked Olivia up and moved her out of the tub onto the floor, unwrapping the curtain from around her. "Oh, my, Livvy." Vivian stood up with the curtain partially wrapped around her wet body. "You have epilepsy. Help someone. Help."

Olivia kept her eyes opened and unfocused as if she were in the midst of an absent seizure. Snake appeared in the doorway.

"What a mess, Viv."

"Oh, honey, she had a seizure. Is she hurt? I can make some warm milk."

Snake ignored Olivia and led Vivian to the bedroom. She dried Vivian off and helped her into her clothes. Vivian's hair had not gotten wet.

"The Keeper was supposed to have you ready early. The Overlord wants an audience this morning." Snake ran her good hand through Vivian's short hair. "How's your legs?"

Vivian stared straight ahead. "Just fine. Why do you ask?"

Olivia blinked and reasoned it was time to recover from her seizure. Snake left Vivian sitting on her bed and came back into the bathroom. "You keep having seizures and the Overlord will replace you. Minus your liver."

Olivia stood up. "It's the stress of traveling and not getting enough sleep. I'll be fine."

"Okay. Wash up and change clothes. There's an extra set of dresses in the closet that will probably fit you. You have ten minutes." Snake leaned down and glared into her eyes. "And this is the last time I'm bailing you out. You're on your own, Olivia. I'm not covering for you again."

33

Steel pounded the table in frustration. When he put the coordinates into a map program the location was in an empty field east of London. Unless Vivian was having a picnic, she wasn't there. Drake had fooled him!

Also, he couldn't get the image of Olivia out of his head. Try as he might, he was unable to ignore Dr. Monarch's pleas for help. While continuing his search for Vivian, he had searched every conceivable word and phrase that might indicate to where Olivia had vanished. He had studied the latest theories of human trafficking. He started to call Ross, but couldn't risk Ross knowing about his encounter with Drake. And to make matters worse, it seemed Jason and Dr. Merchant had fallen off the grid. This could be a good thing, but it also carried ominous implications in view of the death of one of Merchant's colleagues.

Steel left his hotel room and wandered out onto the street. He wore his long coat and a woolen cap to cover his head against the falling snow. It had been snowing again since he left the church and made his way back to his hotel. He had to help Monarch. After all, if it were Josh missing, he would be just as desperate.

But he also had to find Vivian and time was running out.

Steel wandered down the street and looked up as Big Ben sounded out the early morning hour. He paused in front of the huge edifice of St. Paul's Cathredal. Should he go inside and pray? Would God hear him? And, just what should he pray for? To find Vivian so he could kill her? To find Olivia for Monarch? Or pray for a miracle that Josh would be healed? He stood in front on the steps leading up to the huge doors and watched people milling about waiting for their tour guide.

"I would even welcome one of my guardian angels." He said. He glanced around. Not an angel in sight. He couldn't blame them. "I'm not exactly on the side of the angels right now."

He wasn't on a mission for God. Everything he was focused on was against God's kingdom. He sat on a stone wall and felt the cold snow seep through his coat into his legs. He had never been so desperate in his life.

A shadow passed over him and a man in a black, wool coat paused before him. He wore a fur fedora, and his face was covered with a dark gray scarf and his eyes were hidden by mirrored sunglasses.

"Mr. Steel?" He said quietly.

Steel looked at his reflection in the man's glasses. "Who's asking?"

"I am an associate of someone who can help you in your hour of need." The man said.

"Oh, really?" Steel rasped. "Are you an angel?"

"Far from it." The man wore black leather gloves and he pointed to a taxi sitting at the curb. "If you would be so kind as to allow me to offer you a ride, I can explain."

Steel towered over the short man. "You expect me to get into a taxi with a total stranger?"

The man tugged the scarf from his face and lifted his sunglasses with one hand. "I am not a stranger."

"Ishido?" Steel whispered.

"Please, Jonathan. We must hurry before anyone realizes who I am."

Steel followed Ishido to the taxi and climbed into the back seat. Ishido slid in beside him. "You know where to go."

The taxi took off into the traffic and Ishido pulled the scarf down and took off the sunglasses and the hat. "I am taking a great chance, Jonathan. But I have learned something you should know."

Steel blinked. "Ishido, it is dangerous for you to be in London. The authorities are looking for you. You were supposed to leave after you brought Monarch the memory card."

"Yes, and after you learn what I have planned, you will see I am doubling down on my fugitive status." Ishido nodded.

"Does Max know you are here?"

"Max knows many things." Ishido said. "For instance, Max informed me that *two* people need your help."

Steel's brow furrowed. "Who?"

"Olivia Monarch and Vivian Darbonne."

Steel gasped. "I've been looking for Vivian. And I just found out last night Olivia was missing. How did you know?"

Ishido smiled. "Jonathan, you are man who constantly needs assistance, and you fail to ask for it. You are the most stubborn person I have ever met. So, Max has asked me to help you."

Steel's heart raced. "I found out the physical location of Vivian so that means Olivia is there also. But it's just an empty field on the map. There has to be a hideout there."

Ishido nodded to the taxi driver, and he pulled up to a curb and stopped in front of a building. "We will need army to march into that field. I have found us one." He motioned to the old brick building before them. "When we go into the building in a minute, you will be greeted by the gang that sought to recruit me so many years ago. When I learned of what was going on, I approached them, and I have allied myself with them after all these years."

"No, Ishido." Steel said. "I can't allow you to do that."

Ishido's dark eyes glittered. "Is Josh in trouble?"

"Yes."

"Is his life in danger?"

"Yes." Steel hissed.

"I lost my family to the very people I have now pledged my allegiance. I did this so that you will not lose your family. When we go inside, I have told them you are willing to pay a ransom for two victims. All you have to do is provide them with the physical location. Do not worry about the money. I have sufficient funds in a private account on this phone." Ishido pulled a cell phone from his coat pocket and handed it to Steel. "You are the client, Jonathan. You must play the part of a nefarious American mobster who desires these two women for his, shall we say, harem."

Had he ever been a criminal? He looked out the frosted window of the taxi at a closed door. A pale painting in faded colors covered the door. A tall snow covered peak, possibly Mount Fuji? And a serpiginous figure coiled over the face of the mountain looked back at him with serpentine eyes and long whiskers. A dragon? A door with a dragon? Where had he seen that before? The library! Etched in the doors to the library of his home! He felt a tingle in his palm and glanced down as it glowed with blue light. Something flickered in front of his eyes. His "palm" wanted to show him something. "Show me." He said.

❧ 34 ❧

"So this is the famous library." Clay said as they walked through the open doors into the huge room. The library was cold. In spite of a huge fire burning in the enormous fireplace, the air was filled with an unearthly chill.

"Yeah, my father has only let me in here two times in my life." JJ said.

"But, it's part of your house, man. And that door with all the cool etchings! Like a Lovecraftian nightmare." Clay threw the hair out of his face and gazed around at the room. "Look at all of this stuff!"

"Listen, my father told me to meet him here so when he shows up, you'll have to leave." He said.

Clay sighed. "Man, that stinks! I'm your best friend, dude. You need someone that has your back because it may get really bad."

"I'll be fine. Just don't touch anything while you're looking around."

JJ had only been in the library on a few occasions as a boy. He had been forbidden to enter the room. There were too many priceless artifacts and ancient books for a young boy to mess up. He had stood outside those closed doors on many occasions and peered through the crack to watch his father conduct business with other men. The tobacco smoke would so fill the air, wisps of it would seep through the cracks and cause him to cough. He would run away in fear of discovery.

Now, at the age of sixteen, he could only enter the library at the invitation of his father. He stood in front of the fire and tried to find some warmth from its flames. The walls were lined with shelves that stretched to the second floor ceiling. A walkway around the library gave access to the higher shelves. Access to the walkway was through a brass spiral staircase.

The lower level of shelves shared their book space with glass cases and bell jars. Within were various artifacts from ancient civilizations and far lands. As a child, he had tried to see the contents of these glass enclosures, but he had been too short. Now, he walked around the room peering through the dusty glass into the interior.

One wall was filled with an odd collection of pipes from distant times and faraway lands. Another wall contained scrolls of documents tightly sealed within airtight glass. Before he knew it, he had walked around the room and stood before the door.

Unlike the warm mahogany and oak woodwork around him, the door was armored steel with huge rivets the size of mushroom heads. The door was painted with a deep black shiny paint and its surface was covered with a sheen of dust. Not even the maids were allowed to touch it to clean away the dust.

"What's behind this door?" Clay asked.

"I don't know. It hasn't been opened in years."

"Dude, that is totally creepy." Clay squinted at the door. "Like, why is it locked?"

"Something really bad happened there that involved my grandfather. They say it drove him mad." He reached out toward the black surface and his fingers almost touched the cold metal.

"What are you doing?"

JJ whirled as his father entered the library. The Captain, as everyone called him, wore his ever present white Panama hat with a wide brim. His fierce turquoise eyes burned with anger. "I told you to never touch that door!"

"Yes, father." He said as he stepped away from the door. But something pulled at him. Perhaps it was the allure of the unknown. Perhaps it was the unanswered question of his heritage. Perhaps it was something more, evil?

"Who's your friend?" The Captain glared at Clay.

"Uh, Clay. He's been over here before, father. But you weren't here." You're never here, he thought.

The Captain raised an eyebrow as he studied Clay. "Well, Clay, it's nice that you accompanied my son. It's good to know he has at least one friend. But our conversation is totally private. I'm afraid you'll have to leave."

Clay nodded and swallowed. "Sure. Hey, dude, I'll catch you on the downswing." He slipped around the Captain. "I'll show myself out. I know the way."

The Captain watched Clay disappear through the doors and then he slowly shut the doors to the library. He turned and regarded his son.

"Sit down." The Captain said as he took off his hat and hung it on a brass hat rack. His short reddish blonde hair was cut in a fierce crew cut. Spikes of gray glistened in his hair as he ran a hand through it. The Captain wore a white button down shirt and dark pants. He paced in front of the fireplace and pulled his meerschaum pipe out of a pants pocket. He stopped in front of a humidor on the mantle and scooped tobacco into the pipe. He lit the pipe and puffed on it, expelling huge clouds of smoke into the chilly air.

"I suppose you've already heard the test results?" He glared.

JJ squirmed on the couch and averted his eyes. "Mother told me. Everything was normal."

"Yes, normal. I've already chastised your mother about with-holding this information from me." His father began to pace again. "Anything peculiar about your behavior is of utmost importance."

JJ looked up. "Why?"

The Captain paused and glared at him. "That doesn't concern you."

"Of course it concerns me!" Anger boiled up within him and he clenched his fists. "Why won't anyone just tell me what is going on with me? All these unanswered questions. All this subterfuge and mystery."

The Captain stopped and raised an eyebrow as he puffed on his pipe. "Good. You're angry. And, you haven't passed out. Yet."

"What is that supposed to mean?" He stood up.

"What do you think is happening to you?"

JJ drew a deep breath and walked across the room to the door. "That is happening to me. Grandfather went mad. He killed someone behind that door. Am I going crazy? Will I kill someone?"

The Captain stood silently on the other side of the room, pipe smoke drifting away toward the far ceiling. He blew a huge cloud of smoke and walked across the room. He placed a hand on the boy's shoulder.

"What happened in that chamber is of no concern to you. The lives that were taken that night were because of his poor choices. He was not insane. He was merely evil."

JJ slowly pulled away from his father's grasp. "But the stories of his ravings and his tantrums."

"All true. Of course, today he would have probably been diagnosed with multiple personality disorder. One moment, he was a loving, caring man. The next, he was a demon in flesh. Sometimes, he seemed to be speaking with another man's voice." The Captain turned away and walked back to the fireplace. "Or, it could all have been an elaborate ruse."

JJ studied the black door and shivered. "Multiple personalities? Father, what if that is what is wrong with me? What if when I black out, I take on another personality?"

The Captain whirled around and his eyes danced with fire.

"Don't say that! You are who you are and no one else! Do you understand?"

JJ blinked. "But?"

The Captain raced across the room and grabbed his son with an iron grip, both hands squeezing his upper arms. "Listen to me, boy. You are who you are. You are a good person. You have your mother in you, not me. Not your grandfather, do you understand?"

JJ grimaced in pain under his father's grasp. "Father, you're hurting me."

The Captain's gaze broke and he released him. "I'm sorry. You're just tired. Too much studying and too much stress at that school. Next year, you'll go away to a boarding school. There won't be any bullies or any thugs to threaten you. You are a good boy, understand? A good boy!"

JJ shook his head in confusion. "Go away? I don't want to go away."

The Captain's face stiffened and he straightened. He walked over to the fireplace and tapped the spent tobacco out of his pipe. He tucked it into his pants pocket. "You don't have any choice. I've allowed your mother to be the dominant influence in your life. I wanted you to make the right choices. But now you must become a man and stand on your own two feet. I realize I have made a mistake not being more of an influence in your life. I know you will miss your mother, but there will be no discussion on this matter. You have two weeks of school left and then we will start looking for a prep school somewhere on the Eastern seaboard."

The Captain never turned around and walked over to the library doors. He opened them and motioned outside. "You may leave now."

JJ wanted to protest, to cry out in anger and frustration. He wanted to unleash the angry being within when he had the photograph album. Ah, the album!

"I need to tell you something." JJ said.

The Captain's eyes filled with fiery anger. "I told you to leave."

"I found grandfather's journal."

The Captain froze and for a second fear crossed his features. "Where is it?" He hissed.

"I threw it away. Into the woods behind the church. There was something in that journal. Something, I don't know, evil. Was it the spirit of grandfather?"

The Captain hurried across the room and looked into JJ's eyes. "You know where it is? Then, come on. We have to get that journal back. How long ago was it?"

Something about the Captain's manner was deeply troubling. The man was scared, desperate. "Several weeks."

A servant appeared at the door. The Captain flinched at his arrival. "What is it, Hobbs."

"You have a visitor and he insisted meeting you, ahem, in the library."

The Captain's eyes blazed with anger. "Did you let him in the house?"

"Come, come my good friend." A voice echoed in the hallway outside the library. "Since when am I not allowed to visit my own home?"

A man stepped into view, short and with a receding hairline. He was stocky and wore an outdated bowler hat. He carried a wrapped package beneath his arm. The Captain gasped and stepped back. "Nigel?"

The man must have been in his late sixties and he glanced at the boy. "Your son, I presume. I believe he lost something. It was found by a stranger who noticed my name in the back cover and he contacted me.

Nigel moved past the Captain who was paralyzed with confusion and, yes, fear. Nigel placed the package on a table and tore off the wrapping. He motioned to the travel journal. "Young man, you really should take better care of family heirlooms."

"Who are you?" JJ asked.

"I am Dr. Nigel Hampton. I was your grandfather's bene-
factor and traveling companion. He allowed me to collect artifacts from all over the world." Dr. Hampton stepped closer to
the boy and his pale blue eyes bored into the boy's eyes. "You are
very special, JJ. This journal was left by your grandfather for
you." He glanced at the Captain. "And you alone! Please take
better care of it."

"I didn't see your photo in the journal." JJ said.

"My dear boy, I was the photographer." Hampton smiled.
"The camera is not kind to my portly figure."

JJ glanced at his father whose mouth was open and whose
eyes were frozen in fear and indecision. Hampton but a hand on
the Captain's shoulder. "Why haven't you told the boy about our
special relationship, eh?" Hampton turned back to JJ. "I'm your
grandfather's brother. I built this house along with your grandfather. These are my artifacts I have allowed to stay here in the
states. I take it from my accent you have deduced I am not from
the continent. I have put together a museum to display these
artifacts. I could use a good assistant, JJ. You could come live
with me London." He glanced at the Captain. "Instead of a
boarding school."

How had he known about the boarding school? Hampton
smiled and tapped his bowler. "I will leave now. I think your
father has a lot of explaining to do." He turned to the journal
and tapped it with a finger. "Don't let this out of your sight, my
boy. It will change your future for the better."

As the man let himself out of the library passing the motionless and speechless Captain, JJ felt an unmistakable, yet familiar
wave of evil pour out of the journal and over his mind and soul.
A voice spoke quietly in the back of his head.

"I'm back!"

35

Steel felt a cold wave pass over him and he looked up into the face of Ishido. "I had a flashback. A memory. Dr. Nigel Hampton was my grandfather's brother, my great uncle." He leaned forward in pain and fought for breath. How could this be? This explained Hampton's exhibit of the figure that resembled his grandfather. Surely Hampton had lied about the date in that exhibit. In fact, Hampton had lied about a number of things. His elixir was the Elixir of Lies! He looked up into Ishido's face. "Ishido, I can't do this."

"Jonathan, you are my friend and we have been through much together. I do not know what your past has done to you. But I know what my past has done to me. Josh needs you in the now, the present. Whatever this Hampton was to you; whatever he did in the past, he is now controlling your son. You know what you must do. Forget the past for a moment. You can and you will do this. When the time comes you will put your finger on the phone screen, and it will transfer the funds to my new colleagues. Then, they will lead an assault on the location you will give them and take the drugs and the other humans but give you Vivian and Olivia."

Steel sat back, his mouth open. "Ishido, I can't let anyone

who is in captivity just go from one criminal element to another."

"I know, Jonathan. I have a plan on how to ensure my colleagues fail once they acquire the location. You must trust me. But I cannot reveal any more information to you." He put a gloved hand on Steel's arm. "You realize you are not a good liar."

"I know."

"For Josh's sake, you must become one now."

With what Steel had done in the past few days, being the evil criminal was going to be far too easy. He followed Ishido into the building.

They passed through two red doors into a foyer that led backward into a ballroom. The wallpaper had peeled away from the walls and the windows were grimy allowing dirty, yellow light into the room. There were at least two dozen men and women lined along the walls and the back of the room. They all wore black clothing and black bandannas covered their faces.

A table sat in the center of the room. A woman sat at the table. Her face was pale and heavily made up. Her hair was pulled into rolling buns on the top of her head. Without the makeup, she would be unrecognizable in a crowd. She stood up and a red kimono shimmered in the dim light of the room. She motioned with a well-manicured hand to a chair opposite her.

"Mr. Stone, I presume." She said and smiled.

Steel nodded and bowed slightly. "Yes."

"Your associate has vouched for you and if you disappoint me or my friends, you will pay with your life. Painfully." She sat back down. Steel sat in the chair.

"I understand."

"The assault will be costly. We believe the location is heavily guarded and there is the matter of transportation to the site."

Steel glanced at Ishido and tried to hide his surprise. "I was not informed of all the details." He felt Ishido tense at his side. Steel needed his anger, his fury. He thought of Drake dancing in the furnace room and his anger built. "You said you believe the location is heavily guarded. Either it is or it is not!"

The woman tensed and two men stepped forward behind her. She raised a hand. "Do not speak to me that way."

Steel stood up and stepped forward and one of the men moved toward him. Before the man could reach Steel, Ishido had spun around Steel and had grabbed the man by the throat and held his dagger to his Adam's apple.

Steel raised his hand much as the woman did. "Please forgive my tone, but I am the one with the money that YOU want. Call off your men."

The woman nodded and her men stepped away. Ishido released his man and the man glared at him above his mask. "Mr. Stone, we have an approximate location for the operation. The one known as the Overlord has successfully kept his fentanyl farm and his 'harems' hidden away. We know it is the country-side east of London.

Steel smiled. "I have the coordinates. I do not have the personnel to retrieve the two persons I am interested in. As well as eliminating OUR competition." He pointed to his coat pocket. "May I remove one of my phones?"

The woman nodded. "Carefully and slowly."

Steel removed his phone and brought up the map app. He placed the phone on the table before the woman. Her eyes widened and she smiled. She spoke something in a foreign language and a man behind her rushed forward. He pulled a piece of paper from a pocket and jotted down the coordinates. The woman nodded at Steel.

The woman pushed the phone back to Steel and he retrieved it. "The location is indeed one we suspected but something has hidden the goings and comings of people in and out of there."

Probably demonic power, Steel thought. "I came by this knowledge from a man who knows the location intimately."

"Is he still alive?"

"Unfortunately." Steel said.

"Well, that will not matter for long unless he has warned the Overlord." She turned as the man with the paper returned and handed her a tablet. She studied the screen. "Just as I thought. We have long suspected the one who calls himself Overlord had overtaken an abandoned amusement park. We were looking for a church."

"Now that you have the location thanks to me, you will help me acquire my, uh, assets?" Steel said.

"For the right price, Mr. Stone."

Steel looked around at the gathered "warriors" behind the woman. There was more to this than money. "I understand. And, if you somehow acquire the Overlord's other possessions in the process that is of no interest to me."

The woman smiled again and tilted her head in a slight bow. "Then, we do have an understanding. Without your financial support, we could not obtain the necessary equipment to approach the location. It is in plain sight in an open field. Hiding in plain sight! I have wanted to acquire the Overlord's business for months since he infringed on my territory. What I have lacked was sufficient funds and the location." She leaned toward him. "Tell me, Mr. Stone. Where do you get your funds from?"

Steel felt sweat trickle down his temple. He had to sell this. "Ever heard of Anthony Cobalt?"

The woman's eyes widened. "Yes. I heard he died in the explosion of his space station."

"I'm the one who blew it up." Steel said channeling as much of his anger and disgust as he could. "He had lured my son into his cult. And the spoils of his Sunstone energy initiative are now mine. Have you heard of the Sunstone?"

The woman looked over her shoulder at someone in the group and nodded. She looked back at him. "There is one who was in the space station. He survived the explosion."

A tall, thin man stepped forward. He looked at Steel. "Who is your son?"

"Joshua Knight." Steel said with as much conviction as he could muster.

He nodded. "I knew of him." He nodded down at the woman. "He is telling the truth. I saw the Sunstones and they are worth millions."

"Are you implying I am a liar?" Steel growled. Ishido gently prodded him and shook his head. Too much! The man who spoke stepped toward Steel with closed fists.

The woman lifted her hand quickly to stop the man. He bowed his head and retreated into the group of warriors. "That will be enough." She studied Steel. "If you do control the Sunstones, then you have piqued my interest. Perhaps, in addition to the financial support you can also give us the Sunstones."

Steel stiffened and his fists closed. The warriors tensed behind the woman. "I am not here to bargain over Sunstones!" He said. "I thought we had a deal for the two women. If not, then I'll take my business to someone else. Perhaps, the Captain?"

Steel had no idea why he said that. The woman bolted to her feet and put a restraining hand up to the warriors behind her. "You know the Captain?"

Steel pointed to his eyes. "Where do you think I got these eyes from?"

It was hard to imagine the woman's pale face could get any whiter. She suddenly bowed and nodded. "Our transaction will proceed as agreed upon. Forgive me for showing an interest beyond our original agreement."

Steel looked around at the warriors. One by one, they seemed to relax but he noticed some of them were trembling and had averted their eyes. "Then, we have a deal? No more questions asked?"

"Yes." The woman said. "All that is left is the transaction."

Steel pulled out Ishido's phone and placed it on the table. He put his finger on the phone and it opened into a banking app. He tried to hide his shock at the number waiting for his approval to transfer to the woman's account. He turned the phone to her. "Is this the agreed upon fee?"

She smiled and nodded and then typed in her account number. Steel pressed his finger one more time and the money figure disappeared. "Now, bear in mind that you do not want to disappoint me." Steel pocketed the phone. "Or my father."

Steel turned and strode from the building accompanied by Ishido and prayed he would not collapse before they reached the sidewalk.

※ 36 ※

Josh opened his eyes to bright sunlight. His breath steamed in front of him, but something was off about his nose. He started to move his arm and felt a hand on his.

"Don't even move, Josh!" Someone whispered close by. "They think you are sedated. I'm sitting right next to you, and we are facing out away from the clinic. They can't hear us out here, so if you talk, keep it to a whisper and don't move a muscle."

Josh cut his eyes to his left. Faye Morgan sat in a chair next to him, her face turned out toward the rolling hills. "What is in my nose?" He whispered hoarsely.

"A feeding tube."

"Why?"

"You've been sedated for two days. I had to give you the sedation after all. The doctors were too observant. Hovering like vultures! We had to feed you through the tube."

Josh fought the desire to scream in outrage, but he suddenly realized he could feel his legs. "I'm not paralyzed!"

"I know. We found out the reason for your paralysis was NOT the post viral syndrome. The infusion was supposed to be a cure, but it was the cause of your symptoms. They wanted you comatose and paralyzed! What is going on?"

Josh felt tears run down his cheeks. "I'm going to live?"

"Yes." Faye's voice filled with emotion. "Jason and Dr. Merchant figured it out."

"Are you keeping the medicine from me?"

"Yes. I managed to switch out the intravenous bags. But the three doctors insisted on injecting the sedation themselves! I'm so sorry."

"You can't keep doing this, Faye. You're placing your life in danger."

"It's the only way I can get you out of this place and back to Mr. Steel." Faye whispered.

"Have you heard from him?"

"No. But they took your phone away. I managed to find the necklace you were talking about. I have it in my pocket." Faye said.

Josh swallowed slowly and felt the irritation of the tube down his throat. "Dr. Hampton has a plan to make me a petri dish, a lab experiment. They are taking my blood for some reason." Josh whispered.

Faye tensed beside him. "That is why you are anemic! Oh, Josh, I'm so sorry."

"Well, how is our good boy doing today?" Josh heard the much too chipper voice of Hampton behind him. He closed his eyes and tried not to move.

"I'm sorry. Who are you?" He heard Faye say.

"I'm Dr. Nigel Hampton. I developed the boy's cure." Josh felt the man's shadow fall over him along with a chill that came not from the cool air but from the man's evil nature. "You are nurse practitioner Morgan? Correct?"

"Yes."

"I have a proposition for you. How would you like to double your salary?"

Josh heard Faye gasp. "What are talking about?"

"I'm afraid we are going to have to move Mr. Knight."

Josh stiffened a little and hoped Hampton didn't see it. Faye stood up beside him and he felt her step between Dr. Hampton and himself. "What? Why?"

"I'm afraid it is a monetary issue." Hampton said.

"I thought all treatments covered by this clinic were taken care of my donations." Faye said.

"Well, certain donors have become aware of Mr. Knight's unusual treatment and the cost and have demanded he be moved elsewhere. So, I am having him moved to my home and he will need excellent nursing care. I would like to hire you to take care of him."

Faye was silent for a moment and Josh knew she was weighing the pros and cons. He wanted to blurt out 'no' so she would not place herself in anymore danger.

"What about Mr. Steel?"

"Mr. Steel unfortunately is persona non grata. We have been unable to reach him and since there are no other relatives, I have appealed to the state for intervention, and they have agreed. Will you accompany Mr. Steel to my home?"

"Not if it is in London." Faye said.

"Oh, pish posh. I have dual citizenry, Ms. Morgan. I have a palatial manor north of Austin, Texas less than a three-hour drive. I understand you have no children or other dependents, and I can assure you that within the week, Mr. Knight's treatments will be at an end."

Josh felt Hampton's hand touch his shoulder and he fought the need to shrug it off. "I'll leave you to think on it but please bring Mr. Knight in soon. We have to complete preparations to move him."

Josh heard him walk away and he felt Faye lean against his back. "Oh, my! I'm blocking their view Josh. I have to get you out of here."

"Not until I hear from Jonathan." Josh whispered opening his eyes.

"If they take you, I won't have any way to help you. I'm going with you until we hear from Mr. Steel or Jason." He felt her hands grip his shoulders. "I'm your care giver, Josh. I never abandon my patients! I can withhold the sedation now. I can change out the infusion for simple fluid. And, I will need a male assistant. I will demand Hampton hire Dudley." She took the necklace out of her pocket. The sliver of bloodstone caught the sunlight and it glittered. She put it carefully around his neck. "Maybe this will give you hope."

Josh smiled. It would give him power!

❧ 37 ❧

Vivian chafed under the dress and the harsh, tight underclothing from the 1950's. How had women endured that decade? Still, she hid her discomfort behind the false smile. Keep up appearances, she thought. Not a problem. She had been doing this most of her life. Only now did she feel the true depth of truth in her life. The presence within her was not the sickening, cloying stench of evil. It was a sweet aroma of God, the Holy Spirit. It warmed her. It comforted her. Most importantly, it strengthened her as she left the apartment for her next meeting with the Overlord.

"Aunt Viv, would you like to hold my hand?" Olivia said. Vivian took the young woman's hand and tried not to squeeze too tightly.

"Thank you, Livvy. I can't wait to see the Overlord." Vivian said and bile filled her throat. She swallowed it back and tried to imagine how she would handle the upcoming encounter.

The Crimson Snake walked ahead of them, and she paused to glance out the grimy windows at the debris laden hallway below them. Vivian shifted her eyes carefully and also saw the flickering of something moving in the shadows. Snake put up a hand to stop them.

"What's wrong?" Olivia asked and then the girl trembled as she looked around them. What was she seeing? Whatever Olivia saw terrorized the girl. Her hand tightened on Vivian's.

"Livvy, what's wrong? Are you having a seizure?" Vivian leaned over and brought her lips close to Olivia's face. "What is it?"

"I see demons!" Olivia whispered. "Everywhere. I can see them now."

Vivian stood up. "Livvy, just hold on to my hand. You can trust me to take care of you just like you've taken care of me."

Snake motioned them forward. "I thought I saw something. The Overlord is waiting. Come on!"

Vivian followed Snake onto the elevator and then out into the courtyard. The night air was cold but dry for a change. Snake led them across the empty courtyard to the church and stopped. She looked over Vivian's head from the top of the wide stairs. "Olivia, take Vivian inside to the Overlord. I need to check something out."

"Yes." Olivia tugged Vivian up the stairs and Vivian tried to survey the surrounding shadows. A full moon filled most of the courtyard with pale light. The doors to the church opened and two of the Enochians motioned them in. Vivian tried not to shudder as she felt the unmistakable touch of evil. In the past, it had been a painful if not welcome presence. Now she was repulsed by it. She noticed Olivia staring at each Enochian as they passed.

"What's wrong, Olivia?" Vivian said quietly.

"More of them!" Olivia whispered. "They're everywhere."

Vivian nodded. "Well, the Enochians are the Overlord's protectors. They should be everywhere."

Vivian entered the main throne room. The Enochians who had previously been in some kind of trance or prayer were now alert and standing among the pews. Vivian kept smiling as she neared the throne. Lucas wore a blood red robe and his bare white arms and face once again dripped blood and pus. Two children attended to his wounds and his crimson eyes glared at Vivian.

"You are late!" He hissed as Vivian and Olivia stopped at the edge of the stage. Lucas stood up and shooed away the children. "Keeper, I told you what would happen if you displeased me again."

"I'm sorry, Overlord." Vivian said as calmly as she could. "I insisted on choosing my own dress just for you." She lifted the edge of her pink dress and curtsied. "Olivia tried to hurry me, but I knew you would understand. Don't you like my dress?"

Lucas' gaze moved from Olivia to Vivian. "I don't like pink. I told you that before." He clapped his hands and blood showered onto his robe. One of the children approached. "Bring me the kitchen knives."

The child ran to the side of the stage and reappeared pushing a metal cart with some difficulty. Vivian saw the light gleam off knives of various sizes and shapes. The cartwheels squeaked and filled the chamber with the obnoxious noise. Lucas closed his eyes and clapped his hands. "Stop! I thought I told you to oil those wheels."

The little boy froze, and tears poured down his cheeks. "I had no oil, master."

"Then use your own blood." Lucas glared at the child.

Gunshots from outside the church broke the silence and echoed around the chamber. Lucas flinched and his Enochian guards all turned toward the doors. More gunshots echoed from outside along with screams. The little boy glanced once at Vivian, and she pointed to the door. "Run!" She mouthed.

The little boy and the other child disappeared behind the stage. Lucas clapped his hands. "What is going on? You!" He pointed to the nearest Enochian. "Go find out what is happening."

More gunshots now closer and louder. The Enochian glanced once at the closed door and then bolted around the stage into the darkness at the back of the church. The other Enochians followed suit. Lucas hurried down the stairs and stood just inches from Vivian.

"What did you do?"

Vivian slowly smiled and began to laugh. She laughed and laughed. "I have no idea. But I know who I am now, Lucas. My memory has returned. What do you see, Olivia?"

Olivia looked around the chamber. "Hundreds of demons. All kinds and sizes. They're converging here."

"Good. Lucas, you have been the bane of my existence for years. You've misled and destroyed the lives of hundreds with your demons. The Master exiled you. You are now alone and defenseless. The demons are gathering against you. I have no idea where the shooting is coming from, but if I were you, I would run."

Lucas stepped back and before he could take a step up the stage, Vivian released Olivia's hand. "On second thought, why don't stay a while. I'd like to tell you a story of redemption. Mine!"

He paused and regarded her with a hate fill glare. "You think you can escape from hell? You think you can walk away from all that you have done? Look at me! I was the apple of the master's eye until you came along. Now, I am exiled, and I endure unending punishment because of you. I will not allow you to enjoy this forgiveness you have claimed. Your soul may belong to another now, but your body is still in this world, and I can tear and rend and wound you." He said. Spit showered from his lips and spackled her face.

"Go ahead, Lucas. Have your way. You can destroy my body, but you cannot take my soul. I have given it to a new Master." Those words seemed so wrong to her old self, but she knew it was true. Never in her life had she believed in something so powerfully as she did in the certainty that nothing mattered any more but her relationship with the man who had conquered the cross and the grave because he loved her. She moved up the steps and stopped right in front of Lucas. She closed her eyes and lifted her chin to expose her neck. "Go ahead. Kill me!"

Lucas' skin bled cold air as his fingers clutched her neck. And then, he screamed. He lurched back from her, and his hands were covered with blisters. He began to tremble as the wave of blisters poured over his body. He screamed and screamed until every wound gushed blood and he fell to the floor. He writhed in exquisite pain until he was still. His chest no longer moved. For a second, Vivian saw a ghostly image of the man's soul leave his body. It hovered over its lifeless form and its red eyes turned toward her. They suddenly filled with a fear and revulsion.

"They are coming for him." Olivia said and she covered her eyes.

"Please." He heard the ghostly figure say. "Give me another chance. Please."

Two huge hands appeared from behind the ghostly image. The fingers were long and multi-jointed with dark, red scales and bright yellow talons. The hands closed around Lucas' mouth and torso and stifled his screams.

"We have waited long for this one." A coarse voice echoed in the room followed by laughter. Lucas' spirit body reached toward Vivian and his hands almost touched her. She almost felt sorrow for this creature she had once hated with all her heart. He had made his choices and they were the wrong ones.

The doors behind burst open and Vivian whirled ready to fight the remaining Enochians. But the person she saw was the last man she imagined would show up. Jonathan Steel ran down the aisle with the one known as Ishido right behind him. Vivian's heart pounded and she ran to meet him. They met in the aisle, and she threw herself onto Jonathan Steel, her arms wrapped around his shoulders, her face buried in his chest.

"On, man of steel, do you have perfect timing or what?"

Steel was stiff as a board as she hugged him and then he seemed to melt. "I thought I'd never see you again."

"What's happening?" Olivia said as she joined them.

"An assault. By the Geisha and her ninja warriors. Jonathan, we need to go. Now." Ishido said.

Vivian pulled back from Steel and looked at his bright, turquoise eyes through tear filled eyes. "Lucas is dead. He's gone. I'm free, Jonathan."

Steel nodded. "Great! Now let's get out of here."

Ishido led them behind the throne stage just as the windows burst in from ninja warriors converging on the chamber. Steel, Vivian, and Olivia followed Ishido down a long winding corridor beneath the old amusement park. The walls were covered with moisture and mold and the floor was slippery.

"This is an old service tunnel I found on the blueprints on the Internet." Ishido said over his shoulder. "Not a safe place to stay but it comes out at the rear of the park at the old loading docks."

Behind them Steel heard voices and the clash of metal against medal. The warrior ninjas were cleaning up behind them. Ishido paused at a metal door, and it took both of them to open a round wheel. The door creaked open before them onto an open space beneath a fallen roof. Ishido led them through the twisted debris illuminated by the full moon. "Dr. Monarch is over there." He pointed to a gate in a dilapidated metal fence.

They ran across the weed choked road and through the fence. A van waited for them. Dr. Monarch and Steven stepped out of the van.

❧ 38 ❧

Olivia gasped for breath praying very hard that her hyperventilation would not cause a seizure. She tried to ignore the pulsating, gyrating figures of demons all around her. As they neared the van and she saw her mother and her brother, she ran faster. Her mother embraced Olivia and she pressed her face into her mother's neck and let the tears pour. She felt Steven's arms around her.

"Olivia, I thought I'd never see you alive again." Monarch mumbled as she sobbed.

Olivia pulled away. "I'm so sorry, Mom. It was the demons. I saw them everywhere and I had to get away and I wasn't paying attention and I got off at the wrong stop."

"Demons again?" Steven wiped at his eyes. "I don't see any."

Olivia punched him in the shoulder and moved to sit on the floor of the open van. She gasped for breath and her mother sat beside her, putting her arm around her shoulders. Olivia leaned into her mother and watched in the distance as a sudden burst of lights from hovering drones illuminated the old amusement park. Assault vehicles appeared from behind them and moved around the van toward the park.

One vehicle stopped and a man waved at Monarch. "Glad

you found her, Dr. Monarch. Thanks for the heads up. We've got this covered."

"You're welcome D.C.I. Dewinter." Monarch said. "The officer I spoke to when you disappeared. He'll clean up the mess."

As the vehicles rammed down the perimeter fence, Olivia tensed at what approached. The band of demons was a bizarre mix of jumbled up creatures and hovering blobs. Some were human like and others had definite leathery wings and gargoyle like faces. Olivia stood up and ran to Steel. She pointed. "Demons! Dozens of them coming this way."

Steel looked away from Vivian. "What?"

"She can see demons." Vivian said. "I guess that makes her one of us."

"One of us?"

"Christ followers." Vivian smiled.

"I don't want to see demons." Olivia said and watched the ragtag army of demonic beings approach.

"What a git that one was." A demon with bat like features and bulging eyes said in a high squeaky voice. "Glad to be rid of that one. Watched his soul dragged off to you know where." The demon laughed.

Another demon walking beside the bat demon looked like a deformed centaur with multiple eye stalks arising from its flanks. It had the head of a goat. "I was in the throne room. Thought we had seen the last of Lucas for good. Bunch of us tried to drag his soul to the Ravagers waiting to drag him off to Tartarus."

"Lucas isn't dead?" An amoeboid demon oozed up beside the other two.

"He's cursed. Can't die. His soul snapped back into his body like a yoyo." The goat demon said.

Olivia gasped as the demons passed by them and a dozen or more moved toward the van. She pushed away from Vivian and ran to her mother. She stood between her mother and her brother and faced the demons.

"Stay away from them." She shouted. Some of the demons glanced up at her. They all licked lips and saliva drooled but they looked away as Olivia shouted again. "In the name of Jesus, go!"

The hoard hurried on their way and were soon out of sight. Olivia slumped onto the van floor and her mother put her arm around her. "What was that all about?"

Olivia's heart raced and she felt the aura of a coming seizure. "I was protecting you from the demons, Mother. I can't keep doing that. You and Steven have got to change for the better."

She felt the wave of confusion and shaking pass over her and fell into the dark pit of a seizure.

⚜

FAYE PUT A HAND ON JOSH'S SHOULDER. "JOSH, UH, WE ARE moving you to a new facility." He tensed and almost opened his eyes.

"Don't worry. I will be right here with you and so will Dudley." Faye leaned close to his face. He felt the warmth of her breath as she spoke.

"I am going to sedate you. Can't take a chance you will react to all the moving about. When we get to where we are going, I will leave off the sedation and you've receiving no more of the infusions. We'll leave right after this next bag of simple saline solution. Don't worry, Josh. Dude and I will watch over you."

❧ 39 ❦

Steel clicked the fountain pen and placed it in the middle of the old operating table in Hampton's lower theater. Monarch had taken Olivia up to Monty's room to lie down after her seizure. Cassie and Monty hovered nearby whispering to Steven as he filled them in on the details. Vivian had gone with Monarch to clean up in Monty's apartment. Thank goodness Margaret was nowhere to be found.

"I've been told the unholy triad is no longer listening in on me. But I don't believe them. So, now we can talk." He took out a burner phone he had picked up on the way to the museum and dialed Jason Birdsong's cell phone.

"Jonathan?" Birdsong's voice filled Steel with joy. He put the phone on speaker.

"It's good to hear a friendly voice, Jason. I have you on speaker phone. There are others listening but the most important thing you need to know is I am using one of Max's surveillance dampeners so no one can hear us. Are you secure?"

"Yes, Jack and I are in the basement at the lake house. We've been waiting to hear from you."

"Sorry I couldn't call. I couldn't take a risk with Josh. How is he?"

"Jonathan, it's Jack. Josh is fine right now." Dr. Merchant said. "We found out he isn't really sick at all. The virus from Hampton was a ruse to get him to the states. The infusion is what has been keeping him in a paralytic state. There's nothing wrong with him, Jonathan. At least not now. We have to get him out of the clinic."

Steel closed his eyes and resisted the urge to scream obscenities. He felt a hand on his shoulder, and he turned to see Vivian had entered the room. Her hair was wet and her face clean and she smiled at him.

"Honey child, no cursing in front of the children." She whispered.

Steel sighed. "What did you have in mind, Jack?"

"Jason here. I have already been in the clinic once in the guise of a nurse. I can do it again. We have someone on the inside. Faye Morgan."

"Josh's nurse practitioner right?" Steel said. "Can she be trusted?"

"Yes. She helped me escape the clinic and she told me she would watch over Josh." Birdsong said.

Steel nodded and his mind whirled. Now that Vivian was here, he had to decide how to handle the last request from the unholy triad. If he could get Josh out of the clinic, he could spare Vivian's life. "Jason, I'm working on an idea. The last request of the demons hinges on whether or not Josh is safe. I can't take a chance that we might fail. Even though you and Jack have figures most of this out, Josh is still right where seven, six, and five want him to be. He is still under their control, infusion or not. And we have no idea what Hampton is up to."

"Yeah we think Hampton has a totally different agenda from the demons." Birdsong said. "Not sure what that is but Jack has an idea."

"Keep working on how you can get into that clinic and get Josh out of there, Jason. I'd suggest heading to Dallas as soon as possible and I'll call you in a few hours. Wait until you hear from me to make any move. I don't want to take any chances with Josh's life."

"Ok, boss. Man, God is with us." Jason said.

Steel swallowed back emotion. "You have no idea how good it is to hear your voice." He ended the call. He turned to Cassie and Monty. "Cassie, Monty will you take Dr. Monarch and Steven up to the foyer? I need to speak to Vivian. Alone."

Cassie blinked back tears. She knew what he had to do. "Of course." They left Steel and Vivian alone.

Steel turned slowly. This was harder than he imagined. Vivian's hair was still wet and she had washed the makeup from her face. She wore one of Monty's long sleeve tee shirts and a pari of sweat pants. She was different. He could see it. He could feel it. Vivian raked her dark hair back from her face with her fingers and glanced up at him.

"What do we need to talk about?"

Steel motioned to a chair. "Why don't you sit, Vivian. We need to talk."

She sat down. "Talking I can do. Sleeping, not so. He had me back there on a slab." She pointed to the small room between the theater room and the furnace room. "While my brain was trying to recover." She hugged herself and shivered. "That creep Hampton." She looked back at Steel. "I don't think I have slept, really slept since I woke up from Numinocity."

"Nightmares?"

"Dreams? Maybe. Visitations from angels. A fall into hell. Lucas dressing me up like a 1950's fashion doll." Vivian stared at the floor and a tear ran down her cheek. "I thought demons were bad. It's the guilt, Jonathan. I never had to contend with it before." She looked up a him with moist eyes. "I seem to have a conscience now."

"It's called the Holy Spirit." Steel said.

"Never thought I'd have *that* kind of spirit in me." Vivian smiled. "I even remember a few Bible verses or two."

"I found part of the Bible once." Steel said. "In the African prison camp. I was assigned to clean the latrine every day. The guards were using the Bible for toilet paper. I saved most of the book of Romans."

Vivian was silent for a moment. "Do you believe me, Steel?"

"Believe what?"

"That I'm changed. I cried out to God, and he answered. I gave my heart and soul to Jesus Christ. I can't believe it sometimes. I mean, after all I have done, he can still forgive me."

"At least you remember what you have done." Steel said. "I don't know what terrible things I've done."

"Hey, honey child, you okay?" Vivian put a hand on his arm. He wanted to jerk it away. He tensed and she pulled back her hand. "I get it. You hate me. I can't blame you. There are a lot of people who hate me. When we get back, I want you to call up your FBI buddy. I have a lot to confess."

Steel's eyes were directed away from her. "It's not that, Vivian." It was what he had to do to Vivian to save Josh.

"I don't blame you. I once used a situation like mine as an argument against God. Why would God forgive someone on their deathbed who had a lifetime of crime and dishonesty? I mean they lived their entire life the way they wanted to and then with one whispered prayer, the doors to heaven were thrown open."

"Assuming they were genuine in their repentance." Steel said. Would the doors be thrown open for him one day? How could God overlook what he was doing now?

"But it makes sense, Jonathan." Vivian said. "I have so many regrets. So many things I did wrong. So many right things I could have done. If I had my life to live over, I could make such a difference."

Steel finally really looked at her. "You're being totally honest, aren't you?"

Vivian's eyes filled with more tears. "Every passing minute, I feel the weight of every wrong thing I ever did. And yet, with every passing minute, I feel this Holy Spirit you talk of comforting me, reassuring me that God's forgiveness is greater than anything I could ever have done wrong. I mean, it would have to be, right? If God couldn't forgive a 'sinner' as you call them on their death bed, how could he forgive me when I'm still drawing breath and he knows what evil I am capable of?"

Steel sat on the table. "God, I'm miserable."

"Why?"

Steel studied her eyes. They were filled with a level of honesty he had never seen. "You don't know what I have to do to."

"It has something to do with Joshua Knight."

Steel closed his eyes. "Yes. Demands from Seven, Six, and Five. The Unholy Triad! And, I have to become *you* in order to save Josh."

"What?"

"They want you to die, Vivian. And they want me to 'end' you. That was the bargain, and I gave my word." There. He said it and his heart sank. Would it have been easier if she were still a disciple of Satan?

Vivian blanched and sat back in her chair. "Well, looky what the cat dragged in! My, my, Mr. Steel." She trembled and her voice shook. "Promise me you'll make it quick. One tap to the forehead."

"Argghh!" Steel groaned. "Why did you have to go and find Jesus? Why did you have to become the good one?"

Vivian stood up. "Isn't it what you wanted for me? You threw yourself in front of me in Numinocity and took my pain, Steel. That is when it finally made sense to me." Vivian said. "But, if you do kill me, what price do you pay? What does it do to your soul?"

"I don't care, if it saves Josh. That's the dilemma, Vivian."

"Then, I accept my fate. I'll do it myself. That way, you won't have to taint your soul."

Steel studied her face. Her eyes were filled with unshed tears. Her face red with emotion. "You're serious, aren't you?"

Vivian nodded quietly and reached out and took his hand. Her skin was warm and moist, and she placed her fingers between his. "You know I've always loved you, don't you?"

Steel stiffened. "What?"

"From the moment you walked into Ketrick's office with those exotic turquoise eyes and that steely, defiant manner. I knew right then there was at least one man in this world who could best me. I knew, Jonathan. That's why I've fought you so hard. I couldn't admit the love that has grown in my heart for you. I know it will never be returned and I totally understand. Only God could love someone like me."

Steel's breathing quickened and he closed his eyes. "Don't do this, Vivian. Don't say this."

"Why? I'm tired of lying, Steel. Satan is the father of lies and I don't belong to him any longer. I will speak truth from now on."

Steel felt his heart race and his breathing quickened. He looked at Vivian. "Vivian, I have only loved two women, April Pierce and Claire Knight. But my feelings for you have ranged from pure hatred to — ."

"What? Grudging tolerance? A smidgen of fondness? You don't have to say any more, Jonathan. You don't have to love me back. I am not a lovable person." She laughed nervously and swallowed back emotion.

"My feelings are at best mixed." Steel said hoarsely.

"You took the sting for me. That will have to be truth enough." Vivian patted his hand. "Now, see sweetie, that wasn't' so hard. This is for real. As real as I've ever been. I don't want Josh to die any more than you do. What I did to him when I introduced him to the thirteenth demon is unforgivable. I will do anything I can to make up for that."

"Even die?"

Vivian blinked. "Yes. I'm tired, Jonathan. I'm tired of fighting for power and glory and riches. I'm tired of being the puppet of your father. I'm tired of jostling the pieces just right on the chess board of international and corporate power. I'm tired of juggling demons and playing one against the other. Let's face it. There is nothing left for me but incarceration and punishment and pain and humiliation and I deserve every minute of it. But if there is another way out; a way that can redeem my wasted life, then I will take it." She looked back at him. "Josh is young, and his entire life lies ahead. I will not be responsible for taking that away from him."

Grasping for desperate alternatives a thought came to mind. "You worked with my father! You said he was on the Council of Darkness?" Steel said.

"Yes. He is."

"Then, he has some influence, doesn't he?" Steel felt a brief flash of hope. "Maybe he could intervene with the unholy triad."

"I don't know, Steel. The demons on the council seem to have their own agenda. They really don't obey anyone. Besides they may not even know he is on the Council. Everyone keeps their identity a secret unless they form an alliance like the unholy triad."

"But, if you're valuable to him, he wouldn't want to lose you." Steel said.

Vivian glared at him and sat back, pulling her arms up and wrapping them around her. "Oh, no! I will not go back to working for him! That would be worse than death. Let's make it clean and simple."

Steel shook her. "No, listen to me. Vivian, you have valuable knowledge. Ross can get you a deal. You turn evidence on these corporations. You tell them what my father coerced you to do. You could redeem yourself in so many ways."

"And do what? Go into witness protection? Disappear like that?" Vivian leaned into him. "Steel, they will find me no matter what. They have demons everywhere. You alluded to that yourself. *Something* is always watching. I could never hide from the Council."

"Then, take it down. That is what you have been doing from the beginning. Use the Captain to reinsert yourself onto the Council. Go undercover, if you want to call it that. Learn what you can and destroy them!"

"It's tempting, Steel. But there are billions of demons and there are always more demons to take the place of the twelve. You cannot do away with the Council as long as Lucifer wants it to exist." She said.

"There has to be a way to save you, Vivian." Steel growled.

Vivian smiled a crooked smile. "Listen to you, honey. Who would have thought Jonathan Steel would go to bat for little old me?"

"I took the pain in Numinocity." Steel said quietly.

"Yeah, why?"

"I guess I cared more for you than I thought. Everyone deserves a second chance." Steel's voice was barely above a whisper.

Vivian wiped at her eyes. "Yes, you did take the pain for me. That was my deciding point. That was when I understood what Jesus Christ really did on the cross." She looked into the distance and sighed. "I almost met him, Steel. He looked right at me. Such love, such power, such compassion. It almost ended me right then on those rat filled streets of Jerusalem."

Steel looked at his left palm. He held it up and a faint blue glow pulsed under the skin. "I know. Your Grimvox shards penetrated my hand. I relived your memory."

Vivian stood up and took his hand in hers. "I don't have the shards anymore. I'm free and clean." She looked up into his eyes. "Would you look at us? You working on the side of demons and me working with the angels. Who would have thought?" She touched his cheek and pushed a stray strand of hair off his forehead. "You need a haircut, Mr. Steel. Don't be Samson and lose all your strength selling your soul to my old boss. Be careful, sweetie."

Steel's phone rang and he studied the caller I.D. Jason Birdsong. "Jason, I told you not to call me. They might be listening!"

"Jonathan, I had to take a chance. I just got off the phone with Faye. They moved Josh from the clinic!"

Steel glanced at Vivian. "What?"

"He's at one of Hampton's stateside homes in Austin, Texas. Faye is with him. She volunteered to be Josh's nurse and she's making sure he's okay. She said he's safe right now." Jason said. "What do you want us to do?"

"I don't know. I'm calling Hampton now!"

Steel ended the call and turned to the surgery table. He had placed his jacket on the table the night before. Maybe the day before. He wasn't sure. The past few days were such a blur.

"What are you looking for?" Vivian asked.

"Hampton's phone number. It was on the contract I signed for Josh."

Vivian put a hadn't on his arm. "I have a better idea. Come with me." She led him into the other room and over to a shelf. She moved aside some artifacts and picked up a tablet. "It's still here. His iPad Pro." She unplugged from its charger and handed it to Steel. "Pandora is the password. Give him a video call. I'll wait in the other room."

Steel watched her leave the room and activated the tablet. He initiated the video call and it only took a second for Hampton's beaming face to appear on the screen.

"There you are, my good boy! I was hoping to hear from you. Now, it seems Mr. Birdsong has informed you of Josh's relocation." Hampton said.

"He better be okay!" Steel said.

"My good man, I have nothing but the boy's best interest at heart. He is *my* future! I knew of Ms. Morgan's loyalty to the boy and counted on her coming with Josh. You may not realize it, but I have protected Josh from those three demonic doctors who are even now flying to Austin where I have assured them you will meet with them. It seems they've performed too many teleportations?"

"How did you know?"

"You were coming here? Well, I understand you've completed the three tasks and have been withholding some of the results as leverage. Smart boy! I have arranged for a transport airplane out of Heathrow. A private flight. Bring whoever and whatever you need but it leaves in less than an hour, Mr. Steel. You'll be here in twelve hours. You'll be reunited with your son, and we will see the end to this whole sordid affair. Margaret will be in the foyer shortly with the information on the flight. Looking forward to seeing you." The screen went blank.

Steel went back to Vivian his mind whirling. What to do now?

Vivian sat in her chair, her gaze focused on her hand. She held up her empty palm. "If I still had access to the Gimvox I might be able to explore some of its memories, find you a loop-hole, Jonathan."

"I need a loophole right now, Vivian. They are expecting me to bring your dead body on that airplane." Steel said.

Vivian stood up and tried to smile at him. "It's okay. You will do what you have to do. The Grimvox is gone. Now, I will no longer have access to those memories." She froze and held up a finger. "Just a minute. Let me try and remember what it was like for little old me to be wily and conniving. It shouldn't be that hard. I've gotten out of worse situations?" She smiled and her eyes brightened. "Now, tell me exactly what the unholy triad said to you."

"I can do better. I have a recording. Why?" Steel said.

"There is a contract, Steel. Either the details go into the Grimvox for permanent storage." She held up her empty palm. "Or they get you to sign something the old proverbial contract with the devil."

"I didn't sign anything." He pulled out his cell phone. "It was a verbal agreement."

"Just as binding. Let's hear it."

Steel played the voice recording. Vivian looked up from his phone screen and a smile twisted her face. "Oh, sweetie, do I have a proposal for you."

❧ 40 ❧

Steel had precious little time to prepare. Margaret showed up less than ten minutes after the call. Cassie and Monty stayed behind after loading the third crate onto the museum truck. "To watch over the other two crates." Monty had said. He was planning on loading the artifacts back into the crates to return to America.

He called Jason and laid out the plan. Birdsong and Merchant left for the six-hour drive to Austin and would meet them at the airport. Monarch joined him on the flight along with Olivia and Steven. They were anxious to get back to the states. Hampton had arranged a transport plane from, of all people, Miller Avionics. Within two hours, all was loaded on the airplane and they sat around an open cargo bay with the crate strapped in the center.

"Here is the memory card." Monarch opened her palm. Steel took the card and tucked it into his shirt pocket. No spider drone peeked out!

"Thank you for taking care of it. I wasn't sure I could trust you." Steel looked away. "I've never really trusted anyone until I met Cephas."

Monarch sat beside him and was very quiet. "I don't blame you, Jonathan. We all have our secret agendas."

Steel glanced at her and then retrieved his iPad Pro from a backpack tucked beneath his seat. He pulled up the address given to him by Hampton on Google Earth. The "house" was a sprawling mansion built on a hillside overlooking a valley north of Austin in the hill country. Only one road led up from the highway to the mansion. One way in and one way out.

"You need to sleep." Vivian said as he turned off his iPad Pro. She sat on the other side of him from Monarch.

"I know." He patted her hand and tried to quell the uneasy emotions she now evoked in him. "Are you comfortable with the plan?"

"Honey child, I've been in worse predicaments."

Steel nodded and the fatigue swept over him like a tidal wave. He breathed a prayer for Josh and closed his eyes. This time, there were no dreams. This time, there were no flashbacks.

☙❦❧

Jason Birdsong and Dr. Merchant met them at the Austin airport, and they loaded the third crate into the back of the truck. Steel glanced at his watch. It was seven o'clock in the evening and the waning full moon filled the darkening dusk. A cold wind poured in from the northwest and clouds were flowing over the distant mountains. A cold front was moving in.

"Dr. Monarch is going to the hotel to get our rooms. Jack, do you have the supplies?"

Merchant nodded. "I gave them to Dr. Monarch and once we get Josh, we'll take him to the hotel where I can check him out. If we have to go to a hospital, I've already contacted an old colleague of mine in the emergency room of a nearby hospital."

"I have a rental car waiting." Monarch said.

"Mom, I want to go with them." Olivia walked over and stood by Steel.

Steel turned to her and took her by the shoulders. "Olivia, we can't afford you having a seizure in a dangerous situation. The best thing you can do is be there when Jack brings Josh back to the hotel room. He'll want to see you. I need a friendly face there when he arrives. I need you to do that for me."

Olivia bit her lip and a tear trickle down her cheek. "I know. I know! I just had to try."

Steel, Birdsong, and Merchant loaded up in the truck and headed away from the airport. Birdsong drove through the winding hills northwest of Austin following the directions from his GPS. Steel was quiet, praying his plan would work. In the back seat Dr. Jack Merchant was humming to himself.

"What are you humming?" Birdsong asked glancing in the rearview mirror.

"Amazing grace. Universally accepted song of grace. We need all the grace we can get." Merchant said quietly.

Steel's gaze was directed at the road and his thoughts were moving just as quickly as the stripes in the center of the highway. He reached beneath his seat and found a metal box. He pulled out the box and placed it in his lap. Birdsong glanced over.

"Jonathan?"

"I knew you would bring it. You were on a private flight from Arizona when you arrived in Shreveport." Steel tapped the box.

"I wish I'd had it on me when Raven showed up." Birdsong said.

Merchant leaned forward from the back seat. "What is it?"

Steel sighed. "For Jason's ankle holster. This lock box holds the lightest semi-automatic pistol going, the Kel-Tec P32. It's a double-action-only pistol with a polymer frame and a 2.68-inch barrel. It holds seven shots and weighs a mere 6.6 ounces." Steel glanced at Birdsong. "Did I remember it correctly?"

Birdsong nodded. "Yes. But I'm not giving you the combination."

Steel's face warmed with anger. "Yes, you are. I'm not going into this without a weapon."

"That goes against everything you've ever told me." Birdsong said.

"This is different. I've gone too far already to protect Josh. If I have to go all the way, I'm willing. Now, Jason, give me the combination."

The air was tense and quiet only interrupted by road noise. "Uh, I hate to disagree with you, Jason, but I'd feel much better if Jonathan had a gun."

Birdsong sighed and recited the combination. "Jonathan, you only use it under extreme conditions. There will be a room full of innocent people."

Steel keyed in the combination. "There are no innocent people, Jason."

⟡⟡⟡

AN HOUR LATER, THEY TOPPED A RISE IN THE ROAD AND AHEAD on the open hillside stretched the expanse around the mansion. Steel gasped as they drew closer. "That's the house in my flashbacks."

"What?" Birdsong said.

"The house in my flashbacks." Steel could hardly speak. "It's my house. The one I grew up in."

Birdsong slowed the truck and they paused at open gates in a long, stretching black wrought iron fence. The huge mansion sat before them illuminated with outside lighting. The moonlight died out as the clouds moved in and rain began to dot the windshield. "Do you want to back off?" Birdsong said.

"No." Steel said hoarsely. "It's all coming together. Everything is coming together."

Birdsong drove along a winding driveway up to the concentric half circle of stairs leading up to the double front door. Gas lights guttered on either side of the doors in the sudden rainy wind.

"Bro, are you okay?" Birdsong said.

Steel glanced at Birdsong. "I don't know. I saw this house in a recent flashback. A very disturbing one. This was my home. And

Hampton is part of my family. He traveled with my grandfather. I'm still trying to digest all of this, and I don't have much time. I have a very bad feeling about this."

The front door opened, and an elderly man appeared in the yellow light from within. He opened an umbrella and shuffled down the stairs. He paused at Jonathan's window. His hair was wispy, and his skin was dotted with age spots. His rheumy eyes were limpid and seemed to float in the meager light.

"Welcome home, Master JJ." He said in a weak voice.

Steel opened the truck door and stepped beneath the umbrella. "You know me?"

"Of course, Master JJ. They are all waiting inside. The servants can bring in the necessities."

"Servants?" Steel glanced at Birdsong.

"We got this. Just go." Birdsong said.

Steel followed the stumbling old man up the stairs and through the front doors. The foyer was foreign to him. He had barely seen it in the flashback. Two sets of winding stairs encircled the huge open foyer to the second floor and beneath the upper balcony an archway opened into a huge living room. The old man led Steel to the left side of the living room and paused before two doors Steel recognized.

"The library?" He said.

"They are assembled inside and waiting for your arrival." The old man said. He still carried the open umbrella. The doors opened and Dr. Hampton smiled at Steel. He wore a three piece suit with a medal pinned to his left pocket. He opened his arms in a welcoming gesture

"Welcome home, my great nephew." Hampton mailed and then glared at the old man. "Hobbs, you fool, close that umbrella and bring us some tea."

"Yes sir." Hobbs fought with the umbrella and clumsily closed it and shuffled off across the living room. Steel felt the cold metal of the pistol in his pocket and resisted the urge to point it at Hampton.

"Enough with your games. Where's Josh?"

Hampton stepped aside and brandished his arm toward the library. "Right here, Mr. Steel."

Steel walked through the doors and his heart raced. The shelves of books surrounded him. The same sofas and chairs dotted the floor. Across the library were the two huge black doors and in front of them was a hospital bed with Josh beneath a blanket. Standing beside the bed was the woman Birdsong had referred to. Nurse Practitioner Faye Morgan had a hand resting on Josh's arm. The look on her face was a mixture of relief and fear.

Steel started to rush across the room and the unholy triad converged between him and Josh. "Not so fast." Shutendoji said.

"I have fulfilled my end of the bargain." Steel said.

Shutendoji wore her white coat over her scrubs, her hands pressed into her pockets. "The dossier?"

Steel took the memory card from his shirt pocket and offered it up in his open palm. "Everything you need to know is on this card. If you take it, my part of this deal with you is done. Correct?"

"If the card checks out, yes." Shutendoji motioned to a nearby "orderly". Steel froze. Dude brought forth a laptop. For a fleeting moment he felt relief. The green scrub clad man took the memory card and placed it in a slot. Dude held the laptop before him. Shutendoji tapped on the keyboard and studied the screen of her laptop.

"It asks for verification." She glanced at Steel.

"So do I." Steel said. "I want to make sure Josh is cured."

Shutendoji glared at him. "His last dose of medication is even now running in. When it finishes, he will be cured."

"Then, you will not object if I wait to make sure you are not lying."

"Not good enough." Shutendoji said.

Steel nodded and walked quickly across the room. Shutendoji actually stepped back, and Steel placed his finger on the exposed edge of the card. Steel looked up into the eyes of Dude and the angel did not change expression. Shutendoji's hungry eyes turned from him to the laptop. She smiled.

"Yes, the data is all here." She said.

Steel grabbed the laptop from Shutendoji and slammed the lid shut. Shutendoji reacted and hissed at Steel. She grabbed at the laptop and her hand touched Steel's bare arm. Blisters formed and Shutendoji screamed in pain. She glared at him. "What is this?"

"Righteous anger." Steel held up his left hand and the glowing blue light pulsed. "I used this to defeat the ninth and eighth demon. Now, we have a bargain. You can have the laptop and the opened dossier contents once Josh is cured and is cleared by my physician."

On cue, the door to the library opened and Dr. Jack Merchant walked in. "That would be me."

Hampton standing by the fireplace rubbed his hands together and giggled. "This is getting most interesting, Mr. Steel."

"Shut up!" Shutendoji massaged her swollen hand and glared at Merchant. "You! You lied to me."

"And you had a very good friend of mine killed in the most heinous way possible." Merchant said. "I am exactly who I said I was. And I will make certain you clear Josh of his ailment before Mr. Steel returns the laptop. And then we will see to it you pay for that crime."

Gumijo put a hand on Shutendoji's shoulder and pulled her back away from them, all the while whispering in the woman's ear in some vile dialect. Gumijo stepped forward.

"Mr. Steel, you made an agreement with us. If you are as 'righteous' as you say, you will keep your end of the bargain. My rod?"

Steel nodded toward the door. "Jason?" He said out loud.

Jason Birdsong pushed the third crate into the room. Shutendoji cursed when she saw him. Birdsong ignored her and pushed the crate right up to Dr. Gumijo. "Yeah, I was there, too, demon sister. So don't even go there." Birdsong said.

"What is this?" Gumijo said.

"You know what this is." Steel said. He handed the laptop to Merchant. "You know exactly what is in the crate." He turned his gaze on Hampton. "I want the box with the stone. I want the virus."

Gumijo glared at him. "You are in no position to demand anything."

Steel leaned close to her, and she pulled back away from his face afraid to touch his skin. "Shall I tell them what else is in the crate?" He whispered.

Gumijo stepped back, shaken and wobbly. She regained her composure. "Hampton, what is this box and stone he is talking about?"

Hampton retrieved a small wooden box from a nearby shelf. He held it delicately in his hands. "Well done, Mr. Steel. I did not know you had it in you."

"The box?" Steel said.

Hampton held out the box toward Steel. "The real Pandora's Box."

"Containing the virus?" Merchant asked.

"Well, sort of. I placed the viral agent in a syringe attached to the, ahem, other box. But the substance in the syringe is also in this box."

"Careful." Merchant said. He handed the laptop back to Steel and fished gloves from his pockets. He took the box and examined it.

"I wouldn't open that if I were you." Hampton said and frowned. "We would all die. Except for Mr. Knight who now has immunity."

Merchant nodded at Birdsong. Birdsong left the room and returned with a gleaming metal box. He opened it and Merchant placed Pandora's box inside and sealed it. "Hazmat safety enclosure. We're safe, Jonathan."

Gumijo whirled on Hampton. "You gave them the virus! What good is the rod, the serpent now?"

"Oh, pish posh!" Hampton shrugged. "I have more of the virus, you fool. Can't you see what this human is doing?" Hampton said. "He's turning you against each other."

"We can now create a vaccine for the virus." Merchant said. "You can do what you want with the artifacts. It means nothing."

"It meant everything!" Gomijo hissed. "Once the virus was released, we would use the artifacts of your religion to forcing people to come to us for the treatment."

"I told you your plan wouldn't work." A voice came from the doorway. Steel whirled and gasped. The Captain stood just inside the open doors. The Crimson Snake stood beside him.

❧ 41 ❧

Hampton fell silent and actually seemed to shrink. Gumijo pushed her colleagues aside and for a moment, her face twisted into the image of the true form of her demon. "You have no reason to be here, old man."

"On the contrary." The Captain paused and stoked his pipe. He tilted his panama hat back away from his face. The red glow of the pipe painted his turquoise eyes in fiery anger. "You have violated the consensus of the Council. Just as your defeated companions did, you have chosen your own path."

"Our plans are of no concern to you." Shutendoji stepped up beside Gumijo. "We have the permission of the Master."

The Captain ignored Steel. Steel was frozen, paralyzed by the sight of the man he had been pursuing. The Captain motioned to Hampton with his pipe stem. "And what would the Master think if he knew you had chosen one of the opposition as your partner?"

All three doctors looked at Hampton, their heads turning in unison. Dr. Hampton chuckled. "I have no idea what he is talking about."

"Your eyes?" The Captain said. "What color are your eyes?"

"White." Steel spoke for the first time. "He's a Vitreomancer, isn't he?"

The Captain looked at his son. "For once, you are correct, son."

"Don't call me son!" Steel said.

"Oh, but you are my son. What father wouldn't help out his son."

"What are you talking about?"

"Max accessed one of my anonymous accounts for the funds you paid to the Geisha. I supplied the funds for the rank and file of the assault team that rescued two women from a certain Overlord?"

Steel opened his mouth to speak and shook his head. "You?"

"It was a waste of money. I could have freed them at any time. You see, I control that organization, son. The Overlord answered to me."

"What? Then why did you allow them to storm the Overlord?" Steel croaked.

"To help you with your mission, son." He gestured around him. "To save Joshua Knight."

"I don't for a moment think you are, in any stretch of the imagination, altruistic." Steel took a step toward his father. "What's in this for you?"

The Captain pointed to the crate. "The other item in the crate. I want it."

Steel glanced back at Gumijo. "What else is in the crate?" Santelmo and Shutendoji said simultaneously.

"That is not of your concern." The Captain said. "What you asked my son to deliver, he has delivered. The other item in the crate was never a part of the original bargain. Your companion wanted it for herself, didn't you Dr. Gomijo?"

Gomijo merely snarled at the Captain. He ignored her. "If anything, it was destined to fall in the hands of Dr. Hampton."

"Yes." Hampton spoke quietly. "It was to have been mine if I had been able to open the crate." He pinched each eye and dropped his contacts on the floor. His white eyes glowed. "And you!" He pointed at Snake. "You have betrayed me!"

Snake smiled and touched her lip. "You shouldn't have hit me. I work for the highest bidder."

Steel stepped between the Captain and the doctors. "Look, I could care less about your demonic politics. I only care about Josh. There is a lot I would demand from you, but I don't have time for this." He paused and said it. "Father."

"No, you don't have that kind of time." The Captain gestured to the crate. "Open it. I paid for that other item when I funded the attack on the Overlord. You owe me. I'll take my item and you can let these three vixens fight over the rest of the contents."

"I wouldn't do that if I were you." Hampton said. "Once he gets his hands on the Ark of the Demon Rose, he will have unparalleled leverage over the Council. And the Vitreomancers."

Shutendoji and Santelmo gasped. "The ark is in the crate?" They said in unison.

"And you hid this from us?" Shutendoji said to Gomijo.

"You were pursuing your own agenda?" Santelmo said.

"No honor among thieves." Merchant said.

"My patience is growing thin." The Captain glared at Steel. "I'll just have to use my little phrase."

Steel pulled the pistol from his back belt and cleared the space between them in five short steps. He pressed the barrel of the pistol between the Captain's eyes. The Crimson Snake started to react and the Captain put out a restraining hand.

"You say one more word and I'll pull the trigger." Steel said. If the Captain spoke a particular phrase, Steel would forget everything around him. Just thinking about the phrase made his head swim with dizziness and nausea gripped his stomach.

The Captain smiled and raised a hand. Steel backed away keeping the pistol pointed at his father's head. The Captain nodded. "My word I will not speak the phrase." His father said quickly.

"I hear the first word of that phrase," Steel fought back sudden nausea, "And, I pull the trigger."

"You are good with a gun. I taught you well."

"One of my few memories of you." Steel's heart raced and his palms were sweaty.

"You realize that if the Captain gets his hands on the ark, he will have complete control of the council. There will utter, complete chaos." Gomijo said.

"And the Dark Council isn't for chaos?" Steel said.

"Of course not." The Captain said quietly. "Each of the twelve demons has a plan approved by the Master. Or, at least in theory. The present three demons seem to have moved on without the Council's consent."

"That seems to be a recurring theme." Steel said.

"The Council is in disarray!" Shutendoji said.

"We banded together to get something accomplished." Gumijo said.

"By using Steel instead of letting him get in the way." Santelmo said.

"And all the while you were in league with a Vitreomancer." The Captain pointed to Hampton.

"We had no idea." Shutendoji said.

"You hired Niles." Steel said over his shoulder. "He was one of them. And speaking of Vitreomancers, I had a flashback." Steel said to the Captain. "You were at the Lion King musical with a woman with white eyes. I believe Dr. Sno."

The three doctors each gasped. Hampton chuckled. "My good man, we are all pursuing our own agendas, it seems." Hampton said.

"And what is your agenda?" The Captain said to Hampton. "I find it hard to believe your interests line up with these three fools since you are from the rival council."

"Prions." Birdsong said. He stepped up beside Steel. "Jack figured it out."

Steel glanced at Merchant and then back at his father. The pistol never wavered. "Jack?"

"The virus was short lived and was just an excuse to get Josh in a vulnerable position." Merchant looked at the three doctors. "He duped all three of you. The infusion did not 'cure' Josh. The infusion is what kept him sick. I isolated a neuropeptide in the fluid that is related to prions. I'm not entirely sure what Hampton was up to, but Josh was basically a living human experiment."

"Well done on your part." Hampton clapped his hands.

"And the virus in the Pandora's box is what made Josh sick?" Steel said without taking his eyes off his father.

"A mutation of the Protovirus." Hampton said dramatically. "Ask your father. He knows all about it."

Steel glanced back at his father. "What is he talking about?"

The Captain shrugged. "I have no idea, son."

Steel shook his head in confusion. "Dr. Monarch said something about a protovirus and her husband. Is it possible somebody in this room paid Raven to kill him?"

The Captain froze and glanced over at Hampton. "I paid for that assassination. It was to erase any connection with me. But you say her husband was working on the protovirus?"

"That's what she said." Steel felt his hand trembling. "What is this protovirus?"

"Only the key to everything." Dr. Hampton said cryptically. "The key to the past. The key to the present. The key to the future. The key to the Elixir of Life."

Steel glanced over at Josh's limp form. "Ms. Morgan, did you know about this?"

Faye shook her head. "Josh and I talked about demons." She glanced at the triplets. "I didn't believe it at first, but I saw something when one of them got angry. I believe now, Mr. Steel. I believe these demons were controlling Josh for some reason. I came here to make sure Josh was not harmed any more than they already have harmed him."

"We knew you were up to something." Gomijo said to Hampton. "That is why we ordered sedation."

"Josh kept mentioning Pandora." Shutendoji said.

"A vile and ancient evil spirit." Santelmo said. "We suspected you were trying to use that spirit on Josh."

"Go stop the infusion, Jack." Steel nodded toward Josh.

"I wouldn't do that." Dr. Shutendoji said.

"Josh will die." Dr. Gumijo said.

"I don't trust anyone in this room but Dr. Merchant and Jason Birdsong." Steel said. He strode over to the crate, keeping his pistol pointed at his father. Steel slammed his palm against the glass panel and the crate hissed open. He motioned to his father. "Over here. Now."

The Captain approached the crate and Steel reached inside the crate. Cold mist obscured the interior. He pulled out the box cradled under one arm and slid it onto a nearby table. "Take the ark and leave. Now! I'm done with you and your trickery. I hope your council self-destructs."

The Captain took the wooden box from the table. "I see the proper combination of box and compass has been restored. Dr. Lawrence?"

"Me. I put them back together. I will regret this someday but if it creates more chaos for your condemned soul and all of your heathen demons, then it will be worth the price."

The Captain cradled the ark. For a moment his features softened, and he frowned. "If it is any comfort, I think you are making the right decision, son." The Captain slid his cold pipe into a shirt pocket and disappeared through the library doors with Snake close behind him.

Steel pointed the pistol at the three doctors and Hampton. "Jack, are you done yet?"

Dr. Merchant hovered over Josh. "I turned it off. So far nothing is happening."

"You actually believe them, don't you?" Hampton said. "The Master is the father of lies. Do you want to take a chance your doctor friend is right? How do you know they didn't give Dr. Merchant the blood and fluid they wanted you to find? After all, if you kill Josh, you've done their work for them, and you will be to blame."

"Shut up!" Steel said.

Dr. Gumijo stood silent and sullen as her two companions glared at her. "You betrayed us." Shutendoji said.

"And you made a deal with Steel for the memory card." Gomijo hissed. She turned to Santelmo. "What deal did you make with Steel? Have you betrayed us also?"

Santelmo stepped away from Gumijo. "I will guarantee Josh will recover completely, Mr. Steel if you have delivered on my request."

Steel glanced at Josh's still body. "Come on Josh. Wake up."

❧ 42 ❧

Josh heard whispers in the dark. He blinked and squinted trying to see who or what was around him. The past few hours or days or whatever they were had passed in alternating waves of slumber and fighting the urge to jump out of the bed. The profound weakness he felt had been the only thing keeping him from doing that. Faye had appeared now and then, and she had given him more sedation for the move to wherever he was now. Sleep had taken him after awakening for only a few moments in a shadowy room that smelled of books and fire and ash. And now, he had no idea if what he was feeling was real or a dream.

"Josh? May I speak to you one last time?" The voice echoed from the darkness. It was Pandora. She was back. He thought he had banished her for good. She was asking to enter his mind. That was a good sign. Josh had an idea of where to take her and now he knew how to control her instead of her controlling him.

"Yes."

Pandora materialized out of the darkness before him, and they stood in a hallway he recognized instantly. She walked down the hallway and Josh followed her.

"Why are we here in your old house?" Pandora said. "Well,

never mind. I'm loving an old memory of yours." Her long, flowing robe changed into a pair of sweatpants and a huge tee shirt. Her hair was now piled on top of her head. "Who do I remind you of?" She paused and glanced over her shoulder.

"My mother. Don't do that. Or I will say his name."

Pandora shrugged. "These clothes are surprisingly comfortable. Let's just leave it at that, shall we?"

The surroundings changed and Josh found himself in his old bedroom. "This is my bedroom. When I was nine." His heart started to race as he saw his lightsaber, his Xbox in the corner, his gaming posters. "Wait a minute! This is not what I had planned. I don't want to be here. What did you do?"

Pandora plopped down on the bed and smiled. "This is your memory, Josh. I didn't bring us here. You did. Why?"

"There was a memory here I wanted to share." He glanced around at the room. The toys and posters were far earlier in his timeline than he had planned. This memory was too early! "No! I don't want this. My father disappeared, and my mother came to tell me." He did NOT want to relive this memory!

"Josh?"

He whirled and suddenly he was shorter and younger. His mother stood in the doorway to his bedroom. Her eyes were red from crying. She wore the same tee shirt and sweatpants as Pandora. "I need to talk to you. Tomorrow, there will be a memorial service for your father. We have to go." She gasped and suppressed a sob. "It will be bad."

"No!" Josh screamed and ran to the corner of his room. He did not want to do this! Somehow, Pandora was moving him deeper into a memory he had not wanted to recall. How? He opened the closet door and closed it behind him, burrowing into the corner of his closet. The memory was so sharp and painful. "I can't do this." He screamed. "I can't do this."

"Son, you can do anything you put your mind to." A man said.

Josh opened his eyes. He was standing next to a table covered with cookies and drinks. The man before him wore an Air Force uniform. He blinked and looked around. He was at his father's memorial service. At least, the reception after the memorial service. The man had been one of his father's friends? The name tag read Miller. He ruffled Josh's hair and turned and walked away into the crowd.

Josh looked around. Most of the people's faces were blurred and their bodies moved in jerky motions. These were memories tainted by the sorrow and despair. Pandora appeared beside him.

"Bad day, huh?" She wore a black dress, and her hair was pulled back in severe tightness.

"Why are you doing this?"

"Honey, I'm not in control." She put a hand on his shoulder, and he realized he was indeed small compared to his current age. He jerked out of her grasp and ran to the corner of the reception room at the church. He hid underneath the table. These memories were so painful! His heart ached and his thinking was blurred by the grief at the loss of his father. He had lost control of this memory! How was he doing this to himself if he was in control? Something was very wrong!

Then he heard the voice. Strikingly familiar! He peeked out from under the corner of the tablecloth. Two people stood alone in the corner not far from him. A man in a dark three-piece suit had his back to Josh but his pale white hairless head was unmistakable. Lucas!

Lucas spoke to someone else. The man facing Lucas had striking exotic features and spoke in a faint accent. Anthony Cobalt! Both of them had been at his father's memorial?

"I have searched far and wide. He is either dead or he has succeeded in disappearing." Lucas said.

"And the children?"

"Also missing." Lucas said.

"I need that genetic material." Cobalt said and sipped a cup of tea.

"We could have taken Knight before now." Lucas said,

glancing over his shoulder. Josh cringed at the sight of his red eyes.

"Knight was too public." Cobalt said. "We could use the son."

"With Knight's disappearance, the security will be too tight." Lucas said.

"He does share his father's genome and we could harvest part of what we need from him." Cobalt said quietly.

"Or we keep searching for a man presumed dead. After all, Knight turned on us and then the children disappear."

Cobalt nodded. "I have useful information that someone at the assault triggered Knight's conscience." Cobalt sipped more hot tea. "It couldn't have been the Captain. He has no conscience."

Lucas leaned closer to Cobalt. "The Captain hired an assault team and one of the members was a man with turquoise eyes."

Cobalt tensed. "Really? Our old friend, perhaps?"

"Certainly not the Captain. Too young. This man was the only surviving member of the assault team. He has also disappeared." Lucas said.

Josh pulled back under the table. When he was younger, this conversation had meant nothing to him. But now, in hindsight, the conversation was chilling. They had suspected his father wasn't dead! And someone with turquoise eyes had been at an assault on the children? Had convinced his father to fake his own death?

"Well, I didn't see that coming."

Josh flinched and he was standing in the hallway of his house next to Pandora. "You! Stop this!"

Pandora shrugged. "It's not me, Josh." She motioned to the hallway. "These are all your memories. These are experiences and memories of things you've heard and seen that, at the time, did not seem important."

"Why are you so interested in my father's memorial?"

"Your father underwent some kind of genetic manipulation, didn't he?" Pandora said.

"I don't know for sure. I met my half-sister during my imprisonment by Cobalt." Josh sighed. "Look, I know my father wasn't perfect. I know he must have cheated on my mother but, looking back, they had a rough time in their marriage. Mom went to California and found out she had multiple sclerosis. I went with her and spent a week at a summer camp for kids. It was only after I got older that Mom told me that my father had an affair, but she forgave him. At the time I had no idea he fathered one of the Nephilim."

"This memory you just had." Pandora pointed behind her at his bedroom as if the memorial was still going on in the room. "What do you think Lucas was talking about when they discussed your genes?"

"I am related to my father." Josh said. "But from Jonathan Steel told me, the children of the Bloodstone were conceived while my father was under the influence of a demon that altered his DNA."

"And you have also been possessed by a demon." Pandora raised an eyebrow. "Right?"

Josh stepped away from her. "What? I haven't gotten anybody pregnant! Wait! Are you suggesting the changes are permanent and not just temporary during the possession?" Josh stepped further back until his back was against the wall. "That makes no sense. Millions of people have been possessed over thousands of years so the world would be full of Nephilim."

"You don't sound much like a teenager, Josh." Pandora said quietly.

"What?"

"You've grown during our time together. You've matured. You've accessed memories long suppressed and they have illuminated much about you and your family lineage. They can tell you much about your future." Her voice had changed in timber and quality. Pandora touched his chest with a finger and the bloodstone appeared on a chain around his neck.

"I know you have your father's bloodstone around your neck.

I know you tried to hide it with a prayer. It is important you understand the power of the bloodstone and the legacy of your father." Pandora said.

"Well done, Pandora." A masculine voice said.

Pandora panicked, glancing around at the shadows in the hallway. "No! You said I could have him! You said I could be free!"

"I lied." The voice continued. "Go back to your urn, Pandora. Your usefulness is at an end."

Pandora put her hands to her head. Her eyes bulged and she opened her mouth to scream but nothing came out! Her image wavered, flickered like an old television set desperately seeking a channel. She flickered out of existence and a man stood before Josh in her place. He was a tall, elderly man with bright turquoise eyes, a chiseled face and a shock of short, white hair.

"Who are you?"

"I am the true spirit to which you have been speaking." He said.

"Then you can go now." Josh said.

"Patience, Joshua Knight. You need to understand that in your initial dream of drowning when you called out for help and reached for a hand, you actually invited me to come into your mind." The man smiled. "It's not what you would call possession. My demon friend can't dwell in your body, but a demon can be invited to, shall we say, eavesdrop."

The man wore a khaki jacket over a white shirt and khaki pants tucked into heavy duty boots. He carried a pith helmet in one hand. "Now you can demand that we go, but before we go, and I will go willingly, you must know more of what is really transpiring." He winked at Josh.

"I don't want to hear another word from you. You have said nothing but lies. And I know who you serve, the father of lies."

"He was right! You were the best choice." The man said to the air around him.

Josh froze. "Who was right?"

"In time, in time." A wicker chair appeared behind the man. He he sat in the chair and crossed his legs and put the helmet on his knee. He snapped his fingers and the hallway disappeared and they were surrounded by a jungle setting. He motioned to a stump.

"Have a seat. So where to begin?" He massaged his mouth and the sound of frogs and birds filled the air. "I don't want to give too much away. It is important that certain facts remain in the dark for you. Let's say it all began with your father."

Josh sat slowly on the stump and his hand closed on the shard of the bloodstone. "My father? He's dead."

"Oh, that is what everyone wanted you to think. But he surprised us all. Clever man." The man shifted in the chair. "You see long before you were born, he was chosen by Lucas, the man in your memory just now."

"The 'pale devil'." Josh said. "Worked with Vivian and the thirteenth demon."

"Let's just say that Lucas is far more than mere flesh and spirit. He is far more than the demonic spirits that inhabit his body for passing on to others. Although now, he is an outcast from his Master. As you have surmised, Lucas had the vision of finding the genetic material that made the Nephilim a possibility. After the affair with the tenth demon, did you read your Bible?"

"Yes. To understand about the Nephilim." Josh said.

"Yes, 'the men of old'. The 'giants in the land'. The 'sons of man' who had children with the daughters of Eve." The man tapped the helmet. "You know the Philistines were descendants of the Nephilim in that the same remnants of demonic powers sired their ancestors after everyone but Noah's family died in the flood. Goliath was a giant. Not quite as powerful as the original Nephilim or the children of the Bloodstone because of the diminished power of these demonic spirits."

The man leaned forward. "Lucas did not know about genes. He predates that knowledge for he is very ancient. But once the knowledge surfaced, he went in search of the genetic material. He took your father to Patagonia. Did you know that?"

"No."

"He brought back samples of the Patagonian giants. Your father was approached by Lucas not because of his knowledge but because of your father's genes. Your father contains certain genetic material that was essential to the success of Lucas' plan. The children of the bloodstone came from thirteen different men. What Lucas never told your father is the other twelve men all perished. Died within weeks of passing on their altered genes to the mothers of the children of the bloodstone." The man grimaced. "Quite gruesome, I should say. Accelerated genetic mutations, cancers, growths unknown to modern medicine. Their deaths were very painful." The man leaned forward and his bright, turquoise eyes gleamed. "And here is the secret only you now know. Your father lived. He survived the procedure because of his own genetic material. Which he passed on to you, my dear boy."

Josh's heart raced. "What kind of genetic material?"

"In time, in time." The man sat back. "You're wondering why Hampton allowed you to undergo all of this."

"He said to force my brain to change. Make me a petri dish."

"Yes, yes, to eliminate the hardwired part of the brain that clings to God. Bring about the goddess, Pandora!" The man waved his hand dismissively. "If that succeeds, icing on the cake but mostly mumbo jumbo." He smiled. "No, the real reason was to force your mind to awaken to new possibilities. Your mind and body, Josh. You have unlimited capacity for a level of intelligence known to only a few people in the history of the world." The man nodded. "Yes, I have to admit that exposure to extra dimensional spirits can do that. How do you think twelve simple men called by the Son changed the world?"

"The Holy Spirit." Josh said.

"Yes, yes! Now imagine what prolonged indwelling of any kind of spirit would do to a man."

"Besides lead him to death? Bro, your kind kills the host before the host even knows what is happening."

The man frowned. "Humans are fragile, I'll grant you that. The corrosive power of demonic possession is dangerous and ultimately deadly. But if a man could live long enough. Ah, that is the reason the flood occurred. Did you know that? People lived for hundreds of years and the evil of men manifested itself exponentially. Long lives breed great evil, Josh! Man's life span was limited to one hundred and twenty years! Why? So that if demonic possession occurred over a long period of time, the body would perish more quickly. Let's face it. History has shown that men who give themselves completely to the evil of the Master soon burn out and die more quickly!" He shook his head and chuckled. "Demonic inspired vices are quite deadly."

The man sat forward and winked at Josh. "Now, if a man had certain genetically determined resistance to those corrosive effects imagine how useful would that be to the forces of evil? Neuroplasticity, remember? Epigenetics! There could come a day when demons and humans could coexist without damage to the human body. This was the true goal of Hampton's experiments."

The man frowned. "Although, this fact was hidden from him. The unholy triad wanted a viral agent that could inflict greater harm on humans than any previous epidemic and then they would hold up the serpent as a symbol of healing posing as angels of the Creator. All would bow before them. At least that was their plan. Along with the other things."

The man tapped a finger on his chin. "And, Hampton, bless his heart, truly believes the spirit of Pandora lives in his stone. He truly wishes to see the ascendance of the Goddess and he would be her new Messiah. He has always been far too ambitious to see the long game."

"Why are you telling all of this?"

"You need to know that I and my demonic partner have had a very long time to think and plan all of this. We have ascended beyond the petty battles of the Council of Darkness or the

Vitreomancers. We have had a very long view of mankind and we are very patient. I am not like Pandora's spirit. She is a manifestation of the Elixir of Life passed down for thousands of years and is now in the possession of Hampton."

"What is the Elixir of Life?"

"DNA, viral agents, biochemical soup kept alive by my spirit, protected from decay as through the centuries knowledge and genetic material is incorporated into the fluid. Hampton thinks this Elixir of Life will grant immortality. It is merely a repository of arcane knowledge, a biological version of the Grimvox."

"The what?"

"Ask your 'Daddy' about his palm. He'll tell you all about it." The man put his feet down and leaned forward, playing with the pith helmet. "Hampton is deceived. His Elixir of Life is actually the Elixir of Lies, my boy."

"So, you're in the Elixir?"

"Part of me. However, my human part is very much alive hidden away from the prying eyes of man." The man stood up. "There is a spiritual battle coming and you and the man known as Jonathan Steel will be at the epicenter. What you have been through so far is nothing compared to what is coming. You will lose heart. You will be discouraged. You will possibly lose your faith. I tell you all of this because you are so important to my cause and you must endure to the end."

"I will endure to the end, but I will never denounce my Savior." Josh stood up and walked slowly, haltingly toward the man. "My God and my Savior have gotten me through this ordeal. Bro, you may have messed in your pants with this one. Revealing to me what is going on was not wise. I will never renounce my faith. I will never walk away from Jonathan Steel. And I will never serve you or Satan."

The man put his helmet on his head and tapped it. "Excellent! My goal has been achieved. You are now prepared to deal with any type of demonic influence. After all, to prepare you for any eventuality was one of the most important reasons I have

BRUCE HENNIGAN

paid you these visits." His turquoise eyes glowed with mischief. "You see, there are many demonic factions in this universe. As long as you are prepared for the faction that is coming for you, I can breathe easier. After all, the enemy of my enemy is my friend." He disappeared and Josh opened his eyes.

43

"Jonathan? What are you doing?" Josh sat weakly on the side of his hospital bed steadied by Dr. Merchant. Merchant was removing the i.v. lines. "Why do you have a gun?"

Steel gasped as Josh sat up in the bed. His eyes watered and he swallowed hard to repress the emotion that threatened to engulf him. "I'm getting you out of here." Steel said.

"With a gun? What is wrong with you, dude? You hate guns." Josh said weakly. He looked around the room and blinked to clear obvious confusion from his mind. "What is going on?"

"I'm doing what I have to do." Steel motioned toward the door with his head. "Jack, get him out of here. Now, please." He had to process his thoughts without this troublesome emotion!

Josh slid unsteadily out of the bed in his hospital gown. He had lost weight since Steel had seen him last. Merchant put Josh's arm over his shoulder and Faye took up the other side. "Just a minute. I'm not going anywhere, bro, until you put the gun away."

Steel felt the old rage boil up within him. "Josh, I'm not going to tell you again. Get out of here! Now!"

Josh pulled gently out of Merchant's and Faye's grasp. He

walked unsteadily across the room and stood in front of the pistol. "What are you going to do if I don't? Shoot me?"

Steel drew a deep breath. He wanted to drop the gun and hug Josh! "Josh, I have unfinished business here. Please. You have to you trust me. Please." He said through trembling lips.

Josh blinked a few times and looked around the room."Hey, bro, we need to talk about these demons. I've learned some things while I was under. Okay! You don't have all the facts. Besides," Josh pointed at the gun. "This isn't you." Josh said quietly.

"You don't know that."

Josh closed his eyes and wobbled a bit. He put his hands up and opened his eyes. "There is more going on here than you know, Jonathan. We need to get out of here and talk."

Steel shook his head. "Josh, we will talk. Now that you're okay. But there is something else that has to be done before this is over. Trust me." Steel tried to look Josh in the eyes, but he kept shifting his gaze back to Hampton and the triplets. "Jack, can you help me with Josh?"

"Josh, let's get you out of this room." Merchant moved up beside Josh. "I'm Dr. Merchant, a friend of your daddy."

Josh flinched at the word and looked at Merchant. "I remember you. You were there with Jason."

"Yes. Jason is right over there. He will be here with Jonathan. We can explain every thing but we need to trust Jonathan to work this out." Merchant put a hand on Josh to stabilize him. "Hey, Josh, I was the doctor who did your spinal tap. I've been her from the start. You are my patient, okay? I will take care of you. I promise. And I always keep my promises."

Faye moved up on his other side and put one of his arms around her shoulders. "He's telling the truth, Josh. It's best we get you out of here so Dr. Merchant can make sure there is no residual problems from what you've been through. You need to let this play out." She said.

Josh nodded and glanced across the room at Dude. He

nodded. "Jonathan, I hope you know what you're doing and who you are doing this for! Let's go." With Merchant and Faye at his sides, he hobbled through the double doors.

"Jason, it's your turn. Take care of Josh." Steel said as his anger cooled, and he fought for control. Josh was safe. That was all that mattered. Whatever happened now no longer mattered to him.

Birdsong had taken the laptop from Merchant, and he handed it back to Steel who put it under his free arm. "I hope you know what you're doing." He said and left the room.

Santelmo's face lit up with a small smile. "Well, looks like we got more out of this than we bargained for. Your soul is truly tainted."

"Yes, the real Jonathan Steel emerges." Gumijo stepped up beside Santelmo. "Ruthless, cold killer."

"I told you once he agreed to help us, we could bring out the worst in him." Shutendoji joined her sisters.

Dr. Hampton paced behind them. "Interesting. I do believe, Mr. Steel, this entire affair was far more than just about acquiring the dossier and the rod and serpent of Moses. It was about you. The triplets wanted to resurrect the true you. I believe your memories confirm what we have long suspected." Hampton paused beside Dr. Shutendoji, his white eyes gleaming. "I may have betrayed these three demons, but we have a common enemy: you. And the best way to defeat an enemy of your caliber is from the inside out. You have had flashbacks, yes?"

Steel tried to control the shaking in his hand. He blinked, fighting for control. He desperately wanted to pull the trigger, to kill all four of the things before him. Almost, the old voice from the journal returned, urging him on, filling him with red, hot hate.

"Who did you remember killing, Steel? Was it some deserving criminal? Or was it someone close to home?" Hampton said. He crossed slowly to a shelf. "Allow me one indulgence, if you will." Steel tracked his movements with the gun and stepped closer to the crate to keep all four of them in the range of his pistol.

"Move slowly."

Hampton took something from the bookshelf and held it up. "Your grandfather's photo album and journal. I returned it to you so long ago and lost track of it. When I returned the other day, I found it here tucked away with the rest of the books." He held it out. "I offer it to you as a peace offering."

For a second, Steel heard voices echo and he closed his eyes in confusion. He opened his eyes and gazed at the journal. How he longed for it! How he wanted to hold it! "No! I don't want it. Put it away! It is no peace offering! It is only pain and suffering and voices in my head." Steel said.

Santelmo raised her arms. "Stop, Hampton. We can toy with him later. Right now, I only wanted him to kill one person. Have you fulfilled my demands, Steel?"

Steel fought for control, and he was back in Numinocity facing the eighth demon. The difference between defeat and victory had been the armor. Yes, the full armor of God.

❦

Steel glanced back at the eighth demon. It moved toward him, and its hands dropped the implements of royalty and they filled with darts, knives, spears. It began to hurl them at Steel. Steel hopped up onto the end of one of the slabs and moved around Thakkar's body to the end opposite the direction of his friends. The shield deflected each of the implements. The eighth demon now had his back to his friends. Good, it was distracted.

"I'll finish up your friends when I finish with you. What is this armor you have constructed with your imagination?" The eighth demon's voice thundered.

Steel held up the shield. "This armor did not come from a computer program. Nor did it come from my imagination. It came from the Word of God." He thrust the gleaming blue sword into the air, and bright, blue light shot outward in a circle. A voice echoed from the heavens, shattering the monoliths and cracking open the ground.

" Humble yourselves, therefore, under the mighty hand of God so that at the proper time, he may exalt you, casting all your anxieties on him, because he cares for you. Be sober-minded; be watchful. Your adversary, the devil, prowls around like a roaring lion, seeking someone to devour. Resist him, firm in your faith, knowing that the same kinds of suffering are being experienced by your brotherhood throughout the world. 1 Peter 5:6-9."

The eighth demon actually looked stunned, and his lionlike face filled with fear. "What is this?"

"Your end." Steel said.

๑๕๛

I T WAS TIME TO END THIS! H E RECITED THE VERSES UNDER HIS breath, and he felt the calm, the peace, the control come over him. He looked over at Dude standing quietly in the corner of the room. He had almost forgotten about Dude. He had almost forgotten about God!

"I believe you asked me to take care of Vivian Darbonne. What were your exact words?" Steel said with growing confidence. He took his phone out of his pocket with his other hand and played the voice recording.

"Vivian Darbonne, Mr. Steel. She is a thorn in my side. I want her neutralized. She hasn't been seen since the disappearance of number eight. We believe she is planning something heinous to take apart the Council. You will find her, and you will take her out of the equation. Do you understand?"

Steel said. "You mean, eliminate her? I am not an assassin."

Santelmo's voice. "I wouldn't be so sure of that, Mr. Steel. We do not want Vivian to return to the Council, Mr. Steel. She has special status with our master so only you can deal with her. It must seem as if you are the avenging angel, if you will. And, hurry, Mr. Steel. Josh is growing weaker by the hour."

STEEL ENDED THE VOICE RECORDING. HE TURNED AND pointed the pistol at the crate. "I have delivered. Inside the crate." Santelmo glanced at him skeptically and Steel gestured with the pistol at the other two. "Are you two going to trust this one? Each one of you have betrayed the other. I suggest all three of you confirm I have delivered on my promise."

Hampton glanced once at Steel. "I take it I am not included in this conjoining?"

Santelmo hissed at him in some unknown demonic language. She smiled. "Vitreomancers are inferior. We will deal with your betrayal in a moment."

Dr. Hampton moved toward the two great doors of the library with the journal under his arm. Steel motioned with the pistol. "Birdsong is right outside. Don't get any ideas about leaving just yet. The fun is just beginning."

Hampton's white eyes gleamed as he blinked and nodded. "Of course."

"Number Five? What will it be? Go it alone or allow your sisters to confirm you, alone, have not betrayed them?" Steel said.

Santelmo stiffened and nodded quickly. "Very well. All three of us will confirm Vivian is dead. I am hoping what we will see in the crate is her body."

"Or, better, just her head." Gomijo smiled and the teeth of a fox appeared as she licked her lips.

Shutendoji closed her eyes and moaned with pleasure. "Finally, Vivian Darbonne is gone, and we will rejoice." Then she glared at Steel. "And then you will give me the laptop and Gomijo will take the artifacts?"

"Yes." Steel said. He lowered the pistol. "Go ahead. Enjoy yourselves."

The triplets approached the crate in unison. They paused and all three heads turned down toward the crate.

"All I see is mist and fog." Gomijo said.

"Where is Vivian?" Santelmo said.

"I had to keep her body cool." Steel said. "Bend over and look deeper. Wave the fog away."

What happened next was exactly what Steel had hoped all three of the triplets would do. Once again moving as one, they each put a hand deep into the crate to wave away the mist. A green light lit up the interior of the crate and all three of their faces twisted in pain. The screech that came forward from their mouths rattled the bookshelves and on some of the shelves, vases shattered.

Vivian Darbonne sat up from the depths of the crate, both hands closed around all three of the triplets' hands, two in one and one in the other. "Hello sweeties!" She said. "Cat got your tongue? Or is it the Holy Spirit?" On each of the triplets' arms, the skin began to bubble, and all three demons screamed in agony. Shutendoji and Gumijo tried to pull their hands from Vivian's right hand. Santelmo tried to pull away from her left.

"No, my pretties. I am not dead although I deserve to be. No, I serve another Master. Since I now serve the one and true Prince of Peace and not the Prince of Darkness, Jonathan Steel has indeed fulfilled his contract with you. He made sure I would never return to the Council. Just as you requested. Now as to my new Master, He has died for my sins and in his name, the name of Jesus Christ, I commend all three of you to Tartarus. May you burn in hell, sisters!"

"I'll take it from here." Dude stepped forward from his corner. His face glowed with a holy white fire, and he grew in stature. His green scrubs burst away from him and revealed a white tunic upon which sat a golden breastplate. His feet were shod with sandals of gold and jewels. His hair was long and golden white, and a sword and shield appeared in his hands. "I don't often get the opportunity to minister to humans." His voice was strong and made the very base of Steel's skull vibrate. "You would know me as Michael, the archangel and I am looking forward to escorting these three to Tartarus."

What happened next would always be a blur to Jonathan Steel in the years that followed. He would try and remember the battle that took place between three of Satan's most powerful demons and the archangel Michael. The battle took place across two space continuums and the blurring of the margins failed to register on Steel's perceptions. He recalled each demon emerging from their human hosts: Shutendoji as the giant multi-horned, multi-eyed beast, Gomijo as a ravenous multi-tailed fox with huge fangs, and Santelmo as a towering humanoid made of flame and lava. The library reverberated with the clash of their bodies with Michael's shield. His sword flashed with blue lightning and each time it touched the demons' flesh, words sprang into the air from the verses of the Bible. The words were in their original language, but Steel understood them as if an inner voice translated them into thoughts he could understand. The Holy Spirit was truly living inside of him in spite of his betrayal of all he had done that God would never have approved.

Books flew off of shelves! Vases and glass cases shattered. Steel tossed himself over into the crate with Vivian and they both hovered in the cool mist as the lightning and shadow battled around them. But in the end, the winner was inevitable as God's righteousness will always triumph over the defeated demons whose master is already beaten and truly powerless. Steel heard the demons screech and light filled the room. He huddled against Vivian, eyes closed as tightly as possible. He felt her arms wrap around his chest and her faced pressed against his back. He still gripped the pistol and it seemed forever before the light faded and the room grew silent.

Steel sat up and peered over the edge of the crate. The room was back to its original condition. All books sat in the bookshelves and the cases and vases were intact. The only difference was the absence of Nigel Hampton. The huge black doors were open just a crack and for a second, he saw Hampton's face as he peered out.

"Sorry to have to leave you like this, my good boy, but well done! The Vitreomancers thank you." The doors slammed shut even as Steel hopped out of the crate and ran across the room. He bounced against the closed doors and pounded on them in frustration. He felt a hand on his shoulder and turned to find Jason Birdsong behind him.

"Bro, let it go. We're done. We gotta get Josh out of here to the hotel room."

Steel looked up into the eyes of his partner, his most recent joy at the disappearance of the demons vanishing with the escape of Nigel Hampton, his long-lost great uncle and the journal. And he had been face to face with his father. Someone took the pistol from his hand.

"I'll take this."

Steel looked up into the face of FBI Special Agent Franklin Ross. "Ross? What are you doing here?"

Ross tucked the pistol into his black overcoat. "Jason called me. Thought you might need some help, but I only just got here. Couldn't get through the library doors when we heard all the commotion and then silence. That's when the doors opened. By themselves! Just opened! I have a dozen agents outside securing the perimeter." He turned and surveyed the room. The human triplets were unconscious on the floor.

"Those the doctors, Jason?" He asked.

"Yes, sir."

Ross snapped his fingers and two agents appeared through the library doors. "Cuff them and take them to the van. There are three arrest warrants out for them." He glanced at Steel. "Insurance fraud for one. I'm sure there are other charges once we finish our raid on the clinic. Dr. Merchant tipped us off to that place. Turns out most of the patients were part of an assassination ring. They needed a place to heal after their assignments. We'll shut it down for good."

Vivian appeared at Steel's side. "The air tanks worked flawlessly, Jonathan. So, what about me?"

Ross frowned and looked like he was gargling broken glass. He motioned the two agents to leave. "Jason, help them carry the bodies to the van, will you?"

Birdsong nodded. Once they were out of the library only Steel and Vivian remained with Ross. He pulled out a cigarette, lit it up and blew a cloud of smoke into the library. "I'm afraid we will have to lock down this entire mansion, Jonathan. I know you want to check it out. Jason said you thought this was your house?"

"Yes. What about Vivian?" Steel said.

"Seems Interpol has worked out a deal for her."

"What kind of deal?" Vivian said.

Ross paced around the room and gripped a statue of Prometheus with a white knuckled grip. "Mind if I hurl this across the room?"

"What?"

Ross threw the statue against the wall, and it broke into a dozen pieces. Vivian flinched at Steel's side. "I'm not happy about this. Not at all." He turned his glare on Vivian, the cigarette bobbing in his lips as he spoke.

"You deserve to be buried under the jail. At best, you should spill your guts about every illegal deal you've ever pulled and the accomplices who helped you." He paced back and forth, nostrils smoking like a dragon. "But no! This Max pulls a few strings and demands you be put under her authority. Something about a dossier? The same one, I presume that you were looking for?" He pointed at Steel. "The dossier that contains every assassination performed by Raven?"

Steel glanced at Vivian and back at Ross. "What are you talking about?"

"Max's deal. She is going to track down every family, every

survivor and take blood money to repay them for the loss of their," He almost gagged, "Loved one!"

Vivian put a hand to her mouth. "What?"

"No prison for you. But at least I get the pleasure of knowing that you will have to look into the faces of those who suffered from your kind and their evil deeds." Ross took the cigarette from his mouth and ran a hand through his hair. "I guess that will be punishment enough. And I want you to hurry. The dossier is promised to me when you are done." Ross dropped the cigarette butt into a vase. He pulled out a pair of handcuffs. "I do get the pleasure of cuffing you."

"Wait!" Steel said. "I need a moment with Vivian. Please."

Ross rolled his eyes. "Really?"

"Ross, give us a minute. Please." He said.

Ross huffed and started toward the library doors. "Five minutes. Don't get any ideas. My agents have the house," He paused with hands on the library doors as he glanced around the huge room, "Mostly surrounded." He closed the door.

Steel looked at Vivian. "What now?"

Vivian took both of his hands. She looked into his eyes. "Thank you, Jonathan for not giving up on me. Thank you, Jonathan Steel for taking my pain. I must do this. It is far too small a price to pay for the pain I have caused."

Steel felt his heart twist in agony. Why? He had only loved two women he could remember, Claire and April. Why did he feel this way about Vivian? "I don't know how I feel."

Vivian put a finger on his lips. "Honey child, I don't deserve you. You have a lot to process. This is your house? The memories will start coming back. Hampton is your great uncle? Where did he go? What is behind those doors? That knowledge has to cause you some pain. Josh was a lab experiment? There's no telling what he will go through getting over this. You have a full plate and more. Max will be an unforgiving warden. I will probably wish for jail after she gets through with me."

She leaned toward him and pressed her lips against his. She

pulled back and looked into his eyes. "I love you, Jonathan Steel. I always have and I always will. But you have more important tasks ahead of you. Hampton still has the virus. Your father has the Ark of the Demon Rose. There are four more demons on the council and I will say you ain't seen nothing yet! You must focus all of your strength and all of your efforts, and all of your God given goodness on the days ahead. Our world will need it. I know. I once tried to take over that world. And I am just one of many."

Vivian nodded and crossed to the library doors. She paused at the door. "Oh, by the way, there is a false floor in that crate. Dr. Lawrence has left something under the false floor." She smiled and left the library leaving Steel alone with his past and his thoughts and his confusing emotions.

Steel walked over to the black doors and leaned up against the metal. He pressed his ear to the warm surface. He thought he heard voices, maybe laughter? Or was it sobbing? He tried to open the doors and they did not move. He turned back to the crate. He made his way across the library and bent over the edge of the crate. A small air tank sat in the corner along with the other items he had promised to three demons who were now experiencing eternal punishment. He rapped his hand on the bottom. A hollow echo answered.

"Jonathan?"

Steel stood up and turned back to the library doors. Josh stood there with a blanket wrapped around his shoulders. "Is it over?"

Steel's heart swelled and an emotion he had felt very seldom in his life overtook him. He ran across the library to his son. He swept him up in his arms and hugged him tight. "No, it isn't. But we will face whatever comes together."

❦ 44 ❦

The enticing fragrance of roast turkey drifted down the stairs and filled the basement. Steel sat at Cephas' desk and studied the tiny flecks of dark blue imbedded in the skin of his palm. What was he? How was he able to summon holy light from his palms? Most importantly, was he a killer? The pistol had felt all too comfortable in his other hand!

"Dude, aren't you hungry?"

Steel glanced over his shoulder. Josh and Olivia came down the stairs hand in hand.

Steel smiled. "Well, what is this?"

Josh's face reddened and he cleared his throat. "I'm not letting her go. For a while."

Olivia smiled and leaned into his shoulder. "And I like it. Josh is going to tell me all about what it means to be a Christian."

Steel motioned to the two chairs at Cephas's desk. "Have a seat. Tell me all about it."

Olivia sat and glanced once at Josh. "When we first met, I told Josh how mad I was for God allowing me to have seizures. But I can't blame God anymore. God didn't pull that trigger. Raven did. And really, whoever hired her is to blame."

Steel blanched. His own father had hired Raven to pull that trigger. "I'm sorry, Olivia."

Olivia patted his hand. "I'm making peace with it. I just don't understand why I can now see demons."

Steel nodded and shuffled through the folders on Cephas' desk. "I asked Monty about that and he sent me this article. I printed it out so you could read it." He picked up a stapled sheath of papers and handed it to her.

"It would have been easier to text it to me." She said and then she smiled. "No, that was nice, Mr. Steel."

"Jonathan. Call me Jonathan. I read it and there are many people who have the gift to see demons. And angels. Don't know why. But the article does mention that eventually you will be able to control that ability. You won't see them unless you really want to."

"Besides you wouldn't be able to see them if you weren't on the right side." Josh said.

Olivia took the folder and nodded. "Thank you again for rescuing Vivian and me."

Steel looked away. "Your mother approached me and asked me to help. I hate to admit it at the time that I was focused on finding Vivian." He looked back at Olivia. "But God changed my mind. I couldn't let anything happen to you."

"We have moved back into our house here in Shreveport for now. Steven wants to finish his senior year and I have an apology for a band of bad girls at school." Olivia said.

"Yeah, I need to check on Buck. I heard he's home and recovering from the gunshot wound." Josh said.

Olivia drew a deep breath. "Jonathan, when we were waiting at the van, I saw a group of demons leaving the Overlord's place. One of them said something about Lucas."

"Lucas is dead." Steel said.

"That's just it. They said his soul came back into his body. They said he was cursed and could not die."

Steel tensed. "What?"

"I don't think they were making it up. They had no idea I could see or hear them."

Steel stood up and paced across the room. "I hope this isn't true. Lucas can't die? What is he?"

"I don't know, Dad." Josh said.

Steel whirled. "Dad, huh?" He smiled. "I like the sound of that. It will take some getting used to."

Josh fidgeted nervously and then leaned over toward Olivia. "Olivia, I really need to talk to Jonathan alone. Is that okay?"

"Sure, babe." Olivia said. She stood up. "I'm looking forward to Thanksgiving. My mother and brother and I have never celebrated that holiday even in the states. But now that I have so much to be thankful for," She squeezed Josh's shoulder. "I'm looking forward to it." She leaned over and kissed Josh on the lips and climbed up the stairs.

"Babe?" Steel said.

Josh looked back at Steel with a dreamy expression on his face. He blinked a few times and then cleared his throat. "Dude, that was awesome!"

"I'm happy for you, Josh." Steel sat back at the desk. "I know if anyone should be hungry, it should be you. What is so important we need to talk about?"

"First, I wanted to check on you. I'm feeling stronger. Even gained some of my weight back but you're down here hiding in the basement. Why?"

"I need to think. Josh, I compromised myself. I made deals with demons."

"Yeah, to save me. Bro, they had you by the spiritual, well, you know. Thanks for saving me. I know it cost you a lot. But you are a good person, Jonathan."

Steel looked up at Josh. "Am I? I was willing to kill to save you."

"Sort of like when Dr. Monarch was willing to do that surgery on you to help her family?"

Steel tensed and glared at Josh. "It's not the same thing."

"Like her accessing the memory card when you asked her not to because she wanted to know who hired Raven to kill her husband?" Josh said.

Steel stood up, his fists clenched. "Josh, it's not the same thing!"

Josh stood up and wobbled a bit. "Jonathan. Dad! I get it. You did what you did because you cared about me. You said it. You told me."

"Told you what?" Steel tried to slow his breathing.

"Told me that you loved me, bro!" Josh blurted out. "I know that was hard for you. I mean, after all, your father didn't set much of an example."

Steel sighed and released his fists. He slumped and looked down at his feet. "I did say that."

"So, is it true?" Josh stepped closer to him.

Steel looked up and felt moisture in his eyes. "I couldn't lose you, Josh."

"I know. You did what you had to. I understand. Dude, so does God." Josh put his arms around Steel's chest and leaned into him. "We both understand. And I thank you for that. I know it cost you."

Steel relaxed and put his arms around Josh. "I don't know how to do this."

"You're doing just fine."

Steel slowly pushed him back. "And what was that nonsense about letting yourself die to protect me?"

Josh smiled and slumped into his chair. "Good one, bro. I was willing to die if those devil sisters had gotten what they wanted. You know, I had a battle to fight too." Josh said. "If I hadn't gone down in the basement to see Dr. Hampton open Uncle Cephas' crates, I would never have touched that Pandora's box."

"That wasn't your fault."

"Yours either." Josh said. "Man, these things just seem to happen to us. And it turned out good. Olivia is safe. Vivian is a Christian now. Who would have thought that?"

"God." Steel said.

"Yeah, and if God can forgive her for all she has done, I think he can overlook your little dalliances with evil. Bro, it's okay. We made it." Josh reached out and tapped Steel's palm. "So, what's up with your super palm here?"

Steel looked at his left hand. The pale blue light pulsed. He closed his palm. "I don't know. It comes and goes." Steel sat back down and felt the pain throb in his palm. "Listen, Josh, I had a flashback to when I was a teenager. I did some violent things. Maybe. I wasn't sure from the flashback. I was having blackouts back then." Steel swallowed hard. "I might have multiple personalities." Steel turned his gaze on Josh. "I think we need to contact Judge Bolton and find you a new family."

Josh's mouth fell open and he sat back. "No way, dude! You're crazy. I'm not staying with anyone but you."

"You're not safe with me." Steel said.

"Bro, look at me. I was diagnosed with a horrible virus that turned out to be a hoax. I was never really in any danger. You forget something, Jonathan. I am a child of God. The Lord is watching over me. They couldn't touch me. They couldn't really infect me. I was safe all along. You need to remember that, dude. In the future, God's got our backs. Okay? So, no, I'm not going anywhere. I'm staying here with you. Believe it or not, I'm safer with you than anywhere out there. No matter which personality you are."

Steel glared at him.

"Jonathan, you have only personality. Jonathan Steel." Josh said. "If anything is consistent in this universe it's you. Unlike me!" Josh looked away. "Hampton had me fooled the whole time. Talked about taking over my mind. But I learned something."

Josh stood up and leaned across the desk. "Hey, and remember this. Satan is the father of lies. You bought into their lies. You let them deceive you out of love for me. I get it. That's a father's love, dude. You are my new father whether you like it or not and I'm not going away!"

Steel nodded pushing the thoughts of his mental state far into the back of his mind. "Fine, so tell me more about what happened to you in that clinic."

"Hampton's Pandora Stone housed some kind of demon. I accidentally invited it in, and it tried to take over and remake my mind." Josh rubbed his temples. "Pandora was in my head. But I was able to turn the tables on her just like you did on the unholy triad. I used my good memories of mother and Uncle Cephas to my advantage." He smiled. "Jonathan, I made peace with my mother. At least my memory of her."

Steel looked away. "I'm glad, Josh." His heart ached at the memory of the loss of Claire Knight. And, then a deeper feeling surfaced. Could he ever make peace with his father?

"Bro, it actually made me a better person. More confident. More focused. More mature even. And that is what he told me would happen." Josh said.

"He? You mean Hampton?" Steel looked back at Josh.

Josh shook his head. "No, this other guy. Turns out he was pretending to be Pandora. He fooled me and Hampton."

"A new demon?"

Josh wore a puzzled look. "Bro, that is what is so strange. He claimed he and his demon had been working together for a very long time and that his human spirit was the one talking to me at the end after the demon pretended to be Pandora. He said I was special and that some kind of plan was coming together."

"Who was he?"

Josh's eyes widened and he glanced at Steel. "He was an old dude with turquoise eyes like yours."

Steel froze. "What?" His mind went back to the display in Hampton's museum. There couldn't be a relationship! The sign said that man had lived in 1832. "That makes me very nervous, Josh. Between this man in your head and my father, things are happening we have no knowledge of, much less control of."

"This Elixir of Life that Hampton claimed he had. That dude in my head said it was really the Elixir of Lies!" Josh said.

Steel nodded. "I said the same thing to Ishido. We can't believe anything we learn from these creatures."

"Well, there are only four more demons. We have that to be thankful for. And you said your father took the Ark of the Demon Rose to dismantle the Council of Darkness. Bro, the two of you may be on the same side."

Steel shook his head. "Don't forget the Vitreomancers. There are two factions involved in this mess, Josh. I don't want either one of them to come out on top."

Josh put a hand on Jonathan's shoulder. "Dude, today let's forget about demons and go eat. I'm hungry. Our family is waiting."

Steel nodded. Our family. That sounded good. He knew that upstairs Dr. Elizabeth Washington, Jason Birdsong, Faye Morgan, Dr. Jack Merchant and his fiancée Pam along with Dr. Monarch, Steven and Olivia were waiting. Cassie and Monty would join them by FaceTime and have an evening meal in London. A huge extended family of very good, dedicated people. Some of them had committed very bad deeds in the past. But, for today he would accept that they were forgiven and for that he was thankful.

As Josh walked ahead of him up the stairs, Steel glanced once more at his palm, and it gleamed with light for just a second. He looked at his other empty hand that had recently brandished a pistol.

"I don't know what I am, but I know I'm not a killer." His words echoed hollowly in his ears.

❧ 45 ❧

Jonathan Steel had never carved a turkey in his life. At least that he could remember. The dining room table was resplendent with food. Dr. Elizabeth Washington had returned for her Thanksgiving break and promised to spend Thursday with her "extended" family before returning to her home to spend Saturday with her biological family.

Steel held the knives in front of him and tried not to shake. "Thanks for coming, Mama Liz." He said.

Liz sat next to Joshua Knight. Her salt and pepper hair was closely cropped to her face. She smiled at Steel and nodded. "It's good to be home. Every time I leave, something bad happens. But for today, we will be thankful for each other and our new family members."

Across the table sat Jason Birdsong and by his side was Faye Morgan. "We all agreed we need to be here today." Jason said. "For Josh. And you, of course."

"I'll be seeing my huge family tomorrow." Faye said. She wore an orange and brown blouse and she had put a cluster of red leaves in her hair. "I wasn't going to pass up this opportunity to watch Josh eat real food!"

Dr. Monarch and Steven sat next to her. Josh and Olivia sat

together. At the end of the table, a laptop screen revealed the image of Cassie and Monty. "We just wish we could be there in person." She said.

"But we have each other." Monty blurted out and then turned red. "You know what I mean."

Steel cleared his throat and placed the knives back on the table. "Before I attempt to cut the bird, I want to say something."

Steel looked around the room at the most important people in his life. "It has been rough the past few months. We've been through a lot. I was beginning to wonder why God called me into this odd profession. But God also showed me I could turn something evil into something he could use for good. All good things work out for good for those who love the Lord." He paused as he lost his voice. He pushed back the emotion. "I've learned a lot about God and about myself. Mostly, I've learned that God's ways are not our ways. It is because God sees the big picture. He has written the story and all we have to do is play our part in that story. We're not puppets. We are fully fulfilled human beings made in God's image who are helping to write that story by becoming the person God designed us to be. And in that becoming, we find peace and true joy."

"Amen!" Liz said.

"Not yet, Mama Liz." Steel put up a hand. "I just wanted everyone here to know I appreciate you. I thank you." His voice broke. "And I love you."

He sat back in his chair as they all clapped and then his phone rang. He snared from his pocket. The caller I.D. said Ruth Martinez. He smiled. "It's Ruth Martinez! I hope she is talking to me again." He answered the call and put Ruth on speaker. "Ruth! Happy Thanksgiving!"

"Jonathan, listen up. They are coming for you. Right now. They are coming because of the murder. I wasn't supposed to tell you, but I needed to warn you."

"Murder?" Steel stood up. The room fell silent, and the call ended. His mind whirled with memories and images. "What murder?" He blurted out and pain shot through his left palm. He felt the memories take him to another time and place.

❧ 46 ❧

"**S**o, nothing has happened for two weeks?" Clay asked.

"Just the new car." He slapped the hood of the car they sat on.

JJ looked out over the river far below them flowing through a valley. Opulent homes had been built along the lower reaches of the river side. Some were almost as big as his 'manor'. His father had refused to talk about Hampton after his visit and had proceeded with plans to send him to boarding school. The new car was a peace offering.

For his last day at school, his father had bought him the car. It was small and efficient, a blue convertible with a hybrid engine. His excitement at receiving the car was subdued with the news that he would soon be sent off to a boarding school. He would need the car. That was why his father had given it to him. Not because he had finished the tenth grade and was now old enough to drive. From their conversations at the dinner table, he realized his father had not yet mentioned the boarding school to his mother. What was he going to do?

Right now, he didn't care about the future because for weeks he had not had a single absent spell. His father had taken the journal and put it in a safe in the library. The voice was still there in the back of his mind but rather subdued. JJ had driven Clay to the park along the ridge of the valley overlooking the river. How was he going to tell his best friend he probably wouldn't be back in the fall?

"That's really cool. I mean, my dad never bought me anything new like this." Clay leaned back on the hood and rested his head against the windshield. "If I had a car like this then Amy would pay attention to me for sure."

"Amy would still think you're a loser." JJ said and laughed. But the laughter died away with the realization he had to tell his best friend he was leaving in the fall.

"Hey, what's eating you? New car, dude. You should be chilled!" Clay sat up on the hood and punched him in the shoulder.

"My dad wants to send me away to a boarding school in the fall." There, he had said it out loud and his good mood faded quickly.

"That sucks!" Clay hit the hood. "There's no way you're going off to a boarding school."

"It's because of my blackouts."

Clay sighed and slid off the hood. He paced in front of the car. "We've got to come up with a plan. You can't go. You're the only friend I have."

JJ sighed. "My dad says I'm under too much strain. He thinks I might be having some kind of multiple personality thing going on."

Clay stopped and laughed. "That's crazy. You don't have one personality much less multiple."

JJ smiled. "Nice try. Something is going on. I wake up and lose time and something bad has happened. I mean people say they've seen me doing these things. What if it's true?"

Clay leaned against the hood. "Bro, it hasn't happened in weeks, right? I mean, don't you have to be seriously screwed up as a child to do that?"

"My dad thinks it's my mother's fault."

"Oh, yeah, they always blame the mother. Look at me. My dad bailed when I was nine. My mother raised me and I'm perfectly normal. We all know your mom is the coolest mom around. And she's hot."

JJ slapped Clay on the arm and frowned. "This isn't funny. I mean, what if I hurt someone I care about while I'm having one of these blackouts?"

Clay slid back up onto the hood next to him. He gazed out at the afternoon sun settling lower on the horizon. "If you did have multiple personalities, then sooner or later you will hurt someone who is standing in your way. At least, that is what always happens in the movies. Whose is standing in the way of your, you know, other self?"

He glanced at his best friend and shrugged. "I don't know."

"Look, you said that your dad is sending you to a boarding school. Maybe your alter ego wants to take him out."

"That can't happen. He's gone on another of his oversea trips and isn't supposed to be back until July."

"OK, I know this is twisted, but what if your evil side wants to take out your mother?"

JJ shivered and looked out over the city. The thought had crossed his mind. "That makes no sense."

"Sure, it does. Your dad said that she was the reason you are the way you are. See, your evil side wants to get her out of the way and then he can take over."

JJ shoved Clay with all his might and his friend slid over the side of the hood. "Cut it out! Don't say that about my mother, dude!"

Clay tumbled to the ground. There was a profound silence and JJ slid off the hood and walked around the car. Clay lay on his side, his head at an odd angle. Blood was pooling across a rock at the top of Clay's head.

"Clay?" He squatted beside his friend. He lifted his head off the rock. A cut leaked blood onto the ground. Clay's eyes fluttered open, and he groaned. Inside the car, his cell phone rang. He grabbed the phone.

"Hello?"

Heavy breathing came over the speaker. "Son, is that you?" It was his mother. "Listen, don't speak. I'm in trouble. Come home now. I think someone may be in the house." She whispered. The line went dead.

JJ looked at the phone and started the car engine. He tore out of the gravel and dirt on the side of the mountain road and headed down the mountain. While he was driving, he realized he had a phone to call the police. He reached for it and had to lean all the way over the passenger seat to reach it. The car swerved with his effort, and he straightened up as a huge, hairpin curve came into view. He slammed on the brakes and the car spun on the asphalt, slipping sideways toward the guardrail that separated him from a deadly drop. There was a huge impact, breaking glass, the sound of metal on metal and his head thudded against the steering wheel. Blackness came as he remembered leaving his best friend on the side of the road.

⚜

WHEN HE AWOKE, IT WAS PITCH BLACK. HE SAT UP IN THE driver's seat of the car. He was in the driveway of his home. He blinked in confusion. The night sky was above, cool and filled with stars. What had happened? He had been sliding toward the edge of the road and then there had been a crash.

JJ stumbled out of the car and examined the passenger side. The fender and door were caved in and scraped probably by the guard rail. But the car was still drivable. Then, he noticed the blood on his hands. He studied the blood and recalled Clay. He had left him on the side of the room with a blow to the head. He had to call for help.

Wait! His mother had called. Someone was in the house! He started toward the front doors and felt a sharp pain in his heel.

He glanced down. He was barefoot. What had happened to his shoes? It was then he noticed the bloody footprints. They led down the steps from his open front door and toward his car. He raised up his foot. It was covered with blood.

He ran up the stairs and through the foyer. "Mom! Mom! Where are you?"

JJ glanced around. More bloody footprints led across the living room toward the library. The library doors were open. Bloody handprints covered the door knob. Bloody footprints led into the library. He hurried in and followed the prints across the floor. The black doors were open!

JJ stopped in shock, his mind reeling, his heart racing. The black doors were open! The bloody footprints led inside. He calmed his racing heart and his breathing and hurried through the doors. The inner chamber was a small foyer crafted in marble and black wood. Five doorways led off from the main foyer in different directions. He noticed the pentagram inscribed in the tiled floor in black marble. He had entered between the two bottom points and the other points all pointed to the remaining five doors. But, across the center of the pentagram, the footprints led to the opposite door. It was open onto darkness.

JJ hurried across the cold marble feeling his feet stick in the clotted blood. Were these his footprints? He paused at the threshold of the door. It opened onto a stone stairway that led downward into shadowy darkness. Far below, a single light bulb swung from a tether. The footprints led down there.

JJ slowly made his way down the stone stairs into a creeping cold that permeated his bones. Far below him, the stairs descended into a fine mist. From the depths of the stairs, he heard a moan of pain. He hurried into the mist and stumbled down the stairs. His feet squished in the blood and moisture from the mist.

A pale green light filled the chamber at the base of the stairs. The room was hewn out of the raw rock of the mountain behind the mansion. In the center of the chamber, a low platform of smooth rock swelled out of the ground. Its surface was salt and pepper colored and shaped like a huge flattened egg. At the far end of the stone, an oblong slab of flat black shiny rock towered as tall as a huge door. Draped across the slab was the body of his mother.

He hurried through the mist and slipped in the blood. He looked around the chamber. There was blood everywhere. He gasped, his heart racing. He knelt beside his mother's head. Fine speckles of blood splattered her white skin. A huge golden knife protruded from her lower chest. He grabbed it and pulled it out of his mother's chest and tossed it aside.

"Oh, my God!" He sobbed. "Mother, who did this?"

Her eyes flickered open, bright jade green. She tried to smile, and blood appeared on her lips. "I love you, little man. I love you."

The life faded from her eyes. "Who did this?" He screamed. He was still crying when the first policeman appeared at the bottom of the stairs.

❧ 47 ❧

When Steel opened his eyes the first person he saw was the last person he expected to see. Inspector Goudreaux stood over him with hands on her hips and a huge smile on her face. She was a short, trim woman with coffee-colored complexion. Her wiry hair framed a plump face. Her dark brown eyes gleamed with malice. She wore a tight, dark blue business suit with smartly creased slacks and a white shirt buttoned to her neck beneath a matching blazer just as he had remembered from their first encounter in Switzerland. Steel sat up from where he had fallen to the floor. Behind him, his friends and family still sat at the table.

"You can run but you cannot hide, Jonathan Steel." She handed a folded piece of paper to another man standing beside her. He was a middle-aged man with a U. S. Marshal badge on his belt. He wore a cowboy hat and a khaki shirt and jeans.

"Jonathan Steel, you are under arrest for a murder in London, England of Margaret O'Malley and also for the deaths of over 200 passengers on flight 4551. Also, for aiding and abetting the escape of a known international criminal, Reginald Drake." He said.

Goudreaux stepped closer and leered at Steel. "And an accessory to the murder of Dr. Faust."

Steel froze. "What? Faust is dead?"

"Murdered by your accomplice." Goudreaux grinned from ear to ear. "Not to mention associating with a known criminal mastermind known as the Geisha. You can't get out of this one, Steel even with the help of Max. And, we have an arrest warrant for her, too!"

Another man appeared behind her from the kitchen door. "Stop!"

Steel looked up into the face of Special Agent Franklin Ross. "This man is under arrest for federal crimes."

Groudreaux and the U. S. Marshal froze. Goudreaux shook her head. "Oh no, Ross. This is of no interest to you. I was here first."

Ross stepped between her and the U. S. Marshal. "This man," he pointed at the marshal, "Knows that any arrest made on U. S. soil for crimes committed here in the U. S. takes precedent over international crimes. Jonathan Steel belongs to me."

"On what charges?" Goudreaux growled.

"For one, assaulting a federal office." Ross looked at Steel. "More than once. And aiding and abetting a known criminal, Theophilus Nosmo King. And there are many more." He held up an arrest warrant. "You can call my office to get a copy of this list." Ross helped Steel to his feet and turned him around. He whispered in Jonathan's ear.

"You owe me big time!" As he put cuffs on Steel, he recited Steel's rights to him. Ross turned Steel back to Goudrueax.

"Officer, I protest." Goudreaux said.

The U. S. Marshal handed the arrest warrant in his hands back to Goudreaux. "I'm afraid Special Agent Ross is correct. He has precedence. You can file a grievance with the American Embassy and seek extradition."

Goudreaux slapped the paper out of the man's hands. "I've already done that, or we wouldn't be here!"

"I'm afraid all of this is now null and void pending the FBI's case against Mr. Steel." He took off his hat and tilted it toward Goudreaux. "Good day, Ma'am."

Goudreaux screamed in frustration. "I am not a Ma'am!"

The Marshal let himself out and Ross pushed Steel toward the door. "You are in a heap of trouble, and you need the best lawyer money can buy, Steel. This arrest will only delay things a short while."

But the words were lost in the whirling and buzzing in Steel's mind as he reeled under the knowledge that his other self; his violent self; the man in his heart was correct. Who cared who was dead now? He had murdered his own mother!

EPILOGUE

Two Days Earlier

DRAKE WAITED PATIENTLY IN THE DARK ALLEYWAY. THE night was cold and clear with a new moon hanging on the horizon. The narrowed streets in front of Hampton's Museum of the Weird ran directly toward the moon. It was as if the sleepy eye of Satan were looking down upon Drake.

He had cleaned up very well thanks to the little man who ran a small clothing store. Drake had resisted the desire to prolong the man's pain and had made his death short and sweet. The suicide note would make it look like the man had taken his own life. Not that Drake really cared about keeping a low profile, but his newest ally insisted upon it.

He wore a three-piece wool suit with a nice dark shirt and a shiny golden tie. The little man's bathroom had all Drake needed to shower, shave, and brush the nasty stench from his mouth.

"I'm hungry." The demon Phleabite hissed in the back of Drake's mine.

"We needs some more fun!" The other demon, Toepain joined his companion.

"Shut it!" Drake hissed. "I've got to concentrate. You'll get yours shortly." He studied the front door of the Museum and saw the light in the foyer flicker out. The door swung open and the dumpy woman, Margaret, stepped out and locked the door. She started down the street and Drake stepped out of the alleyway.

"Hello, love." He said.

Margaret froze and glared at him. "There you are! I found your anklet in the furnace room. Wonder where you'd got off to. Boss wants you back in your cage."

"I'm afraid not, Margaret. Your boss doesn't need you anymore."

Margaret blinked in confusion and put a hand to her face. "No! I'm not ready! You promised me more! I want Hampton's love." She spoke to nobody in particular.

"Sorry, love, but Hampton will have to wait. He'll join you in hell soon enough." Drake said. He held up the golden knife in a gloved hand and then raked it across Margaret's throat. She tried to scream, her stubby hands going to her neck. She stumbled back into the alleyway and fell into a pile of rotting garbage. She gurgled and then grew silent.

A wind swirled down the alleyway driving grit and trash ahead of it. Drake felt the pelting of the trash on his face but ignored it. He was exulting in the kill! The demons within suddenly fell silent. In fact, he felt them leave his body! Phleabite and Toepain had fled the building! He stumbled back as weakness came over him with their departure. He had not realized how strong they made him feel. Cold fingers caressed his face in the wind. A voice spoke to him.

"You have done well." The voice hissed.

Drake gasped at the touch of the evil presence around him. "Who is here?"

"The fulfillment of your deal with Hampton." Came the voice that swirled around him in the whirlwind of trash and dirt.

"You made a deal with my opposition not realizing who you would answer to."

Drake's heart raced. Could it be? The wind wound more tightly about Margaret and a dark figure emerged from her dead body. "You mean, you were in Margaret?"

Laughter echoed around the alleyway. "Sometimes the best place to hide is in the most unassuming individual possible. I needed to keep an eye on Hampton until we could work things out."

"We?"

"One of us is known as Four. The unholy triad failed but we will not."

"I don't understand." Drake said.

"The knife you used was last in the possession of someone else." The dark figure said.

Drake smiled. "Jonathan Steel!"

"Yes. That man is my sworn enemy and I plan on removing his influence."

"By killing him?"

Laughter echoed around him again. "No. I have something far worse. They will come and arrest him as they did once before when I had influence over his soul. Now leave the knife with the body."

Drake smiled as he tossed the golden knife next to Margaret's body. "Am I to be your new host? Am I to be on the Council?"

"Oh yes."

"Who are you?" Drake squinted into the trashy whirlwind.

"I am known as the third demon."

Drake threw open his arms and smiled. "Welcome to your new home."

LESSONS TO BE LEARNED

I receive email questions quite often. In those questions, my readers seem to sense certain themes and situations in the story that I don't always agree with. However, I am an imperfect writer and often my meanings and messages may not come through. To that end, I have decided to add a new section to this book, "Lessons to be Learned". These "lessons" are the themes I have tried to bring out in my writing and I invite the reader to enjoy this discussion time. Go to the Bible. Read the scriptures. Do you own research on the topics in this section. I pray that God will enrich your life in Christ.

Bruce Hennigan

Question #1: Is it believable that Vivian Darbonne could change so abruptly after her "conversion"?

Read Acts 9:1-22

Consider:

Was Saul truly an evil person? What had he done in the name of his religious beliefs that was detrimental to the growing Christian church?

What was the singular event that changed Saul's life?

How quickly did Saul become a follower of Jesus Christ and begin to preach the Gospel?

Discussion: We see that Saul was very devout in his persecution of the new Christian "cult". He oversaw the stoning of Stephen. His intent was cruel and quick to end the lives of these new heretics. The event that changes his life so quickly and abruptly was a face to face encounter with the risen, resurrected Jesus Christ. In fact, this one moment of monumental, unbelievable conversion is one of the most powerful evidences for the risen Jesus Christ. Let's face it, if God can forgive Saul, he can forgive anyone of anything. Forgiveness is truly accessible to anyone who will claim it at any time in their lives.

Question #2: Did Jonathan Steel make the right choices? Were there other alternatives to his decision to work on behalf of the three demons? Are there times when you might feel like you are boxed in and coerced to do something that is against the will of God? How do you handle that kind of situation?

Read Acts 8:9-24

Consider:

Who was Simon?

What was "sorcery"?

Did Simon change his ways?

Discussion:

Peter confronted Simon with the warning:

Peter answered: "May your money perish with you, because you thought you could buy the gift of God with money! You have no part or share in this ministry, because your heart is not right before God. Repent of this wickedness and pray to the Lord in the hope that he may forgive you for having such a thought in your heart. For I see that you are full of bitterness and captive to sin." Acts 8:20-23

Peter told Simon to have a loyal and clean heart toward God. God expects us to fully serve him in our thoughts and deeds. We cannot be double minded. The agony and conflict Jonathan Steel felt throughout this novel represent the struggles all Christ followers experience. As we navigate the culture and world around us we are constantly tempted to compromise our devotion to Christ and His teachings to achieve a given result. Jonathan Steel's choices are certainly fictional and magnified but just as representative or our own struggles.

How much did Paul suffer with the guilt of the Christians whose death he had overseen? How many times did James, the brother of Jesus, regret the harsh words and doubts he spoke about his brother once he met the resurrected Christ? How did Peter live with the guilt of his betrayal in the courtyard the night of Jesus' trial? We have all been there and we have the hope of grace; unmerited favor; and forgiveness.

What all followers of Christ must do when confronted with these circumstances is NOT to act as Simon did. Tradition states that Simon did not change his ways. Instead, he intensified his devotion to sorcery and in his namesake, Gnosticism emerged as an early Christian heresy.

My prayer for my reader is that as you struggle with the choices we must make every day, we realize there are always more alternatives than we initially think. If we focus on the will of God, we will make the right and correct choices. But in the event we do not, there is always forgiveness and love to be found at the foot of the cross!

Question #3: How do Christians handle unforeseen adversity?

This is more of a rhetorical question. Excellent authors (and I am NOT among that group) have the ability to tell compelling stories in which their message becomes clear to the reader. One of the important rules of good writing is "RUE - resist the urge to explain". Good writers are able to bring the reader along with their characters' stories and have the reader discover the message along with the characters. Even writers who do not intend their stories to have a message by their very nature transmit their own "worldview" through the circumstances of the story.

What am I talking about? I have gotten many questions about my characters and stories and perhaps I have muddled my attempt at communicating that book's messages. Therefore I will NOT resist the urge to explain!

With this book and "The 7th Demon" I wanted to bring Jonathan and Josh to the most dangerous part of their journey. My goal was not to cause the reader suffering. Instead I wanted the reader to see how Jonathan and Josh handled what has been the most devastating challenges to their faith.

King David had Bathsheba's husband killed so he could possess her. What a horrific deed! And yet, David was called "a man after God's own heart". My message in these two books comes down to how we, as Christ followers, handle ourselves in the most trying circumstances whether these are of our own doing or from an unforeseen unavoidable source.

Josh, in his very sick state was oppressed by a demonic spirit intent on overcoming his mind and body — what would have happened to him if he had not renounced the 13th demon in the first book. His journey through this landscape became one of self discovery. He managed to take control of his painful memories and turn the table on this spirit. He came out of this near deadly experience a stronger and more mature person.

Jonathan Steel was faced with an impossible situation: allow his adopted son to die or agree to work with the very demonic forces he had pledged God he would fight. How was he to navigate these circumstances?

Way back in 1995 I underwent an all consuming descent into depression. I talk about this in detail in my book, "Hope Again: A Lifetime Plan for Conquering Depression" (www.conquer-ingdepression.com). Never in my entire existence did I plan on being this depressed! Never did I imagine that my daily choices would begin to accumulate like cholesterol in a clogging artery until I was completely shut down. I found myself powerless, fearful, and isolated by my depression. Thank God, my wife, my family, and my friends helped me see how to work my way out of that darkness.

After emerging from a two year period of painful counseling sessions, I was stronger and more mature. I made much better decisions. My pastor and good friend, Mark Sutton asked me to help him write a book on depression. We did. That first book,

"Conquering Depression" came out in February 2001 by Broadman & Holman Publishing. For twenty years, this little book of our struggle with depression ended up helping thousands! Weekly emails came to us from those who claim "your book saved my life".

Who gets the credit for this? Certainly not me! I never planned on going through depression so I could get three books published! God alone knew the path I would walk. God alone knew the pain I would suffer. God alone knew that, with His help, I would conquer depression! And, God alone knew I would take that experience and turn into something to help others!

That is the message I hope to convey through these two books. As you will see in the coming books, Josh is now a more mature young man. Unfortunately, although Jonathan Steel learned the importance of telling the ones who matter to him "I love you", he still has to pay for his poor choices (with Drake). His struggles are far from over. But, as the reader saw in the final chapters, Jonathan Steel is no longer alone. Unlike how we saw him in the first book where he confronted evil on his own (granted with a little bit of help from Dr. Cephas Lawrence), Jonathan Steel is now surrounded by a host of people who care about him and want to help him. And, Josh, of course.

You may be in dire straits as Jonathan Steel or Josh Knight were in this book. Unforeseen circumstances may keep you in a powerless condition as it did Josh. But God is always there to turn that perceived failure into a victory, a triumph. If nothing else, there is someone else suffering as you are and you may be able to reach out and help that person! You may have been forced to make poor choices thanks to unforeseen circumstances. Your life is not over. You can still battle for strength and determination to get out of that situation. God can turn the tables for you. God can show you how to turn your poor choices, your "Bathsheba", into a Goliath! The battle can be won if God is your strength and comfort.

Remember the life of Joseph. Betrayed by his brothers, sold into slavery, thrown into prison, betrayed by Potifer's wife only to find himself the most powerful person in that region. When his brothers came before him, he could have had them killed instantly, or better yet, tortured as he had been. Instead he said:

> Then Joseph said to his brothers, "Please, come near me," and they came near. "I am Joseph, your brother," he said, "the one you sold into Egypt. And now don't be grieved or angry with yourselves for selling me here, because God sent me ahead of you to preserve life. For the famine has been in the land these two years, and there will be five more years without plowing or harvesting. God sent me ahead of you to establish you as a remnant within the land and to keep you alive by a great deliverance. Therefore it was not you who sent me here, but God. He has made me a father to Pharaoh, lord of his entire household, and ruler over all the land of Egypt. Genesis 45:4-8

When we are in the midst of terrible situations, it is impossible to see God's hand sometimes. But when God has brought us out of those circumstances, whether in this world of the next, we see clearly His plan and His power.

AFTERWORD

I want to thank my readers for sticking with me for these past nine books. Many of the "flashbacks" featured in this novel come straight from previous books in "The Chronicles of Jonathan Steel". Two characters, Ruth Martinez and Reginald Drake come from "Death By Darwin" a prequel to the Chronicles. My intention is to complete Jonathan Steels story in two more novels.

Dr. Jack Merchant's backstory will debut in the upcoming novel, "Shadow Merchant".

There are two very important topics covered in this book and the prior book, "The 7th Demon: The Pandora Stone". I don't venture much into politics but I want to recognize my son and daughter in law who have embarked on a bold journey into the world of fostering. Since Mother's Day 2017, they have fostered eight children and every one of them came from a traumatic background. They have adopted three of three of those children.

I know that in our culture there are unwanted children, both born and unborn. Infertility has reached new levels in our country and there are many couples wishing to have their own family. I want to encourage my readers to support your local foster programs. Help families grow who desire to love and raise children desperate for this kind of love.

Adopted for Life: The Priority of Adoption for Christian Families and Churches By Russell Moore

The Gospel & Adoption by Russell D. Moore, Andrew T. Walker

Called to Care: Opening Your Heart to Vulnerable Children-- Through Foster Care, Adoption, and Other Life-Giving Ways By Bill Blacquiere, Kris Faasse

The other important topic is the existence of the mind versus just a brain. There are several good books I would recommend on this important topic. As I discussed in "The 8th Demon: A Wicked Numinosity" science now recognizes "human exceptionalism". Humans are more than just highly evolved animals. We have a "mind" or, as some consider it, a "soul".

The Soul: How We Know It's Real and Why It Matters by J. P. Moreland

Am I Just My Brain? (Questioning Faith) by Sharon Dirckx

Switch on Your Brain: The Key to Peak Happiness, Thinking, and Health by Dr. Caroline Leaf

Winning the War in Your Mind: Change Your Thinking, Change Your Life by Craig Groeschel

However, I really want to emphasize the importance of being aware of human trafficking! Mike Dellosso, an excellent author promotes the following website for Women At Risk International, https://warinternational.org .

CPSIA information can be obtained
at www.ICGtesting.com
Printed in the USA
LVHW020420110222
710675LV00011B/158

9 781736 141052